SONGS OF SNOW
L.J. THOMAS

Forestedge Press

First Edition: June 2024

Forestedge Press

Cover illustration by Elaine Ho | artofelaineho.com

Cover design by Mallory Rock | rocksolidbookdesign.com

Copy editing by Vicky Brewster | vickybrewstereditor.com

Songs of Snow

ISBN 978-1-7332610-6-7 (Paperback)

ISBN 978-1-7332610-5-0 (eBook)

www.ljthomasbooks.com

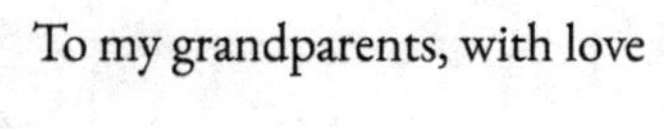

To my grandparents, with love

ALSO BY L.J. THOMAS

We Survivors: A Story from After the End
The Bloody Key: A Bluebeard Retelling

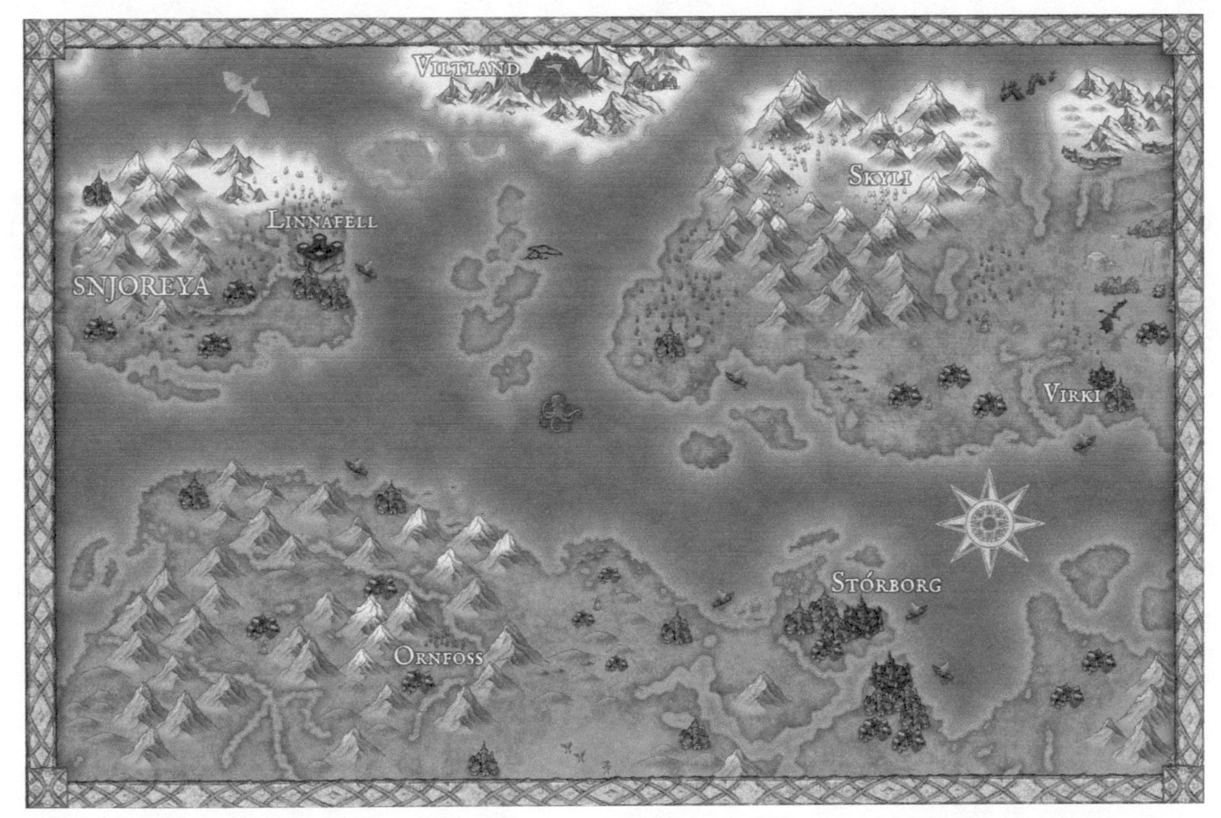

VILTLAND
SKYLI
VIRKI
LINNAFELL
SNJOREYA
STÓRBORG
ORNFOSS

TALES OF THE STORMSINGERS

Elín

"We are the last, Elín," Revna said, her frail hand clasping the blanket. "The last of the Stormsingers."

"Please, eat," Elín coaxed. She sat on one of their two chairs, a spoon of hot broth in her hand. Her grandmother shook her head; she didn't want food. Lately, she hungered only for stories.

Elín sighed and replaced the spoon in the bowl, then tenderly brushed aside a strand of her grandmother's silver hair, which had come loose from its plait in her last coughing fit.

Despite the warm glow of the candles, Revna's face looked pale and drawn. The rest of her thin body was hidden under a pile of knitted blankets and furs. Wind howled against the walls of their home, but the fire in the hearth kept them snug against the cold. Elín had been industrious on the last day they'd had snow-melting weather, chopping enough wood to keep them warm for several weeks.

"We are the last," Revna repeated, her voice rattling from the cough Elín could not cure. "This magic was always to become rarer. A Stormsinger can gift it only to one of their grandchildren. If something happens to that grandchild, or the Stormsinger does not have children, the magic dies . . ."

"Yes, Amma. So you've said. Rest now—don't exert yourself." Elín attempted to feed her more broth. "Your voice is growing hoarse."

Revna's cloudy blue eyes, so often distant now, fixed on her granddaughter. "Do you not see? This gift has become so rare that you and I are the last of our kind. The last of the Stormsingers."

Each night, the old woman told Elín stories of fanciful creatures and brave deeds dared long ago. The tales of the Stormsingers, who could control storm and snow and sea with songs from an ancient book of spells, were never far from Revna's lips. Over the winter, she had taken her whimsy to new heights, ending her tales each night with this "revelation" about the powers she and Elín supposedly possessed. Sometimes, she claimed to have sung the special song each night to Elín when she was still in the womb, passing on her magic.

Elín gave up, setting the bowl and spoon on the small table beside the bed. She did her best to hide the tears pricking at her eyes. Her grandmother was not long for this world, and Elín's only wish now was that she would leave it as herself, not as some foolish old woman who believed in children's tales.

Perhaps it would be better for Revna if Elín played along—pretended to believe that they were both powerful snow sorceresses—but it hurt her to see her grandmother like this. When Elín was a girl, Revna would tell her stories like these every night, especially after the somber time when her mother, Signý, finally slipped away into the world of the spirits. She had never been well, as long as Elín could remember, and Revna said her mother had finally died of her broken heart.

Elín had loved the stories then. She'd believed them wholly, until she grew older and learned that such things were impossible, that magic did not exist. They were just happy, dreamy tales to help young ones sleep at night. Had Revna always believed in them so fiercely? There was no way to know, now.

"They will come for you, child. Else, you must find them. You must help—must learn . . ." Revna trailed off as a cough overtook her. "Above all else, remember . . . the things I have taught you."

Revna's mind must have become even more addled than Elín had feared; she was hardly coherent anymore. Elín wrapped her arms around her grandmother, feeling every bone in her ever-thinning frame. "Alright," she whispered, a tear slipping down her cheek and into her grandmother's silver hair. "I will remember."

Revna took a few more ragged breaths. "I wish to go outside."

"It's snowing and very cold. Perhaps tomorrow."

"Please," Revna said softly. "Open the door. I would like to see the moon, the snow."

Elín pressed her lips together. She'd done all she could to keep Revna and their home warm, to overcome the bitter winter. But she also felt the words her grandmother didn't say: *one last time.*

"Very well," she said finally. "But only for a moment."

Revna nodded, her eyes brighter than they had been for days. Elín stood and opened the wooden door. A swirl of snow and cold air spilled into the cottage, but Revna didn't seem to mind. Her eyes were focused on the silver disc of the moon, the way it limned the bare branches of the trees and made the snow glitter. She sighed once, contentedly, and settled back into the bed.

Sweeping the snow that had entered back outside before it could melt, Elín shut the door tight against the cold once again. She returned to her grandmother's side and told herself that her eyes stung from the burst of chill air, not from the solemn finality of the evening.

Revna's thin, wrinkled hand worked its way out of the blankets and up to Elín's cheek. Her cloudy eyes now seemed far away. "I love you, Elín. You . . . Signý . . . my family is the best thing I have done."

Elín pulled away, sniffing back tears and wiping her eyes. She attempted a smile. "I love you, too," she whispered.

The next morning, when Elín awoke and found that Revna had passed on, she was not surprised. She had gone peacefully, with a faint smile on her lips. After sitting a moment, awash in long-expected heartbreak and guilt-laced relief, Elín brushed away her tears, bundled up, and left the house. She rode her little white horse over to the farm of their neighbor, Arn, who had promised to help her when the time came.

She looked back, once, at the swirl of smoke from the chimney and the empty fields in the golden glow of dawn. Strange how, now that Revna was gone and Elín would live there alone, the word "home" no longer seemed to fit her little cottage.

The funeral took place the next day. It was a lonely affair, with only Arn, his son Haakon, and the priest standing beside Elín in the sacred forest. As she stood over her grandmother's grave, her arm laced through Arn's elbow, it was easy to notice the two strangers at the edge of the clearing.

Had Elín felt less wrung out from her grief, she might have sent them away or asked what they thought they were doing, casting shadows over her grandmother's final resting place. Instead, she welcomed the distraction. Anything to keep the loss, the emptiness, at bay.

As the priest thanked Lady Destiny for filling Revna's life with family and love, and Lady Luck for its length and many fruitful harvests, Elín examined the intruders. One was old—perhaps even older than her grandmother had been—with a wispy white beard and a light gray robe. The other was much younger, his dark hair and black cloak silhouetted against the bright snow.

As the priest continued, asking Lady Legend that Revna be remembered well by all those who had known her, Elín clutched the bundle of birch twigs and winterberry branches she'd gathered to her chest, along with a kerchief she'd embroidered with her grandmother's favorite wildflowers. She whispered her farewell to the last of her family, then gently placed the items onto the coffin.

With shaky hands, she took the shovel from Arn and let the first portion of dirt fall into the frozen earth. She stood a moment, hands clutching the wooden handle and eyes pricking with tears. Then she handed the shovel back to Arn and turned away so she would not cry as he and the priest took turns filling the grave.

Elín's mare, Ský, was tied up just off the path from the village, and Elín could only see glimpses of her white hide through the trees. Seeking distraction elsewhere, she examined the strangers again, trying to place them among the residents of Ornfoss. In a village as small as hers, new faces were a rarity. The men were doing nothing of interest, only standing with their gazes on the burial. Elín watched them anyway to avoid her tangled emotions—the loss, the creeping loneliness, the crushing-but-familiar pressure of keeping the farm going on her own.

Finally, Arn tamped down the last of the earth over Revna's grave. The priest blessed Elín and left. Arn and Haakon began carving an oak tree with the mark that would let Revna's spirit know, should she go wandering, to stay within the clearing. No one else from the village had come to see Revna off to the spirit realms; Elín's family had always kept so much to themselves.

She regretted that now, as she stood alone in the small glade of the sacred forest. Those families that had lived in the village of Ornfoss for generations had broad clearings full of ancestors deep in the woods, plenty of help in times of need. Revna and Signý had arrived when Elín was only a little girl, the rest of their family laid to rest in some other land.

Elín made her way through the snow to her mother's marking on a pine tree near her grave, and ran her fingers along the weather-worn grooves.

How was she to manage now, without them? For as long as she had known her grandmother's time was slipping away, why had she not thought beyond the moment she would lose her? Stronger, even, than her grief was a terrifying, hopeless question:

What now?

"We've traveled far to find you." A voice startled Elín. She jumped and turned to face the speaker, her back against the tree.

The two strangers stood a few paces away. The older man's expression was peevish, but the younger wore the hint of a smile with his wide, hopeful eyes.

"I'm sorry," she said, trying to compose herself. "You must be looking for someone else. I can take you into the village . . ."

"That won't be necessary," the younger man said.

Now that she saw him up close, she was sure she'd never seen him before. The angles of his face—the high cheekbones, the dark, sweeping brows—were unfamiliar. His skin was the same light brown as the traders from the southern lands who came through the village in the summer. She was unsettled by the way he looked at her, with something close to reverence.

He lowered his voice. "Elín, isn't it?"

Her eyes widened, and she became aware of her rapid heartbeat. "How do you . . . ?"

The elder stranger took over, saying quietly, "Your grandmother must have told you we would come." He was tall and thin, pale and wrinkled, and would have fit in well in her village if not for his strange robes.

"I don't know what you mean." Elín glanced at Arn and Haakon, who were nearly finished with her grandmother's tree-mark. They would come to her aid, surely, if these strangers meant her any harm. She leaned into the tree, her hand against the rough bark, ready to push off and run if need be.

The younger man knelt on one knee, despite the snow. He took her hand in his gloved ones before she could react. "We have found you at last," he whispered, a note of awe in his voice. "Songstress of Storm and Snow."

GLORY IN LIFE
Kata

Drops of blood had stained the snow crimson and, in some places, melted the top layer into little hollows with its warmth. The drips were far apart at first, but grew closer together as the elk slowed, leading Kata deeper into the woods. Her calfskin boots floated gracefully above the frozen top layer of snow. Her father was far behind her now, but she was not afraid. This was far from her first hunt, and she had grown tall with the saplings of the forest.

The sunlight turned to burnished gold and reflected in sparkles across the snow as she pursued the elk. The shadows of the trees stretched long, intertwining and merging with each other in a lovely lattice. She was scanning the familiar trees around her, standing very still, when she spotted it. There, through the boughs of a spruce, she could just make out the dun hide of the elk. She exhaled slowly to steady herself. Her breath condensed, swirling upward in the chill air. Then she moved in for the kill.

As Kata approached the wounded beast, she first reached for the knife tucked into her boot, but then straightened. She wouldn't need it; her shot had been true, and the elk was dead already. Placing one palm against the animal's side, she pulled out her arrow, grunting at the force the movement required. Then she pierced the arrow into the deep snow to clean it and slid it back into her quiver.

All that was left was to bless the hunt for Lady Legend. She knelt next to the deer and placed a gloved palm on its forehead, between its impressive antlers. Her eyes closed and she waited, trying to recall the words of the blessing. Her father usually said it for both of them, so she had to imagine his voice to remember how it began. When she had the words, she bowed her head and said them reverently:

I thank you, creature of the woods
For giving your life to sustain my own
May you find peace in the spirit realms
I thank Lady Destiny for my stealth and my bow
I thank Lady Luck for allowing our paths to cross
I thank Lady Legend for the hunters who have come before
And ask her to let you live on
In the stories of those who once knew you

Then Kata rose and whistled the birdsong she and her father used to communicate in the King's Forest. As she waited, she remembered herself, no taller than her father's knee, listening to the blessing for the first time. He'd warned her not to forget to bless any game before using it. One must honor their prey, and if one were faithful, Lady Legend would transfer the animal's glory in life to the hunter.

This elk had surely had some glory among his kind. Each antler was crowned with eight points, and he was nearly twice as broad across the chest as Kata.

She should be proud of herself, but she could not help but wonder how much more glorious she would feel if the animal in front of her was a griffin or a nykur instead of more commonplace game. The hunt would be so much more challenging and, therefore, more rewarding when successful—especially considering how scarce magical creatures had become, the king's decree having been in effect for over ten years now.

Maybe she should mention her aspirations to her father again. Last time, the most unusual expression had come over his face, and she had wondered why he wasn't happy to see her follow in his footsteps. He was too humble to speak of it himself, but others had told her spectacular tales from when he was the most successful unicorn hunter in the land. She sometimes wondered, when he was still and quiet in the woods, and seemed to look far beyond anything she could see, if he missed that life.

Serving as Huntsman to the King was certainly an honor, but it never felt like an *adventure*, the way she imagined tracking and outwitting magical creatures would. Kata even suspected that her father's fame throughout Linnafell for his daring bounty hunter escapades was a large part of the reason the king had declared him Royal Huntsman. Did he not wish her to have the same chance?

Kata stood and scanned the forest for her father, but her attention was quickly caught by the movement of something large and white in the trees to her left. But as she listened, watched, every muscle of her body taut, nothing happened. The forest was silent and undisturbed.

She snorted and shook her head. *Perfect.* Her wish to bounty hunt had grown so strong, she'd imagined an ice bear where there was only a falling snow drift.

A few minutes more and her father, Njáll, approached. Long before she saw him, Kata heard the steady crunches as his feet broke through the iced layer of snow. When he was closer and she could see his weary eyes and hear his tired breathing, she knew she would not broach the subject of becoming a bounty hunter that night.

"Kata, my little dove," Njáll said, smiling despite his exhaustion. "You've become much too fast for an old man like me."

"It's the snow hindering you," Kata said. "And the chill." Though she knew that was only part of the cause.

"Did you speak the blessing?"

"Of course."

He eyed the wound as he approached the elk and said happily, "Your aim was true. Almost as good as mine, and yet you're still a girl. Imagine when you are full-grown."

"I'm not so far from full-grown now, Pabbi," Kata reminded him. "A whole fourteen winters."

He studied her as if he didn't see her every day, scratching his close-cropped, graying beard. Then his eyes crinkled into a grin. "You're younger than you think. Don't hurry to grow old like me."

She knew from experience that there was no arguing him out of one of his sentimental moods. Afraid it was a tear she'd seen glinting in his eyes, she turned away and said, "Well, shall we drag him home before dark?"

Njáll untied the sledge from his back and laid it at the feet of Kata's quarry. After tying its front legs together, he handed one end of the rope to Kata. Together, they heaved the elk onto the sledge. "This was a good hunt, Kata," he said. "The king will be well-pleased. We should stop in the tavern on the way home to celebrate."

"Really, Pabbi?" Kata asked, her face alight. "But it's not our usual day, is it?"

"No," he said. "But this is not a usual buck. It is not every day my daughter cleanly takes down an elk four times her size—or at least, right now, it is unusual. I suspect the future will hold many more."

Kata was no longer listening, embarrassed to hear her father's praise. Let her hunt dangerous magical beasts and *then* be praised. Could she ask him about her dreams now? *No. Better to do it after the tavern, when his belly is full.*

She untied the rope from the buck's legs and swiftly threaded it through the sledge. She threw the other end to her father. On his signal, they both grabbed their ends of the rope and began to pull the elk-laden sledge through the snow.

The tension of the rope heavy on her shoulder, Kata could no longer stay neatly above the iced layer of snow, and she sank halfway to her knee with each step. She frowned; how difficult everything was in winter.

Her father kept a steady but slow pace, and she hoped they would arrive at the tavern before the seats nearest the blazing hearth were taken. As they trudged on through the white drifts for half a league, the sun glanced ever lower through the trees. Her father, still in his sentimental mood, had begun singing one of the old mountain songs, and despite her unskilled voice, Kata joined him.

STAY ROOTED FIRMLY

Elín

Elín yanked her hand away, staring in confusion at the strangers. Then, a sickening thought slowly dawned in her mind. They knew her name and where she lived. They must also have known about her grandmother, somehow known what she believed at the end. They were *mocking* her grandmother and her childish fancies, the tales of magic she so loved.

Everything she'd been stubbornly trying not to feel that morning bubbled over. Her face heated with an anger she'd never felt before, her fists clenched, and she found herself shouting.

"How dare you mock a confused old woman! She cherished those tales long after she could tell what's true from what isn't. And you come here to ridicule her after—after we've only just laid her in the ground."

Arn's strong arm wrapped around her, and for the first time that day, she burst into heaving sobs, soaking Arn's coat.

The younger man stood and brushed the snow from his knees, sheepish. "I'm . . . sorry for your loss. I should have started with that."

As anger gave way to embarrassment, Elín tried to stop crying and wriggled out of Arn's embrace. Wiping her eyes roughly with her hands, she regained some of her composure. "What do you want?"

The older man was even less friendly toward her now. His lips pursed together, and he turned toward Arn. "Can we speak to her alone?"

"Elín?" Arn asked.

She hesitated, then nodded her assent. Best to find out what they wanted and send them on their way so she could go home. Or, at least, to the place that had once felt like home.

Arn addressed the strangers. "Sure you want that? She's rather . . . distraught." He looked at her sideways, the way he eyed horses that were not yet broken. She couldn't blame him; she'd never had such an outburst of emotion before.

"Yes, it would be best."

"I'll wait for you," Arn said to Elín, then he wove through the trees toward the village path, joining Haakon near her horse.

She crossed her arms and glared at the strangers' boots, breathing slowly to keep tears of frustration away.

Clearing his throat, the younger man said, "Let me begin again. Hello, Elín, my name is Týr." He held out his hand. When she refused to shake it, he let it fall back to his side. "I'm apprenticed to Björn." He nodded at the old man, who pursed his lips even tighter.

"Again, we're sorry for your loss," Týr went on. "Our timing—arriving today at your grandmother's funeral—is regrettable, and we apologize. I know this must be a shock for you, but we've been traveling for years to find you."

The hair on Elín's arms rose, and her eyes narrowed in suspicion. "Why did you need to find me?"

He hesitated, glancing toward Björn. The old man's expression soured further, but Týr seemed to be doing his best to salvage the introduction. "Because . . ." he began, then cleared his throat again. "Well, because you are the last Stormsinger, and we are the Keepers of the Tome that holds their spells."

"I am not a child or a fool," Elín said through clenched teeth. She took a few steps toward the path, then turned back around. "Tell me what you really want, or leave me be."

"Truly, we do not mean to insult you or to mock your grandmother," Týr said levelly. "I have spoken the truth."

Elín threw her arms out at her sides. "I'm not a sorceress. There's no such thing. I'm just a girl, one without even a family now. And you're not—what did you say? A 'Keeper'?"

"Yes," he said. "Although Björn is the Tomekeeper. I've not yet finished my training, but someday I will be one, too."

"Oh really?" Elín said, crossing her arms. "Then show me. Where is the Kirja?" That was the Tome's name in the ancient tongue, or at least, so her grandmother had taught her.

"Ah, so you have heard of it. You even know its true name," he said, then looked down and ran his fingers through his dark brown hair. "We . . . don't have it."

"Of course not." She turned her eyes skyward.

"This is why we found you, child," Björn said. "We must get you to safety and then retrieve the Tome." His voice was reedy and sharp, and his tone said he was not used to disobedience.

"Very well," she said. "You found me. I'm returning home now. I'm perfectly safe, and you may go off on your quest for your magic book."

"You're in more danger here than you realize." Týr glanced at Björn, rubbed the back of his neck, and said, "We'll bring you to a safe place, where others of magical abilities hide from those who would destroy them—"

"No," Björn interrupted, turning his piercing gaze on his apprentice. "We'll take you to a truly safe place, in the remote lands where the Kirja is hidden. There, you will learn to wield its power."

They hadn't even agreed on where to take her? Perhaps it was best to play along with their harebrained ideas, as she had with her grandmother's. "May Lady Luck be with you on your wild goose chase," Elín said sharply. "But I'll be staying here. I have a farm to run."

"Please, Songstress," Týr said, a note of desperation in his voice. "We searched so long for you and your grandmother. We've come too late for her, but we did find you. Snowsong—stormsinger magic—is not yet gone. And there are those who need your help."

"If you think I can do magic . . ." Elín shook her head, taking a step back from them. She had the odd sense now that these men weren't mocking her but really believed in the farfetched legends her grandmother had loved.

"Not yet, but once we retrieve the Kirja, we can teach you its songs." Týr's eyes were alight in a way that confirmed he honestly believed his own words.

She was nearly at the edge of the clearing now. Arn and Haakon waited for her on the path, Haakon holding Ský's reins.

But she hesitated. Could these men be the people Revna had mentioned her last night, the ones who would come for her? Elín had given no more credit to those words than she had her grandmother's other ramblings, but what if . . . ?

She turned, leaning her shoulder against a tree, and sized up the men again. Týr may look nothing like the Keepers she had imagined, but this grizzled old man did.

"I've completely botched this," Týr said, glancing at Björn. From his expression, Elín guessed the old Tomekeeper had advised against this plan. "We shouldn't have come to the funeral—I see that now. But we'd just arrived, and I was so anxious to see you, to make sure you weren't in danger . . ."

Danger? The longest nights of winter had already passed, and she had enough food to survive until spring. Especially now that her grandmother was gone, though she'd eaten so little toward the end in any case. What other perils did they imagine? Elín let out a slow breath and relaxed her shoulders.

"Why don't you get the book first and come back here once you've found it?" Perhaps *then* she could believe, and if not, at least she'd be rid of them for a while.

"No," Björn cut in, voice sharp and unyielding. "You'll come with us Now we've found you, it's our duty to protect you, and we cannot leave you alone again. Growing up here in this little farming community, you don't realize the danger you're in. Your family chose this place well when they ran."

Elín blinked in surprise. Somehow, this dour-faced man seemed to know more about Elín's past than she knew herself. The thought of things her grandmother hadn't told her—and now never would—stung. She bit her tongue to keep from asking what her family had run from, not wanting these strangers to learn how little she knew of her own past.

Björn's downturned mouth and disapproving gaze were still aimed her way. Clearly, Elín did not meet whatever expectations he had for a Stormsinger. Which was all very well, since she was *not* one, however much her grandmother had wished for it in her last days.

"I don't know how you know so much about me or what you really want—"

"We've explained," the old man interrupted.

"But," she continued, with the sternest expression she could muster, "I don't want any part in your business. I'm going home." She pulled her cloak tighter around herself and strode out of the clearing.

"Wait—there's one more thing," Týr spoke again. "Is there an inn nearby?" They both followed a few steps behind, their boots crunching in the snow. Arn and Haakon were listening keenly.

She sighed, closing her eyes and bringing her fingers up to rub her temples. "There's no inn for leagues."

She remembered her mother's and Revna's rules about hospitality. Always treat a guest well, as one never knew when they might be attending to a member of the huldufólk in disguise. Mistreat them, and they'd retaliate with their mischievous magic. Elín wasn't sure whether she wanted to laugh or cry as she realized that, though she was gone, Revna was still filling her head with fairy stories.

Opening her eyes, she saw Björn simmering with silent rage. Týr, however, looked crestfallen, and that look convicted her. Whether or not she believed in the huldufólk, whether she believed these men's wild tales, she didn't feel right turning them out into the cold, without offering them shelter or at least a meal.

Luckily, Arn stepped in first. "You must stay the night in my home. There's more room for you there."

"That would be wonderful," Týr said, smiling now.

Elín felt a twinge; for a moment, she had thought it might not be so bad to have guests in her home. Last night had been terribly lonely.

"It has been a hard day for Elín," Arn said. "We must give her some time to herself."

"Very well," Björn assented. "We'll leave her for now. But she must speak to us again before nightfall. We have grave concerns for her safety."

"Elín, do you think you could manage an evening visit?" Arn said, smiling. Clearly, he took the hospitality rules as seriously as her grandmother had.

She sighed again. "Yes. I'll be over later, to cook our guests dinner," she replied, surprising herself. As mad as these strangers clearly were, they were also the most interesting thing that might ever happen to her in Ornfoss. If nothing else, they could tell her stories of the broader world—a welcome distraction from her loss.

"We look forward to seeing you again," Týr said, briefly bowing to her and managing a crooked smile.

She turned away from the strangers and toward her neighbors. "Thank you, Arn and Haakon. You don't know what your help these past days has meant to me."

Elín mounted Ský without another word, urging the little mare on faster through the snow, her cloak catching the wind behind her. When she looked back, the four men had already become lost in conversation as they headed toward Arn's house.

As the familiar snow-covered landscape rushed by, she remembered that her home would be empty when she arrived. Revna was really gone. Elín kicked her horse on faster, hoping to reach the warmth of her cottage before her tears froze to her cheeks.

Needing to steady herself after an eventful morning, Elín spent the afternoon drawing water from the well to take a bath. She filled her soup pot and kettle and placed them over the fire, then trekked out to the well again with the two good buckets she owned. By the time she returned, the water in the kettle and pot had boiled. She poured their steaming contents carefully into the washbasin. After refilling the kettle and pot and repeating the routine twice more, the washbasin was half-filled.

Elín realized how wasteful of her firewood she had been, especially as she had bathed the day before to prepare for the funeral. But surely, being alone in the world warranted some allowances. She must take comfort in whatever small things she could. An unbidden thought made her grimace: if she did leave with Týr and Björn, her dwindling supply of logs wouldn't matter anymore.

Her frown deepened as she untethered her hair from its plaits. The "Keepers" were surely as mad as her grandmother had been near the end, but there was a knot in her stomach that loosened when she let herself consider a journey with them. Unburdening herself of the harsh life on her farm, even temporarily, held some appeal. Had she not sometimes felt confined in this small home in the narrow valley and longed to know what was beyond the mountain peaks? Perhaps, out there in the world, she could learn about the mysterious past of her mother and grandmother. And it wasn't as if there was anything here for her now.

She sighed and pushed these thoughts aside as she slipped her arms out of her fur-lined dress and wriggled off her wool underclothes. The chill hit her quickly, raising bumps on her arms, so she stepped into the washbasin and submerged as much of her body as she could.

The water was disappointingly tepid. She felt sudden tears of frustration prick her eyes and wiped them away, feeling foolish. Most of the afternoon and a half dozen extra logs had been spent in this endeavor, but her planned dose of solace had failed.

Her grandmother had always helped her ration food and firewood through the winter. How was she to manage now, suddenly mistress of the farm? It was small, and she had already managed it these past years, with her grandmother's wisdom and a little help from Arn, but the burden of it weighed on her. She had never done it with no family to brighten her days.

A fresh wind of grief blew over Elín as she recalled the song Revna had always sung for baths. This time, she let herself cry for a few minutes as she wrapped her arms around her knees in the lukewarm bathwater. When the tears subsided, she sang the song all the way through. Her voice trembled at first, and she hesitated on a few words, trying to remember the syllables of the strange, ancient tongue, but by the end of the melody, her voice rang out clear and true. It sounded quite like Revna's. She felt a little better after singing; the bathwater almost seemed warm.

After scrubbing, she stepped out of the washbasin and stifled a shiver before wrapping herself in a thick wool blanket. Though she wanted to linger in the bath—perhaps for hours, lost in memories of her grandmother brought on by the honey-and-juniper scent of the soap—she needed to give herself time to prepare dinner at Arn's.

Elín moved to the fire, still wrapped in the old blanket, and pushed her hair to one shoulder. She gently untangled it with her fingers as the fire dried it. Impractical though it was for winter baths, she had been unable to cut her hair since her mother had died. The chestnut color was one of the only traits she and her mother had shared, and the waves now hung to her elbows.

When her hair was suitably dry, she donned her clothing again and set to work on packing for Arn's. As she pulled stores from her shelves, she tried to be grateful that what she had left would more than last her the rest of the winter. It was a hollow sort of comfort.

As she gathered supplies from around her kitchen, Elín suddenly broke down. She'd been relieved to scrounge up another pair of bowls for her unexpected guests when she realized she only needed one extra, not a pair. Without thinking, she'd packed a bowl for her grandmother. She collapsed into a chair and stared into the fire, frozen by her sorrow.

Hello, Grief, she thought, *it's you again.*

She needed to hold onto everything she could from her grandmother, especially her songs, and she knew it was Grief that made her feel this way. After Signý had passed on, Elín had slept with her mother's carved-ivory hairbrush to keep her close. For the first time in her life, she'd begun the ritual her mother had always both followed and done for her: one hundred strokes with the hairbrush each night.

Back then, she hadn't understood how many of her actions had been the result of mourning for her mother. Grief had been an unfamiliar and unwelcome stranger then—*not unlike Björn and Týr*, she thought with a mirthless grin.

"Still unwelcome," she said to the empty house. "But no longer a stranger."

At some point, she became aware that the fire was going out, only a few wisps of smoke curling from the log and tickling her nose. Elín jumped up and threw on some tinder, nursing the fire back ablaze. Then she peeked out the door to see the sun angling low—more time had passed than she'd realized.

Compose yourself, Elín.

She closed the door and smoothed her skirts, determined to show Arn and her unwelcome guests that she would carry on and could bear her loss with dignity.

She shoved her ingredients—onions, dried peas, and salted pork—into her rucksack, along with a three-day-old loaf of bread and her wooden bowls. She scanned her home, ensuring that she hadn't forgotten anything, when her eyes landed on the rickety little table that had always stood at her grandmother's side of the bed. The one whose drawer she'd never been allowed to touch.

Yes, *this* was what she needed to bring herself back to normalcy. She'd said goodbye to her grandmother, they'd buried her and marked her tree, but Elín had avoided even looking at her side of the cottage. Now, she would sort through whatever precious things Revna had kept in the drawer, and it would be done.

If the strangers who had intruded on her grief had to wait a little longer for their dinner, so much the better.

She approached the drawer and curved her fingers around the handle, admiring the worn-smooth feel of the wood. Best to do it quickly, like pulling out a bee sting. She tugged open the drawer, only to laugh at herself when she found it almost empty.

There was a piece of birch bark, which, on closer inspection, revealed one of the drawings of their horse Elín had always been making as a child. The drawer also held a stone and three locks of hair tied with string.

Elín picked up the little bundles of hair carefully and laid them in her palm. Two were the same deep red-brown as her hair, so they must have been from her and her mother when they were girls. The third, though, was a sunny gold that Elín was sure she hadn't seen on anyone in the village. Arn and Haakon were blond, but theirs was much paler than this. It could be Revna's own hair from when she was a babe. For as long as Elín could remember, Revna's hair had been silver-streaked white, but it certainly must have been another color before.

Placing the locks of hair back in the drawer gently, Elín held the stone in her palm. Why, by Lady Destiny, had Revna kept this?

It was unusual, that was true. The stone was black with hints of red, its surface not smooth but rough and pockmarked. Elín had never seen such a stone—or had she . . . ?

She remembered now: a peddler had come through the village once when she was a girl, advertising a stone that could "help one find their way". Her mother had been in a hurry to return home, but Elín had seen the stone as the man held it out to her. It was not the same shape—not the same stone—but it could have been the same material as Revna's.

What else had the man said about it? Elín sat on Revna's side of the bed, brushing her thumb over the stone, and tried to remember. It was called a . . . lodestone, that was the word, and it helped travelers to find north. What else? Before her mother had pulled her away, the man had said something more in a conspiratorial whisper. "This stone," he had said. "It will also cling to iron . . . *as if by magic.*" She remembered him winking as her mother herded her toward home.

Elín stood abruptly and scanned the cottage for something iron, noticing the metal bands that held together her wooden buckets. She knelt beside one and took a deep breath, then slowly moved the stone toward the band.

Nothing happened at first. But, when the stone was a finger's width away, it leaped out of her hand—as if by magic, as the man had said—and attached itself to the bucket. Elín jumped back in surprise, accidentally kicking the bucket and knocking it over. It rolled back and forth a few times, the stone still attached.

So, it *was* a lodestone. But why did Revna have such a stone, and why hide it? What kind of adventures had she kept secret all these years? Maybe these strangers who seemed to know so much could tell her. If there were such things as this, that were *almost* magic, what else might there be out in the world beyond her valley? Perhaps even a book of spells that, well, if they could not control storm or sea, might do *something*.

She shut the stone up tight in the drawer and left the cottage with her supplies. As she rode over to Arn's, she reflected on her tangled emotions. Since the strangers had come with their tales of magic in her blood, she felt as if she stood at the edge of a precipice, and she could not know until she leaped from it whether she would fall or fly. Faced with that chance, surely it was best to stay rooted firmly on solid ground.

THE TAVERN

Kata

Kata knew her father didn't particularly enjoy going to the tavern with the hunters at the end of a long day, often complaining that it was noisy and crowded. But as neither he nor Kata had ever learned to cook beyond roasting meat or throwing grain, water, and berries in a pot over the fire and christening it "porridge," it was their one day each week to enjoy their sustenance.

She, on the other hand, loved to listen to the hunting tales of the men and women in the tavern. Kata knew how exaggerated most of the stories were, but she loved to hear them all the same—and imagine herself having similar adventures when she was grown.

During these times, she also loved to sit against the wall and watch the tavern's patrons. She was often the youngest person there by many winters, and all the old hunters treated her as their little pet, giving her trinkets found on their hunts—porcupine quills, bear claws, bits of bone or antler they had carved, interesting stones—that she kept in a box at home.

She'd often observed that the hunters' personalities seemed to match their prey's. The dragon hunters were strong, fierce, and miserly with their gold. Those who hunted phoenix had tempers that could flash in an instant. The griffin hunters were prideful and often dressed extravagantly. The nykur hunters were sullen and watchful, and the unicorn hunters, as her father had once been, were quiet and secretive.

Many of those who had been bounty hunters in the old days had moved on to other professions as magical game became scarce, the evil of magic almost wiped out from King Karvel's lands. They relished these chances to boast of their old successes and the ways Lady Legend had blessed their hunts. There were few of

Kata's age who had the skills or desire to pursue their line of work, so they were proud to see her interest. She imagined they were happy she was there to pass the traditions to, though if any ever tried to say so her father would stop them.

That evening, the glow of the tavern and the din of its occupants greeted them while they were still far out in the forest. Kata smiled and quickened her pace. The hunters who spent each evening in the tavern would know this was not their usual day; they would want to know the occasion, and she could show them the elk she had taken.

They left the sledge outside the tavern. Her father tied a kerchief with the royal insignia to it. It was unlikely anyone would try to take the elk, but no one would dare even think it when they knew it was taken by the Royal Huntsman, its destination the palace. Even an elk that would feed as many people as hers wasn't worth the risk of losing one's hands—or, if the king was in one of his vengeful moods, one's life.

The warmth of the roaring hearth and the din of a dozen hunters making merry greeted them as they entered and shut the door against the cold. Bergdis, the barkeep, was sliding mugs of ale or mead to guests, but she smiled and waved to Kata before giving a sharp reply to one of the rowdy men at the bar. Across the room hung trophies from hunts—the heads of elk, bears, and boars. Kata studied them, her cheeks and nose stinging from the heat, and noted that the elk she had tracked and taken was nearly as big as those decorating the wall of the tavern.

Njáll chose a table between the hearth and the bar. Bergdis left her post to bring ale for him and warm milk for Kata. She slipped back to the kitchen and returned bearing two steaming bowls of fragrant stew and a hunk of bread.

"How are you, Bergdis?" Njáll asked as he tore the bread in half, splitting it with Kata.

She wiped her hand on her apron, then drew the back of it over her forehead. Bergdis's cheeks reddened at Njáll's attention, and Kata smiled to herself.

"I am well, Njáll. What have you and Kata been up to today?"

"My girl has taken a large elk for the king," Njáll said, smiling proudly at Kata.

"That's wonderful," Bergdis said. She asked if they needed anything else, but as they'd already tucked into the food, they only replied with shakes of their heads and appreciative grunts.

Bergdis slipped back behind the bar as a gust of cold air blew over them. Helga and Gunnar, two dragon hunters of old, had stepped into the tavern.

"It's a cold one out there," Helga announced as she came in, stomping snow off her boots and unwinding her scarf from her neck.

Several patrons responded with "Here, here," and raised their mugs in her direction before drinking deeply. She spotted Kata and Njáll and moved in their direction, leaning her hands on the back of the empty chair at their table.

"Quite an elk you've got out there, Njáll."

He shook his head, rubbing his beard to obscure his proud smile. "It isn't mine."

"That was your doing?" she asked Kata.

"Yes," she said, beaming as she wiped her mouth on the back of her sleeve.

"Attagirl!" Helga patted her roughly on the back. "I've got something for you, too." She rummaged in the pocket of her bear-hide coat and pulled out a flower.

"Oh, thank you," Kata said, cupping the bloom in her palm. "It's beautiful . . . but is it real? Can anything blossom at this time of year?"

"This is a special plant that blooms in the winter and early spring. Summer may not be so far away as it feels," Helga responded, then turned to the bar to order. Gunnar had already placed his.

"Wait," Kata said, addressing Gunnar. "Aren't you going to tell me a story?" Her father suddenly seemed very interested in the piece of bread he was soaking in his stew.

Gunnar approached the table in his stomping, lumbering way and stroked his beard. "You want a story, do you?" he asked, his eyes twinkling.

Kata smiled and nodded. Most of the tavern patrons were listening as Gunnar began.

"When I was just a mite taller than you," Gunnar said, indicating his height with his hand. "I snuck out into the woods and was away for three days. I journeyed to the mountains off to the west, because I'd heard tell of a dragon who lived in them, and I believed those tales."

At a glance from her father, he added, "I was a bit young to be hunting the likes of dragons then, mind you. It was before the bounties, anyhow. And the thing was—'twas not the dragon I was after. I wanted the treasure."

He looked around the room, a gleam in his eye as he enjoyed the rapt attention of his growing audience. "I climbed the mountain and found a cave. It was a passage, really, and as I wriggled through it, I swear I could see the glow of the dragon-gold. It led me on. The passage narrowed as I went, and I had to leave my weapons behind to fit through. The thrill of adventure tingled through my hands as I crawled. I could hear something now—the heavy, fire-laced breathing of the dragon as he slumbered—and I knew I had to see the beast and its hoard."

Kata grasped her bread tighter, thumb breaking through the crust as she leaned forward.

"Well, that passage just kept narrowing," Gunnar continued, moving his hands closer together as he peered through them. "At the end of it, I could barely move, but I could see—and what a sight there was for seeing. The dragon lay curled in its piles of gold pieces, licks of flames spouting from its nostrils as it snored. The beast was huge—it was the first I ever saw, and quite as big as one of the castle turrets. Amid the gold pieces were gemstones big as my fist, royal regalia—crowns and scepters and whatnot. Chests full of silver coins, engraved goblets, strands of pearls and jewels. Enough treasure for a kingdom."

"What did you do?" Kata breathed, entranced.

"Well, I had no weapons with which to take the beast—I'd left them further back in the tunnel, you see. I could barely move, I was pinched in so tight, and I feared waking the dragon. So, I shimmied my way back out, retrieved my weapons, and tried to find another way into its lair from outside the mountain. After two days of searching, I gave up. I needed food, and my father would be wondering where I was, so I returned."

"But what about the dragon? The treasure?" Kata asked, on the edge of her seat.

"We should be heading home, Kata," her father said, his tone unnaturally even.

"Well, that's the thing, isn't it, lass?" Gunnar said, stroking his long beard again. Helga handed him his mug of mead and stood beside him. "Helga here went back with me many years ago to find the dragon. I couldn't fit through that passage anymore, but we dug it out bigger. And when we got inside, to that room full of treasure? There was no dragon, and further, there wasn't any treasure either!"

"Oh, Gunnar," another old hunter said. "You couldn't fill a cat's nostril with what little truth is in your stories."

"I swear on Lady Legend that the dragon and the treasure were there when I was a lad. I've no idea what happened since, but it was there, and years later, it vanished."

His statement was met with a few more friendly cries of protest. The spell had broken, and the other hunters resumed their chatter. "We should go, Kata," Njáll said, already standing. "It's getting late."

She'd forgotten her bread and stew while enraptured by Gunnar's story, so she finished them in a few gulps. When she scraped her chair back from the table, a man who had been lurking in the corner of the tavern hurried to occupy it and lapped up what little was left in her bowl.

His clothes were tattered, and in his eyes was a hunger Kata had never known. He scared her a little, but her father called, and she forgot about that look as they ventured out into the night, retrieving the elk on their way home.

"Pabbi?" Kata asked gently as they neared home. "Why didn't you like Gunnar's story?"

"He exaggerates," Njáll said briskly.

"All the hunters do," Kata said, shrugging. "Except you. Why don't you share your stories, from your unicorn hunts? You'll tell the king, but you won't ever tell me."

"You're too young."

"I'm *not*," Kata said indignantly. "This is my fourteenth winter, and I've been in these woods, following you on your hunts, since my fourth."

They were home now, and they hung the elk in a tree out back, to be cleaned and brought to the castle the next day. Njáll studied her, his eyes weary, and then said, "Perhaps that was a mistake, my little dove."

She pulled away from him. "How can you say that? This is the only life I've ever known, and you're saying it was a *mistake*?"

"Kata, please, let's have this conversation another time. We are both fatigued, and there are things you don't know—"

"Because you never tell me anything. Not about your hunts or your past, not about *my mother*."

He winced, then let out a heavy sigh. "Someday, Kata. Someday soon. But not tonight."

"You don't want me to hunt unicorns like you," she said. "You don't want me to have the glory you had. You're afraid I'll have stories to tell the king that will be better than yours!"

"That's enough, Katrín," he said, his tone suddenly fierce. She knew she was in trouble whenever he used her full name. "There are things I cannot explain to you yet—you're too young. I forbid you from mentioning this again."

She stomped into her room and slammed the door, then lay down on the bed and tried not to cry. She was thankful for the cabin with its divided bedrooms; before her father became Royal Huntsman, their small home had but one room, and she wouldn't have been able to shut the door on her father. Exhaustion soon overtook her, and she fell asleep before taking off her boots.

Kata left the house before dawn, without telling her father where she'd gone. It was her habit whenever they had an argument. She stalked through her familiar woods, searching for a clear head at least as much as she was looking for game.

Just as the cold set in, numbing her legs, Kata glimpsed a moving blur of white up ahead. She froze. Her heart raced with anticipation—she wasn't imagining it this time. There was something there, something brighter than the snow . . . She'd never seen a unicorn before, but she knew that's what she was tracking. Swift and silent, she crept forward, moving the way her father had taught her when she was no higher than his knee.

Finally, through a clearing in the thick evergreen trees, she saw the beast. It had lain down beneath two large spruce trees. She just stopped herself from letting out a gasp when she saw—the unicorn had *wings*.

She'd heard of such a creature once, called an alicorn. But everyone had laughed at the grizzled old man telling of the alicorn he'd seen, his stein filled and emptied several times before he'd started the tale. Kata had been fascinated, but her father had told her that, if alicorns had ever existed, they'd long since flown from the kingdom. Another example of her selfish father hoarding his knowledge.

Well, he would see that she was old enough to hunt magical beings now, and she didn't need his help to do it. She thought of the handsome reward she would receive from the king for her service, and then of how she would finally have a tale worth sharing with the other hunters in the tavern.

Her shaking hands steadied.

She drew her bow and aimed her arrow at the spot where the alicorn's heart would be, a hand's width below the base of its great wing. The alicorn was still awake. It looked in Kata's direction from under its spruce-bough shelter.

When its eyes met Kata's, an immense sadness pierced her heart. She suddenly felt that to kill this pure creature would be an unforgivable act, a stain she could never wash from her conscience. She tried to shake the thought away—she had been hunting with her father her entire life; this was natural for her—but the feeling would not leave her.

Her hands trembled on her arrow and drawn bow until she released the tension and replaced the arrow in her quiver. *What is wrong with me? Think of the wealth—the fame.* The king, all the other hunters, and even Pabbi would be so pleased. He would finally see that she could do this.

Suddenly, she heard her father's voice, calling her name through the forest.

"No," she whispered to herself. She couldn't let him find the alicorn, though whether because she must prevent him from killing it or because she wanted to take it herself, she didn't know. With a last glance at the strange creature, who had laid its head down in the snow to sleep again, she turned and followed her father's voice. She sent a prayer to Lady Legend that the alicorn would still be there the next time she got a chance to slip away.

UNTETHERED

Elín

"Would you like some warm milk?" Arn asked as Elín entered his home. "Haakon and our guests are out bringing in the herd."

"Yes, I would," she said, shutting the door and cutting off the swirl of snow. If Elín were someone who believed in Lady Luck, she would have thanked her for keeping the strangers out of the way for a while.

She set her rucksack on the table and removed her cloak and mittens. Arn filled two sturdy mugs and placed them over the fire. He helped her add dried peas to the bubbling broth in his stewpot, and they began cutting up the onions and pork in companionable silence. Elín had always appreciated that about Arn, the way his slow, steady gestures could put one at ease. He was the closest thing to a father she'd ever known.

Once the pot hanging over the fire was full, Arn passed her a mug of milk, took one for himself, and they both sat at his table.

"Well," Elín said finally, wrapping both hands around the warm mug. "Have Björn and Týr told you what they want?"

Arn nodded. "They want you to travel with them."

Elín pursed her lips, trying to find the right words. "These strangers I've only just met want me to join them on a journey to find something I don't believe exists. They think I'm in danger here." When she said it aloud, it really did seem like she should say "no."

"I see," Arn said. "What do they want you to find with them?"

"A book," she said, biting her lip. "It has the spells of the Stormsingers. They think . . . They think I am one. A Stormsinger."

She was surprised when Arn seemed unperturbed by this. "Why don't you want to go?" he asked.

"Because it's ridiculous!" Elín looked away from his bearded face and sighed. "You don't look like you think this is ridiculous . . ."

He sipped from his mug. "I don't."

Elín raised her eyebrows. "You can't tell me you actually believe in the Storm-singers. Do you really think I'm in danger here?"

"I'm a simple farmer—what do I know about such things? Although I will say, most legends are rooted in some form of truth." He sipped his milk again and wiped his blond mustache with his sleeve. "You're not in danger here, that I know of, and I cannot say the same for elsewhere. But I think you should go."

"Why?" she asked. "I don't know them, and it sounds like such a long journey. What about my farm?"

"Haakon and I can take care of your farm. We've already been helping with the planting and the harvest since your mother passed. Besides, you'll be back before the ground thaws anyway."

"Really? They said that?"

"The younger one seemed to think so."

That gave her some relief. If it were a matter of leaving only for some number of weeks and returning home after . . . perhaps she could make this journey after all. Elín sipped the heated milk, not knowing what to say. The rough wooden mug was warm and familiar in her hands, like home.

"Do you think I am what they say? That I have . . . magic?" She felt silly even speaking the word aloud.

Arn shook his head. "I wouldn't know anything about that. But I've talked to Týr a bit now, and he's a good lad. I think our guests are trustworthy. You can make your own choice, Elín. But you've spent your whole life here, caring for first your mother and then your grandmother. A little adventure could be good for you."

She studied him over her mug, wondering how his words could be so close to her own thoughts. Arn had never seemed the adventurous type to her—just their strong, dependable neighbor. "Did you ever have any adventures, Arn?"

He guffawed and slapped the table. "Of course, I did. I got into all sorts of trouble in my younger days, often with your father—" He stopped short, and Elín choked on her milk.

"You knew my father?"

He kept his eyes on his mug, frowning.

Her heart raced. "Arn." It was half command, half plea.

"I . . . yes. I did." His frown deepened, and he ran his hand over his eyes, looking defeated.

"Why did you never tell me?" Elín tried, but she couldn't keep the betrayal out of her voice.

"Because I promised your mother, may she slumber well. And now I've broken it . . ." He let out a long, weary sigh.

"But why? Tell me about him! Oh, please—you must."

"I shouldn't, Elín. I can't—I promised her."

Elín held his gaze. "I have nothing left, Arn. Please. If I have family from his side, out there somewhere, if I can at least know something more about my past . . ."

Arn studied her, then finished his milk with a gulp and nodded. A decision made. "I'll tell you only this: your father would want you to go, to have adventures."

"Why?" she asked, trying to stabilize her shaking hands by squeezing them around her mug. He'd said "would want," not "would have wanted"—was there a possibility her father was still alive? That she wasn't alone in the world?

"Please, Elín. Do you want to live your whole life here, alone in that house, until you marry my son or some other local boy? Or do you want to see more of this world? Have a chance to find out what you want from your life?"

Elín had to press her lips shut to stop herself from saying that anyone with eyes could see Haakon had been sweet on Sven's daughter Yrsa for the past two years. But really, Arn's point stood.

She'd been so busy and exhausted caring for the health of her mother and then her grandmother, from running the farm, that she had never given much thought to what came *next*. Her mind had never been free to consider what more she might want. Now that it was, she felt odd. A little afraid.

She supposed Arn was right. Marrying someone and, together, eking enough from the unfrozen ground to survive the next winter, year after year, was what one did when they were grown, as she nearly was now. It was enough for everyone in her village, wasn't it? For her, too, it must be enough.

As the soup began to fill the cottage with its hearty aroma, her thoughts became more unsettled. Arn said nothing, letting her take her time to answer him. Another thought came, unbidden: she wasn't from this village, even after all her years there. Her family's small clearing in the forest that morning had shown as much. Maybe she was, as Týr put it, destined for more.

"I guess I want that," she admitted eventually. She'd never seen Arn speak so passionately, and it added to her interest. "But I think I'll tell them they must retrieve the book first before I will go with them. If I could see the spells and the runes of the ancient language with my own eyes, then perhaps I would believe."

"Seems like a sensible plan."

She scowled. "But what about my father? You truly won't tell me about him?"

"I can't."

"At least tell me this—is he still alive?"

Arn grimaced. "I can't tell you anything more. I promised your mother, Elín."

Her frown deepened. Why, even long after her death, was her mother still keeping secrets from her? If he *was* alive, she had to find him, did she not? Elín was still calculating a way to get more information out of Arn when the door let in a burst of cold air, followed by Haakon, Björn, and Týr.

"Songstress," Týr said, bowing his head to her. She fought the urge to roll her eyes.

"We can't get the last of them in," Haakon said. "Stubborn old beasts. Elín . . .?"

"What is she to do about it?" Björn sneered.

"She knows the old herding songs," Arn said, a slight edge to his voice that hadn't been there before. "The cows come when she calls."

Elín was already pulling on her cloak, but Björn's comment evaporated any hesitancy she had about singing in front of these strangers. She stepped out into the cold and walked to the edge of the fields, her dress trailing through the snow. Haakon and Týr followed her out.

Light, floating snowflakes fell, catching in Elín's hair and eyelashes as she looked for the animals in the darkness. A few cows were down in the little valley between two hills, near the hot spring. Her nose stung in the cold, and her breath crystallized in the air.

She filled her lungs with wintry air and began to sing.

The handful of herding melodies she knew were different from the other songs her grandmother had taught her. The words had no meaning, either in Elín's language or the ancient tongue. Her high-pitched, haunting tones echoed across the fields, even covered in snow as they were. The eerie notes returned as an echo. The faint sound of one cowbell reached her ears. As the herd followed their leader, the lowing of the cattle and brassy ring of their bells mingled with her song. One by one, the cows rejoined the rest of the herd in their sheltered pen.

Haakon secured the gate. "Thanks, Elín," he said, his ruddy cheeks rounding as he smiled. He started to say something else but was interrupted by Týr.

"What *was* that?"

Elín crossed her arms, bristling. But then she saw his face. If he had seemed reverent, awed by her before, he was verging on worship now. Instead of snapping back at him, she blushed and said, "It was nothing. Let's go in and have dinner."

"I'm supposed to believe you're not a Stormsinger *now*?"

"It's not magic—they're just notes that generations of village women have found their cattle respond to. All the village women know them. Right, Haakon?"

"True," he said, his breath clouding in the air. "But most of them don't sound as nice as you."

"I imagine not," Týr said, following her and Haakon back toward the house. "That was . . . unearthly. Beautiful."

Elín was glad he couldn't see the proud smile tugging at her lips. It was the closest thing to magic she knew. She loved the trust of the cows and the feel of her lungs full to bursting before she emitted the lilting, resonant sounds.

The smile didn't last.

"Has the girl come to her senses about joining us?" Björn asked as they entered, addressing Arn and making Týr wince. "We want to leave at first light."

"I have decided," Elín said. "I will go, but only after you first retrieve the Kirja. If I see it with my own eyes, perhaps then I can believe you."

Björn's nostrils flared. "We cannot leave you here, unguarded, for several weeks while we retrieve the Tome. And even if we could, such an important object would not be safe here."

His gray robes were pristine, only a little damp at the hem, whereas Týr and Haakon were muddy. He hadn't helped with the cattle at all.

Elín wondered how the book—if it existed—could be considered so important with no Stormsinger to wield its magic, but she guessed commenting on that would get her nowhere with Björn.

"Very well then," she said instead. "You have your answer. I'm staying here. I won't uproot my life for a fairy tale."

Björn opened his mouth to speak, furious, but Týr stepped in.

"Will you join me by the hearth, Songstress? I can give more details about an alternate plan as we warm up. One that might not take you away for so long."

She pulled her chair over to the hearth, and Týr took one that was already there. The flames danced across his face, casting shadows in the hollows of his cheeks and over his angular nose. Before she hadn't noticed his brown eyes, but the fire reflected in them drew attention to their warmth.

Elín wished she hadn't noticed as something warm unspooled in her belly. She cleared her throat. "What more do you have to tell me of this quest?"

Týr pulled his chair nearer hers. He rested his arms on his knees and mustered a smile.

"Songstress." He looked as if he would reach for her hand but thought better of it. "I know this is all strange to you and that you don't believe us. Perhaps we should have stayed away until tomorrow, to allow you time to grieve. But this journey—this 'quest,' as you call it—is vitally important. To many more people than just you and me."

She considered arguing that this quest wasn't important to *her*, but she held her tongue. At the very least, he was kinder than Björn, and didn't deserve to be yelled at as she had done that morning. "To whom?" she asked.

"It's a long tale, but in short, more than ten winters ago, a group of those blessed with gifts of magic were banished from their kingdom. They have hidden themselves in a mountain wilderness, and they could use the help of the last Stormsinger now to win back their homes."

Elín started to roll her eyes—now not only must she believe that she had powers, but that a whole group of other magic wielders needed *her* help—but Týr held up a hand. "I know, it's hard to believe. But look at how the cows came when you sang to them. You insist it's not magic, but then perhaps snowsong isn't either. Why shouldn't snow and the rain respond when called the right way? And this sanctuary . . . I promise, you'll believe it when you see it for yourself."

"I'm afraid I won't, because even if it exists, I'm not going."

"But I haven't told you the best part of my plan," Týr said with a quick sideways glance at Björn, who was sitting at the table, slurping down soup as Arn and Haakon watched. "It would allow you to return home in a few weeks."

Elín crossed her arms. So this must be what Arn had mentioned. "How?"

"The people of this sanctuary have a plan to defeat the king who banished them. The same king who would send bounty hunters after you if he knew you lived. I don't know the details, but I've heard they're close. If they accomplish it, the world will be safe once again for those like you—for anyone with magic. You could return here then, if that is what you wish. There would be no more danger." He leaned in and lowered his voice. "Please, think on it, Songstress. Just a few weeks away, to keep you safe, in a place full of marvelous creatures. You can begin to learn your powers there, and, in time, you might embrace your role as Stormsinger."

The boy was good. He'd woven a tale Elín wanted to believe. She remembered the lodestone and wondered what other mysteries the world might hold if she just stepped out of her village to find them. His low voice did something strange to her heartbeat, and she began to really consider the journey.

All she'd ever wanted was to take care of her farm and her family, but now . . . there was little for her here. What was a few weeks away—"a little adventure," as Arn had called it—in exchange for a world of snow magic and wicked kings and magic hideouts? She'd never been outside of Ornfoss, that she remembered, so how could she truly know the world beyond it wasn't as he said?

The spell Týr had cast was broken when Björn intruded on their conversation. They both straightened in their chairs as he approached, his hands on his hips, and asked, "Well?"

"I . . . I think she is considering the Skyli plan," Týr said. Then, glancing at Elín for confirmation, he added, "If we can return her home after helping them."

"No," Björn said, his voice cold and sharp. "We will not take her there."

"But it's the safest—"

Björn grabbed him by the collar and pulled him into the corner. They began to argue in hushed tones. Elín jumped up, seeing a chance to leave. When she stood, they both turned toward her. Björn's forehead was scrunched and angry, and Týr held out a hand as if to stop her.

"I've had enough," she said boldly. "If you two can figure out a plan—one you can *both* agree on—you can ask me about the journey once more tomorrow. Until then, I bid you good night." She donned her cloak in one smooth motion, then shouldered her empty rucksack. There'd be time to fetch her wooden bowls tomorrow. Grief and annoyance had robbed her of her appetite, so she didn't regret leaving without having any of her stew, either.

She nodded to Arn and Haakon on the way out, and shut the door firmly behind her. Then she leaned against it and let out a laughing exhale. That had felt good, refreshing. Maybe there was something to what Arn had suggested.

She may not know exactly what she wanted yet, but she knew she did *not* want to spend weeks in the bickering company of those men.

The snow sparkled softly in the moonlight as Elín rode Ský home. Once inside, though, the feeling of spidery, crawling emptiness returned. She threw another log on the embers, watching until it burst into flames and hoping the house would seem more welcoming when it was brighter. It did not.

She tucked herself into bed, but sleep eluded her. She tossed and turned until she finally gave up and threw off the blankets. Elín took her mother's hairbrush from its usual place on the mantle and tucked it into a large pocket of her underclothes, not quite willing to let herself hold it to her chest as she slept, as she had as a grieving girl. After pausing a moment, trying to convince herself it was too silly and sentimental a thing to consider, she opened her grandmother's drawer and slipped the lodestone and locks of hair into her pockets, too. Finally, she pinned the birch bark drawing to the wall over her bed.

After all, there was no point resisting these childish impulses, these desperate attempts to hold her mother and grandmother near, when she might at least allow herself a good night's sleep after this heartbreaking, maddening day. Besides, no one would ever know.

As she finally drifted off to sleep, one thought kept returning. Arn had been right about one thing: if she did want adventure or something different from her life, she wouldn't find it in Ornfoss.

Elín awoke early, just as dawn was beginning to paint the snow in soft reds and golds. She glanced around the empty home and felt hollow. Slipping out of her cottage, she mounted Ský, not bothering to saddle her for the short ride to the edge of the sacred forest.

After securing Ský to a sturdy oak branch, she wove through the trees and knelt beside Revna's grave. It had snowed in the night, so the mound of earth over her grandmother's resting place was covered, helping it blend into the landscape.

Her breath swirled above her, up into the sky, as she steadied herself. She had often visited her mother here, but the loss of her grandmother was fresh. There was a deep ache in her chest as she wondered whether Revna could have hung on for a few more days. Elín would have loved to have her here, helping her deal with these Tomekeepers. Even in the later days, when Revna's mind was confused, she had been a comforting presence.

Elín placed a gloved hand on the snow-covered mound, as if she could draw strength from Revna's love, lying latent in the ground. She closed her eyes and felt the chill breeze tickle her nose and lift strands of her hair. Then, she moved to do the same to her mother's grave. Her other hand went to the pocket where she'd stashed the hairbrush, lodestone, and locks of hair, and she smiled to herself. It was silly, but who was to know she was keeping these trinkets so close?

She approached the little carved votive stone, shooing birds away and brushing crumbs out of its hollowed-out cup from past offerings. Then, she placed a fresh piece of bread with a little of her precious honey into the stone.

"I don't know yet if I'll go," she said softly. "But if I did, I would be back in a few weeks. In a few more, there will be flowers that I can lay here for you. May you slumber well, Amma and Mamma."

Imagining that she did feel a little stronger for having visited them, she stood and turned toward home. Movement in the trees at the edge of the ancestral clearing caught her eye, but when she looked, there was nothing there. Perhaps it had been a deer.

Still, she felt on edge that someone could have been watching her, and she hoped Björn and Týr had not followed her here under some misguided notion of protecting her.

As she rode back to the cottage, she saw the strangest sight: Týr running out the door, his eyes wide with panic and his satchel bouncing against his side. Björn came out from the barn, more composed than Týr but still looking upset. When Týr saw her ride up, he nearly collapsed against the wall of the cottage and let out a heavy exhale that swirled in the cold.

"By Lady Destiny, what ails you?" Elín asked. Ský's ears flicked back and forth, uncomfortable with these strangers, and Elín gave her a comforting pat on the neck.

Týr caught his breath and said, "We were afraid something had happened to you. That you'd gone." His hand gripped the strap of the satchel he wore, turning his knuckles white.

She arched an eyebrow. "What, you thought I would run away . . . *from my own home*?"

"Not run away," he said, his expression still deadly serious. "I was afraid you were taken. Songstress, you don't understand. If certain people knew what you are, what you could do—you're in so much danger."

Elín stopped herself from responding snidely, as the poor boy truly seemed to have had a fright. Björn stormed over, his face blazing. Ský shied away from him, but Elín was glad she was still on her mare and could look down on the old man instead of shrinking away.

"You foolish, careless girl," he sneered. "Do you not know the worth of the blood in your veins? Are you not grateful for our—" He was cut off as an arrow pierced his neck.

A thin mist of blood splattered Elín and her horse, who reared and whinnied as another arrow flew past her head. Týr shouted, "Master!" and tried to support Björn's weight as the man crumpled to the ground.

Elín's heart slammed against her ribs. Time slowed to a glacial pace. She touched a shaking hand to her cheek and stared at the crimson blood running down her fingers when she pulled it away. Týr was still shouting, distantly. Another arrow whizzed by, narrowly missing him. Björn had been shot through the throat—it was already too late for him.

We're going to die.

The realization pulled Elín back to reality, and time once again moved too quickly. She turned her eyes to the trees, searching for their assailants, as her horse paced restlessly. "We have to go!" she shouted to Týr, reaching her hand down.

He knelt beside Björn, his hands and tunic covered in blood and face frozen in horror.

"He's gone, Týr—we will be, too, if you don't come with me!" Ský pranced, wanting to run from the danger. "Týr!"

He looked up as if he'd barely heard her. Then he shook his head, grabbed her blood-slick hand, and swung himself onto the back of her mare. Elín kicked her on, and the horse bolted away as another arrow missed her, embedding in the door of Elín's home.

As they escaped, she looked over her shoulder. Björn's lifeless form stained the snow red, and she thought she made out two figures in the trees, bows drawn. The shadowy arcs of arrows flew toward them, though her horse quickly took them out of range. Metallic fear filled her mouth, and she felt so, so foolish. Why had she believed herself so safe here in Ornfoss, and disregarded the warnings of danger?

If she had just gone with them when they asked, if she'd believed her grandmother, Björn would still be alive.

THE CROWN PRINCE

Kata

As Kata trudged through the snow to rejoin her father, she chided herself for not being able to kill the alicorn. *I was so close, my bow drawn, the arrow aimed . . .* It must have some strong magic that protected it, that kept humans from harming it. She must learn to overcome it if she was to become a huntress of magical beasts.

Overall, however, she was not dissatisfied with her encounter. It was her first sight of her desired prey, and just the thought of it sent her heart racing. Overcoming its strange magic only made it more exciting, more of a challenge.

"There you are, Kata," her father said as she approached. "We need to take the elk to the king this morning. It's wanted for a royal feast today." His eyes locked wary, afraid of another argument. When none came, he added, "You might have some time to chat with the prince, too."

She nodded and followed him back to the cottage.

On the way to the castle, she considered telling her father about the alicorn and asking him for advice on defeating its protective magic. But she stopped herself—after their conversation the evening before, would it not just anger him? Or worse, what if, convinced she was too young, he set off to take the alicorn himself? *I won't let him.* The thought burned fiercely in her mind as she and her father dragged the elk along to the castle.

But she could ask Prince Stefán, her oldest friend. They'd both grown up apart from the other children of Snjoreya—Kata, with the freedom of the woods and rough manners of the hunters, the prince shut up in the castle—and had grown close over the years. He would keep her secret and would certainly have no desire to hunt the beast himself.

Most of Linnafell, Snjoreya's capital, lay south of the river, while the castle sat imposingly to the north. The river wrapped around its southern face and hugged its grounds as it flowed northwest through the island. The barriers to the other sides of the castle were formed of cliffs over the sea to the east and the King's Forest to the north, which Kata knew well from hunts with her father.

After delivering the elk to the castle kitchens, they proceeded into the public chambers so her father could greet King Karvel. He always expected Njáll to sit with him and exchange gruesome stories of hunts past, either of magical beings or forest game. The rumor was that her father had the king's ear more often than his own council or the clan leaders did, so often did they go ignored.

Kata and her father bowed to the king upon entering his chambers. The king was a tall, wiry man with pale skin and dark hair. He wore a purple cloak lined in what Kata thought was ice bear fur. His gray eyes studied Kata until she squirmed under his gaze. Then, with a flick of his wrist, he dismissed her. "Run along, girl, while your father and I reminisce."

Usually, it was Njáll who sent her away, as he forbade Kata to listen to his hunting stories. Much as she wanted to hear them, running off with Prince Stefán was always a welcome consolation. Today, she didn't dare protest, exiting the room and heading further into the castle to find the prince and tell him her news.

He would likely be in the library or one of the castle balconies. She passed a group of servants, their arms full of bedding, on her way to the library. He was not there, so she retraced her steps, nodding to the castle guards as she passed the king's chambers again. Her father's deep voice and the king's laughter met her ears, and she bristled with jealousy for all the tales she never got to hear. Finally, she ran into the prince on the spiral staircase of the tower closest to the balcony overlooking the gardens.

"Kata," he said, smiling. "It's good to see you."

"I must tell you something, Stefán," she whispered, trying to listen for any footfalls on the tower steps. "I mean, Your Highness."

The prince extended his arm up the staircase. She passed him, and he followed her up the stairs and out to their favorite balcony.

Once sure they were out of earshot of any servants, Kata hurriedly began her tale. "I found something in the woods—"

She stopped short. In the bright daylight, she could see that all was not well. Stefán's quiet demeanor wasn't unusual, but she couldn't overlook his swollen eye, tinged several shades of purple. "What happened?" she asked, instinctively reaching out to examine the wound. Kata stopped herself from touching his face just in time—it was so easy to forget he was the Crown Prince.

"I'd rather not discuss it. An accident," Stefán said, his eyes flicking out to the horizon. "What were you going to tell me? You found something?"

"You must be more careful," she said, trying to look less concerned than she felt. She missed the playful Stefán of her childhood—the one who would run along the beach at the foot of the castle's cliff or through the hedge maze with her. They were growing older, that was true, but he was also growing more solemn. These puzzling injuries had become more frequent, ever since the one that had broken his ankle years ago. It had healed improperly, leaving him with a limp.

"Really, Kata, you mustn't worry about me," he said, probably seeing that her brow was still furrowed. "Tell me your news."

She pursed her lips, not wanting to drop a subject so important. He must take better care of himself. But he was waiting for her news, and eventually, the urge to share overpowered her concern. "Alright," she said, her face lighting up again. "It has finally happened! I saw a magical creature in the woods."

Stefán touched her arm, gently guiding her further away from the stairwell, where they could hear an echo of the king's laughter at some tale of Njáll's. The part of her forearm where his hand had been was oddly warm, even after he let go. "You must not speak of such things in my father's hearing."

"Oh, but I will—I'm going to hunt it. Think of the reward he'll give!" She clasped her hands together and imagined it. How proud all the hunters would be of her. How delighted the king would be. And her father would have to admit he'd been wrong.

Stefán paused and looked out over the snowy kingdom he would rule one day. His hand with the missing fingers—that way since birth—clasped the balcony's rail. "What sort of creature is it?" he asked quietly.

"An alicorn," Kata said, keeping her voice low. "No one was even sure they existed; no one has been able to hunt one. Imagine it! A winged unicorn, and I've found it." She breathed in, and said, almost reverently, "Stefán, what if it's the last one in existence?"

"You've seen such a beast, and yet it lives?" Stefán asked, attempting humor, though his smile did not reach his eyes. "This surprises me."

"Yes, that's why I need your help. As I was about to shoot it looked at me and . . . it stopped me. I don't know how exactly. It must have some sort of protective magic. You can help me overcome it. With all your books and studies, you must have some idea of how this can be done, some advice to give me."

Prince Stefán had grown bookish as he matured, and often when she visited the castle now, he would be up in the library, poring over some old manuscript or map. Though she had little interest in such things herself, she loved to see him studying such materials, especially the moments when his face would light up with some new discovery that he would then eagerly share with her.

Stefán still gazed out over the balcony, his hands on the rail. He turned to her. "Yes," he said quietly. "But we shouldn't discuss it here. Come to my chambers."

It had been years since she had last seen his room, but Kata still remembered the way as he led her through the drafty corridors of the castle. When they neared the door to his chambers, one of the servants passing by gave her a strange look, one she couldn't decipher.

He paused for a moment at the door, as if nervous to open it. She considered suggesting the library instead, but guessed he had chosen his room for a reason. Either for privacy or because he'd stashed some excellent information about alicorns there. Finally, he opened the door and led her inside, shutting it tight behind them both.

The room was still familiar, though there were subtle changes from the last time she had visited, as a young girl. The bed was still curtained with embroidered fabric, and the large stone hearth took up a good portion of the space, its fire bathing the room in warmth and golden light. But the little bronze soldiers and the carved wooden elk they'd once played with were gone. A desk sat against the window now, piled high with books and parchment, quills and ink bottles.

She felt she should make some comment on the room, but couldn't think of anything to say. When she turned toward him, though, she saw that the prince wasn't silent because he awaited compliments on his decor. She knew that expression; he'd been determining how best to say something difficult.

"Kata," he said gently. "If you want my advice, it's this: forget you ever saw the beast."

Her mouth dropped open. "But how can I? It was the most incredible thing I've ever seen! And think of the money . . . My father is growing old; I could let him retire from hunting and rest."

"I know it won't be easy," Stefán said. "But I believe it's best you forget this creature. I've been reading, and I think we may be wrong about . . ." He trailed off, then looked at her with his unblinking gray eyes. "Whatever happens, you and your father shall not want for anything, Kata. The King will see to it, and I shall as well, after he is gone." He gave her an odd, earnest look.

"You don't understand." Kata shook her head and paced in front of the hearth. "First, as generous as it is, neither my father nor I will ever accept your charity."

"I'm not speaking of charity—"

"Please," Kata said, then mellowed, realizing she'd just interrupted the future king. Talks with the prince were peppered with these strange realizations more and more often lately. She didn't like to feel that their friendship would ever change, but she knew that it must someday. When he became king, or perhaps before then, when he was expected to take on the duties of an adult Crown Prince. But today, all was still the same.

He had stopped talking and waited for her to finish with a frown.

"There was something about the alicorn," she continued. "When I looked at it, I just—I somehow knew it would wait for me in the woods. It was almost as if . . ." She paused. It was almost as if it *wanted* something from her. But what could an alicorn want from her besides its life? She shook her head, clearing away the thought. "The point is, I can find it again. And if I slay it, my whole life will change for the better. Don't you see? I'll finally be doing what I've dreamed of my whole life."

"You still dream of this? Of becoming a bounty huntress, as you did when you were a child?" The prince sighed and ran a hand through his hair. "You haven't realized there are better things—how much *more* you could do?"

She swallowed and tried to keep the hurt from her face, then crossed her arms. "Like what, *Your Highness*? What's better than what I want for myself?"

But they were interrupted by a knock on the door. A servant, summoning her back to her father, who must already be out of stories for King Karvel. She bit back a frustrated groan, then hurried out of the room and down the spiraling stairs, Stefán following close behind her.

"Good day to you, Prince Stefán," her father said and bowed, then continued out the door of the main gate.

"Good day, Prince," Kata echoed, her tone dismissive.

"Kata, I've upset you, and I didn't mean to—" Stefán started.

"All is well," she said briskly, though her tone belied the words. Lately, there were so many misunderstandings between them, and she longed for their simple days spent exploring the castle and its grounds, hand in hand.

Stefán reached out and caught her arm as she turned away, pulling her back toward him. In a gesture very unlike himself, he kissed her hand. She felt herself blush, her stomach flipping at the gentle press of his lips. But he'd only done it so he could get close enough to whisper, "Do not kill the alicorn, Kata. I command you as your prince."

She bristled; Stefán had never commanded her to do anything before. "Good day, Prince Stefán," she repeated, her voice icy, and followed her father off the castle grounds.

Kata found herself more convinced than ever that she must hunt the alicorn. She would simply have to devise a way to overcome its magic on her own. Then they would see—her father, Prince Stefán, even the king—they would *all* see she was stronger and braver than any of them thought.

HOW WIDE THE WORLD
Elín

Elín had not directed Ský or known where she wanted to go besides "away," but they'd soon crossed the bridge over the river, left behind the valley's fertile fields, and reached the wooded foothills preceding the mountains. Týr seemed an inexperienced rider, but he'd clung to her for dear life and managed to stay astride the horse.

"Where now?" Elín asked, her voice trembling. "We can't go back." The weight of the statement sunk in—her home was gone. She repeated softly, "I can't go back."

"Circle back that way," Týr said, pointing. "They won't be able to track us. We need to go north, but let's throw them off our trail first." The blood on his tunic was already drying from crimson to dull brown.

"What's north?"

"Skyli, the land I told you about."

"But I don't want to go there!"

She expected him to argue, but he was silent, only wrapping an arm tighter around her waist as Ský galloped on. Then he said, gently, "We can't stay here. Skyli is the only safe place I know."

They'd reached the trailhead for a path Elín knew wound northward. She'd never ventured up it before. Ský slowed to a trot, then stopped when Elín pulled on the reins. Týr slid off the horse and then helped her down. Her hands wouldn't stop shaking, and her blood rushed in her ears.

"I don't suppose she could join us?" Elín asked, her voice small. She already knew the answer.

Týr grimaced and shook his head. "This and many other parts of the path are too tricky for a horse to navigate."

Elín wrapped her arms around Ský's neck, burying her face in the mane and breathing in the horse's familiar earthy smell. She'd already lost her mother, her grandmother, her home . . . how could she lose this too? "Go home," she whispered. "Go to Arn. I'll come back when I can."

Tired now, the mare walked to the river and slowly followed its path along the snow-covered ground. Once, she turned and looked back at Elín, who called out to hurry her on. Her voice cracked, but she at least kept the tears at bay.

Týr used the ankle-deep snow to clean the blood from his hands, and Elín did the same, trying not to be sick. He wiped the blood from her face with the cleaner of his tunic sleeves. "Will she be able to find her way?" Týr asked, nodding toward Ský and switching his satchel to the other shoulder.

Elín nodded. "Arn and Haakon will take care of her." Her face paled. "Oh, Týr, when you don't return, they'll look for you. They'll find Björn and—what if the archers are still there?"

Týr shook his head. "No. The bounty hunters aren't interested in them. They'll follow us. That's why we can't delay any longer."

"Bounty hunters," Elín repeated numbly.

Týr nodded. "The king I told you about—he would have sent them."

He walked into the woods and came back with two branches, the right height and width for walking sticks. He handed one to Elín, and she took it absently. Her gaze was still fixed on Ský's path home, and she prayed to any of the goddesses or ancestors who would listen that Arn and Haakon would be safe from the archers. That poor, sweet Haakon would not be the one to find Björn.

"We need to go," Týr said, placing his hand on her shoulder. "If we hurry, we'll make it to another village by nightfall and can hide ourselves there. We have enough food and coin here"—he patted his satchel—"for the journey. I promise, when it's safe, I will bring you back here."

Turning to him, she bit her lip and searched his eyes. "You will?"

"Yes, Songstress. I swear it by Lady Luck."

"Týr," she said softly. "I'm sorry."

He squeezed his eyes shut and shook his head. "I can't think about that right now. There will be time to grieve later, when we're safe."

They set off on foot and, before long, were on top of the mountain—or what the villagers called a mountain, but was only the largest of the foothills.

Elín, looking down on her cottage and the fields of her farm, and Arn's, and the river snaking through the village of Ornfoss, and the sacred forest at the edge of the valley, wished farewell for the first time to everything she had known. They continued down the other side of the hill, and, in a moment, her whole world was out of sight.

As they crested the last ridge, taking Elín ever further from home, she gasped at a landscape more splendid than she ever could have imagined. An immense, crystal-blue stretch of water with evergreen trees along its shores stretched before them. Across the vast, semi-frozen water, she could see jagged snow-capped peaks reaching up toward a cloudless blue sky.

"Is that the sea?" she whispered, spellbound.

A laugh barked out of Týr. "You—you think that's the sea? Have you really never seen it?"

"I . . . have rarely left home," she said, her spine stiffening.

"I'm sorry," he said, making a palms-up gesture when he saw her hurt expression. "But what can I say?"

"Sometimes it's best to say nothing at all," she snapped, turning away from the breathtaking view before her. "Oh—I'm sorry," she said, remembering his loss, the violence they'd witnessed only that morning.

"Please don't look at me like that."

"Like what?"

"Like you pity me." Týr's voice was thick with emotion.

"But I'm so sorry about what happened this morning. Týr, you must know—I didn't believe you. I thought you were both mad, really, and I never thought anything terrible would really happen."

"I know. I'm not sure I really believed it would happen, either, until it did."

"And . . . I know what it's like to lose someone. Not just someone, but someone who might as well be *everyone* because they're all you have."

He swallowed, eyes down on the path. Then he looked up at her. "Please, Songstress. If you want to do something for me, just treat me exactly as you did yesterday. As if what happened this morning . . ."

She pursed her lips, studying him. Well, if that was what would help him right now. She arched an eyebrow and put a hand on her hip. "Would you please stop with that? Call me Elín. Try to imagine you are a reasonable person."

She could tell he was fighting a grin, so she continued, "I cannot spend the next few weeks in the company of someone who treats me as you do." As she said it, she desperately hoped it *would* only be a few weeks. To be back home in time for planting, as Arn had said, was all she could hope for now.

"That's better," he said. "And I'm sorry for laughing at you—I was just so surprised. But you may be right about me needing to hold my tongue more often than I do."

His eyes were haunted, but he seemed to be holding himself together rather well for someone who had just seen his mentor killed. Better than Elín was managing, anyway. Every time she remembered Björn's blood staining the snow scarlet, she thought she would be sick.

It was best not to dwell on what had happened to Björn. Elín cleared her throat. "What is the sea like, if this is nothing like it?"

"Ah, so you don't mind *some* conversation," Týr said, the corner of his mouth tugging up. "Just as well. This will be a tiresome journey if we aren't speaking. The sea is . . . big." He laughed, looking out over the alpine lake again. "It's beyond me to describe it. Anyway, you'll see it for yourself tomorrow—and sail on it, too—if we make it."

"Sail? You didn't tell me we'd be taking a ship anywhere!" She looked through the trees at the lake, the largest body of water she'd ever seen. How frightening would it be aboard a vessel on the vast sea?

He shrugged. "Unless you know a way to fly us there, a ship will have to do."

Squinting in the sunlight, Týr scanned the path up which they'd come. There was no one following them, yet. Then he continued down the trail leading into the next valley. Elín tried to keep up with him, but it was hard to find her footing as rocks slipped out from under her. She was frustrated at how much more she relied on her walking stick than Týr did his.

He seemed to notice and stopped under the pretense of asking her a question about her farm. She answered it, thankful for the excuse to catch up to him. After that, he slowed his pace and continued asking her questions, learning far more about Elín and farming than he could possibly have wanted to know.

"But you've seen so much more than I," Elín said. "There must be far more interesting places than Ornfoss. I think spending a day and night here was enough time for you to become familiar with its surrounds."

Týr nodded. "It is a small village, but I admit the settled life of a farm fascinates me. I've spent so much of my life traveling."

"What is the best place you have been?"

"Skyli," he said without hesitation.

"Truly?"

"Yes. It's sad when you think about how everyone living there does so because they have no other choice, but the landscape is rugged and beautiful, and the community they've created there . . ." He shook his head. "It's unlike anything else I've experienced. And the market, with all the magic-crafted goods created by giants and gnomes and huldufólk—you'll love it."

Elín had never been to a proper market—Ornfoss was too small to sustain one. Neighbors bartered goods between themselves, and a few times a year, traders came with the few things they could not make themselves. She had never realized before how wide the world was, how little she knew outside of Ornfoss, and it made her ashamed.

Their path wound through the mountains, the exertion and altitude making it difficult to carry on much conversation. Elín thought that at some point she must grow numb to the scenery, but around every turn was a breathtaking vista, another view she couldn't believe was so close to her home. The path was neglected, and rocks had fallen, covering it in many places, but it wasn't impassable. Why had she never explored beyond her village?

Eventually, they came upon a crumbling bridge stretched high over a deep ravine that cut its way jaggedly through the mountains. To their left, thundering torrents of water sped down the cliffs to join the river below.

Elín glanced over the edge, watching the descent of the falls. The drop was much higher than she could calculate—one hundred feet? Two hundred?—but she knew a fall would be deadly.

"Come on," Týr said, starting across the bridge. The wooden slats were icy, worn, and wet from the spray of the falls, and the ropes to each side swung with his movement. "You're a Stormsinger, Elín. You can't be afraid of water."

"It's not the water, it's the . . . falling." Her voice trembled, and she folded her arms so he wouldn't see her hands shake.

Týr's expression softened, and he said, in a tone gentler than Elín had expected him capable of, "Here, take my hand. We'll cross together. This is the worst bridge of the journey."

"There are *more*?" She gingerly stepped onto the bridge. A chill trickled down her spine as the falls sprayed her leg, soaking one side of her dress. *Do not slip, do not slip.*

"Yes," he said, taking another backward step. "A few more. But I've been on less sturdy bridges over much higher drops than this, and I'm still here. There, see? I'll test each slat before you step on it."

Elín slowly made her way across the bridge, but every time she took a step, following Týr, she couldn't help staring at the rocks far, far below. Each time she froze, heart racing and hands gripping the rope railing.

"Don't look down," Týr said. "Look at me."

She raised her gaze to his face and tried to keep it there as she put one foot in front of the other. The angles of his face were much more pleasant than the ravine below, and his eyes really were a nice color: a warm, inviting brown. She tripped where the bridge again met the land. He caught her and laughed, helping her onto the snowy ground.

He grinned. "Did I distract you?"

Elín didn't respond, trying not to blush. Her heart still beat quickly from fear. Or at least, she told herself it was from fear. The foamy river carried on its course far below them both. Now that it was no longer a danger, the rushing water of the falls was quite pretty.

"Are you sure that one was the worst?"

"Yes," he said. "And you did well. Come along."

At the top of the next rise in the path, as he scanned the trail behind them and then the sky, he made a half-laugh, half-snort that sounded rather like her mare.

"What is it?" Elín asked, picking her way along the rocky path.

Týr tipped his head skyward. "The sun and the moon are both in the sky. A sign that Lady Luck is with us. Or at least, I used to believe that."

"Well, we're still alive," Elín said. "But that was because of my horse, not some goddess." She was thankful for the sun, at least. It kept them warm enough not to worry about frostbite, despite the alpine chill.

Týr was quiet for a few footsteps. Then he said softly, "There was just one time in my life that Lady Luck smiled on me. I thought that one time was worth all the rest. But I should have known it would run out."

"Lady Destiny fixes the hour you'll die, but Lady Luck steps in when the hour is nigh," Elín quoted. Then she snorted and shook her head. "The goddesses are a lot of rubbish anyway."

He smiled faintly. "Ah, you leave it all up to Lady Destiny, then. Fitting, for a Stormsinger."

"I pray only to my ancestors—at least they have reason to help me. But if you must assign me any of the goddesses, I suppose she is not so bad. Perhaps you should shift your allegiance."

"No," he said, pushing his hair out of his eyes and squinting in the sunlight. "Lady Destiny doesn't concern herself with people like me. Neither does Lady Legend—she remembers great kings and warriors and Stormsingers."

"And Keepers, I should think."

He sighed. "I'll never truly be a Keeper now—my training wasn't finished. But I wasn't always an apprentice, either. I was—well, something worse before."

Elín frowned. In Revna's tales, the Keepers were trained in a fortress of stone and ice on the barrens of Viltland. Had Týr not been brought there as a child to learn? If there was any truth to her grandmother's fancies, it must be an old truth, of a world that no longer was.

"No," Týr said, as if to himself. "Lady Luck is the only chance for those like me. Although, I suppose if I knew who any of my ancestors were or where they might be buried, I wouldn't mind going to them once in a while."

Elín considered this as they continued, trying to imagine what it must be like to be adrift in the world, with no ties to the past. Perhaps he'd become a Tomekeeper and joined Björn because he was seeking such a connection. As they ascended the next mountain, their breaths grew labored as the air grew thinner. Now that Elín had Týr's silence, she found she no longer wished for it.

There were four more bridges to cross that day, but Týr was right—none were so high or frightening as the first, and she didn't need his help to cross them. It was late in the evening by the time they reached an village inn for the night, so they supped and slept without much conversation. In the morning, they woke early, broke their fast, and continued.

Around midday, they reached a port town, and Týr led Elín to a beach of smooth stones. She sat, wrapped her cloak tighter against the chilly sea breeze, and marveled at the view before her. The sea extended to the horizon, and its waves lapped the gray stones in front of her. She could hear the distant din of the docks and the calls of seagulls overhead. A slight sulfur smell tickled her nose, and she tasted salt from the breeze on her tongue.

Týr sat beside her, cross-legged, and smiled. It was a tight smile, and his shoulders were tense, but it was genuine. "*This* is the sea. How do you like it?"

"It's magnificent," she said, breathless. "I had never imagined how . . . *endless* it would be. And alive."

"It always seems alive to me, too," he said. "And as if it has a personality—it changes so much with the weather."

There were a few shells nestled among the rocks. Elín plucked one out and ran her finger over the silky mother-of-pearl inside. The beach was gray except for strands of dark green seaweed and branches of driftwood, smoothed by the sea and bleached bone-white by the sun.

During their trek, she'd had plenty of time to contemplate that Ornfoss might never again be safe for her. This was followed by a new and frightening thought: she would have to imagine a "home" that was not her farm. She'd given much thought to it as they followed the mountain paths but had decided on nothing. Now, she thought that if she must choose a new home, it might be nice to live near the sea. To experience its moods, to feel its salty breeze every day.

"Týr," she said, looking at him, then back out at the waves. She wasn't sure if he was ready to speak of this yet. "I'm sorry about Björn. If I had believed you, maybe . . ." She swallowed, unable to speak the words.

"Speak nothing of it," he said gruffly. "If we hadn't gone to Ornfoss, they might not have found you. Or perhaps your grandmother had used snowsong to conceal your location somehow, and as she entered the spirit realms, the protection left you. We can't know."

Elín shuddered to think how close they had both come to death. And why? Because Týr sought a myth and believed her blood had a strange power?

Another thought needled her. If the Kirja and the Stormsingers were not real, why would someone send hunters after them?

"I'm rather afraid," Elín admitted.

Týr gave her a crooked half smile. "Me, too."

Yesterday, she wouldn't have believed him. But last night in the inn, she'd heard his breathing grow ragged from where he slept on the floor. He wasn't taking the death of his mentor as in stride as she had first thought, and perhaps was as overwhelmed as she was at the situation in which they found themselves. Not wanting to embarrass him but needing to provide some measure of comfort, she'd waited until his breathing had slowed, then pulled one of the blankets off the bed and covered him with it.

They'd both lost everything but, Elín realized, Týr's loss was worse for being unexpected, and for being so complete. She still had Arn and Haakon,Ský, and perhaps might see her home again someday. What did Týr have? The myth of a dusty old book and unfounded confidence that she was someone important.

Her heart ached for him, and she vowed to be less exasperated toward him, as difficult as that might be.

She kept her eyes on the horizon and said, "Everything is so new for me. My world was my village, and I feel so silly and embarrassed at how little I know. You've seen and done so much more than me . . . I feel at such a disadvantage."

"Don't worry," Týr said, standing and offering a hand to help her up. She took it and stood beside him. "I was once like you. You'll catch on quickly, believe me. Shall we find our ship now? I am weary of walking, and we'll be safer across the sea."

She nodded, and he led her back into town and along the docks. She did her best not to stare at everything—the ships, the cargo, the nets of fish, the sailors and fishermen about their business—but it was more commotion and more people than she had ever seen before. Sea spray was so thick in the air that Elín could taste salt on her tongue.

Eventually, Týr stopped and called to a man aboard a large wooden ship with a dragon masthead. Shields hung along the sides, interspersed with openings for the spindly oars. Deckhands from the far-flung reaches of the world were busy with ropes or cargo. A stocky, bearded man walked along a wooden plank from the ship to the docks and greeted Týr. They shook hands, and Týr said something, praising the ship.

By Lady Destiny, Elín thought, *we're sailing with vikings!*

FIRST TRUE HUNT
Kata

Following orders had never been one of Kata's strengths.

As she and her father left the castle, passing the stage where executions took place and crossing the narrow bridge back into Linnafell, she began forming a plan to find the alicorn again. It would have to be at night, while her father was asleep, or there was too much risk he'd run across her while he was hunting. She wouldn't be able to drag the animal back herself—it was so large she didn't think even Gunnar would have the strength to pull it on a sledge alone. But that was no matter. She would mark it with a royal kerchief and return home to retrieve her father.

She imagined his face when she told him; he wouldn't believe her at first, but then she'd pull him out into the dark woods to see her prize. He would be proud. Surely *then* he would teach her all the secrets he knew of hunting magical game. After this one succeeded, the next hunt would be easier.

"I'm glad to see you looking happier," Njáll said, seeing the smile on Kata's face. "Did Prince Stefán cheer you up?"

The smile vanished. "No," she said. "I'm actually rather angry with him."

The morning had worn on, and the streets were no longer empty but filled with townsfolk going about their business. "What's wrong, Kata?"

A flame of anger flashed within her when she remembered how Stefán had taken her hand, then betrayed her, forbidding her to hunt the alicorn. But she couldn't explain that to her father. She said instead, "He's always injured of late—he had a black eye today—and he'll never tell me how it happens. As Crown Prince, he must be more careful, mustn't he, Pabbi? He's the only heir."

Njáll pressed his lips together, as if to restrain himself from saying something. Then he looked at her for so long she began to feel uncomfortable, standing in the streets of Linnafell while the crowds bustled around them.

"Kata . . ." he said finally, in a tone too low for passersby to hear. "The king . . . can be a cruel man."

Her brows drew together. "What do you mean, Pabbi?" She had never heard him criticize the king before; it certainly didn't seem a wise thing to do.

He shook his head, not looking at her, then said, "Never mind, my little dove. Let's go home."

Her frown deepened, but she nodded and followed him.

At the edge of Linnafell, an exhausted woman sat with her toddler, another babe in her arms. She held out her palm, and Njáll put a silver coin into it, brushing off her thanks.

Back on the forest path to their cabin, Kata remembered the man at the tavern the day before who had finished her stew. The beggar woman had worn the same expression as him: tired, hungry, hopeless.

"Pabbi?" When he *hmm*ed in response, Kata asked, "That woman back there—why doesn't she learn to hunt?"

Their footsteps crunched in the snow as they passed a bubbling hot spring, and he was silent for so long that she was unsure if he would answer. Then he said, "For many people, things aren't so simple."

His tone didn't invite further conversation, but Kata pushed anyway. "But there's so much game in the forest. Hunting takes some practice, but she could feed her family. When her children are grown, they could help."

They were at their front door now, and Njáll looked over Kata's head down the trail, as if to ensure no one else was there. Then he said, "We may take game from the King's Forest because I am the Royal Huntsman. Others cannot. Most of the best land for game is reserved for the king."

Kata bit her lip. "But you bring meat to Bergdis. Rabbits and fowl and such." Others, too. Now she thought of it, money wasn't exchanged when he dropped them by the tavern. She had assumed it was business of the king's, but . . .

"The king doesn't know of that," he replied. "And you must not mention it to him or Prince Stefán, do you understand?"

When she nodded, he added, "I see that the king has more than he could ever use, so I share some with those who need it more. We are lucky, Kata and because we can help, we *must* help. Do not forget that."

He gave her a long look, the worry lines in his forehead deepening, then turned into the cabin.

Her father had been so strange lately, but *why*? Kata's stomach knotted as she followed him through the door. Surely after she slayed the alicorn, things would be better. Her father would have no need to worry anymore, about the king or anything else.

In the darkest hour of the night, Kata slipped out from beneath her blankets and padded out of her room. She donned her coat, lifted the quiver strap over her head and onto her back, careful not to rattle the arrows, and slipped her hunting knife into her boot. Once outside, she strung her bow and breathed easier. Her father still slumbered inside.

She stood outside her home and looked at the stars. The moon was nearly full that night, but she could still see hundreds of stars through the trees. The moonlight reflected by the snow lit her way through the woods, and with her keen hunter's eyes, she didn't need a lantern.

What a beautiful night for my first hunt. My first true *hunt.*

She made good time trekking to the alicorn's resting place. As she neared, she prayed to Lady Legend that the beast would still be there. These woods looked so different at night, but Kata found herself making her way through them without hesitation, as if the alicorn was pulling her along, drawing her to itself.

When she found the clearing, she stopped and took slow, steady breaths with her eyes closed. She must be completely in control for this moment. When she opened them, she slipped an arrow from her back and onto her bow, nocking it. Then she stepped forward three paces, staying in the shadows. Now, through low-hanging branches, she could see the alicorn. It slept as if nothing had disturbed it since the last time she was there. Its coat was such a luminescent white that it made the snow look dull.

Kata crept forward as silently as possible. Her heart pounded as she raised her bow arm and pulled the arrow back to her mouth. *This is it.*

The same caution she'd felt the last time washed over her. She was ready for it this time, but that didn't make it any less powerful. *I will take this beast and have my reward*, she told herself. But though her arrow was aimed and her arms steady, her fingers ceased to obey. They refused to release the bowstring.

The alicorn's eyes opened. Kata narrowly stopped herself from gasping aloud, though it didn't matter—the animal already knew she was there. It lifted its head in her direction, and when she looked into its eyes, she caught a fresh wave of dread. A bolt of warning said that if she completed her task, she would regret it for the rest of her life. Her heart sank as she realized her hunt would fail yet again.

Driven by a force she didn't understand, she un-nocked her arrow and set her bow on the ground, taking the quiver off her back and slipping the last arrow into it before laying it next to her bow. She felt an irrepressible urge to be close to the alicorn, to feel the soft feathers of its wings.

She slipped through the trees, staying in their shadows, then stopped in the moonlight, standing perfectly still and allowing the alicorn to see her. It stood, and she nearly bolted, realizing how much taller it was than she. Her head only came to the height of one of its legs. It began to move toward her, and she noticed, with a twist in her stomach, how sharp its horn looked.

I must be very still, she thought as she began to tremble.

The creature advanced slowly, as if trying not to spook her. Eventually, she gathered her courage enough to take one last step to meet it. She swallowed when she saw the horn shining silver in the starlight, so close to her that with one swing of its neck, the hunter would become the hunted. *Magical creatures are dangerous*, part of her thought. *If you cannot kill it, you must go home to safety before it kills you.*

But a stronger part of her—a part she thought must be bewitched by the alicorn—took off her glove and reached out her hand. The alicorn allowed her to feel its warm, velvety nose, then rub its neck and stroke its silky mane. Its breath was warm on her cheek as it nosed her shoulder. Everything about it was softer and finer than any horse she'd seen before. Up close she saw that its coat wasn't white, really, but many shades of pearlescent pinks and blues.

Still entranced, she took another step and reached out to feel its glossy white feathers. As she traced her fingers along the edge of its wing, she suddenly froze. She had heard a voice, masculine but strangely ethereal, in her head.

Come with me.

She stumbled backward and fell into the snow, then scrambled to get to her feet again. "Was that . . . you?" she whispered, looking into the alicorn's eyes.

The creature met her gaze, and she had time to wonder whether her mind had become addled. Then, she heard the voice again.

Yes. Come with me.

The alicorn didn't move, but she knew the voice was from him. And it was in her head. "How?" she asked him, her tone full of wonder.

But a thought pricked the back of her mind—what dark magic was this? Should she not be frightened? He was *in her mind*. But she only felt calm, trusting.

You shall have the answers you seek. Come.

The alicorn, in his slow, graceful way, knelt on his front legs. Kata realized she was to mount him. She began to tremble again, but a new rush of that feeling of untroubled safety came over her, and she was steadied.

Her thoughts bubbled beneath the surface of this feeling: *This alicorn could take you anywhere. Somewhere full of danger, with more magical beasts with even stranger powers. You should not go with him. Your father could not find you, nor the other hunters. They don't know where you have gone, and you don't know even where the alicorn will take you.*

But these thoughts could not overpower the sense of peace the alicorn gave her. She climbed onto his back and, in a flash, had to grab onto his mane to stay there. His muscles rippled beneath her as he jumped, leaving the ground. His wings flapped, making strands of her hair blow around her face. Her stomach flipped as they passed the tops of the highest trees and she clung even tighter to the beast she had set out to kill. Kata had left everything—including her bow and quiver—behind.

SAILING WITH VIKINGS
Elín

E lín kept her spine straight, attempting to hide her fear. She also tried to quell her imagination, which had run away with visions of herself cowering in fear as the vikings raided a village.

Stop, she thought. This voyage would be fine. They were escaping the worse dangers tailing them. A few pirates only *might* harm her, whereas the bounty hunters had already killed Björn in trying to get to her . . . In any case, she had nowhere else to go and only Týr to trust.

"I'll help your lady onto the knarr here," Axel, the viking captain, said as he took Elín's hand and she stepped onto the ship. Týr followed, and she had a moment to appreciate that the vessel seemed more spacious once she was aboard than it had from the outside.

Captain Axel's beard, which was streaked varying shades of gray and white, reached to his waist and was braided and threaded through with metal beads and trinkets. He was dressed head to toe in a mixture of brightly dyed wool, leather, and furs. A smile pushed up his ruddy cheeks as he led them through the maze of crates and barrels to their place on the ship. She found it difficult not to stare at this strange man, and at everything the crew did to prepare for their journey.

A line of sailors passed crates hand-to-hand to be loaded below deck, while two fierce-looking female vikings hoisted the sail. Others checked ropes, retying them if needed, applied more pitch to the seams of the planks, or ensured the oars were threaded through each oar port. They were all dressed like their captain, in bright and warm clothing, braids woven through their hair and beards.

"This spot here'll do," the captain said, stretching out a hand. It was a bench behind the oars and shields lining the sides, but in front and to the left of the seat near the tiller, which she supposed Captain Axel would occupy before they set sail. Elín sat close to the ship rail and Týr sat beside her. The sail, striped red and white, billowed out in front of them.

"Now, mind her with the seasickness," Axel said to Týr. "This being her first sea voyage, it's best she eats these before we set off. Don't want her getting sickly after all the work you've done to find her." He handed Týr a kerchief-wrapped bundle, which he opened to reveal a couple of sausages and a brick of cheese.

"Thank you, Axel," Týr said. "Your men won't notice we're here."

"I hope not," the captain grumbled, then winked. He made his way to the front of the ship again. The sea breeze had picked up, but Elín could still hear Axel barking orders to the crew as he went.

Týr broke off some sausage and cheese and gave the pieces to Elín.

"I'm too nervous to eat," she said, pushing the food away and looking back at the dock and the safety of the village. Perhaps there was yet time to disembark and . . . if not go home, go somewhere that didn't require being on a vessel that moved disconcertingly beneath her as it bobbed lightly on the sea.

"Having a full stomach helps," Týr said. "Please, eat some."

She took the bits of food and began to nibble on them. "Why didn't you tell me we'd be sailing with vikings?"

Týr laughed. "This is a cargo ship, not a warship. Axel and his men do go out on raids, but for this trip they're just carrying stores to supply their friends across the sea. We're perfectly safe. And besides, our options are a bit limited—only those operating outside Snjoreya's laws can take us where we're going."

"Oh." The crates and barrels she had imagined full of every kind of weapon seemed mundane now. She caught a glimpse of blue-gray fur as a cat slinked around the cargo.

"Don't you trust me?" Týr said, something catching in his expression, stopping it from becoming a full smile.

"I'm trying to," Elín said.

Something hard glinted in his eyes. "You can trust me. I may not have finished my training and sworn to put the Stormsingers above all else, but I'm still bound by Björn's legacy to protect you. If anything makes you uncertain, ask me about it. I'll never lie to you. I cannot stand any form of dishonesty."

Elín looked back to the port to avoid the intensity of his gaze. "How much longer until we arrive at—what did you call it? Skyli?"

"We should go ashore tomorrow morning. Then we'll trek up the mountain. We'll be there by nightfall."

"It's not as far, then, as I thought." Elín smoothed her hands over her skirts.

Týr nodded, looking out at the horizon as the vikings let loose the ropes, turned the sail to the wind, and put out to sea. Elín's stomach began to turn as the ship rocked on the waves, and she finished her cheese and sausage quickly, hoping it would help as Axel had promised. She watched the other ships and fishing boats, and the village beyond them, grow smaller as they pulled away.

"Will we lose sight of shore?" Elín asked, suddenly worried. How frightening would the sea be if they were so far out that the land vanished? She imagined water on all sides, stretching to the horizon. How would they find their way?

"It's a short journey," Týr said. "The weather is clear, so we'll only lose sight of this coast for a short time before the far coast is within sight." As they finally sailed away from port, he let out a long breath and slumped, likely relieved to have evaded the bounty hunters.

They were silent for much of the day, watching the crew and the lapping of the waves. Elín fed the ship's cat a few bits of sausage until Axel scolded her, saying he needed to earn his keep by catching rats. Týr pointed things out to her, giving her names for some of the crew, the tasks they were performing, and the parts of the ship. She was growing more comfortable with him and found his past intriguing. If she'd been given the choice now, she thought she might have said yes to this journey.

Elín gripped the side of the boat as the shore faded from view, but her fear soon passed. As she looked all around them, nothing but waves to the horizon, she felt unbearably light and free. Movement in the water behind them caught her eye. Smooth, black-and-white shapes slid above the waves and back below them again gracefully. Their markings were so sharp, such deep black and bright white, that they didn't seem quite real.

"Oh, *look*." She tugged on Týr's tunic sleeve, and he turned on the bench.

"Whales," he said, smiling at her. "Orcas. They're amazing creatures."

Elín nodded, still entranced by the breaching whales. What a vast, varied world it was. She'd never known. What else might be out there? Perhaps there was such a place where beings were capable of magic. But *she* wasn't one of them.

They watched the orcas until they faded from sight, then turned to face the billowing sail again. "I can't wait to show you Skyli," Týr said.

Elín attempted a smile, then looked out to where the blue of the sky faded murkily into the gray-blue of the sea. She wasn't so eager to reach her destination, to disappoint him. He'd spent his whole life preparing for this. What would happen when she took it away? When he realized that perhaps the Stormsingers had never been real at all?

"Týr, I know you've seen Skyli," Elín said, turning to him, "but as far as me being a Stormsinger—whatever your master or my grandmother might have told us . . ."

She bit her lip against the stabbing pain of loss she felt when mentioning Revna. And then there was another prickle of guilt—had Björn died for a lie? She swallowed and said, "I have no powers; there is nothing special about me." She ran her fingers along the side of the ship and looked out to sea.

"You do," Týr said without any hint of doubt. "Don't you believe it?"

Elín pursed her lips and gave him a skeptical look. "I believe only what I can see and hear and touch."

He looked around them, and, seeing that the vikings were all busy with their tasks, said quietly, "Perhaps I can show you then."

"Týr, really . . ." Elín started to protest.

"Hold out your hand," he said.

She looked at him doubtfully, but, seeing his determined expression, she stretched out her right palm. He uncorked his waterskin and poured a small measure into her hand. Her expression only grew more skeptical.

"Alright," he said. "Now sing these words—"

"Týr," she said, suddenly feeling frightened. "This isn't a good idea—I cannot do this, and even if I could, what if I do something wrong?" *What will happen when you find out I'm not who you think I am?*

"You won't," he said. "This incantation will freeze the water, nothing worse. Now hurry, before any of the crew see what we're up to." He sang it softly to her.

Elín looked into his confident, trusting eyes. Her brows pulled together, and she asked, "Can you sing it again?"

He did, and she thought she recognized the tune. Amma had sung it a few times when it was chilly outside. Had her words caused the frost to cover the grass, the trees, the cottage? It couldn't be.

Quietly, cautiously, she began to sing the spell, her eyes locked on the little pool of water in her palm. Nothing happened. She felt increasingly foolish but finished the song anyway.

Then, on the last note, she saw something. The surface of the water crystallized, icing over in a snowflake-like pattern. She gasped, stunned that anything at all had happened. But just as suddenly as it had appeared, it vanished. There was only water in her palm again.

Her widened eyes met Týr's. He beamed and squeezed her shoulder. "I told you so. I knew you could do it."

"But where did it go? What happened to it?" she asked in a stunned whisper.

"The spells take practice," Týr said. "And concentration." He glanced around the ship to be sure the crew were paying them no mind, then said, "Try again. Imagine the water freezing as you sing."

She nodded and began to sing again, softly, closing her eyes so she could better imagine the water in her palm freezing. About halfway through the incantation, she felt a tingling in her palm, and she smiled, finishing the song before she opened her eyes.

"But . . . it's gone," she said, seeing only water in her hand. Her stomach felt heavy with disappointment. Did she imagine it the first time? If only it were as obvious as the old herding songs—either the cows came home or they didn't. No half-glimpsed ice crystals or palms prickling from either magic or nerves.

"It's alright," Týr said, wiping the water from her hand with the hem of his tunic. "I think you almost had it. Anyway, you've done it once, and you will again."

"Does the spell work for you?" she asked.

"No. I'm not Stormsinger, remember? I'm a Keeper's apprentice. Or, I was."

"You know," Elín said, "you aren't what I expected, when I heard stories of the Keepers of the Tome."

One of his crooked grins flashed across his face. "You aren't like I expected, either." Before she could protest, he said, "I have no doubt that you are one, but you aren't like the Stormsingers I imagined."

"You must be very disappointed, then."

"Not at all," he said. "The Stormsinger I expected . . . well, she wasn't as easy to talk to as you. Power over wind and water had made her rather haughty. And she didn't have eyes like yours . . . a rare, deep blue. Like the sky just before nightfall."

Elín turned away to hide her blush.

Týr nudged her with his elbow. "What about me? What did you imagine?"

Björn, she thought immediately. But she didn't want to hurt him, so she said, "An old, wise man. I suppose I pictured him rather snobbish too."

It had been too close, still. Týr blinked a few times, his eyes shiny, and looked out to sea.

"I'm sorry," Elín said softly. She reached out as if to take his hand, but dropped her arm to her side instead.

"Does it get easier?" There was a vulnerability in Týr's voice that made her desperately want to say yes.

"No," she said, giving him a sad, knowing smile. She should know, having lost everyone dear to her already. Even Arn and Haakon—would she ever see them again? "It doesn't. But time will soften its edges, and you will grow more able to bear it."

He let out a slow breath, then nodded once, tightly.

The sun was slipping into the ocean, bathing the sky in warm hues. First pastel purple and peach, then rich gold, deep amber, and the red of winterberries.

Living in her valley, hemmed in by mountains, Elín had never seen so much of the sky at sunset, and she could not pull her eyes from its beauty. When the sun had gone, the night became chill, and a heavy weariness came over her.

They had traveled far in the last two days. And perhaps—if she had truly done magic—it had taken more energy than she would have expected. She covered herself the best she could with the scrap of sailcloth one of the vikings had given her. The stars winked awake as the sky darkened, and Elín lay on their wooden bench. She slipped into sleep easily, lulled by the rocking of the knarr on the waves.

When Elín awoke, her shoulder and hip were sore from lying on a hard wooden bench, but she was otherwise surprisingly comfortable. Her head rested against someone's leg, and an arm was around her, draped casually across her side. Elín enjoyed the warmth and comfort for a moment before she became fully conscious and remembered where she was: on a viking ship, with a near-stranger as her guide—and, apparently, her pillow. She bolted upright.

Týr was already awake, leaning against the side of the ship. Her face burned. "Oh—I'm sorry. I didn't mean to—" she stammered.

"All is well," he said with his usual smile. "I wanted to let you sleep; today will be a long one. But look, we've made it."

He pointed off the starboard side of the ship. Elín wiped the last traces of sleep from her eyes as she took in the mountains looming before them. Axel was barking orders as two crewmembers dropped the anchor. Another pair were readying a small boat to take them ashore.

Axel paddled them out himself, chatting with Týr as they went. Elín gazed in awe at the steep mountain. She wondered how on earth they would climb it and where the hideout was. Hopefully, not at the top, which was shrouded in clouds.

"Thank you, Axel," Týr said. "Your help makes all the difference to our cause."

"Of course, lad. Now you two take care. If you succeed, in time, these waters may be safer for all to traverse."

Týr and Elín watched him paddle back to the ship and board again.

On the ship, she'd thought back to the arguments Týr and Björn had had about where to take her. Between the old Keeper's insistence that they did not go to Skyli and the way Axel and Týr seemed to know something about a "cause," Elín felt uncomfortable. Týr had told her he would tell her anything she asked. It was time to test that.

"Why didn't Björn want to take me here?" she blurted.

"Ah," Týr said, grimacing. "I wondered when you'd ask about that."

"What is the other place? The one where he wanted us to go?"

"It's a barren island called Viltland, and it's where the Keepers and Storm-singers before us would train. The Kirja is hidden there, far from the king's reach." She'd heard of Viltland—a land of liquid fire and ice like stone—from her grandmother's stories.

"So, we still need to go there, too. But why didn't he want me to go to Skyli?" Elín asked, crossing her arms.

Týr sighed. "My master and I had different opinions on the responsibilities that should be placed on you."

Elín's blood went cold. "Oh?"

"He thought we should just find you, teach you to wield your powers, and keep you and the Kirja hidden away."

"And what do you think?"

He turned back toward her then, his warm eyes capturing her gaze. "That you have a responsibility to use your gifts for good, so long as you are safe."

Elín swallowed back her panic. "If I do have gifts," she asked, "shouldn't it be up to me how I use them? And where we go?"

"Of course. It is still up to you. But if I took you straight to Viltland, like he wanted, you wouldn't see the good you can do. The people here who need you."

She looked away, seaward again. The viking ship had vanished out of sight. Elín was stranded with Týr and whoever lived at this mountain hideout. Hadn't Captain Axel said, "You found her," when they arrived at the knarr? Even he knew more about Skyli and what was in store for Elín than she did.

Afraid of the hopeless feeling growing within her and too proud to cry in front of Týr, she latched onto anger instead. "Let's imagine for one moment that I actually agree to stay here, and we find the magic book, which I shall pretend exists," she said fiercely. "What then?"

"Well," Týr said, clearing his throat, "they believe you can help them defeat the king and win back their homes. They'll take good care of you here."

"Until they find out I have no powers—that I can't summon storms or calm the sea. Until they find out I can't help them." That she knew nothing of their world. He was silent for so long, Elín wondered if he had realized she was right; whether they wouldn't be friendly toward her when they found out she couldn't wield snowsong. "Why did you bring me here when I was safe and happy and—" She struggled to find the word. When she realized it was "small," she bit back tears. "I was safe back home in Ornfoss. Before you led hunters to my home and dragged me away."

Týr winced. "Perhaps it felt safe there," he said gently. "But I promise that this is the safest place in the world for you now."

"I don't even believe this place exists. That any of it exists."

"It does," he said. "Please, come with me and see it for yourself."

She shook her head. "Tell me first. Tell me the whole history of this place and that other kingdom. I'm tired of knowing nothing."

He glanced to the side and said, "Look, Elín, there are those here who can explain things to you better than I can. Let Eldri or one of the other leaders give you the history."

"No," she said, shaking her head. "I want to hear it from you. I won't take another step until you tell me everything you know."

Týr sighed and sat against a boulder. He patted the ground next to him, but only shrugged when she refused to sit. "Alright," he said. "Where to begin . . . ?"

THINGS YOU MUST SEE

Kata

The wind rushed against Kata's face in great gusts with each flap of the alicorn's wings, blowing her shoulder-cropped hair into her face. Her knuckles went white from clasping his mane. She spent a few minutes repositioning her knees over his shoulders until she found a place where she could use them to hold tight. When she looked up, the night sky filled her vision. She'd never seen the vast sky unhindered by trees or village lights before, and she found herself breathless as she took in the thousands of stars, hung like jewels on black velvet.

When she managed to make herself look away, down toward the earth once more, her stomach lurched. They were high up now; the kingdom grew smaller as they soared upward, and both her fear and her wonder grew greater. It was so strange to see things like the castle and the river from above. Kata was reminded of a map of the kingdom Prince Stefán had once shown her. Before seeing the map, she had never envisioned her homeland from a bird's eye view, and she had been amazed.

Now, though, it was night, and she could see each part of the kingdom as it had been drawn on the map: Linnafell, the river, the King's Forest, even a glimpse of the western mountains. She suddenly felt a great pain of homesickness, like an arrow through her heart. *Will I ever return to this kingdom, my forest, my father, again?*

But even as she thought this, a fresh wave of that peaceful feeling rolled over her, and she was able to enjoy the sensations of flight again. Now that the alicorn was flying faster, her hair stayed out of her eyes, whipping behind her. She breathed in the brisk night air, which was cool but somehow didn't make her shiver. It smelled clean and fresh. Since the alicorn was no longer climbing but flying levelly over the ocean, she carefully stretched out her arms and closed her eyes, imagining the wind carried her without the need for magical beasts.

When she opened her eyes again, her island kingdom was out of sight. They were still over the sea, flying eastward. Her stomach lurched, and she panicked. "Take me back," she said to the alicorn. When he didn't respond, she said it louder. "Take me back! Return me to the forest!"

The alicorn turned his head, eyeing her. Then, his slow, steady voice entered her mind again.

I cannot. There are things you must know. Things you must see to believe.

Kata swallowed, remembering all the tales of bounty hunts she'd heard over the years—the ways magical beasts could trick not just your senses but your mind. Even as she thought of her fears, her pulse did not race, and that feeling of calm returned, like a blanket over her sense of panic. Could alicorns control emotions as well as speak into minds?

She cleared her throat and said loudly, to be heard over the wind, "When I have seen these things, will you return me safely to my father?" She realized she had nothing to bargain with if he said no, but she tried to keep her voice sounding brave.

The alicorn said nothing for two more beats of his wings. She felt his hesitation; there was more he wanted to say, but he held back. Finally, she heard his answer in her mind.

Yes.

She let out a breath. That was the best she could hope for—but what good was the word of a magical beast?

Kata ached for her bow and quiver. She was so accustomed to wearing them that the places where they would have lain across her back felt too light and empty. If the alicorn should turn on her, what would she do?

Suddenly, she remembered her hunting knife, tucked into her boot. Slowly, so the alicorn would not feel her move, she untangled one of her hands from his mane and slid it into her boot. The knife was there, the handle real and solid as she wrapped her hand around it. She would not be completely defenseless if this beast attacked her.

Turning her attention back to the sea below them, a shore had emerged on the horizon. The new land was soon below them. As the alicorn started to descend, mountains she'd never seen before rose in front of them. She slipped her hand out of her boot and back into his mane. *Be ready*, she thought. That was what her father always told her—be wary, be ready, and your hunt shall succeed.

The alicorn landed as gracefully as he had alighted, and Kata slipped off his back, giving him a questioning look.

We haven't arrived. He answered, holding eye contact with her. *But we must rest. We'll continue our journey tomorrow.*

I could kill it now, she suddenly realized. She was close, and it would not suspect her. She could kneel, pretending to adjust the strap of her boot, then leap, knife in hand . . .

But there it was again. That ache in her heart when she thought of killing this beast. Its pure white coat that dulled the snow, stained with blood . . . she had to stop herself from shuddering at the mental image.

Maybe it was because, aside from the ability to speak with in her mind, the way he spoke was so unexpected. He had an intelligence that the other game she hunted did not. Even if the elk or boars were able to speak, it would not be in the way he did. So like a human.

The alicorn looked back at her, indicating she was to follow. The mountains loomed around them, but he led her into a forest, to a snowless cove beneath one of the tallest trees. The ground beneath was made soft with fallen spruce needles.

She climbed under the branches and curled up. The alicorn laid down against her back, one wing extended over her, as if in protection. She found she was tired and had no idea what to feel anymore. It was impossible to tell which emotions were hers and which were from the powers of the alicorn.

Her eyes opened wide as she realized there *was* a way. *If I work myself into a panic and the alicorn calms me . . . I will know.*

And surely she had enough fuel for panic. She had disobeyed her father, and now he would wake alone at home. She would be gone, and he would be so afraid. All the hunters would be out looking for her. The only trace of her left would be her bow and quiver, left in the woods. Would he go to the king? Would King Karvel offer his men in the search? What would Prince Stefán think—would he fear for her, too?

No. Prince Stefán would know. He would know she had gone after the beast. She had told him and only him about the alicorn. Would he tell the others? If he didn't, they'd never find her. But if he did, they would go after the alicorn, and he had wanted to protect it. How long before they gave up the search? And then a question that stung: *would Prince Stefán protect me or the alicorn?*

Her throat went dry, and her hands clammy. Her heart beat faster now, but then the now-familiar feeling—which had to be from the alicorn—intruded, covering her panic. She could swallow again, and her heart slowed, but her thoughts remained free.

He will drag me to the ends of the earth, and I will feel calm all the way. He will keep me from receiving that special power of fear—the extra strength that comes when your pulse races, the crystal-clear focus you gain at the end of the hunt, when you are so close. Without that, how will I defeat him?

But her eyes were heavy, and she was warm beneath her shelter built of alicorn wing and evergreen boughs. She felt peaceful under the alicorn's spell and drifted to sleep before she could decide what her next move should be.

In the morning, when Kata woke, the alicorn was gone. Next to her was a leather pouch which she found to contain dried meat and berries. The food looked familiar to her—dried venison, most likely, and bilberries. As she wondered whether to trust food from the alicorn, her stomach protested. She took a few careful bites and, experiencing no ill effects, wolfed down the rest.

Her mind felt clear, free from the influence of the alicorn's power. She realized now that she had been in a haze, ensnared by the wonders of the alicorn: the flying and his strange powers. Now she could evaluate the situation again, and she saw what she must do. *When he comes back, I will stab my knife through his heart. I must do it quickly, before he realizes what I'm about and stops me with his magic. I must not feel panic—I must be steady.*

Having a plan made her feel steadier already. Though there were details she did not have: how would she get back home, across the ocean? Were there people nearby? There had been no sign of any from the air, only endless wilderness, probably haunted by magical beasts worse than him. If she did make it home, she would need some evidence of her hunt for the bounty. Maybe the horn and some feathers from the alicorn's wings after she slayed it.

But she had little time to think over these things before the alicorn returned, and it was time to attack. Before thinking, before giving herself a chance to feel the fear it would sense, she drew her knife and jumped toward the beast, ready to thrust her blade into its chest.

The alicorn went still and gazed into her eyes. She was still, too, her knife drawn back. All she had to do was extend her arm, forcefully, and the creature would be dead, would be hers. What stayed her hand?

Your father could do this. All the people you love do this. They will be proud. Songs of your prowess as a huntress could make their way to the king's chambers. The bounty will secure your father's comfort in old age.

But as she stood, her hand holding the blade began to tremble. The alicorn could just as easily pierce its sharp horn through her heart, and yet he remained still, allowing her this chance. Slowly, she realized the full depth of her fear was present. He was not using his magic to comfort her now.

Her hand slackened, and the blade dropped to the ground. A tear dripped down her cheek and she collapsed, kneeling in the snow under the weight of both what she had just done and not done. "I'm sorry," she whispered, though whether the words were for the alicorn, her father, or herself, she couldn't say.

Rise. She felt the alicorn's command, and she obeyed, her eyes on the ground. Would it kill her now? She hoped it would be quick.

You will have many chances more, if my death is what you desire.

She looked up and met his eyes. She had so many questions that she didn't know which to ask first.

We'll reach our destination today. Answers await you there. Come. He knelt, bending his front legs as he had the night before.

Kata slipped her knife back into her boot, watching for a reaction from the alicorn as she did so. He gave her none. Then she stepped forward and placed her hand flat against his forehead, his horn between her thumb and forefinger. She closed her eyes, not quite knowing what she wanted to do, then tried to say, "I'm sorry," without using her voice. Maybe he could feel her emotions, since he was able to change them.

The alicorn shook out his mane, and she heard him whisper, *So it is true.* But she didn't know what he meant. She felt that he'd forgiven her, though, and climbed onto his back. He straightened his front legs, lifted his wings, and asked, *Are you ready, Kata?*

"Wait," Kata said, lacing her fingers into his mane. She wondered how he knew her name, and suddenly felt ashamed that she didn't know the name of this creature who had carried her so far and shown her kindness when she threatened death.

"What's your name?"

Magni, he said, and then launched off the ground, taking Kata soaring over the mountains.

SONGSTRESS OF STORM AND SNOW

Elín

"Many years ago, a king rose to power across the sea." Týr began his story gazing off into the distance, as if it would allow him to see back in time. Elín recrossed her arms, shifting her weight from foot to foot.

"King Karvel feared magic. He feared those able to wield it would become more powerful than him. So he banned it. Stormsingers and human-like creatures such as mermaids and huldufólk were banished from his kingdom. A bounty was placed on other magical beasts, and many in his kingdom began to earn their living by hunting them."

Perhaps it was only the winter chill, but Elín shivered, the hairs on her arms rising. It sounded like other fanciful tales her grandmother had told of those who sought to destroy magic generations ago, and the ways the Stormsingers had fought back.

"Your family lived in that kingdom. Snjoreya," Týr said, meeting her eyes. "About twelve winters ago, your mother and grandmother fled with you. They made a home in your town of Ornfoss, hidden far away from this king."

"How do you know all this?" Elín asked, biting her lip and looking away across the sea. Surely she would remember having crossed it before.

"Björn," Týr said, his voice catching. "He spent years trying to find your grandmother after the other Stormsinger he knew of died. But they chose your hiding place well. Or maybe your grandmother used her magic to keep it secret."

"Týr," Elín said, her brows pulling together. "They never spoke a word of this to me. If I'd escaped from this king, and was living a quiet life in Ornfoss, why did you and Björn come for me now?"

He stood and came to her side, arms crossed, looking out at the sea as she did. "Because the king did not satisfy himself with expelling magic from the borders of his kingdom. In recent years, he has sent hunters further afield, offering more and more bounty for each magical being killed."

"Is that who came after me?" She let out a heavy breath and wrapped her arms tighter around herself.

He nodded. "I think they were after Björn and me. I hope they don't yet know about you. The last Stormsinger—the last one besides your grandmother and yourself—was killed under the king's orders only a few years ago. He believes the Stormsingers are all gone, and prides himself on having wiped out your race. If he knew that you still lived, with your powers . . ."

"He would quickly remedy that mistake," Elín finished for him.

He nodded, then turned to her. "I'm sorry I didn't tell you all this sooner. You already doubted me about the Kirja and the Stormsingers and all of it. Björn thought if I told you all at once, you'd never come with us."

"I understand," Elín said, putting a hand on his shoulder briefly. "But from now on, you must tell me all you know. No more secrets."

"Of course."

She took a deep breath. "Then tell me—what do you know of my father, of the rest of my family?"

"I'm afraid very little," Týr began, and Elín's shoulders fell. "Your father stayed behind in the kingdom of King Karvel. I don't know why. If he or any of your other family still live, I don't know anything about them. Björn was focused on the safety of your grandmother and, especially, you."

Elín tried to hide her disappointment. Would Arn, at least, tell her what he knew? Surely he would after all she'd been through—if he and Haakon hadn't gotten tangled up with the bounty hunters. She ran a hand down her braid and asked, "So, this mountain safe place . . ."

"Many of the creatures who fled came here, if they could. In the dead of winter, it is connected to the other kingdom—Snjoreya—by ice. The journey over that northern ice field was very long and cold. Many didn't survive, but those who did stayed here. They have been waiting, planning . . . looking for a way to overthrow the king so they can return to their homeland."

Elín swallowed, and her eyes widened as she realized what this must mean. "They were waiting for someone like me. With the spells in the Kirja . . . they'll expect I can do magic. That I can save them."

She shook her head and took a few steps backward. Týr's eyes said "yes" even as she saw him struggle to phrase it differently, to soften the blow.

"No, Týr, I cannot do this! I hardly believe I possess any magic, and if they think I can save them . . . I have nothing against a king and his army!"

"Elín, please," Týr said, his hands reaching out. "One step at a time. First, we keep you safe. Then, I'll find the Tome. The others will help us plan, help you learn to use your powers. It won't come all at once."

She crossed her arms and turned to gaze up at the mountains, looming tall before them. The vikings had left, and she had no way of getting home. Even if she did, it wasn't safe there anymore. It wouldn't take long for the king's hunters to ask why Björn and Týr had been there . . .

And if she went elsewhere without at least seeing this mountain hideaway, would she not always wonder what could have been?

If the king succeeds in his plans, and I did not help them in whatever ways I could . . . She bit her lip and fingered the end of her braid. She knew what Revna would do.

"Alright, Týr," she said, sighing even as his face brightened. "Lead the way, and I'll take this first step, though I cannot promise I'll complete the whole journey. I doubt I'll be able to help."

"The first step was leaving Ornfoss with me," Týr said. "I know your hand was forced there, but this next is important as well. You must see this place for yourself and stay here, where you'll be safe, while I retrieve the Kirja."

She shook her head. "No," she said. "I'll go with you to get the Tome. We need to stay together."

He pressed his lips together and said, "It's too dangerous."

"But Björn wanted me to go where the book was hidden."

Týr grimaced. "He and I disagreed on that point. I believe you're safest here, with other magic users to protect you. The Kirja is in a remote place that we hope the king's men will never find, but it's unguarded."

"Your plan was to leave me here alone?" Elín asked, her voice breaking as another wave of the now-familiar loneliness, that driftless feeling, welled up. "With all these people who think I can save them?"

"Only until I get the Tome. Then I'll return and—"

Before he finished, they both heard something taking the trail down the mountain toward them. Something large that breathed heavily. They turned to look up the icy path and Elín had to struggle to stay upright; her knees buckled at the sight of the ice bear approaching them.

Elín had heard of ice bears before, but she hadn't really believed them real. This one was larger than any animal she'd seen before, his shoulders well above her head. He took slow, lumbering steps on his giant paws. His head swung back and forth slightly as he kept his eyes on them. His fur was thick and, she suspected, warm and soft. The bear took great, huffing breaths, sending swirls of vapor into the cold air. Elín found herself frozen in place, wishing she did have the power to protect herself and Týr with snowsong.

In the corner of her eye, she saw Týr bend to one knee, his right arm in front of him like a shield and his head bowed. He pulled on the corner of her cloak, and she knelt in the snow, attempting to make her shaking, slow-moving limbs imitate his pose. She hoped Týr knew what he was doing; they'd just made themselves easier targets for the ice bear.

But the white bear stopped a stone's throw away from them, and a small creature slid off its back and took a few steps forward. He had pointed ears and delicate features, and suddenly, Elín realized Týr was bowing to *him*, not the bear.

"Where is the Tomekeeper?" The man's voice sounded reedy yet ancient.

Týr shook his head, grimacing. "He didn't make it."

"May he find peace in the spirit realms."

The elfen man stepped closer to Elín, and she raised her head to meet his eyes.

"You've found her, then. She's the last Stormsinger?" the man asked, his voice a little awed as he addressed the question to Týr.

"Yes," Týr replied. There was no doubt in his voice.

The man stepped up to Elín. He was so short that their eyes were level as she maintained the pose of respect. His eyes were a clear, icy blue and surrounded by fine wrinkles. Slowly, he put his hand to her cheek. It was warm, though he wore no gloves or cloak.

"You shall wield much power with your voice, Elín. Welcome, Songstress of Storm and Snow, the last of her kind."

She didn't know how to respond to such a grand introduction. Her heart had finally slowed to a steady pace as she realized the ice bear was not a threat to them, but now she grew anxious again. What incredible things would these people want from her?

Seeing that he expected a reply, she finally managed to stammer, "Th-thank you."

"Elín," Týr said. "This is Eldri. He is huldufólk and the chosen leader of those who live here on this mountain."

Not knowing what to say, she bowed her head again, which seemed acceptable.

Eldri spoke once more, this time to Týr.

"Come," he said as he turned and approached the bear again. "There is no sense in standing here in the cold. Come up, come in, and be warm." Faster than seemed possible, he took his place on the ice bear's back, gave it a signal, and the bear turned back up the mountain path.

Týr rose and offered a hand to Elín, but she refused it and stood on her own, brushing snow from the knees of her dress. She gave him an icy look, then turned to follow the bear.

"Elín, please," he said, catching her hand.

"What, Týr?"

"I was trying to explain . . ."

"Explain how a whole mountain of people are now expecting me to save them? With the amazing powers they believe I possess, when I can't even freeze water in the palm of my hand?" She tried to mask her panic with frostiness, but it showed through at the edges of her voice.

"They've waited a long time to find you. They'll be patient while you learn." Týr let go of her hand and looked over her shoulder. She looked, too. The ice bear was almost out of sight. "I'm sorry," Týr said. "I keep making mistakes. I wasn't ready for this."

Elín turned to follow Eldri and the bear without responding.

"Wait," Týr said, and she barely kept herself from turning her eyes skyward, instead turning her attention back to him.

"What?"

"I know this is more than you knew it would be when we found you in Ornfoss. If it were safe, I would take you home now. And if this is too much . . . we can turn back. I can't take you home, or promise anywhere else is safe, but I will take you wherever you wish to go. If you would rather find a new home."

Elín inhaled sharply. "You will?" That was what she wanted, wasn't it? Safety, a new home. Somewhere she belonged.

"Yes," Týr said.

But where would she go? And wherever she went . . . she'd be alone. She blinked a few times, then her brows drew together. "If I left . . . what about the Tome? And the king—what will the people of this mountain do?" She looked down at the snowflakes clinging to the wool of her dress and asked, quieter, "How will I know whether I can become a true Stormsinger?"

"They'll find another way to do what needs to be done. But they could use your help, and the snowsong you'll learn. As for the rest, that's up to you."

She sighed, realizing she couldn't leave now. Her home was gone, and she had nothing with which to start again elsewhere—only the clothes she wore and the sentimental items in her pockets when they'd fled. Ský might bring her some comfort still, but the animal would be better off with Arn and Haakon.

Even if she could return to Ornfoss, she imagined herself wandering the village, listless, dreaming of the adventures happening far away, to other people. The excitement and impact on the world she would never have. And if she truly could help the refugees here . . . she would try her best.

"You've made your point. I'll stay at least for tonight."

Týr's mouth pulled up into a half smile, and he gestured up the mountain. They could still hear the ice bear's padding steps and snuffling. They followed him up the path, Elín bracing herself for whatever new adventures, whether horrible or wondrous, awaited her.

All Beings Magical and Mundane

Kata

Magni landed on a snow-covered cliff overlooking a valley between two peaks. Kata tried to gracefully dismount, but she still hadn't got the hang of it and ended up sliding off him sideways and thudding into the snow. She stood and brushed herself off, then asked, "Why have we stopped?"

We are here.

Kata's brows pulled together as she looked down into the valley. Nothing but snow, as far as she could see. "Where is 'here'? I thought you were taking me to see other magical beasts." *Don't sound too eager,* she reminded herself. *He'll suspect I want to hunt them.*

Magni snorted and shook out his mane, then said, *Step forward, and be ready to see.*

The cliff edge was only a stone's throw away, and the shape of it was concealed by the snow drifts. Kata felt on edge, and not just because they stood on a cliff. Would he try to trick her into walking off it and falling to her death? She tried to remain calm so he wouldn't send his peaceful emotion to her again.

Slowly, she took a step forward. Then another. They were well above the timberline, in the shadow of the highest peak and surrounded by stones and snow. Below, there was only a small alpine lake ringed with trees and fed by streams at the other end of the valley. She looked back at Magni, and he jerked his head up as if prodding her to continue. When she turned forward again, the scene before her had changed completely. Blinking a few times, she rubbed her eyes, not believing.

The valley was full of magical creatures, bustling about in an outdoor market of sorts. A griffin and several phoenix—two parents and a child—flew overhead. Huldufólk traded goods with gnomes and a couple of giants. A herd of unicorns kept themselves to one side, and a few ice bears lounged near the lake, which teemed with movement. From her vantage point, she couldn't make out what sort of creatures swam in the lake, but she guessed nykur, the horse-like monsters known to lure travelers to watery graves.

Others might see only the color and liveliness of the creatures below, but Kata saw bounties.

If she still had her bow, she could have easily shot down the little family of phoenix before anyone noticed her. The bounty money would buy food and clothing for her father and herself for at least two years. The trick Kata had heard from phoenix hunters was stealth and aiming true enough that the bird was dead before they could burst into flame and be born again.

The griffin would be harder, but also more valuable. It would probably take two or three arrows, and in the meantime, she'd have his beak and talons to contend with. Since she didn't have her bow, though, she would be unable to hunt griffin or phoenix. Maybe with her knife, she could take a unicorn or a nykur from the lake . . .

Magni stepped forward, interrupting her thoughts. There was something in his eyes—sadness, maybe—that made her worry he knew what she'd been thinking. Shaking the idea away, she asked him, "Why have you brought me here? What is this place?"

A sanctuary. A safe place for those banished or bountied by your king.

"So why would you bring *me* here?" Kata asked. She turned away from the valley and looked at him. "You must know what I am—what my father is."

Magni studied her for a long time. A light snow had begun to fall, and the flurries caught in his mane and eyelashes. Finally, she heard him again.

You are more than you know.

Then he turned to walk a path into the valley. Swallowing back her questions, she followed him. Perhaps there were others here who could give her better answers.

Kata was relieved when Magni chose a path that led into a dimly lit cave, instead of taking her into the valley. She'd never seen so many fearsome creatures in one place, and she dreaded walking through the crowd below, especially as she was almost weaponless.

The cave was set up as a little house, dimly lit by a hearth at the back and candles along the walls. An old man sat on a small chair near the fire—except he wasn't a man, really, but a member of the huldufólk, diminutive elves with mischievous magic. He smoked a pipe, but when he heard Magni and Kata enter, he set it down and hopped off his chair.

He approached Kata, and she felt foolish that her instinct was to run away from a creature that stood no higher than her waist. But she'd heard plenty of stories about the huldufólk. There was a reason they—and all those who could practice magic—were banned: to create a safer kingdom for everyone.

"Ah, Magni," the man said, smiling so that delicate wrinkles formed at the corners of his crystal-blue eyes. "You've found her."

Magni dipped his head in acknowledgement, and Kata wondered if he could speak to the huldufólk the same way he spoke to her—inside the mind.

"Kata," the old man said, stepping forward and bowing. "I've waited a long time to meet you. My name is Eldri."

"Hello," Kata replied, unsure what to make of him. "How do you know my name? Why am I here?"

If he was annoyed by her abrupt manner, he didn't show it. "We've waited a long time for a human of your gifts," Eldri said, motioning for her to sit in the chair on the other side of the hearth as he took his own seat again. The chair was a tad small for Kata, but she managed to squeeze into a somewhat comfortable position on it.

"My gifts?" Kata asked, puzzled. "You mean like hunting? Surely an ice bear or a griffin is a better hunter than I am."

Eldri shook his head, smirking. "No, child. We need another of your gifts. Your ability to speak to magical beasts."

"But I can't . . ." Kata started, then trailed off. She had been speaking to Magni since they met, and he understood her, but surely there wasn't anything so special about that? He obviously understood Eldri as well.

"Magni?" Eldri asked. The alicorn had been standing back at the cave entrance. Now, he stepped forward, between them. "Can this child do what we hope?"

Magni must have told him "yes," because the old man smiled again.

"Our alicorn here has the same gift as you," Eldri said, turning back to her. "He can place his thoughts in the minds of other magical beings, a way of speaking to them without a voice."

Kata gasped. "You mean, you think I'm magical because I can understand him? I'm afraid you're mistaken." She struggled to get out of the too-small chair and stood, backing away from the hearth. Magni and Eldri seemed to be having another silent conversation.

Eldri turned to her again and said, "My child, Magni told me you spoke to him in the same way. He doesn't think you meant to, but he heard your voice in his mind. We thought it would take months for you to learn, but if you've already used your powers once . . ."

She turned to Magni and said, "No, you're wrong. I never put words in your head!"

Magni glanced at Eldri, as if making sure he wouldn't overhear the next thing he told Kata. *Yes, you did. This morning.*

Kata shook her head, backing away. She was almost at the entrance of the cave. She could run for it—

Kata, please. Magni spoke to her again, and there was a hint of desperation in his eyes. *You told me you were sorry.*

She froze. She *had* tried to say she was sorry . . . with her hand on his forehead. And he had said something, too: "So it is true . . ."

Try again. You'll see.

He must have communicated that to Eldri as well, because he said, "Yes, try it again. Step up to him, place your hand on him. Of course, once you've had practice, you won't need to touch him to communicate, but they say it helps when your powers are new."

Swallowing, trembling, Kata stepped up to Magni. She brushed her hand over his mane and then laid it flat against his warm neck. She did not want to do this. It could not be true. But if it was, she had to know . . .

She took a breath. "What should I try to say?" she asked, looking to Eldri.

"Anything, child," Eldri said, picking up his pipe again and making a hard gesture to light it. She had never seen magic done before and had to stop herself from flinching when she saw the lick of flame in the pipe.

"Alright," she said. She closed her eyes and imagined her home. The cabin she and her father shared, lit by the glow of the fire on a cold night. The stars through the trees overhead, the candles and fire dancing on the snow through the open door. Her father silhouetted in the doorway. *I want to go home,* she thought.

You showed me your home. Magni said. *You want to go home.*

She stumbled back, opening her eyes and pulling her hand away from him as if he had burned her. "Impossible," she breathed. "No," she said, her eyes wide and the tone of her voice rising in fear. "I don't have powers. I'm not one of you. I can't be. I'm not . . . I'm not—"

"Not what?" asked Eldri gently, blowing a smoke ring.

Kata lowered her eyes to her boots and said, "I'm not evil." The last word came out barely above a whisper.

A creaky sound, like the wind in the bare tree branches, emanated from the old man, and it took Kata a moment to realize he was laughing. She looked at him sharply.

"Oh, child," he said. "What evil could you have done in your short years?"

She considered that for the space of a few breaths. She had certainly done things she regretted, but . . . "I've done my best not to do others harm. To do good, where I can," she told him.

He peered into her eyes, then nodded. "Very well, then. You—like all beings, both magical and mundane—certainly have the potential for wicked things. We all must choose how we live each day, and I think you'll find that many of even the most fearsome creatures here have made the same choice as you."

Kata was still in shock, but she managed a nod. She wasn't sure what to believe, now. Her father, the king, all the hunters . . . they were always telling of the dangers of magic. But here were two magical creatures in front of her who meant her no harm, who told her she was really one of them.

One of them. The words twisted into her like a knife.

"It has been a long journey for Kata," Eldri said to Magni. "Please take her to the room we've prepared for her. She will want to rest."

"Wait," she said. "It's true, what I told Magni. I want to go home. Can't you take me home?" Her voice broke on the last word, and she bit her lip to keep it from trembling.

"I'm afraid we can't do that," the huldufólk man said. "We *will* take you home, I promise you that. Soon, but not yet."

So, she really was trapped here and would need to find a way to escape. Even if the two magical beings in front of her were harmless, Kata knew there were others here that were anything but.

Eldri hopped off his chair again and approached Kata, taking her hand in his small, warm one. "You will find out more when you meet the other girl we have summoned here."

"Other girl?" she asked, lips parted in surprise.

"Yes," Eldri said. "The last Stormsinger. She has just arrived today as well, and you will meet her soon."

Kata managed to stifle her gasp as Magni led her back into the daylight and further down the twisting, snowy path. Her mind raced. Her father had forbidden her to ask about the Stormsingers and made it known to the other hunters that they could not speak of them to Kata. She had always been horribly curious about them—they must be viciously evil for her father to forbid talk of them—and she had eventually begged Prince Stefán to tell her all he knew.

"They're powerful witches," he had said after much harassment. "They can control ice, snow, water—some say even wind and storm—just by singing the right spells, called snowsong. My father says there are none left."

But King Karvel was wrong. There was one, and she was *here*.

HOPES OF THE MOUNTAIN-DWELLERS

Elín

Elín sat alone in her room, which was really a cave within the mountain, furnished with a small hearth, a bed, and a chair. She tried to convince herself that only a few days ago, Revna was alive and she was safe at home. Safe believing that magic was the stuff of fairy tales. She sighed and undid the plait in her hair, which was already half-undone from the journey.

She smoothed the auburn waves out with her fingers, then took her carved ivory hairbrush from her inner pocket and began the hundred strokes her mother had always prescribed. The ritual had been neglected the last two nights, since Týr had found her and she'd been forced on this adventure, so she had to be careful of a few tangles and knots. She was grateful to have something familiar in these strange lands.

When she was only halfway done, there was a knock on the plank of wood that covered the narrow entrance to her cave.

"Come in," she called, hoping it wasn't Eldri. The huldufólk leader looked at her in such an intense way that she could feel all the hopes of the mountain-dwellers laid squarely on her shoulders.

But it was Týr who came into the cave, blinking as his eyes adjusted to the darkness. He took a few steps forward, then stopped as his eyes found her next to the hearth. She paused mid-brushstroke as he stared at her long tresses.

Elín pretended her cheeks weren't flushed from his gaze and set the brush down on the low mantle. "I'm just freshening up from the journey," she said.

Týr nodded and swallowed. "I-I'm sorry. I didn't mean to interrupt."

"Don't be silly," Elín said, gesturing for him to have a seat on the bed. He obeyed, and she asked, "Did you have something to tell me?"

"We're to have dinner with Eldri and a few other guests tonight, including a girl who is also a vital part of their plan."

"Really?" Elín asked. "A human girl?"

Týr nodded.

"Is she a Stormsinger, like me?"

"No," Týr said. "You're the last. She has other powers that will be useful, though. The girl's name is Kata, and she comes from Snjoreya. That's all I know, but we'll learn more tonight."

"If every being on this mountain has some kind of magic, why do they need her? And me?" Elín asked.

"Don't underestimate how powerful snowsong is, what the spells can do that even huldufólk cannot. As for Kata, she can travel freely in Snjoreya as a human," Týr said. "Any huldufólk, or gnome or giant, would be killed on sight if they tried to enter King Karvel's lands."

Elín swallowed and attempted to keep her voice from quavering. "That means if we are captured, if they find us here . . ."

Týr grimaced and nodded again. "But we'll do our best. Eldri has a plan that will work. You'll be safe here. I know it."

"And when do I get to hear this plan of his?" Elín asked, picking up the hairbrush again. The familiar motions steadied her trembling hands.

"Tonight," Týr said, "at dinner."

Elín nodded, and they sat in a comfortable silence for a few minutes, Týr looking into the fire while Elín finished brushing her hair and restored it to its usual braid. She thought a regretful look might've passed over his face as she tied the leather cord to hold it.

"The hairbrush was my mother's," she said softly as she placed it on the bed. "It's the only thing I have of hers. Well, the only thing that matters."

Týr nodded and picked up the brush, running his fingers over the finely shaped handle, the figures of ice bears, snowflakes, and evergreen trees carved into the ivory.

"Well," she said, suddenly feeling awkward. She'd shared too much and grown too comfortable with someone who was, after all, still a stranger to her. "What do we do until dinner tonight?"

Týr grinned and said, "Björn and I were here for a few weeks in the summer—did I tell you that? We came to look for you; we thought your grandmother might have brought you here. You should meet the amazing people and creatures that live at Skyli. Can I give you a tour?"

"Very well," Elín said, standing and straightening her skirts. "Lead the way."

He took her down a different path from the one they'd arrived by. A few twisting turns through snow-laden trees and, suddenly, before them was a sprawling marketplace filled with creatures far stranger than Elín had ever imagined existed.

Her brow furrowed. "But how?" Elín asked. "A moment ago, this was only a lonely mountain, and now a few steps further, and we can see all this." She gestured out at the throng of huldufólk and other creatures bartering at dozens of market stalls.

Týr smiled. "Snowsong. I'm told this was a powerful spell made by the Stormsingers who came before you. She enchanted the water in the air to shimmer and conceal what lay below. Most spells don't last after the death of the Stormsinger who sang them, but she was very skilled and found a way."

Elín let out a low whistle of admiration, finding she did not trust her voice to speak. Her stomach was in a knot—was this the kind of magic they expected her to be capable of? When she couldn't even freeze a palmful of water?

"Come," Týr said, motioning for her to follow as he stepped into the crowd.

He's strong, she thought suddenly, *in a way that I am not.* After her mother had died, she hadn't smiled for weeks. At her grandmother's funeral, she had thought she might never laugh again. But Týr had lost everything, and still he smiled and laughed, finding joy especially in sharing the things he loved with her. The sea, snowsong, Skyli . . .

She followed him, attempting to look everywhere at once. There were a few other humans like herself there to trade food and supplies for the handicrafts of the mountain-dwellers. Stalls and tables were set up ramshackle. One stall boasted herbs and roots, dried and tied to a string that was strewn about the stall like a garland. Their pungent odors tickled her nose, and she wondered if they were for making enchantments. Perhaps there were other lands where potions were used.

Other goods were more mundane. Týr explained that humans brought up wool, and the huldufólk spun it into beautiful, silky yarn, some of which they made into sweaters and shawls. The gnomes traded lovely wood carvings and household tools.

Huldufólk children darted in and out of stalls, dodging around the legs of the much taller beings who walked through the market. Elín was hesitant at first, but as the stall owners smiled and welcomed her, she ran her hands over the beautiful fabrics and sampled the delicacies offered her—new tastes she had no words for.

"Here," Týr said, pulling her attention toward a stall run by a giant.

Elín approached, trying not to stare at the man. Though he was sitting on the ground, his head and shoulders were above hers. On the table in front of him were knives, swords, and axes. Each was forged with intricate designs, weaving together different metals in their hilts. Týr picked up a small knife and showed it to her. She took it carefully.

The handle fit comfortably in her palm. Its engraved design was floral, inspired by the little crocuses that popped up in early spring. "It's beautiful," she said, smiling at the giant.

"You must have it," the giant said, his deep voice booming from his chest.

"Oh, I couldn't," she said, laying the knife down on the table. "I have nothing to trade."

"Take it, Songstress of Storm and Snow, and remember the giant Brokk who gave it to you," he replied, a grin spreading over his features. "You will need protection where you're going."

Elín took a step back and swallowed. Did everyone here know who she was?

Týr gave him a tight smile. "It will be of use if she needs to protect herself here in Skyli," he said. The implication was clear—Elín wouldn't be going anywhere.

Brokk didn't waver. "Another gift, this one for our brave Keeper." He handed Týr a short, sturdy sword. Though not as elaborate as the dagger, it was still more beautiful than any metalwork Elín had seen before.

Týr seemed conflicted for a heartbeat or two, but he took the sword and thanked the giant.

Following his lead, Elín hefted the dagger in the palm of her hand again. The giant handed her a beautiful leather cover for it, and she sheathed the blade. "Thank you, Brokk," she said. "I will make good use of it and remember you when I do."

She had to turn away from him, embarrassed by how *honored* he seemed by her comment. But turning away didn't help.

Elín felt surrounded. She hadn't noticed before, in her wonder at the existence of such a place, but many eyes were on her. Whispers followed in their wake as they walked through the market. She only heard a few snatches here and there, but it was enough to confirm that "Stormsinger" was on the lips of many. More gifts found their way into her hands—a beautiful woven blanket, a sturdy embossed leather rucksack, knitted shawls and embroidered dresses, herbs for healing and a salve for burns.

It took Elín a few turns around the market to realize why she suddenly felt such an ache. She'd let herself imagine this wondrous place as her new home. If she were a Stormsinger, could she not belong here, live among others like herself who understood magic? But it could not be if everyone expected her to save them. She was back to having nowhere safe, no home.

Týr followed her as she walked to the edge of the lake, away from the market. To their left was a herd of unicorns, but she barely glanced at their luminescent coats as she took deep breaths of the fresh mountain air.

"What's wrong?" Týr asked.

"I can't do this," she said, dropping her bundle of gifts at her feet and bringing her hands to her cheeks. "All those eyes on me . . . more people than I've ever seen in my life, and they expect me to do wonders to help them."

"It's true," Týr said, surprising her by not trying to deny or soften it, as he had after she'd met Eldri.

"They don't understand that I'm not a hero; I'm just a farm girl. They don't see me as that at all—I'm just a symbol to everyone here. Of magic they thought was lost."

"Not to me." There was something so intense in his gaze that Elín had to look away.

She kicked at one of the pebbles that lined the shore. "They believe I can save them when I didn't even believe they existed." She shook her head. "I didn't nobly pledge myself to help—I only came here because I had nowhere else to go. They shouldn't pin their hopes on me." She thought of her grandmother, who'd relied on her for everything these last years. Elín hadn't even been able to save her, in the end. She added softly, "I'll let them down."

"You won't," Týr said quickly. "They'll all help you, Elín. They know how much you've been through to get here and will be patient while you learn. Now come back with me. I want you to meet some of the humans here. There's Greta, who skis over the mountains for days to trade here, and Fridolf, who comes here on a sled loaded with food, pulled by his pack of dogs."

Elín took a deep breath, looking out over the lake, which she realized was probably also teeming with creatures and their dreams of returning to their homeland.

"Alright," she said. "Take me to see these dogs."

MONSTERS

Kata

Magni brought Kata to a little room carved out of the mountain with a blazing hearth and a comfortable bed. He encouraged her to rest there until dinner.

There are many here who know you're coming and that you're a huntress. Please stay. I would not wish them to be frightened of you.

Kata stared at him, mouth agape. Surely nykur and griffins and all other manner of terrible creatures would not be afraid of *her*. She was a skilled huntress, but she'd yet to fulfill her dreams of hunting anything magical and did not have her bow. Only a half-grown human girl, no fangs or claws or dangerous powers. What could be so frightening about her?

But Magni hadn't noticed her surprise before he left. She sunk to the bed before the hearth, her thoughts swirling. The dominant one was: *I'm one of them.*

How? How could she, the daughter of one of the best bounty hunters in Snjoreya, have anything to do with magic? King Karvel had banned all those who could do magic years ago. Could she even return home?

And if she did make it home—if she somehow convinced Magni to take her back—would she have to conceal her abilities from her friends, from her own father?

Yes, she thought, imagining the looks of disgust on the faces of Gunnar and Helga and all the other hunters. And her father...he hated magical beasts so much he wouldn't even talk to her of them. At that thought, she put a hand to her mouth, stifling a sob. *It is the only way. I must hide what I am.*

It would not be so difficult. There were few magical beasts left in King Karvel's lands on which to use her powers. She would have to forget this place, pretend it was only a dream. A tight pain in her chest blossomed when she realized she would have to forget Magni, too.

Would anyone notice she was different? Prince Stefán, maybe.

She sat up straighter. What *would* Prince Stefán think?

It was hard to know. He read a great deal about magic, and not because he hated or feared it, like his father did. He was fascinated by it. Perhaps she could tell him when she returned—*if* she returned.

A sinking feeling hit her stomach. She had been so cold to him in their last meeting. If she didn't come back from this strange land fraught with danger, would that be the last he remembered of her? She blanched at the thought, then shook it away.

Stefán wasn't like that. He didn't hold grudges, especially against her. She could trust him with this.

After all, he had always kept her confidence in the past. He had warned her not to kill the alicorn, and that had turned out to be wise advice. Well, so far.

Of course, everything else hinged on the painful twist of that "if"—*if* she managed to find her way home. Kata suddenly felt out of breath as she thought of never seeing Pabbi again. Or Stefán. The day before Magni had taken her, she'd been angry with both of them. What if she didn't get the chance to set things right?

Finally, Kata couldn't take any more of the stifling, thick air of the cave. Despite Magni's advice, she stepped outside. She felt better instantly, breathing in the fresh alpine air. The rooms carved into the mountain opened out onto evergreen forest, and she decided to go for a walk in the woods. Surely, there was no harm in that. The creatures all seemed to have been assembled in the marketplace—a thought that sent her stomach roiling. She planned to avoid setting foot in such a treacherous place.

She retraced part of the path Magni had led her on, then took the first offshoot she found that went into the woods.

The winding path took her to the lake, then stopped. On the distant shore to her right, she could see the marketplace and the white silhouettes of ice bears lounging at the water's edge. She shivered at seeing so many monsters there, hiding from the hunters of her kingdom. A thought tugged at her: *were they really monsters?* She no longer thought of Magni as one. He was almost...her *friend*.

She pushed that thought aside, turning to follow the shore to the left until it met up with a creek. The sound of rapids called her onward, and she followed it upstream. She surmounted a hill, holding onto trees for balance in the slippery snow, and found herself in front of a lovely sight: a waterfall, half-frozen. But she didn't admire it for long because her eyes were drawn to the horse beneath it.

The dappled gray beast stood calmly beside the water, as if waiting for her. Gracefully, he arched his neck to drink from the stream, then raised his head to look at her again. He was a beautiful horse, a well-built stallion, and she found herself taking a few steps toward him, imagining how lovely it would be to ride him.

She'd only ridden horses a few times—with Prince Stefán, at the royal stables—but she loved the feeling of it. Her favorite horse back home was a spirited bay mare, small but fast.

Something stopped her a few steps from the horse. *What is he doing in the mountains, beside a stream?* Surely, the terrain was too steep here... Her stomach dropped. Hadn't she seen horse-sized creatures swimming in the lake?

Her gaze traveled down to the horse's hooves, and, indeed, they faced backward. This was no horse.

The nykur stepped forward, looking as friendly as any of the royal horses, then turned so his side faced her and she could mount him more easily. She wracked her brain for the advice nykur hunters had given for this situation.

She couldn't kill him with her knife; if she got that close, he could easily move against her, and she would be stuck to his skin. He'd dive under, and she'd drown. A distracting sound—music, from a stringed instrument—started wafting from behind her, but she commanded herself to focus. She'd never heard anything from the nykur hunters about music, but it could be part of their deadly magic.

Then she remembered. "Nykur!" she shouted. The creature rolled his eyes upward and whinnied but, slowly, started edging his way toward the stream.

"You're a nykur!" She added for good measure. "You're a nykur, and you'll leave me be!"

With one last regretful glance at her, he slid into the water and disappeared. She breathed heavily, leaning against a tree, thanking Lady Luck that it had only been a nykur and not something worse, that wouldn't shy away at the sound of its own name.

As she calmed, she realized the music hadn't stopped. In fact, it had grown louder. She turned around slowly, reaching for the knife in her boot.

Behind her was a young man. He was tall and wiry, and he played a violin while dancing between the trees. He finished his song—a jaunty tune that had reached a crescendo as he approached—and bowed. Kata stared at him, her foot still propped on a rock and her hand still reaching into her boot for the knife.

"What, no applause?" the man asked, then spun, putting the violin to his chin again and playing a few melancholy notes. He turned back to her and smiled. "I thought for sure that nykur would get you, and I'd have to play the hero."

Slowly, Kata straightened. "Who—*what*—are you?"

"Name's Fossegrim," he said, his violin swinging behind his back as he bowed again and shook her hand. "But you can call me Grim." He winked and released her hand.

Kata was wary; her heart still pounded from the encounter with the nykur. "What foul magic are you planning? To drown me, like a nykur? Or will your music enchant me so I become lost in the woods?" Her voice squeaked, her fear showing, so she stopped and took a few breaths.

He looked hurt. "Of course not... Ah, you must be the little huntress every-one has so much to say about."

He circled, examining her as if he'd never seen a human girl, and she crossed her arms. "What magic *do* you have then?"

"This," he said, grinning, as he began to play again. This time, it wasn't music, or at least not the sort one would expect from a violin. The sounds of nature—a babbling stream, wind in the trees, a few chirping birds in the distance—emanated from his magic instrument.

This time when he bowed, Kata couldn't help but look impressed. "That was...something," she admitted.

"I could teach you, you know," Grim said, a sly look coming into his eye. "All I need is a bit of meat. It must be stolen, though. I'll know if it's not."

"What, by Lady Legend, could you want with stolen meat?" Kata asked.

"Why should it matter to you?" he asked, playing a few more enchanting notes. "Do you not want to learn?"

"No," Kata said. "I think I'll be going."

He shrugged, then played a few more jaunty notes of the first tune. "If you change your mind, you know where to find me: here at my waterfall." He jumped onto the ice, spinning and dancing as he played.

"Of course," she called, already backing away down the path.

Kata pointed her boots in the direction of the marketplace. Though she dreaded being among so many magical creatures, she had to admit there was safety in numbers. She had no desire to come across another nykur while she was alone in the woods. Or another confusing waterfall-spirit.

She followed the lakeshore but gave the dozing ice bears and herd of unicorns a wide berth. Then, at the edge of the market, she spotted a pack of dogs. Someone was playing with them. A human girl, by the looks of it. Close by was a bearded man with his hands on a dogsled, in conversation with a young man with dark hair and brown skin.

She approached the dogs and the girl. "Hello," she called in greeting, her relief at finding other humans here creeping into her voice. The girl, who seemed a few winters older than her, smiled back. "Have you come to trade?"

The girl swiped her long red braid over her shoulder as she gently pushed a dog away from her, laughing. "I'm afraid not . . . I was brought here for something rather different." When Kata didn't respond she added, "I'm supposed to be their 'songstress of storm and snow.'"

"*You're* the last Stormsinger?" Kata asked, her voice sounding equally wary and puzzled. Another thought shot through her like an arrow: *the last snow-witch would command a hefty bounty from the king.* An unimaginable sum.

"I'm afraid so," the sorceress replied, smiling. "But please, call me Elín." When Kata only stood there, staring, she patted the ground beside her—amid the playful dogs—and said, "Come. Sit."

Kata hadn't failed to notice how many eyes around them their exchange had drawn. By the varied expressions on the faces of the huldufólk, gnomes, and giants, she could tell some of them feared her and what she might do to their newly found snow-witch. Others' eyes were greedy and expectant, hoping for a showdown between the two—and not rooting for Kata to win it.

"You must be Kata. Please, join me."

"You know my name?"

"Yes," Elín said. "They tell me we're to be allies in helping the creatures here."

Kata knelt beside Elín stiffly. She was dangerous, full of deadly magic, even if she didn't look it. Two of the dogs leaped into her lap and licked Kata's face. She laughed, surprising herself, then noted the sour expressions on the crowd of onlookers. They didn't seem to believe a dog would enjoy the company of someone as traitorous as her.

Elín noticed Kata glancing around. "Yes," she said quietly, conspiratorially. "They whisper about me, too."

"Because they worship you. Not because they're afraid."

"Believe it or not, I'd trade with you." Elín shook her head and smiled sadly. "Fear doesn't come with so many hopes and dreams attached."

Kata studied her, stroking the thick fur of the dog nearest her. He rolled onto his back and she obliged him with a belly rub. "You know," she said, "you're not at all how I imagined the Last Stormsinger would be."

Elín laughed lightly, rubbing her cheek against the neck of the dog sitting upright next to her. "I must agree with you there." The panting and playing of the dogs occupied them for a few moments. Then Elín asked, "What did you expect?"

Kata stopped scratching the neck of the dog to her right and said, "Someone much older, for one."

Nodding, Elín said, "Yes. My grandmother used to tell me stories about the Stormsingers. I imagined them as these tall, elegant creatures, with pale skin and white hair, crystalline eyes—nothing like me at all."

"I never knew my grandparents," Kata said, her voice edged with longing. "And my father was never one to tell fairy stories."

The young man who had been talking to the owner of the dogs approached. He smiled when he saw Elín laughing and playing with the dogs.

"Eldri calls us all to dinner," he said. Kata felt her expression turn grim at Eldri's name.

"Kata, this is Týr," Elín said. "Týr, this is Kata, the huntress."

"Pleased to meet you," Týr replied, inclining his head.

"These dogs are lovely," Elín said to Týr. "Why didn't we travel here via dogsled?"

Týr smirked. "If I thought we could handle eight rambunctious dogs—or even afford to feed them—I would've considered it."

That brought a smile to Elín's face, but Kata was still worrying about dinner.

Elín must have picked up on her anxiety. "Why don't you come back to my chamber first?" she asked. "I imagine you don't want to attend this dinner in your hunting clothes, and, with everything I've just been given, I'm sure I have something you can wear."

Following a sorceress back to her chamber. *Good idea.*

But Elín had a point. Everyone here was looking at her as if *she* were the monster, not them. Tidying up might help. Besides, she had to admit that she liked Elín. "Alright," Kata said, standing. She stroked one dog's pointed ear and patted another on the head regretfully.

Týr looked like he would object, but Elín silenced him with a smile and told him he could meet them outside her chamber to lead them to dinner.

THE FOUR PROTECTORS OF THE LAND

Elín

"**O**h," Kata said, blushing as Elín pulled yet another leaf from her tangled hair. "I *am* a mess."

"Nonsense," Elín said. "From what you've told me of your journey, you've had plenty of other things to worry about." She ran her fingers lightly over Kata's thick mane and, finding no more leaves, twigs, or evergreen needles, said, "There, now I can brush it."

She pulled her mother's brush from her bag and started running it through the ends of Kata's hair, using longer strokes as she worked out the knots. She wasn't sure exactly why she'd invited Kata in or why she was helping her. Perhaps she had recognized in the girl's forlorn expression something that reflected her own feelings about being brought here. Neither of them had asked for this.

Kata sniffed, and Elín noticed that her eyes were glassy.

She removed the brush quickly. "Oh, I'm sorry. Am I hurting you?"

"No," Kata said, shaking her head and pressing her forefinger to the corner of her eye. "I'm sorry, it's silly, but . . . I found myself thinking of my mother."

A familiar wave of grief resurfaced in Elín as she thought of her own. She stepped in front of Kata's chair and said, "I understand. I lost mine years ago. This was hers." She handed the hairbrush to Kata, who held it as if it were a treasure.

"It's lovely," Kata said as she handed it back. "I didn't lose mine, really, because I never knew her. But, when I was young, sometimes I would imagine her brushing my hair like this. Or singing to me."

Elín nodded knowingly and returned to her task. Kata's hair was thick but much shorter than hers, cropped at the shoulder, so it didn't take long to finish.

Afterwards, she helped Kata into a robin's egg-blue dress, one of the many garments the vendors in the marketplace had piled into her arms. It was too big and too long for Kata, but Elín helped her tie it with a sash at the waist and then braided her hair.

"There," she said, tying off the end of Kata's last braid with a leather cord and smiling at her handiwork. "Do you feel more ready for a dinner with all the magical leaders of this land?"

Kata took a deep breath and let it out slowly. "I feel better than before, but . . . not 'ready' at all."

"I'm nervous, too," Elín admitted, giving her hand a squeeze. "But we'll get through it together."

Kata smiled and exited the cave. Elín heard Týr, waiting outside, say, "Oh, there you are."

Pausing to be sure Kata was gone, Elín stowed the hairbrush in her pack and pulled out the little drawstring pouch where she'd put Revna's treasures. She withdrew the blond lock of hair and examined it before the fire.

Yes, her suspicion was confirmed. The sunny gold was the same hue as Kata's.

"Elín?" Týr called. "We need to be going."

"Of course," she called back, tightening the pouch and quickly returning it to her pack. Then, she straightened her skirts and stepped out into the fading sunlight, rejoining Týr and Kata.

There would be time to unravel these mysteries later.

A young man, tall and lean, played the violin as they entered. When he saw Elín, he abruptly stopped his song and coaxed the most incredible sound of the howling wind from the strings of his instrument. He danced as he played and ended the wind-music as he reached Elín.

"Honored to meet you, Songstress," he said, bowing brusquely, then nodding to Týr. "And you, Keeper. Name's Fossegrim, but call me Grim. Ah, and you, Kata. Well, we've met, haven't we?" He gave Kata a grin, and she glared in reply.

Elín's sight adjusted from the snowscape outside to the firelit cave, and she could now see the group Eldri had gathered for dinner. There were eight guests in all, plus his ice bear lounged outside the entrance to the cavern that served as a dining hall, guarding it. She, Týr, Kata, and the newly met Grim made up half the party.

Then there was Eldri, who sat at the head of the table, which was laden with a vat of porridge with apples, a platter of herring, and baskets of flatbread. Wooden bowls and brass goblets were placed on the table in front of each chair. The huldufólk elder beckoned for Kata to sit to his left and Elín to sit to his right. Magni—who Kata had told her of—stood at the other end of the table, his wings relaxed. He was an impressive sight; his white coat and feathers seemed to glow despite the dim light of the cave.

Grim seated himself next to Kata, and between him and Magni sat a rather frightening woman. The huge black wolfskin she wore was held on by a rough rope wrapped several times around her waist. Her long black hair, though frizzy and matted, was striking against her pale skin, and she threw twitchy, watchful glances at the others in the room.

"This," Grim supplied as he sat and pulled a pipe from his pocket, "is Nattmara."

"And I am Skadi," came the clear, calm voice of the final member of the party, seated between Týr and Magni on Elín's side of the table.

Skadi stood to greet them and had to duck her head to avoid hitting the cavern roof. Strands of her brown hair were twisted and braided on the top of her head, and her arms and calves were bare despite the cold. Behind her chair, leaned against the wall, were a longbow and a huge set of skis and poles. Giantesses had never featured much in Revna's stories, but those Elín had imagined, and those she had seen in the marketplace, were certainly not this beautiful.

"Týr," Skadi repeated when he introduced himself. "I knew your name-sake—a mountain giant from the old days—eons ago. He was a brave and just warrior, worshiped by some as a war god. Bear his name proudly."

He bowed his head to her, then leaned toward Elín and said in a low voice, "Björn decided to call me by that name."

Familiar with the ways grief could accost one from the most unexpected sources, she gave him a sad smile and reached out to squeeze his hand, just once.

She and Kata greeted their new acquaintances the best they could, trying not to stare. When the introductions had finished and everyone had seated themselves around the table, Eldri raised his goblet for a toast.

"Kata, Huntress of Snjoreya, and Elín, Songstress of Storm and Snow . . . welcome to Skyli, our mountain refuge."

Everyone—except Nattmara, who wouldn't, and Magni, who couldn't—raised their cups and toasted them with shouts of, "To Kata," and "To the Songstress." Elín had to stop herself from blushing, especially as Týr met her gaze before drinking his toast.

Dinner commenced. The food wasn't extravagant, but it was hearty and good. The apples were a special treat, and Elín wondered if they'd been preserved by magic. All her farm's apples had been eaten by this late in the winter. Grim, naturally friendly, attempted to make small talk throughout the meal, occasionally aided by Týr and Skadi. Conversation was difficult; they all knew they were there for more than light chatter over dinner.

A pair of women kept the table stocked with food. At first, Elín thought they were human, but then she caught sight of one's cow-like tail swaying out from under her skirt; they were huldra.

"Why are they here?" Kata blurted when she noticed the same thing.

"They're magical creatures," Skadi said. "They were banished from Snjoreya, too."

"Yes, but . . ." Kata seemed like she might not go on, and her cheeks grew red as all eyes turned on her.

"You mean because they can become human, like us?" Elín asked gently, trying to help her.

"Exactly," Kata said. "They just need to marry men, and they'll lose their tails. They could've stayed in Snjoreya and wouldn't have to be monsters."

"You think we'd all transform ourselves into the likes of you if we had the choice?" Natmarra asked sharply, shooting glares at Kata and Elín.

"If it meant safety . . ." Kata said gently.

The two huldra had briefly left the cave, but now they returned. The blonde one held a jar of honey, and the one with tawny skin and shiny black hair held a fresh jug of ale. "Why don't you ask them yourself?" Skadi suggested. When Kata only looked embarrassed, Skadi relayed the question.

The plumper huldra with the long, golden braid smiled and said, "Though we are not so powerful as the huldufólk, we would like to keep the little magic we possess."

"And besides," the other added, "we love each other more than we could love any man, human or otherwise." She took her partner's hand and kissed her cheek, making her blush.

Elín studied Kata, who was now staring at the food in the middle of the table with a wrinkle of confusion between her brows. Of course, Kata lived in the kingdom that had exiled everyone here in Skyli. What did she truly believe about magic and those capable of wielding it?

As they finished, emptying their wooden bowls, the atmosphere grew heavy. Eldri leaned back in his chair and stroked his chin as the huldra cleared the table, then dismissed themselves.

"Elín, Kata," Eldri began, pulling Elín's attention back to the table. "You both have some idea why we've brought you here, but I shall make our plan clearer now."

No one spoke as they waited for him to continue. Elín traced a knot on the wooden table with her finger, anxious not to see the expressions of the other dinner guests. They would certainly ask more magic of her than freezing water in the palm of her hand, and she hadn't even mastered that.

"Perhaps you've heard the legend of the Four Protectors of the Land," Eldri said. Elín had, of course, from her grandmother. A needle of grief threaded through her.

"I hope you won't mind if I tell it again," Eldri continued. "It is one of my favorites from our history."

He stood and walked to the hearth, looking into the flames before turning back to the room. "In the kingdom of Snjoreya, there were once four protectors of the land—landvaettir. The Griffin of the North, the Giant of the South, the Bull of the West, and the Dragon of the East.

"Not so long ago, a rival king sent his skin-shifter to spy on the land, hoping to find an unguarded place to land his warships. The skin-shifter transformed himself into a whale and swam around Snjoreya. He approached the east coast first, but found himself flown at by a monstrous, fire-breathing dragon The landvaettir was joined by a few smaller dragons, and on the shore crawled basilisks, venomous snakes, and lizards. The skin-shifter-whale continued to the north."

Though most in the room had heard the story before, they listened, rapt.

"There, he found himself set upon by the Griffin of the North, who was joined by eagles, phoenix, and his children. The skin-shifter swam on, hoping for luck on the west coast, but there, again, he was met by protectors. This time, the great Bull of the West, who was joined by ice bears, unicorns, nykur, and many other creatures of the land, prepared to fight. Finally, he continued to the south, where he found the frost giant, joined by mountain giants, smoke giants, and trolls."

"Yes," Skadi murmured. "I was there."

"Among all the landvaettir, there were also humans, ready to fight. But they hadn't lived on Snjoreya long and had only recently begun to worship Ladies Destiny, Legend, and Luck."

Eldri pulled out his pipe then and lit it with a flick of his fingers. "Finally, the skin-shifter turned back and brought his king the news that the land was too well-guarded to attack. Snjoreya should have been safe."

Though Elín knew how the story ended, Eldri's ominous declaration made her shiver.

"The king who had sent the skin-shifter was determined to make war. He wouldn't listen to his accounts of how well-protected the island was, sending his ships, loaded with soldiers, to conquer Snjoreya anyway." Eldri paused and pulled from his pipe, then blew another of his perfect smoke rings. "The battle was fierce, and the landvaettir and the first humans of Snjoreya fought bravely. Many died in battle, and Lady Legend ensures we sing their praises to this day. Just when hope seemed lost, a snowstorm came over the land. The foreign soldiers didn't know how to fight in a blizzard, but our people did. They were defeated, and Snjoreya was safe once more."

The room was quiet and still but for the crackling of the hearth. Everyone was entranced by Eldri's storytelling.

"Our three goddesses realized that if these few hundred humans were going to prosper in this land, they might need to interfere. The harshness of the land and snow and sea was Snjoreya's greatest advantage against any foe. Huldufólk already had some power over earth and fire, but the Ladies had not yet granted power over sea or snow or storm to anyone.

"The first humans were a fierce, warlike people, and they would have a capable army someday. They just needed time, and the Ladies decided the best way to grant them this time was to give some of them—twenty-four in all—power over these elements. The Kirja was created, and the first Tomekeeper was chosen. The Stormsingers were born. But they were always meant to fade away, as the humans grew in number and no longer had need of their power."

The huldufólk leader smiled at Elín. "Luckily, you have not faded too soon. We need your power still."

Another pull, another smoke ring that drifted lazily to the stone ceiling.

"Many of the landvaettir were killed in that battle, centuries ago. Many more have been killed by King Karvel's hunters since—the great griffin, the frost giant, and the bull are all gone, though some of the lesser landvaettir and their descendants remain, as you've seen here at Skyli."

"And the dragon?" Kata asked, breaking the silence over the room.

Eldri paused for effect. The light of the fire danced over his features. "That dragon now guards the hoard beneath King Karvel's castle."

THE KING'S CRUELTY

Kata

The silence after Eldri's revelation was broken by Kata.

"No," she said, louder than she meant to, as her mind reeled.

Nattmara slapped her hand on the table and stood, emitting what could only be described as a low growl as she bared her pointed teeth. Kata shrank back, fearing the woman was about to transform into a wolf before her eyes.

When they were children, Kata and the prince had been amused by the legends of Nattmara and the powers of her kind, the dark dreams they brought to people in the night. But Kata wasn't laughing now that she knew they were real.

"That's enough," Skadi said, eyeing Nattmara coolly, her chin high.

Eldri had put up his hands at Kata's outburst, but he lowered them as Nattmara seated herself. She was still glowering at Kata as he turned to her. "Please, child. Tell us why you doubt this."

Kata took a moment to settle her thoughts, looking into Eldri's icy blue eyes and trying to ignore her skin, which felt warm from the waves of hate in Nattmara's gaze.

"Because . . ." she said, then cleared her throat. Elín flashed her a supportive smile, and she continued. "Because I know King Karvel. If he had a dragon, he wouldn't use it to guard anything. He'd kill it and display its bones in his trophy room."

Had she not visited that room many times? She remembered the wicked gleam in the king's eye as he showcased his treasures. Kata had always marveled at the skeleton of a young dragon displayed proudly in the center. The walls were lined with unicorn horns, griffin beaks, and nykur hooves arranged in pleasing geometric patterns. Two mounted ice bear heads hung on opposite walls, over either doorway. *And do I not also dream of adding to its contents, of displaying my kills there, too?* Her stomach churned.

"I'm afraid you're not quite correct, my child," Eldri said gently.

"You've said so yourself," she said. "He seeks to destroy all magic, not use it."

"He seeks to destroy all others who can wield magic," Grim cut in.

Nattmara sneered. "The king has no problem using magic for his own gain."

Kata shook her head, still disbelieving. "But a dragon would never guard a treasure for him. They only hoard their own." This much she knew, from Gunnar and Helga. Her blood went cold at the thought of them, at what they would do to a place like Skyli.

If they found out, she thought grimly, *they'd kill every creature here for the bounty . . . as I would have only a few days ago.* As she perhaps still would if she knew she could escape afterward. A nykur or two, at least.

"Ah," Eldri said. "And here's where you come in." He gestured to Kata, then to Týr and Elín. "The dragon only guards the king's treasury because she believes the treasure to be hers. When the king needs to withdraw anything, he secretly feeds the dragon an elixir to put her to sleep, then takes what he needs. When the dragon awakes, she's always furious about her missing treasure."

"We're thinking," Grim said, grinning and lightly plucking his violin strings, "that if Kata here tells Dreka—that's the name of the dragon—what's been going on and makes her believe it, she'll take care of the king *for* us."

Kata grabbed her goblet and gulped down some mead. She was unused to the taste, finding it too sweet, but swallowed it down anyway. It warmed her belly, giving her something to focus on besides her terrifying thoughts: *I'm to speak to a dragon? How does one do so without being burned alive?*

"A dragon cannot be bound," Skadi added. "She only stays there, below the king's dungeons, because she is content with the treasure and the food brought to her. If she learned what the king does, what happens to her missing hoard, Dreka may be willing to help us. She could easily escape her lair, and that would show the people of Snjoreya the truth of the king's greed and deception. That he not only uses magic, but hoards so much of the kingdom's riches for himself."

Natmarra bared her pointed white teeth in a grin that gave Kata goose bumps. "And if Dreka were to find the king afterward and take revenge for her missing hoard . . . so much the better."

Kata clenched her hands into fists. They expected her not only to listen to this treason, but to participate in it?

"So," Týr said. "Kata will use her gift to speak to the dragon and explain the truth to her. Why do you need snowsong?"

"The Songstress is to help in several ways," Eldri said, smiling at Elín. "She will create a great snowstorm to distract the king's soldiers. We hope it will also protect the people of the kingdom—a dragon's eyesight is meant for nighttime and dim lairs, not the brightness of blizzards. Next, she will use her gifts to help Kata slip into the castle and down to the dragon's den undetected. There is a hidden entrance, from the time when Stormsingers held more power than kings. It is an ever-frozen wall of ice disguised to look like the stones from which the rest of the castle is hewn. A special incantation from the Tome can open it."

Týr blanched. "That's too dangerous a venture for her. Perhaps she can summon the storm from here, but she must not set foot in Snjoreya."

"Even the most powerful Stormsinger cannot summon a blizzard from across the sea." Eldri leaned back in his chair. Týr's face looked quite cross.

Before Týr could respond, Elín, who had gone pale, spoke up for the first time. "But after the king is . . . gone . . . who will rule Snjoreya? The kingdom would descend into chaos."

"The king's council, likely, until the prince comes of age in a few winters," Eldri answered. "We have a few allies on it who will help us."

"And," Elín continued, not looking up from her plate, "what if the prince, after seeing his father killed by a dragon, hates magic even more than the king does now?"

"We'll deal with that if the time comes," Eldri said, and Kata's blood ran cold. "We hope, with the help of our allies in Snjoreya, to negotiate peace with the prince, the clan leaders, and those members of the royal council who may be sympathetic to our cause."

"No," Kata said again. Nattmara let out a hiss but was kept in her seat by Grim's hand on her shoulder. "It's just—I know Prince Stefán. His father can be cruel, but he is not. He cares for magical creatures."

She paused, deciding it best not to go into detail on their exchange about the alicorn. Reminding everyone that, only a few days ago, she'd been out to kill Magni wasn't the wisest idea. "We should tell him our plan," Kata said. "He'll support us. He can help."

Skadi raised an eyebrow. "The prince will support us in a plot to kill his own father?"

The room chilled, the only sound the crackle of the hearth. *Would he?*

The warning of her father—"the king can be a cruel man"—returned to Kata, as well as an image of Stefán's bruised, solemn face the last time she saw him. She wished he were there with her now, that she could apologize for being angry with him, for not *seeing*. The thought of never speaking to him again, of not getting the chance to tell him she understood now, made her bones ache.

And then another memory came to her. From years ago, after the queen's death. She and the prince had sneaked away from a banquet and out to their favorite balcony to stargaze. Prince Stefán had sighed, then turned to her and whispered, "I believe if not for my father, my mother would still be here."

"What?" She hadn't understood then what he'd implied.

"Please, Kata," he'd pleaded in a panicked tone. "Tell no one what I've said. Forget it. Please."

She'd agreed readily, swore on Lady Legend and the others for good measure, only wanting that look to leave his eyes. She was young enough then to have always been safe—to not recognize fear.

Now, she understood.

That cavern in the mountains of Skyli was tense as the assembled dinner guests awaited her response.

Go on, Magni said gently, inside her head.

"Yes," she said firmly. "The king's cruelty has scarred Prince Stefán's life, too."

Eldri studied her, and Kata held his gaze, chin high. A new, terrifying thought crept in: what if they didn't allow her to warn Stefán? If he saw a dragon attacking, would he not try to defend his people and his lands, even his father? He could be injured; he could perish. She would lose him. She worked hard to maintain her composure. Then she felt Magni's calming magic wash over her, steadying her heartbeat. For once, she was grateful for it.

The huldufólk leader's fingers were steepled below his chin, his elbows on the table. "Very well," he said. "If you think the prince will ally himself with us, you can try. But I must warn you that the plan proceeds with or without his cooperation."

Kata inclined her head. "Of course." *But what about* mine? She thought rebelliously. Her powers, nascent though they were, were the key to their whole plan. If she refused, it would fail. But, of course, convincing them she would go along with the plan might be her only way home, her only chance at warning the prince of what was coming for his father and his kingdom. She could not stand by while her closest friend could be harmed.

Almost as concerning as that thought was that the smallest part of her was considering joining them, fighting *for* these creatures. But how could that be? She'd just learned of a treasonous plot on her king, planned by those her friends and family hunted and claimed as enemies. One of whom had tried to kill her only a few hours ago.

"And the nykur?" Kata asked abruptly. "Will they return to Snjoreya, if we succeed?"

Skadi shifted in her chair. "Why do you ask?"

"Because one tried to drown me earlier today," Kata said, failing to keep the accusatory tone from her voice.

Týr gasped and Nattmara grinned.

"And Nattmara and her kind," Kata said with more boldness than she felt. "They torture humans—give them horrible dreams. Are they to return as well?"

"The nykur and Nattmara have agreed not to harm any humans," Eldri said. "Are you sure a nykur tried to attack you?"

"Yes!" Kata said, looking to Grim for support. "He was there, he saw it!"

"Is this true?" Skadi asked him.

Grim smiled, basking in the attention. "Yes, I suppose it is. I was out in the woods and saw a nykur beneath my waterfall, trying to tempt her. She scared it off, though." Turning to Kata, he continued in a mischievous tone, "I suppose there are some here who are none too happy that we've partnered with a girl who hunts for the king."

"Yes," Nattmara said, baring her teeth again. "There are some who might believe putting the girl to death is the safer route."

"Enough," Eldri said firmly. "Kata, I will speak to the nykur. You are here under my protection. Anyone attempting to take your life will find themselves forfeiting their own." He glanced pointedly at Nattmara. Kata wondered if he was protecting her with more than his words—maybe with his magic, too.

But she didn't have time to ask, because Eldri took her hand, then Elín's. In a softer voice, he said, "Kata, Elín . . . this plan and my protection are not all you share. I believe it important for you to know that you also share a mother and father."

No Longer Alone
Elín

*Y*ou also share a mother and father.

Two words reverberated through Elín—*family* and *home*. Somehow, here at the edge of the world, she'd found a way to reclaim the two most painful things she'd lost.

"But how?" Kata asked, her brows pulling together. Most of the dinner guests, excepting Týr, didn't seem surprised. Perhaps they all already knew.

Joyful tears pricked Elín's eyes. Her suspicion had been right. "Is it true?"

Eldri nodded, releasing their hands from his small, warm ones. Using magic to relight his pipe, he leaned back in his chair as he breathed in the smoke and blew out a ring. "Yes, it is. It's a long story, and it's late, so I will only say that your parents split you up to protect you."

"No," Kata said. "My father wouldn't . . ."

"There are many things you don't know about your father," Eldri said levelly.

My father is alive. I won't need to bother Arn about him; with their plan, I could meet him myself! Elín felt something bloom in her chest, so warm that she would not have been surprised if she had actually started glowing.

She stood, smiling broadly, and approached Kata. "Little sister," she said as she embraced her, a tear rolling down her cheek. Kata stiffened at first but then managed to return a light embrace.

"Elín," Kata said, stepping back and looking at her with a puzzled expression. "About our father . . ."

"I cannot wait to meet him. You have no idea—I thought I was alone in the world, but now I find out I still have a family?"

"Yes, well . . ." Kata glanced around the room, and Elín noticed Nattmara's sharp teeth flash in a cruel smile.

"You should both retire for the evening," Eldri said, hopping off his chair and standing before them.

"Yes," Kata said, pretending to stifle a yawn that didn't look quite genuine. "I'm—uh—tired."

Elín's smile faded for a moment, but it had been a rather long day. "We'll speak more of this tomorrow, then," Elín said. "When we're well-rested. We have a great deal of catching up to do."

Magni came to Kata's side and Týr came to Elín's. They slipped outside, Kata still looking worried. The news must have rattled her; she slipped down the path to her lodgings without saying goodbye.

Týr was unusually quiet, too. As they approached their cave-chambers, which were next to each other, he said, "You are right, I think. It's late, and it'll be better to talk when we are rested tomorrow."

His expression was troubled, and she bit her lip. Hadn't they just received good news? The mountain-dwellers had a plan, and she had not only a father but a sister, too!

"Sweet dreams, Elín," Týr said, then slipped off to his room.

Elín woke feeling, for the first time she could remember, excited. After her mother had passed it had seemed her life was on one long, narrow path. Taking care of herself and Revna, the animals, the farm . . . living in Ornfoss. Except for midwinter, it was comfortable enough, but far from exciting. There had been no anticipation for events beyond planting or harvest.

Now, there was plenty. Learning more about the creatures of Skyli, trying to help them. Getting to know her sister, meeting her father. Discovering what powers she possessed and what she could do with them. Finding a new place that felt like home.

She pulled herself out of bed and crossed to the pitcher of water on the mantle. After lifting it and placing it on the rough-woven rug in front of the hearth, she sat in front of it, cross-legged.

Placing her hands on either side of the clay pitcher, she sang the freezing spell Týr had taught her on the knarr—the one she'd heard Revna sing a few times. As she did so, she imagined the water in the pitcher freezing. That tingling feeling entered her fingers again, but, ignoring it, she finished the song.

On the last note, as she shifted on her knees to look into the pitcher, it burst, cracking into pieces. "Oh!" she exclaimed, but then began to laugh.

"Elín?" Týr called from outside her door. "Are you alright?"

"Yes, yes, come in!"

He entered and blinked a few times, his eyes adjusting to the firelight before finding her on the rug.

"Look!" she said, feeling giddy. Seeing was believing, and she now had undeniable proof of her powers, making her hands stiff with cold. She stood and handed him the pitcher-shaped chunk of solid ice.

He took it, confused at first, but then realization dawned over his features. "You froze this? With your powers?"

"Yes," she said, grinning. "I guess I'm a Stormsinger after all."

Týr set the ice down on the chair and grabbed her shoulders, smiling. For a moment she thought he might kiss her. What a strange thought. Instead, he let her shoulders go, cleared his throat, and said, "That's wonderful!" as she took a step back and tried to hide her blush.

"I'm afraid I destroyed my pitcher, though," she said, gesturing to the shards of pottery on the floor.

He laughed. "I'm sure they'll be more than happy to supply you with a new one."

"What next?" she asked. "Teach me something else! I know creating a blizzard is a long way from freezing a pitcher of water, but I can work up to that, can't I?"

Týr glanced sideways. "About that . . ."

Her smile faded. "What? You don't think I can?"

"No, no, it's not that . . . With some practice and access to all the spells in the Tome, you should be able to do nearly anything." He gave her a crooked half-smile, but the anxious look didn't leave his eyes.

"Well, alright. Let's go find it." She needed the Tome for Eldri's plan, to help all the kind people here who believed in her magic and, like Týr said, would help her master it. To make her way to Snjoreya, to meet her father, and to make it safe to return to her farm when she was ready. *If* she was ready, after finding Kata and her father.

"We will," Týr said. It seemed like he wanted to say more, but he stopped and ran his hand through his hair.

"But?" she prompted.

"But . . ." He looked down and brushed some snow from his dark cloak. "As the Tomekeeper, and with you being the Last Stormsinger . . . I must advise against participating in Eldri's plan."

"What? What do you mean?" Elín asked, beginning to pace the room. "You told me before that Eldri had a plan that would work. And you're the one who dragged me out here—so I could *help*."

"I'm sorry, Songstress." Týr sat on the bed and didn't notice her bristle at the title. He put his face in his hands and let out a long sigh. "I didn't know they would ask this of you. Maybe Björn did. Maybe he knew, and that's why he didn't want to bring you here. And I've made another mistake."

"I want to do it."

"Why?" He looked up at Elín, disbelief plain on his features. "You've already lost so much—everything, really. And this could cost you so much more. Your life, even."

Elín sat in the chair and gazed into the fire. He wasn't wrong. She'd lost everything—her mother, her grandmother, her home. But—"Look how much I've gained."

He still didn't believe her. "Like what?"

She smirked. "Besides an annoying guardian?"

"Besides that."

Everything. She thought back to her last talk with Arn. Adventure had done her good. If she hadn't lost her home, if it had always been safe, would she have ever left her village? She might never have seen what else she could do, what more she could be. The possibilities now seemed almost endless. "So much—adventure, using my powers, finding out I have a sister. And this incredible place. I'm so glad you brought me here, and I want to help Skyli's people."

He shook his head. "I brought you here because it's safe. Their plan is too dangerous—leading you right into King Karvel's castle? I can't allow that . . ."

Her cheeks flushed red with anger. "Well, it isn't up to you! I've made up my mind; I'm going to help them any way that I can."

"Please." Týr took her hand, then quickly dropped it, as if he hadn't realized what he'd done. "I need to keep you safe. If there are ways you can help from here . . ."

"I should let my own sister put herself in danger while I shut myself up, safe in Skyli?" She shook her head and walked across the room again. "No, we're going." When Týr looked like he would protest, she said, "Or I'm going, anyway, with or without you."

He sighed. "If you can't be dissuaded, I'll go with you. I am bound to protect you."

"Well then, I release you from your bond," Elín said, throwing her hands in the air.

His face went white and hurt, as if she'd struck him. Something tugged at her heart, and she approached him, softening.

"Týr, you don't understand. After my grandmother . . ." She choked on the words. "I was all alone. There was no one and nothing left for me in Ornfoss. Then you came and, well, turned my world upside down"—she rolled her eyes—"and now I find out there's a whole kingdom here of people who need me. I'm no longer alone in the world. My father is alive. I have a sister!"

Týr kept his eyes on the ground. "It's the same for me. When my master . . ." He swallowed. "All I had left was you." He met her eyes then, and she felt her pulse quicken.

"Then please, Týr, help me to help these people. I'm the only one left with this power, so I have to try. I want to help win them back their homes, even though mine is lost to me."

He stood, turning away from her, and paced to the other side of the cave. His hand clenched into a fist and unclenched. Finally, he sighed and turned back toward her. "Very well. I told you I'd go with you in either case, but I'll do whatever I can, since this is your decision. The first order of business is to find the Tome."

"Yes," Elín agreed. "How far away is it?"

"A few days' journey by land and sea. Please, is there any way I can convince you to stay here while I retrieve it?"

"No. Where you go, I go. Or perhaps it's the other way around," she said, smirking.

He rubbed his eyes.

"More sea travels." Elín crossed her arms and arched an eyebrow. "I take it I'll be seeing more of Axel and our viking friends?"

Týr managed a crooked grin. "Most likely."

"When do we leave?"

"At first light tomorrow. We'll gather the provisions we need today at the market, and I'll send word to Axel."

"Very well. I'll join you at the market after I speak to Kata. She seemed troubled yesterday. I think there was something she wanted to tell me . . . something she didn't want to say in front of all the dinner guests."

"Of course," Týr said. "I'll see you at the market. And may Lady Luck help us if you insist on keeping to Eldri's plan."

"I do insist," she said firmly, attempting a confident smile as he sighed and left her room.

LEARNING MAGIC
Kata

It wasn't until she *knew* her mother was dead that Kata realized she'd always carried a secret hope that she was alive. Still out there, waiting for Kata to find her again. Now, that hope had been snuffed out.

She couldn't bear to talk to Elín. Not just because of her mother, but because of her father, too. How was she to tell Elín her father was a bounty hunter? And how could she justify that side of her father with him marrying into a *witch* family? It all made sense now, why he forbade the hunters to tell her of the Stormsingers, why he refused to speak of her mother. He'd lied to Kata her whole life. About everything.

All Kata had wanted since Magni took her was to go home, perhaps with a trophy or two, but everything grew endlessly more complicated the longer she stayed in this land where monstrous creatures reveled in their magic.

So, when Magni retrieved her before dawn, it was easier to go with him than to wait for Elín to come to her room, eager to speak of the father she hadn't known she had. The father that would probably turn her in to the king for bounty without a second thought.

The scent of cedar tickled her nose as Magni led her to a clearing in the woods on the side of the mountain. Away from inquisitive eyes.

"Why are we here?" Kata asked Magni, shivering in the cold.

Use your mind, not your voice, Magni said. *We're waiting for your training partner.*

"I thought *you* were my training partner," she said, and Magni gave her a sharp look for using her voice. She closed her eyes and took a deep breath. Kata didn't want to be here at all, learning something that would get her banished from Snjoreya. But she'd seen one bright spot in Eldri's plan last night—if nothing else, it might be her only way home.

Fine. Who is my training partner? She tried to send to Magni. But she wasn't sure if it had worked. Before he could respond, she heard violin music wafting through the trees.

She put a hand on her hip. "By Lady Legend, no, Magni. Not him!"

Grim danced his way into and around the clearing, playing his favorite jaunty tune. When he finished, he bowed for so long that Kata nearly found herself clapping just to make him stop. Finally, he straightened, still grinning, and handed his violin and bow to a nearby tree.

Kata's breath caught when she saw the tree lightly reshape its branches to hold the instrument and wrap its finger-like twigs around the bow.

Well, she thought. *If he can command trees so easily, maybe he can teach me to command a dragon.* Even if he *was* friends with Nattmara and had nearly let a nykur drown her.

"Well, Kata," Grim said. "Shall we begin?"

"What do we do first?" she asked, addressing Magni.

Close your eyes. Focus your mind.

Kata obeyed, closing her eyes. Fresh snow had fallen in the night, dampening scent and sound. She couldn't smell or hear Grim and Magni, but there was something . . . a dim presence, almost as if she could feel where they stood in relation to her.

She sensed Magni moving in an arc from in front of her to her left side. She couldn't hear him move, but she felt his change in position. Keeping her eyes closed, she said, "I can feel your minds . . . and Magni, I know you just moved to my left."

Very good. Magni said. *Now, send something to Grim. Images are easier than words alone, when you first begin.*

She nodded and closed her eyes again, finding it easier to focus her message without visual distractions. She imagined the waterfall where she first met Grim and tried to send, *Is this your home?*

Nothing happened. There was no reaction from Grim, so she tried again, imagining sending the message from her mind to his.

"Are you doing it?" Grim asked.

"Yes!" she said, losing the picture in her mind and opening her eyes. "Be quiet. I'm trying to concentrate."

"Alright, alright," Grim said, holding his hands up defensively and wearing his familiar toothy grin.

What did you try to tell him? Magni asked her.

She conjured the picture again in her mind and, this time, tried to send it Magni's way with the same words.

Then she asked, "Magni, did you see?"

A glimpse of a forest scene. Try something more familiar.

She sat against a tree this time and closed her eyes again. A pang of home-sickness came over her as she remembered the tavern. Sitting at her usual table, a hunk of warm bread and a bowl of hearty-smelling stew before her. Surrounded by her father, Helga, Gunnar . . . Bergdis at the bar. The chatter of a dozen hunters. She sent the image to Magni with the words, *Are they looking for me?*

After a pause, Magni replied. *I do not know.*

Kata swallowed, suddenly feeling exposed. She was out here with an alicorn and a water-spirit, and back home, they had no idea what had become of her. Or that she was learning magic, the thing they all feared so much.

Send it to Grim.

No, she thought, unsure if she was still transmitting her thoughts to Magni. It was too personal, too vulnerable.

Go on. This was stronger than the other.

"Alright, Grim," she said. "Be ready."

"I always am," he said, rubbing his hands together.

She closed her eyes and pictured the tavern again, but this time focused on the table, the stew and bread, and sent a different message: *Are you hungry?*

But even as she tried to send the message, she could feel it did not reach him the way her words had reached Magni. Something held them back.

It isn't working, she sent to Magni, but felt that message fail to reach its target, too. Like an arrow released before the bow was fully drawn, falling to the snow between them.

"I'm trying," she said. "But it isn't working."

Grim, sit beside Kata. Let her put a hand on your shoulder. It may help. Magni must have been communicating to Grim, but sent that thought to Kata too. Just thinking about how she could accomplish that—speaking to two people at once with her temperamental powers—gave her a headache.

"As you please, Magni," Grim said as he sauntered over to her. Halfway, though, he stopped and peered at the alicorn. "Are you sure she has the gift?"

Her face flushed in anger. "Of course I do! *He* can understand me."

"Yes, but he's the only one who can. It's only his word that says you even have a gift." He sat beside her, cross-legged, and grinned. "Ah, don't be angry, little huntress. I'm sure our Magni here would never lie about such a thing. His motivations are always as pure as that white coat of his, aren't they?"

Grim stared at the alicorn. His grin turned menacing, but Magni didn't react.

"I won't have you insulting my friend," Kata said hotly. "Magni, there must be someone else to practice with."

Do you think a dragon will be easier?

His words sent a chill down her spine, and she shook her head, lightly. "Fine, I'll make do with him."

But why is it so much simpler with you? She added privately to Magni. This time, it seemed to reach her target. It was becoming easier with him, at least.

It's harder with those who do not share our ability. And easier with those we trust.

The image of her father and their tavern friends came back. Did she really trust Magni so completely?

"I've got nothing over here," Grim said, interrupting her thoughts.

Kata groaned in frustration and gritted her teeth. "I wasn't sending anything. Now be silent."

She reached out a tentative hand and placed it on his shoulder. Shaking away the image of the tavern, she imagined entering the castle to greet the King. The great hall with its colorful tapestries, the sconces dripping candle wax down the ancient stone walls. *Have you been here?*

This time, it seemed easier. He was beside her, her hand touching his shoulder. It should have been simple to place her thought into his mind. But again, she felt something holding it back.

"Still nothing," Grim said, feigning impatience through his grin.

"Fine," Kata said, getting up and walking across the clearing. "I give up. I can't get through to him."

You have walls up. She heard Magni's voice in her head.

Of course I do! She sent back to him. How could she explain? She feared magic—all of her people did. It was ingrained in her. And Grim had only done his best to make her uncomfortable since she first met him.

Just then, Kata, now more attuned to her new awareness, felt the presence of another magical being. She whirled around to see the trees part above her head as Skadi entered the clearing.

"Let her try with me." The frost giantess's voice was deep and resonant.

Grim shrugged and picked up his violin and bow from their resting place across the clearing. They heard angry, harsh notes fade to more pleasant ones as he made his way deeper into the woods.

Kata nodded as she sized up Skadi. This could work. She couldn't completely trust Skadi, but she at least understood her—she who long ago, before the Ladies were worshiped, had been revered as a goddess of mountains and hunting.

Alright, Magni prompted. *Tell her something.*

Kata closed her eyes, hearing a light wind stir the trees and feeling the chill in her fingertips. This time, she pictured her last hunt in the forest, following the elk. He had stopped to strip bark from a tree. She'd unleashed her arrow, piercing him through the heart. *Do you hunt elk?*

For several tense moments, she tried to hold the image, to keep pushing her thoughts along the fragile thread she'd made between their minds.

"Yes," Skadi said.

Kata opened her eyes, her hands clenched into fists in excitement. "Did you really hear me?"

"I saw you hunting an elk in the woods. You wanted to know if I hunt them, too." Skadi said, glancing at Magni as if unsure what to make of this human girl's excitement.

"Yes!" Kata shouted. "I did it. Oh, thank you, Skadi. Thank you!"

The corners of Skadi's mouth turned up in a smirk, and then she knelt so her eyes would be closer to Kata's level. She wore a large satchel and now rummaged in it. Finding what she sought, she stopped and looked at Kata, her hand still in the bag.

"I came because I have something for you."

"For me?" Kata asked, her eyes wide. She had never considered magic creatures, thought to be so wicked, giving gifts. And she certainly had not expected to receive one from an elegant giantess.

Skadi pulled forth a handsome bow, already strung, hewn of pale wood and decorated with forest designs; ferns and foxes peeked through the carved trees. Then Skadi took out a leather quiver, embossed with similar details and filled with wooden arrows fletched with brown-and-white striped feathers.

Kata let out her breath. "They're beautiful." She reached out an eager hand to take them, then stopped. Surely, there was a reason Magni had flown her here without her weapon of choice. The creatures here already trusted her so little . . .

"Go on. Take them." Skadi met her eyes, and there was something in them. Something that said Skadi understood the risk, understood everything Kata had been taught, and wanted her to have them anyway. Wanted her to feel their trust.

"Thank you," she breathed as she took them, running her fingers over the bow's carved limbs reverently and appreciating the craftsmanship.

"But of course," Skadi said, indicating her own bow, which was like a much larger version of Kata's and slung across her back. "A huntress should never be without her weapon. And this one is special. Put it over your shoulder and say the word, '*hylja.*'"

Hesitating, wondering at what point down this magic-learning spiral she would finally stop, Kata slung the quiver over her shoulder and put her head through the bow so it rested across her back, its string bisecting her chest.

She muttered the word, and her shoulders fell when it didn't work. "Nothing happened."

Ah, Magni said. *A wonderful gift, Skadi.*

"It looks the same to you," the frost goddess explained. "But we can no longer see that you have it. No one will know you are armed until you take them off to use them."

Kata tried to smile. This gesture spoke of a far deeper trust than she deserved. She was attempting to force her tied tongue to communicate her thanks when a shriek pierced the sky. Instinctively, she nocked an arrow and pointed it toward the sound. A phoenix! A bird worth its weight in gold to the king. She aimed . . .

As it swooped toward them, she remembered where she was. That these were her friends, now. Or at least, they were no longer her enemies. She thought of Magni's patience, Eldri's confidence in her, Skadi's gift. Elín's warmth as she brushed her hair. A deep sense of shame washed over her as she released the tension from her bow and re-quivered the arrow. Luckily, her companions hadn't noticed—or, if they had, they were giving her the benefit of the doubt that it was only a reaction to the sudden noise.

"What is it?" Skadi asked, stretching out her arm. The phoenix perched on it and ruffled its flame-colored feathers. The giantess pulled a message scrawled on paper from its leg. She didn't tremble, and her face didn't turn any paler, but her voice was harsh and urgent.

"King Karvel's hunters were spotted on the mountain trail."

GIVE FAR MORE
Elín

Elín was sitting in the marketplace, playing with Fridolf's dogs again, when the phoenix cries came from above. The market burst into chaos as people scrambled to pack up their things. Children were snatched up by their mothers, and shouts of people searching for their loved ones resonated through the valley.

"What is it?" Elín asked as Fridolf began harnessing his dogs. He'd already hastily rolled up his goods and lashed the bundle to his sled.

"Danger," he said, slipping the harness onto the lead dog. "My guess is hunters—I need to go. Lady Destiny guide you on your journey, and Lady Luck grant your mission success. And if you fail, may Lady Legend ensure all remember your attempt."

"Thank you!" Elín called, but his dogs had already sprinted off, pulling him away over the snow. *If you fail . . .* His words were only a traditional blessing for people starting new endeavors, but they still made her feel uneasy.

Where's Týr? Where's Kata? Her blood raced in her veins as she wandered through the crowds, searching for his dark hair or her sunny gold. By the Ladies, there was such a large throng of people—where were they all to hide if hunters had found their sanctuary?

The latter question was quickly answered as Skadi stepped out from the woods. "Follow me to safety," she commanded in her calm, sonorous voice.

The hubbub paused briefly. Then the crowd reorganized itself to follow the frost giantess, though they still chattered frantically.

Elín located Kata, trailing behind Skadi, and trotted to catch up with her. "You're alright!" she said, breathless. "Have you seen Týr?"

Kata shook her head. At the same time, there was a shout of "Elín!" Týr's face appeared in the crowd as he pushed his way through to catch up with them.

Skadi stopped near the sheer face of one of the mountains. She placed her hand on it, and a gaping hole appeared, as if the stone had dissolved. "Get in," she said to the crowd around her. "We'll hide here."

"No," Týr said, turning to Elín. "We can't. We need to find the Tome. If the hunters found Skyli . . ."

Elín looked from him to Kata, her forehead creasing. "But . . ."

"They could be hiding for days, Elín. We need the Kirja for Eldri's plan," Týr insisted, looking to Kata for support.

"He's right," she said slowly. Kata seemed nervous, running a hand through her thick blonde hair. "The sooner we execute the plan, the better. Every day that passes means more deaths . . . more bounties."

"If you want to stay here, I'll go—"

"No, I'm going with you," Elín cut Týr off, shaking her head. "But Kata, stay with them—stay safe."

"I will," Kata said. "Magni will fly me to meet you when it's clear to travel again."

"Where shall we meet you?" Týr asked.

Kata glanced around at the crowd, seeing that nearly all had filtered into the shelter. "In the King's Forest, there's a big oak tree near the double bend in the river. I'll wait there each day at high noon."

Týr nodded his agreement.

"Take care, my dear," Elín said, kissing Kata's forehead and drawing her into an embrace.

The last of the magical creatures—a few ambling ice bears—had filtered into Skadi's hiding place as they spoke. "Farewell, Elín," Kata said. But she paused and glanced to the side, rubbing her tunic hem between her fingers. "But first, there's something else you should know."

Elín shook her head. "Tell me when we meet again. There's no time."

"It's about our father," Kata blurted. In a lower voice, she said, "He's known to be the best unicorn hunter in the land. Now he hunts game for the king's table, but before that, he killed *dozens* of unicorns." Kata's eyes went wide.

"No," Elín said, a hand to her mouth. "It can't be." Had she really come all this way, kindled the hope of meeting her father after sixteen long years, only to find out that he was a killer? Her heart sank.

"I'm sorry," Kata said, grimacing and still running her fingers over the hem of her tunic. "I wish we had more time. But he's a bounty hunter—he might even be coming up the mountain as we speak. I thought you should know."

Still stunned, Elín nodded slowly. "Thank you for telling me. Be safe. We'll see each other again soon."

"Lady Luck be with you," Skadi said as she crouched through the doorway she'd made. The mountain sealed behind her, as if the opening had never been there at all.

"Come on," Týr said, pulling Elín along. "The hunters were spotted on the west side of the mountain, close now. We'll double back around so as not to meet them. Let's gather our things and go."

In a few short minutes, they each shouldered their packs. Both Týr's satchel and Elín's new rucksack were heavy-laden with magic-made gifts. They picked their way along the icy path on the north side of the mountain. Týr walked in front, checking around corners and looking over cliff edges to be sure they weren't seen by anyone. While checking the view beyond a frozen trickle of water, he held out a hand to stop Elín, then brought one finger to his lips while his other hand pointed down and to their left.

Very carefully, Elín inched forward until she could see the group of hunters, clad in furs and leather, sneaking along the path far below them. There were two women and three men. Each carried a longbow, and quivers stuffed full of arrows bristled on their backs. Elín felt a chill creep into her fingers. There were enough arrows between them to kill every creature in Skyli.

She studied the men closely, looking for any sign that one of them might be her father. One seemed too young, but the other two were of the right age. They didn't share any features with Elín or Kata, but she stared at them anyway, her heart beating fast. She didn't want to believe what Kata had told her, but could see no reason for her to lie. The sickening thought must be true: she was descended from someone who lined their pockets by slaying the purest of beasts. Who might even be willing to kill *her* for a bounty.

When the hunters rounded a bend and vanished, Týr motioned for them to continue. Elín tucked away all thoughts of her father. They crept their way down the mountain and through the wooded path, back to where Axel had first taken them ashore.

It was a long, cold night spent by the shore, trying to sleep beneath trees for shelter and worrying that the hunters might have found Skyli and destroyed it. Thankfully, Axel and his crew were prompt, arriving just as dawn broke over the mountains.

The captain rowed out to them in the rowboat, sending them a hearty wave. But when it was time for them to board, he was less friendly.

"I'm sorry, lad, but I need payment. The crew knows King Karvel's hunters roam further out, killing any magical beast they come across. They don't want to be tangled up in it."

"We can get it to you after we get the . . . book," Týr said, grimacing. Most of the crew weren't aware of the details of their mission, Týr had told her, so he had to be careful when mentioning the Tome.

Axel's mustache curled up as he smiled sadly, shaking his head. "I need something now."

"How about this?" Elín asked, showing him the dagger the giant had given her. "It must be worth something."

"Aye, that it is, but I can't trade it where we're going. In King Karvel's lands, they ask too many questions about magic-made weapons."

So, she couldn't trade her other gifts from the market either, though few would've been valuable enough to cover their journey. Elín swallowed back the lump in her throat and replaced the dagger in her rucksack, drawing out her mother's ivory-handled hairbrush instead. It shone in the sunlight and she tried to feel glad that she always kept it oiled and polished.

"No, Elín, we'll find another way," Týr said. "You can't—"

"Yes," she said, straightening her spine. "I can. I'd give far more to see our mission succeed."

Axel took the brush and ran his hands over the carved details and smooth ivory, turning it back and forth. "This'll do," he said finally, then motioned for them to step aboard.

"We can buy it back from him after we get the Tome," Týr said in a low voice, searching her eyes. "There'll be some coin hidden with it."

She managed a half-smile. "We can try." Then she bit her lip. If there was one item that hurt her to part with, this was it. She wondered what more she would need to give up to see their mission succeed.

Týr held her eyes for another few moments, then nodded, as if he'd made a decision. "Come, sit," he said, guiding her into the boat with a hand on her back. "We'll be there soon enough."

"By Lady Destiny, are those women out there?" Elín leaned over the rail, shading her eyes from the sun, and tried to make out what sort of creatures were splashing in the sea and lounging on the wave-beaten rocks.

"No," Týr replied. "Mermaids."

Elín inhaled. "Truly? I hadn't thought they were real." Not for the first time, she remembered the thousand apologies she owed her grandmother for not believing the stories she told of strange creatures and powerful Stormsingers. It certainly seemed that more were true than not.

The ship drew close enough for Elín to see for herself that they were mermaids. The women had fish-like tails from the waist down, and their long hair was wavy from the salt. There were nine in total, all striking in appearance. A few of them waved when they saw Axel and his men, and two of them dove gracefully into the water and swam toward the boat.

"Is it safe for them here?" Elín asked, her brows pulling together. "I mean, with King Karvel's hunters?"

"Until recently, anyone was safe as long as they weren't in Snjoreya," Týr replied, a gruff note entering his voice. "Now . . . no one is truly safe. But mermaids have their own tricks to hide from or even destroy enemy ships. Some say they can even tell the future. They mostly live here, now, in the Shallows—islands of stone between Snjoreya and the lands to the east through which ships cannot safely pass."

The two mermaids who approached had long black hair and tanned skin—they must spend a good deal of time in the sun, on their rocky islands above the water. One of them surfaced near Axel's end of the ship and spoke with him. The other swam around the boat, doing a lazy backstroke that showed off her curves to the enraptured vikings. Then she dove under the boat and resurfaced near Elín's seat by the rail.

Up close, the mermaid was even more striking, with high cheekbones and thick, dusky lashes. Her eyes were a vivid purple that matched her iridescent tail, swaying in the water behind her.

"Hello?" Elín said uncertainly.

The mermaid grinned. "They tell me you're the last Stormsinger." Her voice was melodious, but her eyes appraised Elín shrewdly.

"It's true," Týr said, and Elín bit her lip. Freezing a jug of water did not make one a powerful sorceress.

The mermaid kept eye contact, unblinking. "You will fight for us, Songstress of Storm and Snow?"

Once more, Elín felt the crushing weight of other people's hopes resting on her. She swallowed, finding her voice, then nodded. "Yes. I'm going to try."

She inclined her head. "Then you have our blessing to pass through these waters. And I shall give you a gift." The mermaid pulled a strand of woven fibers from the water. A pearlescent, twisted shell hung from it. "This necklace has a bit of our magic. It allows the wearer to wander unnoticed through a crowd. But be warned—ours is different than the magic of the huldufólk. It has limitations, and it will not hide you from the one who knows you best."

"Thank you," Elín said. There wasn't much call for hiding in crowds in Eldri's plan, but she was touched by the mermaid's willingness to help, while also feeling a little burdened by their faith in her.

The mermaid watched Elín put the necklace away in her pack, her colorful tail swaying calmly beneath the water's surface and her arms floating gracefully at her sides. "I was born in the icy sea north of Snjoreya, and I long to return," she said. "My sister, Hronn, is telling the captain that he must not take you there by the usual way, around the Shallows to the south. The kraken waits."

"Thank you for warning us," Týr said. The mermaid's violet eyes flicked to Týr, as if just realizing he was there, before settling back on Elín.

"What's your name?" Elín asked.

"I am called Kolga," she replied, turning to go.

"It was nice to meet you, Kolga."

The mermaid looked back over her shoulder and said, "If you are strong and quick-witted, we may meet again, Songstress of Storm and Snow." Then her arms skimmed the water gracefully, and she dove beneath the waves.

Hronn finished her conversation with Axel and returned to the other mermaids. As the ship made way again, Elín watched them play and swim about the rocks until their figures faded into the distance.

She turned to Týr, eyes bright. "The amazing things I've seen on this journey . . . have you met any mermaids before?"

He shook his head. "No, only heard tales. That was . . . something."

"What about the kraken? Have you encountered it before?"

"No, and I pray to Lady Luck we never will."

"I'm glad they warned us, then."

The day passed quickly as they made their way north. Ice floes appeared atop some of the waves and along the shore. Translucent blue glaciers were visible in the distance. When Axel stopped the ship, they were nearly surrounded by glaciers and spears of ice jutting out from the water. To their right was a strange landscape of snow and ice formed from the volcano that belched smoke from its peak: the icy, barren wastes known as Viltland.

Axel made his way toward the back of the ship. "We can go no further without danger to the ship. We're going to trade, and we'll meet you here tomorrow. Be warned, if you aren't here by sunset, I'll have to leave. The crew distrusts this land." And indeed, the other vikings were scanning the horizon with suspicion, huddled and shivering.

The land seemed colder than Ornfoss, even in deepest winter, but Elín didn't shiver. She was bundled in all her warm clothing, but she also wondered if the snowsong magic in her blood kept her warm.

"Of course," Týr replied to Axel, helping Elín up and into the little rowboat. He waved to Axel and the other vikings, then steered them through the ice floes until they reached ice solid enough to stand on.

She helped him pull the boat ashore and secure it, then surveyed this new land. Ice shards protruded from the ground. Ahead was a path carved into the smooth and curving glacial walls. Farther along, deep tracks were grooved through the ice, where lava had slid across the land. Most had cooled to rock, but here and there, steam rose from the channels. Everything glistened in the fading sunlight.

She turned to Týr, who'd pulled his satchel from the boat and was putting it on.

"Yet another treacherous path?"

He smiled crookedly. "Yes. But with any luck, this'll be the last one for a while."

BECOME THE HUNTED

Kata

The hiding place Skadi had opened with her magic went pitch-dark as she sealed the entrance, but quickly brightened again as Eldri spread his arms over his head and unleashed his magic. Glowing orbs hovered over the dozens of magical creatures huddled together in the cave. If Kata squinted, they almost looked like dappled sunlight through leaves.

Fear kept everyone silent, so though Eldri whispered, his voice carried over the crowd. "Stay here, stay silent, and we shall be safe," he said. "If any of you have concealing or cloaking magic, use it now."

Several huldufólk made gestures with their hands, casting spells over the hiding place. Despite the events of the last few days, Kata felt on edge seeing magic being done so brazenly. Magni caught her eye through the crowd, his coat and feathers bright in the cave, and she felt him release his calming magic over not just her, but everyone hiding with them. Several of the most nervous gnomes fell asleep; maybe his power had more effect on them due to their small size.

The hours passed slowly, and Kata had plenty of time to wonder about worrisome things. Which hunters were out there on the mountain paths? Could Gunnar or Helga be with them? What about her father?

And why were they here? Could they be looking for her? Or had they found out about Skyli, the last safe place for all who lived here? *Am I betraying my people and our way of life by hiding with our enemies?*

Her hands were growing clammy, and she wiped them on her trousers. She could patiently track an animal for hours while hunting, but now that the roles were reversed . . .

Once before, Kata had felt this exchange, had become the hunted instead of the hunter. She'd followed a wild boar to her den when she saw the creature had babies. Turning to go, she'd heard the boar charge, kicking up leaves, and barely managed to scramble up a tree in time. The beast had circled the tree, snorting furiously, before she returned to lay outside her den and glare up at Kata with beady eyes.

She could have shot the boar from up there in that tree, but instead, Kata had carefully climbed down, keeping an eye on the boar the whole way, and dropped to the ground. The beast lifted her head, but she only watched as Kata backed away.

Later, she'd asked her father if she had done the right thing, or if she should have killed the boar. It was one of the king's favorite dishes, after all.

"No, my little dove. Even a boar's children shouldn't be without their mother." Then that glassy look had come into his eye as he gazed at her, his face expressing something like regret.

That conversation had a different meaning now, in light of everything she'd learned. As angry as she was, she missed her father. Kata had so many more questions for him now than she had ever had before. Was it possible he was there now, just outside of Skadi's conjured wall?

Restless, Kata took to pacing the edges of the hidden opening in the mountain, giving the magical creatures a wide berth where she could. It was at the very back of the cave that she saw it: a glimmer of light. From far away, it looked like one of Eldri's hovering orbs, but now Kata could see that it was sunlight, barely streaming through piles of rocks. Skadi must not have conjured a completely new space within the mountain but expanded an existing cave.

There was another way out—or in—which Skadi had missed. Kata turned back, ready to search for Magni's mind in the crowd and let him know Skadi needed to seal the stone there. But then she glanced back toward the light, the opening.

Kata saw her chance. Eldri's plan wasn't her only way home. If she did know any of the hunters out there, she could join them and return home. No one ever needed to know about her powers, about this place. She could forget, and the creatures of Skyli could forget about *her*.

As quietly as she could, she maneuvered through the rock formations of the cave, following the light. Ducking beneath the icicle-like stones of the cave, she found a narrow tunnel that she could slither through on her belly. It was only once she was halfway through it that she realized she could have gotten stuck. By then, there was no other way but forward.

At the other end of the tunnel, the cave widened and then broke out into the woods. The light outside was blinding at first, and the wind was chilly on Kata's cheeks after the stifling air of the cave. Kata filled her lungs with cold, pine-scented air and grinned. She was free.

When she had blinked a few times and adjusted to the light, she saw the valley and lake below her. Everyone had cleaned up well, probably with magical help; there was no evidence of the marketplace that had been there in the morning.

Now, it was just a matter of finding the hunters and convincing them to take her back home. She'd lie about the hidden creatures, of course—though they would be worth a fortune, and though there were still a few she'd have no qualms killing, she couldn't be the reason they *all* perished.

She skirted the edge of the mountain, hoping none of the hunters would mistake her for game. But before she'd made it more than a few paces from the cave, Magni's voice entered her head.

What are you doing outside the mountain?

Kata's teeth clicked together in frustration. She was so close to escaping. *I'm going to the hunters.*

A long pause while she waited for a response. But instead of his voice, Magni himself appeared through an opening Skadi had made in the mountain. She could glimpse the frost giantess behind him, her hand up as she worked her magic. The daylight streaming in illuminated her, even as she was backlit by Eldri's orbs. Her expression was unreadable, and Kata wondered what Magni had told her.

"Get back inside," Kata whispered sharply. "It's not safe, for you especially."

I will, if you come with me.

Kata shook her head. "No. I'm going back home."

The alicorn studied her with his pale eyes. *I'm taking you home in only a few days, remember?*

"Can't you see that I don't belong here? Everyone's frightened of me and, well, maybe they should be."

Magni inclined his head, then shook out his mane. *I didn't only come out to bring you back. Skadi also wanted me to see if the hunters had gone yet.*

Kata's stomach dropped. Had she missed her chance?

But then Magni knelt on his front legs so Kata could climb onto him. When she hesitated, he snorted and said, *You want to see, too, don't you?*

"Yes, but be careful, Magni. If they see you . . . they'll take you as a trophy." She stepped up to him, running a hand along his neck, then swung her leg over. It came more naturally to her this time, and there was comfort in twining her hands into his silky mane. The alicorn took a few running steps and then launched into the air, catching himself with his wings.

Flying was surely as exhilarating as it had been the other times, but Kata was too busy scanning the ground for hunters to notice. Magni swung wide around the mountain, and she peered over his neck, trying to make out anyone on the path below.

There, Magni said, dipping sideways in the direction he wanted her to look. *Five of them.*

She squinted against the sunlight and could just make out the figures of the hunters below. None were recognizable from this height, but she had a gut feeling her father wasn't among them.

We should go before they see us.

Kata straightened on his back and tried to send a *yes* mentally when suddenly an arrow shot up toward them. As if time had slowed, she saw the arrow spin and arc, wood flexing, then pierce Magni's wing, sending a mist of blood into the air.

"No!" she shouted as he lurched sideways, nearly unseating her and whinnying in pain.

Magni stopped himself from tumbling through the air and regained control, then flew as quickly as he could, with his damaged wing hindering him, back the way they had come. They were soon out of sight of the hunters.

He landed much less gracefully than usual in the valley, and Kata dismounted, rushing to look at the wound. Magni was breathing hard, and blood seeped from the hole the arrow had made, staining his feathers.

"What can I do?" Kata asked desperately. This would be her perfect opportunity to escape, to run into the hunters' arms. Whose side was she on—Eldri's or theirs? She didn't know; but she couldn't let Magni die.

No matter, Magni said, his naturally calm voice now panicked and rushed in her mind. *Eldri can heal me. I'll be whole again in a few days.*

Kata shook her head. "No. The hunters . . . they saw where you flew. They'll follow us back here. They could find the others."

Come back to the shelter. He made his way to the wall Skadi had opened before, one wing hanging at an odd angle. A few blood-soaked feathers fell onto the snow in his wake.

"No," Kata said again, a plan forming in her mind. "They know they've injured you. They'll come to . . . finish."

All we can do is hide, Kata. Come.

"Do you have any idea how valuable you are? No one even knew whether alicorns really existed! The bounty the king will pay . . ." Kata swallowed nervously. "They will not stop pursuing you without a very good reason."

Magni stamped a foot and rolled his eyes back in his head. *What can we do?*

"I'll give them a reason. If they're King Karvel's hunters, I'll know them. My father will have told them I'm missing—they might even know I'd seen you in the woods." A plan quickly formed in her mind. Not a good plan, but the best she had at the moment. "I'll say . . . that you took me, and I managed to get away when you landed because you were distracted by your injury."

The alicorn paused in his tracks and turned to her, ears pricked to attention. His blood continued to drip onto the snow—a concerning amount. *Will that be "a very good reason"?*

"I think so." *I hope so.* She stooped to pick up a handful of the bloody feathers from the snow-covered ground. "I'll tell them the wound was critical; that you flew away but won't live long. They can give the king these feathers, and, with my testimony, he'll give them the bounty. That's all they want."

And if they don't believe you?

"We don't have time for this, Magni. You need to go—have Eldri heal you. Besides, I need to get back to Snjoreya and you won't be able to fly me there until your wing is better. The hunters will take me."

I don't like this.

"Neither do I, but it has a chance to work. Now go."

He took one hard look at her. *Ladies Luck and Destiny be with you. And may Lady Legend honor what you are doing for us all.*

There was no time to dwell on the guilt washing over her at that statement, or to decide where her allegiances really lay. She made a shooing motion with her hands. Magni turned toward the mountain, and Skadi, who must have been waiting for them, suddenly appeared silhouetted in the opening she'd made once more in the stone. Eldri's floating orbs of light glowed behind her

As Magni passed through, Skadi met Kata's gaze and raised her fist to her heart in a salute. A blink later, she was gone. The cold, hard mountain wall stood once again between Kata and those she'd always longed to hunt.

Against the Flames
Elín

Viltland was a harsh land of ice and shadows, but it did not lack beauty.

At the center of the island was the cone of the volcano, which bellowed sparks at uneven intervals. Streams of molten lava, cooled and slowed by the icy surrounds, started at its peak and flowed across the land. The red glow of the fiery, liquid rock was mesmerizing. Elín had to keep her gaze from lingering on it and ensure she lifted her skirts whenever they needed to hop over another rivulet of oozing, red-edged black.

They passed the crumbling remains of a once-mighty stone fortress. Revna must have spoken true: the Keepers had lived here and trained the Stormsingers. Týr said it was destroyed years ago by King Karvel. It must have been early in his reign, for the toppled stones were wind-worn, smoothed by time and ice melt.

"Why did the Keepers choose Viltland to hide the Kirja?" she asked.

"Viltland isn't habitable, not really, but it can be made manageable with snowsong," Týr said. "They wanted somewhere secluded. This is where all the young Stormsingers used to come and spend a few years learning the spells from the Tome. It was a secret place, but King Karvel discovered its location somehow. He destroyed the fortress and the original Tome, but there's another, hidden deeper into Viltland. That's where we're going."

She wondered if the last Stormsinger—the one who died before her grandmother, who King Karvel had killed—had revealed the secret of this place. If they didn't know of Elín and her grandmother, they may have believed themself the last of the Stormsingers. Perhaps they'd given up hope of escaping the king; it would no longer matter what happened to the book with no one left to sing its spells.

Waves of blue and green light danced across the starlit sky as Týr and Elín picked their way along the icy path. At the crest of one of the ice hills Elín stopped, breathless from the climb, and stared. The aurora reflected across the glacial landscape, spreading a whisper of their colors across all the eye could see.

"The northern lights," Elín said as Týr came to her side. "I've heard of them, but I couldn't have imagined anything close to them. Have you seen them before?"

"Yes," Týr said, nodding. He looked out at the landscape, then at Elín. "But not quite like this . . ."

She suddenly realized how close they were standing, their breath visible in the chill night air. Her heart beat quickly as she looked out over the curves and hills of the glaciers again. Then she felt Týr's hand reach out, his fingers interlace with hers.

Her face warmed despite the cold, and she found herself imagining their lips meeting. Týr, this boy who had found her and taken her to a mountain hideaway, who had been so calm and patient as she crossed a decaying bridge over a turbulent waterfall, who had shown her Skyli, and the sea . . .

But it wasn't to be. Týr straightened and let go of her hand, spying something over her shoulder. A look of confusion, then panic, crossed his face.

"What is it?" she asked, but she could already see the glow of fire, the plume of smoke in the distance. "Is that . . . ?"

"The Tome is there." His voice was tight, strained by anxiety.

He grabbed her hand again, but this time, it was to pull her along the path toward the column of smoke. They slid and scrambled across the snow-packed ice, racing against the flames.

What had once been a log cottage, hidden in a stony alcove, was now a smoldering ruin. The acrid smell reached their nostrils from many paces away. As they approached, they took in the extent of the damage. The roof had collapsed and many of its beams were burned away. Had anyone been inside, they would have perished.

Týr's face had gone pale, and his feet faltered as he approached the wreck. It had been a small cottage, so it didn't take long for him to circle it and see that there was no one within. A trail of four or five sets of fresh footprints in the snow led up to and away again from the cottage.

"Who did this?" Elín asked, watching bits of ash blow away on the breeze.

Týr had stepped into the wreck for a few moments. He came out holding the smoking sheaf of papers and scorched leather binding that had been the Tome. He pressed his mittened hands against the parts that still glowed red, extinguishing them. From the size of the book's leather spine, over half of the pages must have been completely burned away. The other half were so singed and scarred that Elín doubted a single spell remained intact.

She could see by his trembling hands and ghostly pallor that Týr was crushed, so she didn't repeat her question. Anyway, she felt a sickening sense that she already knew. Who besides King Karvel would order such a thing done?

He walked toward her, leaving the smoking cottage behind him, and sat in the snow. Laying what was left of the Kirja in his lap, he removed his mittens. The edges of the book still glowed orange, and Elín could see the Tome had singed holes in his mittens and raised pink burn marks on his hands.

Still, his shaking fingers traced the outline of the ancient book as if he couldn't quite believe it was gone. "I've failed," he said. Softly, as if to himself.

Elín took a few steps closer to him. "Your Lady Luck was on our side. Had we arrived but a little sooner, we may have been captured—or worse—by the king's men."

"And had we arrived a day earlier, the Kirja would have survived!" he exclaimed, his voice heavy with emotion. "No, I do not call this a victory for Lady Luck."

Elín laughed, but not kindly. They *were* lucky; perhaps King Karvel's men had the same uneasy feeling toward this land that Axel's crew did. If not, they might have lingered to ensure the little cottage burned completely, and been there when she and Týr arrived. "Which would you have—this book or our lives?"

He stared up at her, and the pain in his eyes made her regret her words. "It's only a book—an object—to you. You don't understand."

She let out a sigh and sat beside him in the snow. The northern lights had faded; without their softening effect, the stars looked harsh against the darkness.

"Then tell me," she said, meeting his eyes.

Týr looked at her and swallowed. "This here . . . this is hundreds of years of history, gone. Incantations you could have learned, could have used to save Eldri and his people, to do good. Songs to bring rain or snow, to make a fog roll over the land, to guide a coming storm, calm the roiling sea, or halt the northern wind. All lost."

Ash like snow fell over them, and the smoke from the cabin stung Elín's eyes as he placed the Tome in her lap. She'd never held a book before and didn't know how to read, even in her own language. Without Týr to read the spells and translate the ancient tongue, the book was useless to her.

She ran a finger across the cover. Though it was warped from heat, she could still feel the intricate patterns of frost, snowflakes, and icicles embossed in the leather. It was true that she didn't feel its loss as he did. A small part of her felt relief that no one would expect such grand deeds of her now, but a larger part worried for Kata and her new friends.

"There have been dozens—hundreds, perhaps—of Keepers of the Tome over the centuries," he continued, looking away from her. "And none of them allowed this to happen."

"Týr . . ." Elín said, placing a hand on his knee for a moment. "You mustn't blame yourself." When he wouldn't meet her eyes, she said, "Truly, you must not—you couldn't be in two places at once, and you found me first."

He shook his head. "I thought if I could keep you safe and find the Tome, it might make up for other things. Other failures. But Björn's death, our journey, my studies—it was all for nothing." His voice was harsh on the last words, and he kicked at a rock frozen into the ground.

Elín pulled spare handkerchiefs and the bottle of salve, given to her by a mother gnome with kindly eyes back in Skyli, from her pack. She sat beside him, reaching for his burned hands.

"You don't need to do that—I can patch them up myself," he said, trying to take the jar from her.

She laid one of her hands over his and said, "You could. But why would you when I'm here?"

Týr relaxed his hands, letting her take one in her own. With a fingertip, she applied salve to the burned skin. She tried to be gentle, but he winced. To distract him, she said, "You told me once that there was but one day when Lady Luck smiled on you." Her voice was light, almost a whisper. "When was it?"

He blew out a long breath that clouded in the cold. "It was the day Björn found me. He saw something in me that I hope is truly there."

Frankly, Elín hadn't seen the grumpy, strict old man's appeal, but . . . "He was special to you, wasn't he?" she asked. "Not just because he was training you."

"Yes. He was everything to me. I never knew my parents. I grew up on the streets of Stórborg." His voice went softer, as if he were ashamed. "It wasn't an easy life, and I had to do terrible things to survive. Things I hope I never have to do again. Things that might make you wish you didn't know me."

"Don't say that," Elín said, wrapping the first hand and tying the ends of the handkerchief. She took his other and said, "You were a child, and you were on your own."

"I was alone," he conceded. "Until Björn found me. He saw my potential, even as a little boy. He taught me to read, how to navigate the world beyond Stórborg, about the Stormsingers . . . everything I know." Týr paused, watching her hands bind his wounds. "I've failed him, and all the Keepers before me. And I've failed Skyli."

"You didn't fail," Elín said, tying off the other handkerchief. "You found me, you found the Kirja . . . you couldn't foresee all that would happen, and it was a great deal too much to ask you to do all on your own."

"It wasn't, though," Týr said, looking at his freshly bandaged hands. "It wasn't too much to ask, after everything I'd done before. I thought if I could get this right—find the Tome, protect you—that it might make up for some of the wrong I had done in my old life."

She recorked the jar and returned it to her bag. Then she picked up the ruined Tome, studying it momentarily before she passed it back to him. He took it but continued to stare out across the barren, frozen landscape.

"You're too hard on yourself," she said. "You've protected me. You nearly saved the Tome, and you took on more than he could have expected. Björn didn't want us to join the fight in Snjoreya, but who knows what good we can still do there?"

This seemed to pull Týr out of his reverie, and he looked at her questioningly, a crease appearing between his brows.

"We must do what we can to help Kata, though it may be less than before."

His brows drew even closer together. "You still wish to go to Snjoreya?"

Elín nodded. "To help my sister. And the people we met—" She thought of Brokk, who had given her the dagger, of Fridolf and his dogs. Eldri and all he tried to do for his people. "They need us."

"It will be dangerous," Týr said. "You shouldn't risk it, you're—"

"The Last Stormsinger? What can I do with my one remaining spell? Freeze pitchers of water?" She laughed and ran a hand along her braid. "Besides, I've only been 'The Last Stormsinger' a few days. Surely the humble 'Elín' I've been for sixteen winters can be of some use."

"This isn't your fight," he said. "I thought it was wise to take you to Skyli, that you would be safe there . . . I didn't expect them to ask so much of you."

"I know. I guess we have that in common—the burden of high expectations. But I will fight for them, and with my sister. It's my choice." She stood, clearing her skirts of snow, and offered him a hand to stand. "Kata knows the prince—perhaps there's another way into the castle and down to the dragon that won't require snowsong."

"As the Keeper of—well, what's left of the Tome, I will follow your command. I serve the Stormsingers. But are you sure?"

She understood his doubt. It wasn't so long ago that all she'd wanted—all she could imagine wanting—was to return to her farm. But now . . . "Even without

Eldri's people in exile and my sister facing a dragon for them, King Karvel has hurt me, too. Because of him, I never knew my father or sister. My mother died far from them, her heart broken. I lost my home. This is my fight, too."

Elín took his harm, careful of his injured hands, and Týr let her help him to his feet. Dusting snow and ash from his tunic, he said, "This may not end well for either of us."

"Back in Ornfoss, Arn hinted that my father may be alive. I hoped if I went on this journey, I might learn more about him, and what may be left of my family," Elín said softly. "Now, because of you, I can do even better. I can go to Snjoreya and meet him. Even if he is a hunter, like Kata said, I wouldn't miss this chance for anything."

The stars shone coldly beyond the smoldering cottage; it was still many hours until dawn. A cloud passed over the moon, casting shadows on Týr's face as he said, "Then let Lady Luck be with us."

MOST DANGEROUS PREY
Kata

Tears came easily.

The hunters came into view only moments after Skadi had sealed the mountain and Kata had finished covering Magni's tracks and blood trail with snow. She let the panic she felt at her friend's peril show on her face, let the relief she felt at being found mingle with it, and the tears fell.

Be quiet, be still, she thought at the cavern inside the mountain. The stone walls were probably thick enough to dampen any sound, but if they weren't . . . she needed to move, to lead the hunters away.

"Helga!" she shouted as she recognized her friend, rushing into the older woman's arms. The tension of her days since leaving Snjoreya melted away as she buried her face in Helga's fur coat.

"Kata?" Helga asked, her face incredulous as she wrapped her hands around the girl. "How did you come to be here? Your father is sick with worry!"

The other hunters, including Gunnar, caught up to them. They were all as shocked to see her as Helga had been. Kata pulled away and took a deep breath, roughly wiping the tears from her face. This would be the true test. Could she make Helga and Gunnar, who had known her since she was a toddler, believe her story?

"Pabbi—is he alright?"

"He will be now we've found you, lass," Gunnar said, clapping a hand on her shoulder. "Now tell us, how did you come to be here, at the edge of the world?"

She swallowed and let her eyes show fear. "There was an alicorn, when I was out hunting in the woods."

Gunnar nodded. "The same one I just shot? Never in all my days did I think I'd see the likes of such a rare beast."

Aching as she realized an old friend had been the one to injure Magni, she controlled her expression and nodded. "I don't know what happened . . . it must have bewitched me! I went out at night and it made me ride it, then flew off with me. I was so afraid!"

She allowed herself a few hiccupping sobs then, though, of course, she hadn't been so afraid. Magni's magic had made sure of that.

"Hush, darling. You're safe now. And only moments ago? Was that you on the alicorn's back?" Helga asked, wrapping an arm around her.

Kata nodded. "It fell to the ground, dropping me there"—she pointed to the one spot of Magni's blood in the snow she had left uncovered—"and then flew away again."

"Are you hurt, darling? We never would have guessed it was you up in the sky."

"No, I am well. I just want to go home," she said, genuine tears welling in her eyes as she thought of her father.

"We must hunt down this beast," one of the other hunters said. "Which way did it fly?"

"Over the mountain," she said, sniffling and hoping the lie was convincing. "But there's no need. Gunnar's shot was true; he won't make it far." She drew the blood-soaked feathers from her pocket and laid them in Gunnar's hand. "Will this be enough proof for the king?"

"Oh, never mind that now, child," Gunnar said as he slipped them into his pocket. "We'd best get you home. Your father will want to see you safe, and you're probably half-starved from days spent with that monster."

"But the king—" one hunter said, stopping as Helga threw him a sharp look.

"Are you sure? Whatever the king sent you here for . . ." Kata began, then realized it wasn't an avenue she wanted to pursue. "I would like very much to go home," she said, her voice forlorn. "Please."

"We'll go at once," Helga said. The hunter who had spoken humphed loudly, and the other huntress rolled her eyes, but none of them questioned Helga's decision. Kata took one last furtive glance at the mountain where Eldri and his people hid, then let herself be led down the mountain with Helga's arm around her shoulders.

As she gazed out across the waves, Kata knew the queasy feeling in her stomach wasn't only from the ship as it sailed westward. She agonized over what she would say to her father and what he would say to her. So much had changed. He could lie to her no longer about her mother or sister. Had he also lied about being a hunter? It didn't seem possible; so many in the kingdom knew his reputation. The king's trophy room was adorned with his kills.

How could she reconcile that side of him with what she knew now?

Another wave of sickness passed over her, and she pressed a hand to her stomach. A whole day and night had passed at sea, and she had yet to find her sea-legs. Really, whether magic was evil or not, an alicorn was a much better mode of travel than this.

She could do nothing but wait to see her father. Now that she was with the hunters, though, she had decided to forget all about Eldri and his plan. It wouldn't work without her, and this was the easy way. Týr and Elín *might* find their dusty old book; they *might* make it to Snjoreya unharmed. She would simply send them away again. The creatures could stay at Skyli forever, or find a new hiding place, even if that thought made Kata feel as ill as the waves did.

Maybe she could explain her powers and what she'd seen to Prince Stefán, and he would listen to her. She recalled their last meeting, the cold way he'd commanded her. But he'd also asked her not to harm Magni. He was her oldest friend, and she'd missed him a great deal these last few days. Perhaps he could see a way out of this mess that she could not. He *must* be able to help.

Kata's abilities were not yet finely tuned, but she suddenly felt a flicker of magic and stood up straight, looking out to sea. She hated the way the ship bobbed on the waves, making it feel as if her legs would lurch out from under her at any moment.

There was something there, as she'd felt in the clearing with Magni, Grim, and Skadi. But the spark she felt made whatever creature caused it seem impossibly large. It moved in the sea, far below the ship but pulling nearer. She gasped as she realized what it must be.

Only one sea creature was so large and powerful.

She knew of the kraken, of course; kraken hunters frequented the tavern at times. Rough, hulking men who smelled of salt and sweat and disappointment. Men desperate enough to go after the most dangerous prey of all. Few ever saw it and lived to tell the tale.

The hunters on the ship with Kata were not of their kind. They had made money on phoenix and nykur and unicorn, and didn't know how to fight monsters of the deep. She would have to keep them safe. Surely, it was alright to use her powers to save her friends from a magic far worse than hers.

The flicker was growing, becoming a flame, as the creature ascended from the depths. She closed her eyes and took a steady breath, extending her mind like a welcoming hand. The boat lurched sideways, sending some of the hunters off their legs. There were shouts of "What was that?", "Are you alright?", "Could it be . . . ?"

The sky was blue and clear. It had not been a wave or the wind. A tense silence came over the hunters as they braced themselves, knees bent and weapons drawn.

Please, Kata extended her thoughts to the kraken. *Leave us be.* She hoped it would work, though she had only successfully spoken to Magni and Skadi before. Perhaps because of the kraken's powerful mind, or perhaps because her desperation slipped through with the words, it did.

Who dares speak to me? A mere mortal?

As the words, rough and cold and booming, entered Kata's mind, something burst forth from the sea and sent a sheet of water falling onto the deck. A massive tentacle fell across the stern, pushing several barrels overboard and shattering the railing on one side of the ship. A huntress dodged out of its path, rolling across the deck.

The hunters and sailors had recovered from their falls, but now stood frozen, dazed by the glimmering flesh of the kraken. Kata had always imagined it pale and milky, like the squids she'd seen washed up on shore near the castle. But the tentacle was sunset-orange and studded with pink, gem-like markings that imitated scales. The sheen of the seawater made them glitter in the sunlight as the beast writhed, pummeling their ship.

The vibrant colors declared it unlike any other squid or creature of the deep; this monster had no need to hide or blend into the sea.

Kata gripped the railing, squeezing her eyes shut to concentrate as her heart hammered in her chest.

Please. I am Kata. I need to live—I'm going to Snjoreya to defeat the king, to help your kind. Eldri has sent me. Odd. Even in her desperation, the words didn't feel like the lie they were.

I could, perhaps, spare you . . .

Another tentacle, this one larger around than Kata's waist, landed on the deck and swept a hunter into the sea in one smooth motion. "No!" she yelped, then remembered to say it inside her head.

She did her best to sound fierce, but the words trembled in her mind, edged in fear. *Do not hurt them—they will see me safely home.*

And who are you, halfling, to command me? His voice thundered inside her mind. *What care I for these hunters? For the king, for the troubles of Eldri and his people? I am master of the sea. I care not for the matters of land-beings.*

The hunters were stabbing at the first tentacle, which still flailed along the deck. They used spears, knives, whatever they had. Kata still wore the bow from Skadi, but using it would raise questions she couldn't answer. Anyway, she could see that using force against the kraken was fruitless. Gunnar shot arrows into the sea, as if they could reach the great beast. Kata could feel him still far below, his impossibly long tentacles the only thing in range.

She tried another tack. *Are you not tired of this? Of being hunted, pursued, injured? They will never take you—you are too great. But many try.*

What care I? The voice came quieter, not so rumbling now.

It can end. I will end it—I will speak to the dragon; she will destroy the king who sends these hunters for you.

A scoffing noise came through. *A girl against a dragon?*

Please, just leave us. Let me try.

His tentacle ceased flailing on the deck. Two others floated beneath the water, swaying peacefully, studded with arrows. Finally, he said: *Very well. I gift you this one chance.*

She let out her breath, relieved.

But.

Her hands re-tightened on the rail of the ship as she closed her eyes again.

If you should fail and cross my waters again, I will not spare you or your companions a second time. The tentacle draped across the ship slipped back into the water almost silently, winking red-gold as it sank beneath the waves.

Thank you, she tried to call, but he was already sinking, sinking. She clutched the ship rail as her knees went weak. Speaking to the kraken had left her drained.

When she finally opened her eyes, there was little evidence of the attack. A few barrels bobbed in the sea—the hunter who'd been knocked into the waves had found one to buoy himself. Large gashes of splintered wood ran across two parts of the ship's rail. Most of the hunters and sailors were on their knees, thanking Lady Luck. Others shouted to the floating hunter or searched for a rope long enough to throw him.

All were occupied except Helga, who stared directly at Kata.

No. She knew.

Kata's hands trembled as Helga approached. She was still reeling from what she'd done—lied to the most powerful creature of the seas—but even if she'd had control of her limbs, there was nowhere to run or hide. Helga came to Kata's side by the rail, staring out across the waves like her.

"Did you do this?" she asked quietly.

Kata swallowed but said nothing. She was unsure if it was safer to acknowledge or deny it.

"I saw you," Helga said, turning and gripping Kata's upper arm much too tight. "You weren't fighting with the rest of us. You were staring out to sea, concentrating, and it stopped. We'd barely injured the beast—yet it left us . . . . I've heard of such foul magic, of those who can connect their minds to those monsters, but I never thought I'd see it myself . . . You weren't really taken by the alicorn either, were you?"

Kata looked up at her then, surprise overcoming her fear. This was Helga, after all, who'd been almost a mother to her. She could help. "I was. At first . . ."

"And then?" Her eyes narrowed, and her voice was sharp. It wasn't the voice of the wise huntress Kata knew. "Never mind. We'll discuss it when we make it ashore."

The older huntress turned to go. Beyond her, two hunters were pulling in the one on the barrel using a long rope.

"Helga?" Kata asked, her voice quiet but cutting. She turned, barely. "What are you going to do with me?"

The huntress, who had once had nothing but smiles, stories, and woodland trinkets for Kata, pressed her lips together and looked away. "I'm taking you to the king."

LIFE AND BEAUTY
Elín

Týr squinted at the horizon to the east. Elín saw nothing but undulating dunes of snow and ice. "What is it?" she asked.

He shook his head. "We need to get back to the rowboat."

"We could wait here in the cottage," Elín said, "and leave at first light. There would still be plenty of time to reach shore before sunset. We're both tired, and this was a shock." The flames were gone, and with the cold, what remained of the cottage barely smoldered now.

"This land sees frequent storms. Lady Luck has blessed us with clear weather so far, but we should leave now before that changes." He turned and trudged back along the path. Sighing, Elín followed.

They'd been plodding along for about an hour when the wind picked up. It whipped Elín's braid and pierced through her cloak and dress, raising bumps on her arms. Her teeth chattered, and the path was quickly becoming obscured by blowing snow.

"Týr?" she said, but he didn't hear her over the wind.

Then the sky opened, and snow began to whip around in all directions, carried by the growing wind. The path ahead was gone; she could barely see Týr.

He turned back toward her, grabbing her hand to pull her along.

"No!" she called. "We can't go on in this—we'll get lost!"

"The path is this way," he called back, tugging on her arm.

"We can't see the path! We could fall from a cliff or slide into a lava flow." Her teeth were freezing cold from exposure to the biting wind. They couldn't keep arguing like this.

Even through the raging blizzard, she could see the disappointment and fear on his face. "Alright," he said. "But we'll freeze to death if we wait out in the open."

She nodded, trying to tame her flapping cloak with one of her hands still in his. Ornfoss saw a few blizzards each winter, but she'd never been more than a short ride from the safety of her cottage.

"I saw some ice caves up here," Týr yelled over the wind, guiding her to the left. She had seen no caves but followed him anyway. There was no time for fear, and any chance to be out of the fierce wind and snow pelting her cheeks was worth taking.

After what seemed an eternity of struggling through the shifting snow, they came up against solid ice. Týr led them along a glacial wall, feeling for an opening. After a few tense minutes, he said, "Here! One we can squeeze into."

She nodded, not wanting to speak against the wind that fought to overwhelm her lungs. After feeling her way to the opening in the ice, she wiggled her way through.

The darkness and silence were beautiful. Though dawn had not yet broken, the blizzard outside had glowed an eerie white in the moonlight. Here, all was calm.

Elín prayed—to which goddess she didn't know or care—that the cave was not already inhabited, though they'd seen no living beings since they set foot on Viltland. She quickly established the cave's dimensions by feeling in the dark. The space was large enough to sit upright but not to stand, and to lie down and fully stretch out one way but not the other.

"We made it," Týr said as he finished wriggling through behind her. Her eyes had adjusted now, and in the shaft of light that came from one end of the cave, she saw him pat the remains of the Tome in his satchel. He slumped against the cave wall, exhausted, his usual grin nowhere in sight.

When she sat across from him, her back to the opposite wall, her feet almost hit the wall he sat against. She could've reached out and touched his knee. "Certainly not the most glamorous accommodations of our journey," she said, attempting levity. "And to think I once feared Axel's ship."

He didn't smile as she'd hoped, but put his head back against the icy wall and closed his eyes. "The worst part is," he said quietly, "if the Tome had survived, you could've cast a spell to stop the blizzard."

She huffed out a laugh. "Even if we had such a spell, I imagine it would take me years of practice to do that kind of magic. I would think ending a storm is much more difficult than starting one. Besides, if we had a safer place from which to watch this storm, it would be lovely. Perfect window-weather." When he didn't react, the same weary look on his face, she cleared her throat and tried another tack. "I don't suppose there's any hope of finding wood here, or something to start a fire."

He opened his eyes. "No. Just stone and ice and lava. Nothing that burns." She understood by his defeated tone what he didn't say—nothing to burn but the Keeper's cabin, the Tome.

Elín dug through her pack, finding nothing to burn, though at least there were enough food rations to get them back to the vikings. Her hand bumped the pouch with the locks of hair and Amma's lodestone before landing on the sheathed blade the giant Brokk had given her. She took it out, wanting to trace her fingers over its floral designs, an anchoring reminder of life and beauty amid this barren, stormy land.

When she withdrew the dagger from its sheath, however, she nearly dropped it in surprise. The designs on the side and handle of the blade were glowing. First, a pale green, then a deep blue. The teal of the ocean on a sunny day, then a hint of magenta. She let out a gasp and said, "I didn't know it could do this."

The sight pulled Týr back from wherever his thoughts had taken him. He shuffled toward her, and she gave him the dagger when he reached out his hand. "The colors of the aurora," he said.

She nodded in recognition as he handed it back to her. She set the blade down between them, and its light cast shadows over the icy walls and Týr's cheekbones. They were silent, watching the colors fade into one another so slowly that they tricked the eye. Were the pale blue flowers not a faded green only a moment ago?

Her eyes growing heavy, Elín unlashed her rolled-up, huldufólk-woven blanket from the bottom of her pack. "I think we should sleep," she told Týr. "The storm could rage all night, and we're short on rest." When he didn't respond right away, she pursed her lips and added, "And I know, with nothing better to do, you'll brood all night. That certainly won't help anyone."

He scowled, eyebrows scrunching together. "I wasn't brooding."

"Whatever you say," she responded with an airiness she didn't feel. "Now, get your sleeping mat out so we can lie down."

Týr reached for his pack, but his hand stalled in midair. Then he brushed his hair out of his eyes and cleared his throat. "There's not a lot of room in here."

"The better to keep warm," Elín said. "Keep the heat in."

He unrolled his mat, and Elín had to crawl out of the way so it could spread its full width. Then she lay down on half of it, tossing the blanket over herself. Týr was still crouched in the corner.

"Well?" she asked. "Had enough brooding?" After a long pause, he sighed and lay next to her, their backs together. "I won't bite," she promised. "Unless you kick me in your sleep like my mother used to. Then maybe."

On the coldest nights, Revna, Signý, and Elín had all climbed into the bed, which they had moved as close to the hearth as they could without fear of the blankets catching fire. But lying next to Týr, feeling the hard planes of his back and his warmth through the layers of clothing separating them, was nothing like those nights.

"It's not that," Týr said softly.

She'd been trying to make him laugh, but she sobered at hearing his tone. "What is it, then?"

He cleared his throat. "There's something I haven't told you."

Bracing herself for another secret—and peeved that there *were* any more secrets when he'd promised there wouldn't be—Elín prompted, "Yes?"

"It's about the Keepers and the Stormsingers. They must never become . . ." He took a deep breath and tried again. "They must never fall in love, or marry. All that."

Though Elín could feel the icy floor of the cave through their flimsy bedding, her face flamed at those words. She went still, conscious not to move at all, and struggled to make her tone casual. "Oh?"

"Yes," he said. "My master was very clear on that. He even reminded me of it that night we spent at Arn's farm, after you left. No matter what—if anything were to happen"—he cleared his throat—"nothing *can* happen."

Elín bit her lip to keep from snapping about his insinuation that something *could* happen between them, then realized she only felt snappish because perhaps, deep down, there was a part of her that had begun to wish something *would*.

"Did he say why?" Her voice came out too thick, so she swallowed. "I mean, out of curiosity?"

"Something about the Keeper's duty being the Tome and the spells, and the Stormsinger's duty being to snowsong and the people they serve. Tradition, I suppose."

Elín's first instinct was to say something disparaging about all these traditions, but she bit her tongue. It didn't matter if she believed in them; they'd be as important to Týr as the rest of the Tomekeeper duties. And she didn't want to imply that there were any feelings of that kind to worry him.

But there *had* been something, hadn't there? On the ridge, when they were looking at the northern lights. And before that, a few times on the journey . . . she didn't know when, exactly, but she had come to rely on him and think of him almost as fondly as she had her own family. Or perhaps she was only so alone in the world that she'd imagined more than friendship.

If she could even call what they had friendship. Had he not done everything out of duty, or loyalty to his master?

Her throat suddenly constricted, and she squeezed her eyes shut to keep any tears from falling. The last thing she needed was for them to freeze to her cheeks.

"Elín?" Týr asked, and she was careful to control her breathing, keep it slow so he wouldn't suspect her emotions.

"Yes?" Her voice came out primmer than was natural, but it was better than revealing her tears.

"Are you alright? Is there anything we should talk—"

"No, no, I'm perfectly alright," she said. "Only tired." The cave was small; as much as she tried, it was impossible to ignore his now-familiar scent of leather and parchment and forest. It made her want to roll over, nestle into his chest, and breathe him in. Which would, of course, be a completely mad thing to do. Even before what he'd said about tradition.

She felt him reposition on their mat, their backs still touching. Then he bent his knees and the bottom of their boots pressed against each other as well. It was comforting to have him so close, despite the distance he had just put between them. Elín reached for the glowing knife and sheathed it. The cave dimmed.

"Sleep well," she said eventually, when she realized he would say no more. Elín lay awake for a long time, staring into the darkness and chastising herself for feelings she should not have.

The translucent walls of the ice cave brightened as dawn broke, and Elín blinked, still half asleep. At some point in the night, Týr had rolled over, and he was now pressed against her, one arm thrown over her side. She snuggled closer to him, enjoying the warmth, and his arm tightened around her. Her eyes fluttered closed, and she smiled to herself.

But then her mind really woke up, and she remembered their conversation the night before. That nothing could ever happen between them, because of a Tomekeeper rule and—more painfully—her realization that this was all only duty to him. Her heart sank.

She wriggled out from under him. "Don't worry, there will be none of *that*," she said rather sharply, but he didn't wake. She tore her eyes from his face, but not before noticing the way sleep had softened its angles and cleared the lately ever-present crease from between his brows. *Enough*, she told herself, and crawled to the opening of the cave.

The snow had covered much of the entrance, but she made quick work of digging it out with the help of her blade. When the opening was wide enough, she shimmied through. The blizzard had ceased. All was calm, and the sun was high enough in the sky to be white instead of gold.

Elín would have smiled to see that the storm had passed and that they could leave this chaotic place, but the landscape had changed overnight. The snow had covered any landmarks and was piled in great wind-whipped drifts where yesterday there had been only stone and ice.

The path was gone.

EVERYTHING A GAME
Kata

"Helga, please," Kata pleaded, whispering so the other hunters would not hear.

The older huntress only gripped Kata's arm tighter, her fingers digging in. She flashed a smile at another hunter as they passed. "Have to be getting her back to her father," she said brightly. "He's been worried sick."

When they'd left the docks in favor of the forest path to the castle and, further on, her home, Kata wrenched her arm from Helga's grasp. "Please can I explain?"

First glancing back and forth to be sure there was no one else in sight, Helga crossed her arms. "Explain what?"

Kata took a deep breath. "I'm not sure where to start. Take me to my father and let me explain to both of you. Please, don't take me to the king. You must understand—we're wrong about them, Helga. About magical creatures."

Helga staggered back a step, as if Kata had slapped her. "They've got to you," she said softly. Something like pity came over her features before her expression hardened. "I won't hear such foul things from you." She grabbed her arm, but Kata twisted away.

"Please, Helga. You've been . . . It was only my father and me, and you've been so important, so kind to me. You must know what the king will do when you tell him." Her voice grew desperate, and her eyes widened. "I thought you cared for me."

"I did," Helga said, the words piercing Kata's heart, surer than an arrow

"And you no longer do?" Kata asked. "All for something I cannot help?"

Helga looked at the ground for a long time. Kata waited for her to say something, to take back what she'd said, to reaffirm that of course she cared about her. That Kata was—as she'd always secretly hoped—like the daughter she'd never had.

But instead the old huntress cleared her throat and said, "Are you going to come easily, or do I need to take out my knife?"

Kata's shoulders fell as she struggled against tears. She wasn't like a daughter to Helga, or even a person anymore. Maybe it was proof that Helga had once cared about her that she was bringing her to the king alive, and not as a slain trophy in exchange for bounty. All hope lost, Kata let Helga grab her arm again, dragging her through the woods, right up to the castle bridge.

Kata had entered the castle hundreds of times with her father, always eager to see her best friend. This time, she prayed to Lady Legend and all the other goddesses that Stefán wouldn't see her like this—wouldn't find out she was a traitor to the land. Losing Helga was wound enough; she couldn't bear to lose Stefán's esteem as well.

The guard asked Helga what business she came on, and she made him bend his ear to her mouth so she could whisper to him. He recoiled when he heard and hurried them into the throne room. Kata's face burned with shame.

King Karvel lounged in his throne, a glass of blood-red wine in one hand. He was richly dressed, as he always was, in the finest velvets and brocades. The heavy gold crown with rough-cut gemstones shone against his black hair. His eyes were gray, like Prince Stefán's, but where Stefán's shone with intelligence and kindness, his were like ice—cold and harsh.

"Ah, it's my huntsman's daughter and one of my best dragon-hunters. I heard the expedition returned early, so I suppose you did not find the rumored hideout in the mountains. Have you any new trophies for me?"

"Only one besides her," Helga said, shoving Kata forward.

She tripped and fell on her hands but quickly scrambled back upright. To be treated like this by Helga, of all people . . . it made her anger flare.

"The girl?" King Karvel asked. His bored, above-it-all tone had vanished, and he leaned forward with interest.

Kata examined the tapestries hung on the wall behind the throne so she would not have to look at him. They were bright and new, placed there during his reign, and showed brave hunters slaying dragons, griffins, and unicorns. Once, she'd dreamt of being just like those hunters, but now those images made her feel ill.

"Yes, Your Highness," Helga said. "We found her flying on an alicorn—though she claims she was captured by it. We killed it and have a few of its feathers, but I'm afraid that's the only trophy to come from your expedition. We thought it best for the Royal Huntsman to be reunited with his daughter, and so turned back."

"Please get on with it, huntress." The king said, waving a dismissive hand. "What changed your mind—why is she here and not with her father?"

"She has the power to communicate with those monsters," Helga spat. "Our ship was attacked by the great kraken. We tried to slay him for you, but before we could, Kata spoke to him somehow, and he left us."

The king's gaze was heavy on Kata.

When he didn't speak, she threw her hands in the air. "I didn't want any of this! They tricked me and stole me away from home." She felt her eyes welling with tears but wouldn't let them fall. Not while she was locked in a stare with the king.

His voice was deceptively quiet when he said, "'They.' So the alicorn didn't act alone."

Kata swallowed, a stab of guilt twisting through her abdomen. She'd said too much already. She should have controlled herself, denied having powers at all.

"So, it took you," the king prompted, swirling the wine in his glass. "Where and why?"

"Somehow, they knew about my powers."

One dark eyebrow arched. "Oh?"

"Yes. I don't know how. I didn't even know myself. If I could give them up, I would!"

Those words didn't sit well with her. They were not quite true. And anyway, Helga, Gunnar, and the other hunters would have died by the kraken if not for her.

"Where did they take you?" he asked again.

This was a piece of information Kata could use. Perhaps she could even barter it for her freedom. If the king knew how close the hunters had come to Skyli . . . . But every part of her burned at the thought of betraying the location of Eldri and his people—at imagining them strewn across their once-safe valley, bloody and lifeless, hacked apart for trophies. Had they not been through enough? Even if they *had* kidnapped her and dragged her into this mess.

"I don't know," she lied. "The alicorn enchanted me, so I was blind to the way there."

"And what is 'there?'"

Kata started to thumb the threads on the edge of her tunic but stopped when she realized it made her look suspicious. "It's a hideout. There were other magical creatures there."

"It exists, then." King Karvel leaned forward on his throne, his free hand clasping its gilded arm. "They must have wanted something from you. Tell me what it is, or I'll imprison you in the dungeons."

Kata's knees went weak. She'd asked Prince Stefán to see the dungeons once, when she was young and curious and thought everything a game. He told her "no"—it was one of the first times he'd ever denied her anything. "I wouldn't wish you to see those cells, the darkness . . ." he'd said. "Do not ask that of me." She had to stifle the twisted smile tugging at her mouth as she realized she might get her thoughtless childhood wish.

"They want to overthrow you," Kata said. "They want to return here. They say it's their home." It didn't seem like too much to reveal; certainly, he could have guessed as much.

"And they sent a girl like you, alone, to overthrow me? What use can your powers be when no magic creatures live within my lands? Unless they wanted your hunting skills, which your father says have grown considerably. I rather hoped you would use them to help fill my trophy room, but alas." He spread his hand out in front of him forlornly.

Kata swallowed back the bile rising in her throat when she realized that not so long ago, she had hoped for that, too. Watching a drip of wax crawl down from one of the iron wall sconces overladen with candles, she forced herself to think.

He didn't know they knew about the dragon. How much should she reveal? She had to give him *something*, or she wouldn't walk free of the castle. Even Eldri and his people wouldn't want that. "It wasn't just me. I wasn't really important to the plan," she lied. "They were going to send a Stormsinger, too."

"Impossible," the king hissed. "The Stormsingers are gone."

"I saw her myself, Your Highness."

"Did you see her perform any magic?"

Kata hesitated. "I did not. But they treated her like a goddess, so she must have been powerful." She was endangering Elín to save her own skin. But why should she care? They may be sisters, but she was still a stranger to Kata, and look how easily Helga—who knew her so well—had thrown her to the wolves.

"And this supposed snow-witch," the king said. "She is coming here, to Snjoreya."

Kata nodded curtly.

"Excellent," the king said, downing the rest of his wine and setting his glass on the dais beside him. Then he clasped his hands in front of him. "I have a proposal for you."

This didn't sound good. Kata's hands were shaking, but she crossed her arms to hide it.

"You're a skilled huntress. Is this not so, Helga?"

Helga grimaced but said, "Yes, Your Highness."

"If you kill this Stormsinger for me, I can make this all go away," King Karvel said, sweeping his hands out in front of him.

Kata's jaw fell open, but she caught herself and clenched it shut. *Kill* Elín?

"Before you say something that will get you thrown in the dungeons, think on my offer. Take care of this problem for me, and I'll forget all about your . . .

abilities. So long as you never use them again. Actually, I might even allow you to use them if you promise to do so only to fill my trophy room."

Helga squeezed her hands into fists beside Kata. She was unhappy. Had she really wanted to see Kata imprisoned or executed? Had all the years, all the stories and gifts shared, counted for nothing? Was she angered to miss out on a great bounty in return for the betrayal, and insulted to find the King now offering a legendary hunt to Kata? Kata's heart felt heavy in her chest, but she didn't have time to dwell on this new wound.

Her stomach turned as she thought of killing Elín, her sister, and she struggled not to show anything on her face. Not to let the King know her loyalties might lie elsewhere.

"In addition," the king said, stroking a hand over his chin. "I will allow your father to retire. I know the hunts grow more difficult for him. He can cease spending his days in the woods, and I will ensure his salary is still paid from my treasury. If you want the position of Royal Huntsman, I will give it to you. Then twice as much wealth shall flow into your home. Your father never wanted the opportunity—claiming he needed to spend his time with you—but the Royal Huntswoman could also lead hunts outside of Snjoreya, for magical game."

Kata felt dizzy. Pabbi could retire. Her future as a fearsome bounty huntress would be secure. She could have everything she'd ever dreamed of and more. There was just one little thing she had to do.

Physically, it wouldn't be a problem. She knew where Elín would be at a certain time every day after she arrived in Snjoreya. Kata had taken much larger and faster game. Elín would trust her, wouldn't know what had happened until it was too late. And then, all of Kata's problems would vanish. Even Eldri and the others would bother her no more, trapped in their sanctuary across the sea.

The thought of the dragon stirred her to try her powers. When she reached out, she thought she could feel the creature's presence far below them. She couldn't connect, though. Maybe Dreka slumbered. Just as well. She hadn't wanted to tangle with the dragon anyway, and now there was a way she wouldn't have to.

Kata swallowed, but her throat remained dry. "I want an agreement in writing."

"You don't trust my word?" the king said, shaking his head and feigning sadness. "Not a great start to my relationship with my future Royal Huntswoman. But I see no harm in it." He waved his hand, and a scribe hurried over from the wings with quill, ink, and parchment in hand.

He dictated the contract to the scribe, and as the latter scribbled away, Kata had time to consider her options. If she didn't do this, she'd be thrown in the dungeon, possibly to rot away there. Or executed publicly. Either option—her death—would kill her father, whereas if she just killed the last Stormsinger for the king, their lives would improve dramatically.

If she did manage to escape somehow, what then? If Helga reacted this way, what would her father or the prince do when they found out about her magic? And all the rest of the kingdom, who cared for her less than they did . . . there would be no life for her here anymore.

But if killing a creature as pure as Magni would leave a permanent stain on her soul, the way she had felt that day in the forest with her arrow trained on him, how much worse would it be to kill her own sister?

Kata supposed she would find out.

The scribe held the freshly inked parchment and quill out to her, and she took them, her hands trembling. At the bottom, the king had written an additional number. It was a princely sum, three times what her father was paid in a year and twice what a slain young dragon would command. The bounty for wiping out the Stormsinger line was far more than even she had imagined, back in Skyli when the thought of killing Elín had first crossed her mind.

King Karvel, Helga, and the scribe's gazes were heavy, all fixed on her. There was only one choice.

She expelled a long breath and signed her name to the contract.

AS FIERCE AS STORM

Elín

"Týr, wake up," Elín said, shoving his shoulder after she'd crawled back into the cave.

"What is it?" he mumbled. There was an undertone of fear in his voice as he blinked himself awake.

"The blizzard's over," she said. "But there's no path. I hope you know the way."

He scrambled to his hands and knees and worked his way through the cave entrance she'd dug out. Shading his eyes with his hand as they adjusted, he scanned the horizon. "No," he said hopelessly. "I became so disoriented before, with the wind in all directions."

Týr collapsed to his knees, and she hurried to his side. "Which way do we need to go? What direction?"

"West," he muttered. "We need to go west."

She scanned the sky, but it had turned so hazy that it wasn't even possible to tell where the sun was. "There must be a way."

He shook his head. "I'm sorry. I've failed you. Again."

"Would you *stop*? This wasn't your fault, and your apologies are doing no good. We need a plan." But she admitted to herself that the matter was fairly hopeless; they were in some kind of glacial valley, the walls so high that they couldn't see the cone of the island's volcano or its belches of smoke. There were no distinguishing features besides the ice cave, which was so inconspicuous that if they walked thirty paces across the snow and glacial ice, she would probably lose sight of it, too.

Týr took the Kirja out of his satchel and gently flipped through its charred pages. "There's nothing useful here," he said.

"I don't think wayfinding is a Stormsinger skill," Elín said tartly. "Unless one could call the west wind and feel where it's blowing from."

"I am sure there was a spell for that in these pages," Týr said quietly.

"Could we set off in one direction and just see . . . ?" Elín trailed off. That option was much more likely to end with them exhausted and freezing to death than with a sighting of the shore and Axel's knarr. The days were so much shorter here in the high north, even midway to spring. They only had a few hours to reach shore before the superstitious vikings gave up on them.

She sat beside him in the snow, her hands clasped as she tried to think. Had she ever heard her grandmother call the wind? A spark of an idea there, related to Revna's songs—but what good were lullabies now, with their lives at stake?

Thinking over her possessions, her mind caught on Brokk's knife. It could glow in the darkness. Could it do more? She scurried into the cave again and grabbed her pack, lugging it out through the narrow opening. But as she reached for the knife, her hand clasped around the lodestone. *Oh.*

"Týr," she said softly. "Do you know how to use a lodestone?"

His face lit up as she held out the stone to him. He looked at her then as if she really were the Last Stormsinger, the savior of Eldri and his people, someone who could summon the wind with a simple song.

"Thank Lady Luck," he said. "You've saved us."

"Don't thank her," she said, grinning back at him. "Thank my grandmother."

To their credit, Týr's viking friends seemed relieved to see Elín and Týr alive and rowing out to the knarr. They may have taken Elín's most prized possession, but at least they'd come back for them.

Using the lodestone had been easier than Elín expected. Týr had melted snow in his hands and poured it into a small bowl from their supplies. Elín had supplied a needle, and after rubbing one end of it against the lodestone Týr poked it through the cork from his waterskin and let it float in the bowl. It spun lazily before settling in one direction.

"That way's north," Týr had said, "so we need to go that way." He pointed west.

Elín had been unable to pull her gaze from the floating needle for several moments. The peddler in the marketplace when she was a girl had been right. It *was* like magic, but required no concentration or spells.

Thank you, Amma, she'd remembered to say before she left. She wondered if the lodestone had been saved from when Revna and her mother had journeyed across the sea to Ornfoss.

Now it was midafternoon, and as Axel hauled them onto the ship from the rowboat, he assured them in a cheery tone that he would've given up on them come nightfall. Elín managed a weak smile as she and Týr found their places near the back of the boat.

"Do you need something to eat?" Captain Axel asked Elín.

"No," she said. "I'm more used to the sea now. I won't be sick."

With a grunt of acknowledgement, Captain Axel tromped back to his place at the helm, and Elín sighed, leaning heavily on the rail. The sharp smell of fresh pitch cut through the cold, and when she licked her lips, she tasted salt.

"You're becoming quite an adventurer," Týr said, giving her a crooked smile. "Only a few days ago, the sea terrified you."

She laughed lightly. "You're right. A few days before that, I mistook a mountain lake for the sea. What happened to the timid, pragmatic farm girl I was then?"

"I'm sure she's still in there," Týr said. "Think of all the stories you'll have to tell the people of Ornfoss when you return to your old life."

Elín bit her lip. "I've been thinking about that. If we survive this, I'm not going back to Ornfoss."

Týr's expression turned blank. "You aren't?"

"No," she replied, surer this time. "I have a sister now—and a father to meet. And now that I have a taste of travel, and of my powers . . ."

A crease appeared between his brows. "Your powers are why you *should* go home, or somewhere else secluded. Your family moved to Ornfoss for a reason. You're the last Stormsinger, Elín. We need to keep you safe."

"Good thing I have such a brave Keeper to protect me, then," she said, trying to be playful.

He shook his head. "No, you don't understand. I can't stay with you now. I'm only here until the task at hand is done."

Elín's stomach lurched, and she wished she could blame the sea for it. As she'd feared, it hadn't even been friendship between them. It was all duty, and once he was satisfied he'd fulfilled it, he would leave. She chided herself for being silly—when had she started to want him by her side anyway?

She cleared her throat. "Where will you go?"

Týr picked a sliver of wood off their bench and threw it into the sea. The mermaids had been right: the waves were rougher here, and the ship careened on the waters. The ship's blue-gray cat hid beneath the bench, behind her skirts. Elín didn't mind the choppy seas. She wanted to see all of its sides, to know the ocean as perhaps only sailors knew it.

"Björn once told me of the Lost Library of Safni. It's supposed to be hidden somewhere in Stórborg. It's a sprawling city with winding streets and secret alleys. But I grew up there, and I know it well—I think I could find the library." he said, squinting as he looked off to the cloudy sky over the iron-gray sea. "If I did, I might be able to repair what little is left of the Tome. To fulfill what I still can of the vows I would have taken as a Tomekeeper. There will be other books in the ancient tongue there, too, so I might be able to piece together a few pages, salvage a few spells."

Elín said nothing. Her tongue felt too thick to trust speaking.

Stórborg was said to be ancient, beautiful, and sprawling. Many claimed it the largest city in the world. Elín's desire to see it was stronger than any homesickness she might have felt for Ornfoss. To have Týr show her the place he had grown up, especially . . .

But from the way he spoke, he hadn't been issuing an invitation. He was simply telling her his plans because she had asked, and he would expect her to stay somewhere "safe" instead.

She looked out over the waves, afraid he might read all of this on her face.

I'll never tire of looking at the sea, she thought, and it warmed her a little. There was another thought that she had been trying not to examine too closely, as it had the potential to hurt: *Perhaps I'll never tire of having Týr beside me, either.*

He cared only about restoring the Tome. If only there were another way to recover the lost pages. Her one freezing spell could only do so much.

But the spell hadn't felt like an "incantation" to her. It had been as familiar as a lullaby because she'd heard Revna sing it. A song had always been on Revna's lips—songs for bathing and cooking, for rainy days inside and lovely days in the fields. Was it possible they hadn't been songs but *spells*? Perhaps Revna had found a way to teach Elín the things she would need to know, even without the Tome or the Keepers, or revealing her secret.

"Týr?" she said, sifting through her memories for a song she knew well. She landed on the bathing song, which she had last sung the day before she'd had to run from her home. "What do these words mean?" She recited the first words of the song, careful not to sing them.

He gaped at her. "They sound like words of a spell. They're asking water to warm up. But how do you know it?"

Elín couldn't help grinning. "I think my grandmother may have saved us yet again."

"How?"

"She taught me so many songs. I didn't realize they were *spells*, that she was controlling anything. I know dozens that she used to sing. If I share them with you, and you translate and record them—"

"We can recreate the Tome," Týr said, his brown eyes suddenly sparkling. "Or part of it, at least. And you can start to become the Stormsinger you were meant to be."

She threw her arms around him without thinking, and he returned the embrace, one hand cradling the back of her head. His leather-and-parchment scent enveloped her, and she breathed in deeply through her nose before remembering that this was not the way things worked between them.

Týr seemed to remember at just the same time, because his hands fell away from her. The places where he'd held her felt cold even as her face burned. She needed something to occupy her hands, so she sat back on the bench and began to rework her braid.

Out of the corner of her eye, she could see that Týr's face was flushed too. He sat far enough away that no part of them touched. He coughed. "Right," he said, fixing his gaze out onto the horizon. "This is good news. Let's get to work."

They spent the rest of their sea journey together swapping spells as the ship bounced along the sea, carried by strong winds. Elín spoke the words, and Týr translated them, scrawling the angular runes of the ancient tongue on sheets of parchment from his satchel. They tested a few that wouldn't alert the vikings to what they were doing. Elín warmed water in her hand or called a bit of fog to roll in over the sea. There were gaps here and there where she forgot some of the words, but Týr was so familiar with the ancient tongue that he was able to supply suggestions that fit most of the time.

He soon ran out of parchment, and Elín grew too tired to use any more magic, but she wasn't done remembering. There was even one song they thought could calm blizzards, which would have been quite helpful back in Viltland.

"What about the storm spell?" Týr asked gently. It was the one spell they truly needed—the one that would allow them to execute Eldri's plan.

Elín leaned back against the side of the ship. "I want to believe my grandmother would never call a storm—only calm them. But I think I know which one it is."

She'd remembered a day when she'd come in from riding because a fog had picked up. Her mother and grandmother had been fighting, but they wouldn't tell her what was wrong. Revna had swept out the door, her mother calling her back.

Curious, Elín had followed Revna, staying out of sight. Her grandmother had gone to a field and sang a haunting melody in the ancient tongue. The wind picked up, the snow started to fall and swirl through the sky as she sang. Elín had panicked, cried out, and run to her as the storm whited out her vision.

Revna had wrapped an arm around her, taken her back to their home, and tucked her in. After kissing Elín on the forehead, she'd looked up at her daughter and said, "Never again." Signý had nodded, her face full of relief.

Elín repeated the words she could remember, careful not to picture so much as a snowflake as she did so, but after all these years and only hearing it once, she didn't know the full spell. Týr did his best to fill in the rest, but the result was cobbled together, and they didn't dare test it right then, not wanting to endanger the crew. Then she shared the memory with him.

"I wonder why she created the storm," Týr said. "I don't see how it could have helped your family."

Elín pursed her lips, thinking. "It didn't, and I don't think that's why she did it. I think . . . after so long without using her powers in that way, she just wanted to see if she still could."

Týr nodded.

"I understand it now. The way working magic feels, controlling things as fierce as storm and wind and snow. How overpowering it can be. I've done so little, yet enough that I wonder . . . I wonder if King Karvel is right to fear it, a little."

"He'll have a great deal to fear from you and Kata in a few days," Týr said, smiling.

Elín smiled back but looked out to sea before he could see her expression falter. There were gulls squawking in the distance, so they must be nearing land. She wanted to believe the king could be defeated without snowsong, that there was another way to get Kata into the castle. But she suspected she had much more to fear from a king who exiled hundreds from his lands, who kept a dragon bound, than he did from her.

THE LAST STORMSINGER

Kata

Kata's hunting instincts took over as she left the castle. She still had the bow from Skadi, and it would be concealed until the last moment, thanks to its magic. Her target would be at the riverbend at high noon, as soon as today if their ship had arrived swiftly. It would be simple.

While her mind was distracted, her feet had decided to start her on the path home. She turned around abruptly; the king had forbidden her to see her father until she'd fulfilled the contract. He'd also directed Helga to catch all the hunters that had been on the ship and warn them to say nothing of Kata's return. Though if her father had visited the tavern today, it was likely too late.

What lie will Helga tell him, then, to explain my whereabouts?

Kata felt no sympathy for her—Helga's betrayal still stung. Maybe it always would, now that Kata knew her real mother was gone. There was no one to fill Helga's role in her life.

Well, there was one person. But if Kata wanted to claim a better life for herself—or at least, keep her freedom—Elín wouldn't live long enough for that.

Unable to visit the tavern, her home, or Prince Stefán, Kata quickly realized she had nowhere else to go. At first, she'd enjoyed the familiar embrace of the woods, especially after the tumultuous sea voyage. But as she wandered through the King's Forest, unbidden memories kept crowding in. There was the thicket where the first hare she'd taken had lived, and here was the clearing which, in spring, grew the sweetest wild strawberries. Along this portion of the river's edge grew the brambles where, as children in midsummer, she and Stefán would sneak out of the castle to eat raspberries until their fingers were stained purple.

She banished these memories. They were from a lifetime that now seemed past, and she couldn't see a way to go back to the girl she was then. Especially after she'd done what needed to be done. Seeing that further pacing through the King's Forest would do her no good, she decided to wait for Elín at the rendezvous point.

She wondered, briefly, what Eldri and the others would do when they found out what she'd done. Then she remembered the promise she'd made the kraken—that she would be the one to end this war. In a way, she would be. With their Stormsinger gone, the war would end before it had the chance to start.

It was a warm day for how early in the year it was, and the river flowed free of ice as she followed its path to the double bend. Rocks peeked above the water's surface. She found comfort in the familiar smells of spruce and fir and juniper, the slight whiff of sulfur as she passed a geyser.

Kata sat on a boulder and pulled out the apple and hunk of bread she'd been given as an afterthought as she left the castle. She hadn't realized how hungry she was and wolfed down the food, brushing crumbs from her tunic and watching little birds hop through the snow to peck at them.

When they'd flown away, Kata stood and examined the woods around the riverbank and its large oak tree. The trees and shrubs were mostly leafless, so they wouldn't make good cover. A gentle snow fell, but it was warm enough that the flakes melted as soon as they hit stones or trees. She ventured further into the woods until she found a spot that would do. The forest floor rose slightly there, and a thick log would hide her from view. She was at the edge of the bow's range, but it shouldn't be a problem. An arrow or two loosed, and this would all be over.

She wondered if Elín would be equipped with defensive spells. Had she had time to study the Tome yet? Had they even found it?

Kata froze, her spine tingling and heart pounding. *They*. She'd forgotten about Týr.

Would she have to kill him, too? The thought sent Kata's stomach lurching. It wasn't that she *wanted* to kill Elín, either, but she saw no way around it.

Deep down, she still feared Elín, at least a little. Eldri and Magni had been kind to her, but she'd also been in mortal peril in the last few days thanks to a nykur and the kraken. Magic was to be feared. If they had succeeded in finding the Tome, Elín might be dangerous, too. There was a reason King Karvel had tried to wipe out the Stormsingers.

But Týr . . . he had no magic. The blood running through his veins was ordinary, like Kata once believed—and now desperately wished—hers was. She couldn't do it.

If she shot Elín—

Kata squeezed her eyes shut, but the image didn't leave her: an arrow piercing her sister's chest, blood spilling onto the snow as she fell to her knees. She swallowed back bile and pressed her thumb and forefinger to the bridge of her nose. *Think, Kata. Focus.*

Forcing herself to detach from her tangled emotions, Kata tried to think with the clarity of the hunt. If she completed her task, Týr would avenge Elín. Kata had seen the way he looked at her back at Skyli, but even if she hadn't, protecting the Stormsinger line was his duty.

It was sickeningly clear—either Kata found a way to get Elín on her own and flee when the deed was done, or she would have to kill them both.

A branch snapped in the undergrowth, and Kata whirled toward it. She stood alert for a few minutes, but there was no one there. By Lady Legend, she was on edge.

She flopped onto the ground, not caring that it muddied her trousers as she leaned her back against a boulder.

Getting Elín alone may not be so hard, but it would deepen the betrayal considerably. Kata had seen her eagerness to connect, the hope in Elín's eyes when she'd learned they were sisters. All Kata had to do was ask for a sister-to-sister chat. She could pretend it was something about their father, maybe—

Muddy footsteps reached Kata's ears. Two pairs. It could only be *them*. They must have arrived in Snjoreya that morning, too, and Kata had been too busy planning her kill to realize the sun had reached its zenith overhead.

She scrambled to her feet, adjusting the bow and quiver on her back and whispering "*hylja*" again, just in case. When she was done with this, she would burn the bow and never again deal in magic.

Elín and Týr emerged through the trees, chatting and laughing. Kata's heart raced. She was desperately tempted to run before they spotted her.

But it was too late. When Elín saw Kata, her eyes lit up and she outstretched her arms as if to embrace her. The words Kata had planned—"Elín, I must speak to you alone"—dried up on her tongue. She panicked, stumbling backward. Lightning fast, she removed the bow, nocked an arrow, and drew back her arm.

"Stand back," she said, her voice ragged and wild.

Elín and Týr froze, their mouths matching O's of surprise as they saw the bow. Then Týr drew his sword and Elín's arms, still open for an embrace, slowly shifted so her palms were up, facing Kata and clearly weaponless.

"Kata," Týr said, stepping forward and brandishing his sword. "Put the bow down. Let's talk."

She'd forgotten they might be armed. Kata's knees trembled, but she shook her head and kept the arrow steady, trained on Elín's chest.

At the same time, Elín gestured for Týr to stand down and said, "What is it, Kata? Let's talk about it, whatever it is. Why are you afraid?"

The calm tone—the same she'd used when she'd brushed Kata's hair and readied her for dinner with Eldri—made Kata's eyes sting. Why had this witch ever been kind to her? She bit her tongue to keep from crying out, drawing blood.

"I'm not afraid," Kata ground out through clenched teeth. Her arm holding back the arrow was beginning to shake, and not just from the strain of keeping the string taut.

Týr took another step toward Kata, and she swung her bow his way, the arrow pointed at his heart.

"Týr," Elín said steadily. "Sheathe your sword." When he looked at her, eyes wide in horror, she said in a fiercer tone, "Put away your sword and step behind me. Whatever happens to me, you shall not touch Kata. I forbid it."

"The Stormsinger line—" he began, a cloud of breath whooshing out into the wintry air.

"The last Stormsinger has spoken," Elín said coldly. Her reddish-brown hair was covered in a crown of white snowflakes, and Kata couldn't look away from her. What game was this? Was she preparing to summon snowsong to strike Kata down?

With great reluctance, Týr obeyed, sliding his sword back into its sheath with a dull ring, then retreating one step to the side and behind Elín.

There was fire in his brown eyes, but Kata barely noticed because Elín's deep blue ones were fixed on her. "Kata," she said softly. "My sister. I don't know what has brought us here, but I won't raise a hand to you. A lifetime apart—our family torn in two—has caused such suffering. I will not add to it."

The weight of the bowstring was tiring; Kata's muscles burned. She finally found her voice again and said, in a hoarse whisper, "The king commanded that I kill you."

Elín blinked once but didn't otherwise react. Týr kept clenching and releasing his fists and muttering under his breath.

Even quieter, Kata added, "If I do, all will be well again. My problems gone. If I don't . . ."

Elín must have heard, even over the breeze creaking the trees and the flowing river. "All is well, Kata. Do what you must. I forgive you."

This is wrong. Kata knew that, but she had no other choice. Words her father had spoken returned to her, unbidden: "Because we can help, we *must* help. Do not forget that."

But her father was a killer. He had hunted unicorns, the purest of creatures. She could become a killer, too. Kata had only to chisel away at her heart until it was sharp as glass and kill one snow-witch for the king.

Týr's hand covered his mouth now. Kata felt suddenly fragile, about to break. A sob clawed at her throat.

"I'm sorry," she whispered as she let her arrow fly.

A SAFE PLACE
Elín

Týr tried to push Elín out of the arrow's path. He was too slow, but it didn't matter because the arrow flew over their heads, landing in the river with a dull splash.

Elín took several deep, ragged breaths, pressing the heels of her hands to her eyes as Týr's arm around her waist steadied her. She thanked her ancestors and all the goddesses, not caring whether she believed in them or not. She'd nearly died, and at the hand of her new-found sister. But *why*?

When she'd recovered, she looked at Kata. The girl had collapsed to her knees in the snow, tear tracks shining on her cheeks. Kata wore a look of such anguish that Elín brushed Týr off and joined Kata in the snow. Týr quickly snapped up the bow and quiver Kata had tossed aside, putting them over his own shoulder to keep them out of her reach.

Cautiously, Elín embraced Kata. Some tiny part of her was afraid that this was a trap—that Kata would withdraw a dagger and thrust it into her back—but she ignored it.

Kata leaned into her shoulder and sobbed, her shoulders shaking as she muttered "sorry" repeatedly. Elín smoothed her hair and whispered, "All is well now. Get the tears out—let them go."

She didn't release Kata until her breathing had steadied and Elín's cloak was soaked with tears.

"Now then," Elín said as Kata pulled away. "Why don't you tell us what that was all about?"

The brave huntress was abashed now and couldn't meet Týr or Elín's eyes.

Kata pulled a crumpled scroll of parchment from her tunic and handed it to Elín, who unrolled it and passed it to Týr.

He read it aloud, then said, "Lady Luck has abandoned us again. The king knows you're here." Týr paced in front of them and peered through the trees. "We can't have you out in the open like this."

Kata sniffled. "I think I know a safe place." Her voice was small, hesitant. "For all of us. I can take you there."

"Thank you, Kata," Elín said with a slight smile. She extended a hand to help Kata to her feet.

Týr looked about to explode, probably thinking Elín might as well have agreed to enter a troll's lair, but she silenced him with a sharp look, and they followed Kata into the woods.

The "safe place" ended up being a hunting lodge deep in the woods. It was wide and squat, hewn from dark logs and four times the size of Elín's cottage back in Ornfoss. Dripping icicles hung from its eaves. When Týr asked who it belonged to, Kata replied, "The king."

"You've led us into a trap," Týr said. "He could find us here."

Kata shook her head. "The king rarely hunts himself, and never in winter. We'll be safe here, and we're far from the city."

Týr looked as if he wanted to argue further, but Elín shook her head once, and he stopped. As they stepped inside the dark lodge, it became clear that no one had inhabited it for some time. Cobwebs hung in the corners, and the air was musty. Dust layered the faded tapestries on the wall.

Once Týr had started a fire in the stone hearth, Elín lit candles on the table, and Kata found some blankets in a back room, it was cozy enough. Certainly better than a Viltland ice cave.

"Now," Elín said, "we must tell each other everything."

And they did. First, Kata described Magni's injury and pretended death, traveling by sea and narrowly escaping the kraken, thanks to her powers, and then being dragged before the king and given the contract.

"Oh, Kata," Elín said, and tucked the blankets around her more snugly. "What an ordeal. But it sounds as if you've been very clever to make it this far."

Kata's eyes were wide, and she seemed not to know what to say. Perhaps she was still conflicted over nearly killing Elín earlier.

A scratching noise on the door interrupted Týr and Elín as they began to recount their own tale. Kata sat bolt upright, and they all stared at the door.

"It could be a tree blown by the wind," Elín whispered.

Kata shook her head. "That's an animal. I can hear it breathing."

Týr blanched. "What sort?"

"Something large. An ice bear, maybe?"

The scratch came again, and Elín thought she could hear the beast's huffing breaths now, too. "Týr," she said gently. "Give Kata her bow."

She saw him struggle between his distrust of Kata and his fear of the creature outside, but he did hand it over. Kata took the bow, then silently slid an arrow from her quiver and nocked it. Elín reached into her bag and withdrew her dagger, though she left it sheathed for now. She remembered what Axel had said about magic-made objects raising questions in Snjoreya.

Týr crept to the door, sword in hand, and looked to Kata. She drew back the bowstring and nodded, and he opened the door.

A great wolf pushed its way into the lodge, and Elín gasped, her hand fluttering to her chest. But then there was another sound—of a violin—and a tall, slender figure entered behind the wolf.

"By all the Ladies," Kata said, keeping her bowstring taut. "Get inside."

"Ah, Kata, this is not a very friendly welcome," Grim said with an exaggerated frown. Týr shut the door behind them, cutting off the cold air and snow spilling through.

"I'm not putting my bow down until she transforms," Kata said, teeth gritted.

"Fine, fine," Grim said, setting his violin on the table and nudging the beast, which was larger than any wolf Elín had ever seen. Its head nearly reached Grim's shoulders.

For a terrifying moment, the wolf stood to its full height—or as close as the low-ceilinged lodge would allow—then morphed into a woman. One with a mass of matted black hair, wearing a wolfskin roughly tied at the waist with rope. Elín recognized her from the dinner with Eldri—Nattmara. Elín wondered how the pair had found them, but she supposed there were many things a living nightmare and a water-spirit could do.

Kata put away her arrow and slung the bow over her head again. "Of anyone Eldri could have sent, why did it have to be you two?"

Nattmara's sharp teeth flashed. "Eldri didn't send us."

"Came to check on you," Grim said, peering at her. "You've looked better, but your skills have improved. We ran into our mermaid friends, and the big news is that you spoke to the kraken and saved your ship."

"I did."

"Excellent. I see I've taught you well." As Kata started to protest, he turned to Elín and Týr. "And I see our Stormsinger and Keeper are alive and whole. Have you got the Kirja?"

Elín glanced at Týr, biting her lip. His face fell in shame, and her heart ached. The loss of the Tome was still devastating for him. She cleared her throat. "It's gone. The king's hunters got there first."

Grim sighed. "Well," he said, "there goes our entrance into the castle. Good thing Kata is so cozy with the prince. I'm sure he can get her in."

Kata winced. "No," she said. "I can't go near the prince or the castle anymore."

"Why not?" Nattmara asked, growling low in her throat.

Týr grabbed the scroll from the table and handed it to them as explanation.

Grim let out a low whistle after skimming it. "Quite the sum you're worth, Songstress. I wouldn't command half as much."

"You'd command enough," Kata said, scowling and, Elín suspected, only half joking.

"What are you implying?" Grim asked, a hand to his chest in feigned shock.

Kata plastered on a sweet smile. "I would've killed you for much less." After a pause that was a little too long, she added, "Before I visited Skyli, of course."

Nattmara flashed her teeth again and threw up her pale hands. "Can we focus? The pair of you have shredded Eldri's plan."

"Ah, Eldri," Grim said, tossing the scroll back onto the table. "Perhaps he and King Karvel have more in common than they think. Very efficient, both of them. Minimize their losses by sending just one person to do a job for an army."

"What do you mean?" Elín asked. Then she remembered what Nattmara had said when they'd first come in. "You said Eldri didn't send you . . . so why *are* you here?"

"And where's Magni?" Kata asked, crossing her arms and looking worried. "Is he not healed yet? Why wouldn't he come instead of you?"

Grim shook his head. The merriment left his eyes, and Kata sucked in a breath. Then he said, "He's alive and in Eldri's care. But concealing everyone and lighting the mountain took much from Eldri. He won't be able to heal Magni in time for your mission."

"Does Eldri have a new plan for us, then?" Elín asked.

"Not exactly. As I said, we're here on our own business," Grim said. "Nattmara and I—and many like us—grow weary with Eldri's endless patience. Especially after that close call with the hunters. If you both failed, Eldri's plan was to prepare his people to defend Skyli whenever King Karvel found it. Which would likely be soon."

"We have other plans," Nattmara said, baring her pointed teeth in a wide grin. "If you fail, we will attack Snjoreya. There isn't much time left before spring melts the ice bridge, but there's enough. We will take back this kingdom by force."

"You can't," Kata said, her eyes wide and mouth ajar. "Think of how many will die—on both your side and Snjoreya's."

Grim lifted an eyebrow but said only, "That's why it is vital you succeed. If not . . . blood will be spilled. On both sides, we know, but we believe ours will come out on top. And we're willing to die trying."

"You have no chance," Kata said. "There are so few of you left."

Nattmara smirked. "The trolls will fight with us. King Karvel has nothing that can match them."

"Trolls," Týr said, blanching. "Eldri couldn't convince them to join the others at Skyli. How did you get them to organize with you?"

"The trolls are as tired of the king as the rest of us," Grim said. "And they're willing to do a bit *more* than Eldri is."

"Don't do this," Týr said. "Don't go against Eldri."

Nattmara rolled her eyes. "I'm tired of everyone believing Eldri is so pure. He knows how to take calculated risks as well as any other leader. He's been softer than we prefer, but I was impressed with his plan to bring Kata to Skyli."

"Why?" Elín asked. Nattmara frightened her, and hoped she'd never have to see her in wolf form again, but there was a dark edge of truth to her words. Elín had admired Eldri and believed him a kind and brave leader, but now . . .

A flash of teeth as Nattmara laughed and shook out her black mane. "What do you suppose Eldri would have done had Kata not agreed to help our cause? Or had it turned out she did not share her father's gifts?"

"What are you talking about?" Kata asked, glaring daggers at Nattmara. "My father has no gifts."

Grim smirked. "I guess there are a great many things you don't know about your father. Just as there are many you don't know about Eldri."

Silence fell over the lodge except for the howl of the wind in the chimney and the fire crackling in the hearth. "Eldri isn't like King Karvel," Elín said, though her doubts showed through in her voice.

"I'm afraid he is," Nattmara said. "Your softhearted Eldri would have held Kata hostage and forced your father to speak to the dragon if he wanted her back. I thought it an excellent plan."

"That's not possible," Kata said. "My father has no gifts. He hates magic." But her words sounded less certain than before. Elín looked at Kata, trying to gauge her thoughts, but her sister wouldn't meet her eyes.

"Now, now, Nattmara," Grim said. "It didn't come to that, so there's no use digging up the past. But we must make a new plan. Kata can still speak to the dragon, but we must find a way to get her into the castle. The longer we wait, the greater the risk she or Elín will be caught, the plan discovered, and Skyli's location revealed."

"She's already been caught," Nattmara muttered. She scraped a long fingernail down one of the hearth stones, then turned to glare at Kata. "You didn't reveal Skyli's location, did you?"

"No. I told them I'd been enchanted not to know the way."

"She's cleverer than she looks," Grim said with a mocking grin.

"We just need a way into the castle," Elín said. "I'm sure Kata will take it from there. Right, Kata? Týr and I will help. The last thing any of us wants is an all-out war."

Kata's eyes widened, and she nodded.

"Excellent," Grim said, clapping his hands once. "Nattmara and I shall scope out the castle and try to find another way to get Kata inside."

"Won't that endanger you?" Elín asked.

He shrugged. "I'm a water-spirit. I have my ways. And Nattmara will, of course, return to her wolf form and stay hidden in the woods."

"Let's waste no more time," Nattmara said. In a flash, she was a large wolf once again. The transformation made Elín stumble back against the table, but she caught herself and managed to school her expression into something that wasn't sheer terror.

"We'll return at dawn," Grim said. "Be ready to follow through on your agreements. Just not this one," he said, and pitched Kata's contract from the king into the fire. His eyes, steely, met Kata's, and Elín caught some anger there. Perhaps her sister hadn't been so sure of her choice to spare her life.

Týr opened the door for them again. Through it, Elín caught a glimpse of dark sky and pin-prick stars. The sun had set since they'd arrived at the lodge. She realized only one night stood between them and—well, anything could happen tomorrow. It made her shiver. She drew a blanket around her as Týr shut the door against the cold.

He leaned against it, then slid to a seat on the floor. "Well," he said. "Today has been . . ."

"Yes," Elín said, sighing. "Perhaps it's best we sleep now. Exhaustion won't help any of us tomorrow."

Týr nodded. He stacked a few more logs on the fire, then went outside to check that all was well, that no one had found them. They'd considered lighting more fires and sleeping in the well-furnished bedrooms, but wanted to attract as little attention to themselves or the lodge as they could.

Kata helped Elín arrange the blankets she'd found in front of the hearth, and their packs for pillows. As she spread one of the thicker blankets on the floor she whispered, softly, "I'm sorry."

A corner of Elín's mouth quirked in a sad smile. "I know." She rolled an extra blanket into a pillow, then placed it nearest the fire and patted it, welcoming Kata to lie down.

Kata ducked her head and didn't argue. Within moments, her breathing had slowed, and Elín knew she was asleep. She felt strangely protective of the girl, even though she'd nearly been killed by her hand earlier that day—although, she still wasn't sure whether she had genuinely believed Kata would do it.

Perhaps with her mother and grandmother gone, she wanted someone to care for. She ached for Kata, growing up motherless, surrounded by rough, deadly hunters. She hoped that, when all this was through, they could be friends even if they could not become as close as sisters. Of course, they'd have to survive overthrowing a wicked king first.

A rush of cold air and the sharp scent of pine blew over Elín and made the fire flicker as Týr reentered the lodge. "All is well?" she asked.

He nodded, then took Kata's bow from where she'd dropped it on the table and disappeared into one of the other rooms. When he returned, Elín looked at him with crossed arms and pursed lips. "Was that necessary?"

"It's a precaution. I still don't trust her—you saw the contract."

"She had her chance," Elín whispered, glancing at the last fragments of parchment, turned to ash in the fire. She blew out the candles on the table, so the room was only lit by the red glow of the hearth-fire.

Týr collapsed onto his place on the pile of blankets, exhausted. "Please, Elín. Let's not argue." He adjusted the pack under his head and closed his eyes, warm firelight flickering over the angles of his face.

"I don't want to argue, either," Elín said, lying between Týr and Kata and cocooning herself in blankets. They should be warm enough through the night, even though their fire was small.

The sleep Elín desperately needed eluded her. She would have blamed the excitement of the confrontation with Kata earlier that day, but she knew that wasn't the true cause.

No, it was the memory of Týr pushing her out of the arrow's path. Had Kata's aim been true, he would have been shot instead of her. She mulled it over and was both excited and disappointed by the moment's possible implications. Had he done it only out of duty, like everything else he did, because she was the last Stormsinger? Why bother when they did not have the Tome? Without him to interpret the ancient tongue, the few spells she did know were not much use.

She wanted to think he had done it for another reason. A word she didn't want to speak, even in her own mind, lest it foil something that might be growing between them.

Still, he had been so sure about leaving. About searching for the lost library. If Elín knew what was good for her, she would start distancing herself from him now. If only she could.

"Týr?" she said softly to the smoky, near-dark room.

He mumbled a sleepy, "Hmm?"

"Sweet dreams."

He rolled over and pressed his back to hers, as he had in the cave. "You too, Songstress."

This time, when he said it, she didn't mind the title.

BY THOSE DEAREST

Kata

Kata woke before dawn. It took a few moments for her to realize where she was. Not in her own home, not in the cave at Skyli, but in the king's hunting lodge with Elín and Týr. The fire had dwindled, so she placed another log on it before getting up. The others were still asleep, Týr's arm draped across Elín.

She knew now that she could never kill Elín. Maybe she could never kill a magical creature, either. It didn't matter, really. Those dreams were gone, the contract burned, and what she needed now was to survive. Entering the king's castle and confronting a dragon didn't seem like the best way to do that, but where else could she go?

Sighing, she slumped into one of the wooden chairs. She'd considered sneaking out while the others were still asleep and going home, but she couldn't bear it if her father turned her over to the king. Helga's betrayal had been hard enough.

On the other hand, discussing her situation with Prince Stefán would surely help. He had a way of coming up with solutions, of piecing together bits of information in ways she could not see. But going near the castle was a death sentence now, and she wasn't entirely sure he wouldn't turn her over to his father—a sharp, painful thought.

There was also the threat of a war over Snjoreya. King Karvel had strong forces, but could they face trolls and whatever other unsavory creatures Grim and Nattmara had dealings with? Kata's heart twisted—Prince Stefán could be among such a war's casualties. The hunters would surely get involved, and she couldn't bear to see her friends or father killed in battles she might have helped prevent.

She'd just resigned herself to staying with Elín and Týr, making the best they could out of Eldri's original plan, when rough scratching on the door cut through the silence.

Yesterday, Nattmara had scratched the door a few times lightly, but today, she clawed it. It was loud enough that Elín and Týr stirred in their sleep.

"Who's there?" Týr asked.

"I think it's Nattmara again," Kata said, approaching the door. She *hoped* it was Nattmara, because whatever clawed the door was giant and frantic. Then, she scowled, realizing she was *hoping* to see one of the two most annoying people she knew. "Where's my bow?"

Týr gave her a sheepish look and started toward one of the back rooms. It was too late; the force of the beast outside had broken the door latch and wolf-Nattmara burst through, growling from deep in her chest.

She transformed, but looked even angrier in her human form than she had as a wolf.

"Grim's been captured. I try to tell you about it, and you're all here, asleep!" she spat. She started to go on but was interrupted by Elín.

"Captured? How?"

"A guard caught him when he transformed after working his way into the castle in his water form, through the river," Nattmara said. "The guard restrained him in iron shackles before Grim could turn back and escape."

"Where is he now?" Týr asked.

"The dungeons, I assume, but his execution has already been announced in the city. Even now, people flock to the castle to watch." Nattmara's words were bitter, and Kata couldn't blame her. She'd never witnessed such an event herself—most of the magical creatures were safe in Skyli long before she was old enough to understand the law—but she had not thought them barbaric until Skyli had opened her eyes.

"He's a water-spirit," Elín said. "Surely a sword cannot . . ."

"The iron shackles," Týr said. "They'd keep him from his water form, and he would be as human as you or I when it comes to"—he swallowed—"execution."

Elín ran her hands down her braid. "How can we save him?"

Nattmara paced in front of the hearth as she spoke. "If we can free him from the shackles, he could transform and make his way to the river. There, he'd be safe. But if you could conjure something to disguise his escape, that would help."

"I can summon fog," Elín said, though her face paled. Kata wondered if this was the first time she'd really be testing her powers.

"But how do we get someone to undo the shackles?" Kata asked. "The execution block will be surrounded by people. There's no way to do it without being seen."

Týr and Elín exchanged one of their private glances, and then Elín pulled something from her pack. "I think I have a way," she said, holding out a shiny shell hanging from a strand of woven fibers.

Kata had been selected as the one to sneak onto the execution block wearing the necklace. It was not because she cared about Grim most, of course, but because Nattmara had agreed to provide a distraction in the moment Grim slipped away, and Elín was to provide a layer of fog to help disguise his escape to the river. Týr had offered to do it, but he'd been horrid at moving quietly, whereas Kata's hunting experience had trained her well for such a task. And there was a chance Kata could use her power to speak to Grim and instruct him, though it hadn't worked so well back in Skyli.

Thus, Kata wore the shell necklace as the trio joined the throng of citizens headed toward the castle's outer grounds. There was a time when her skin would have burned from using an object imbued with magic, but now, she met it only with weary acceptance. Still, if she could have seen a way to do this without the necklace, she would have.

Nattmara crept along, a shadow at the edge of the woods, as the three of them merged into the crowd. She hoped there were so many people only because of the day's warmth—it seemed they were having the first false spring of the year—but she knew many were there for the spectacle, too. To see the evil of magic punished and purged from their home.

When they drew near enough, they saw Grim, his hands bound in shackles as he knelt on the stone where criminals were beheaded. King Karvel and Prince Stefán stood on the wooden execution stage alongside a group of advisors and the executioner, who was dressed in black.

Something stirred in Kata when she saw the prince. His mouth was a grim line, and his hands were clasped behind his back. She wondered what he thought of all this, and, more painfully, whether she'd ever speak to him again.

Among the advisors, she spotted her father. Her heart twisted, and she turned her face away. The others had said the mermaid's magic wouldn't work on the one who knew her best, so she had to be sure Njáll didn't see her. It also hadn't worked on Týr or Elín, probably because mermaid magic was a slippery thing, and they already knew she wore it.

She nudged Elín and pointed him out. "That's our father. Njáll, the Royal Huntsman."

Her sister's eyes widened, but she said nothing. Perhaps Kata shouldn't have told her; there was plenty else to worry about right now.

Elín and Týr found a place at the edge of the crowd and began their work on the spell. Kata continued toward the stage, relieved that the magic of the necklace seemed to work. Though she saw familiar faces from the tavern, their gazes seemed to glide over her as if she weren't there at all.

A man stepped forward on the stage, and the crowd stirred. Seeing it was her father, Kata ducked behind a tall woman so she wouldn't be seen. Njáll called the crowd's attention. They quieted and turned toward him. He was a respected man, not just for his position with the king and his prowess as a hunter, but for the good he did among the people.

"Friends," Njáll said, his deep voice ringing out over the crowd. Its familiarity made Kata ache. "I stand before you to ask the king's mercy for this water-spirit's life."

Kata couldn't help but gasp; luckily, there were so many other gasps and murmurings in the crowd that he couldn't have heard hers. She wiggled between a few more people, drawing closer to the stage while staying out of her father's sight.

Elín must have cast her spell, as a light fog slowly came over the crowd. It was thicker near the river, hopefully enough to cover Grim's escape.

Njáll continued, "For those creatures most closely resembling us, with near-human forms, the punishment has always been banishment. Perhaps this water-spirit stumbled into Snjoreya by accident. I ask you, Your Highness, to consider banishment, a punishment more in line with your mercy and benevolence."

Kata sneaked a glance at the king as murmurs rippled through the crowd. Most were surprised that a well-known unicorn hunter would say such a thing. It surprised Kata, too. Others grumbled that they'd come for a show, but a few seemed to think his argument reasonable. Remembering what Grim had said about her father sharing her gift, Kata wondered if that was why he spoke for the irritating water-spirit. She still found it difficult to believe that her father, the famed unicorn hunter, could speak to these creatures as she did.

But there was little time to wonder about it now; her moment of opportunity was fading fast. The king stepped forward to respond. His face was stony; he had not been moved by her father's plea.

Kata wove her way through the last few people between her and the stage for a better view. As she stepped up to the execution platform, she ensured she did so at an angle where her father would not see her.

Fear sang through her when she first pulled herself up onto the stage. She was afraid the magic would fail once she stepped out of the jostling crowd and stood alongside the smaller group of people on the execution stage. But no one observed her, not even Grim, and she was able to move toward him undetected. Everyone's attention was on the king now, anyway, as he defended his choice to execute Grim and assured the crowd that keeping the kingdom safe from magic was worth a little spilled blood.

She reached inward for the tentative thread of her magic and tried to tie it to Grim's.

I'm here to rescue you.

A pause, in which she stepped closer to him, wondering if her magic would work now, when it hadn't back in Skyli under much less strenuous circumstances. She thought the message had gone through.

The shackles on Grim's wrists were clamped together with a bolt, so all she had to do was pull it and urge him, with a whisper, to make for the river. Nattmara was to show herself then and howl, drawing the crowd's attention away as Grim transformed and escaped.

When I pull out the bolt, transform and flee.

Grim gave an almost imperceptible nod. Good, he'd heard her. Kata took a few cautious steps toward him, reaching for the shackles.

She glanced over her shoulder, then wished she hadn't.

Stefán saw her. It was unmistakable; his eyes were on her, not on Grim or anything behind her. She froze, mentally begging him not to react, to say nothing.

It turned out the glance was enough. The king stopped his speech about justice and the law, seeing his son's eyes fixed on something. That was enough to overcome the magic. He saw her, too.

Useless necklace.

With three swift steps, King Karvel grabbed her by the arm. Perhaps recognizing what it was, he ripped the shell from her neck. Several familiar faces in the crowd—including Bergdis and Gunnar's—blinked in surprise as they recognized her. She looked her father's way. His face was carefully blank, but she knew he saw her now, too.

"Look," the king said with something like glee. "This girl, who has lived among us all her life—even she conspires with them. We can trust no one. Let her death, and the death of this foul creature, be an example to you all. This kingdom will not tolerate dealings with evil."

Kata panicked, her eyes going wide and her heart racing. He was going to kill her. *Now.*

She looked out to the crowd for help. Týr and Elín were whispering frantically, poring over scraps of parchment. But even if Elín could summon a blizzard, what good would it do Kata now? The rest of the crowd seemed stunned, too.

They shuffled back and forth and muttered to each other. Some eyes were angry, some wide with surprise or even fear.

Kata looked at Stefán, but his face was impassive. He would not return her gaze, could not see the plea in her eyes. This was his fault—he'd drawn the king's attention to her. What a terrible misstep. How was she to know that Stefán knew her better, even, than her father? Were the last days of her life to be a string of betrayals by those dearest to her?

Njáll stepped forward and dropped to one knee before the king. "Please, Your Highness, spare my daughter. Whatever she has done, I know she is loyal to you." His voice had been clear and true, composed and convincing, when he spoke for Grim. Now, it was ragged, edged in fear.

The king smirked, and Kata glared at him, trying to cover her fear with rage. "Justice must be served, my huntsman." He turned to the crowd and said, "Let this be a warning to all of you. Magic must be rooted out. I cannot stay my hand, even for my own people, if they become entangled in its evils."

To their credit, the crowd didn't seem happy with this decision. She realized the king had not revealed her gift, so to the crowd she was only a regular girl caught up in the dealings of magical beings. There were looks of horror, murmurs of dissent, even some tears for Kata from some of the hunters she recognized. But none of them spoke for her. Her father could do no more. They shared one short, desperate look, just enough for Kata to take comfort in the fact that her father still wanted to save her, despite her dealings with Grim. Then he stood upright again, shoulders stiff, and took his place among the other advisors.

Nattmara, perhaps, could have still saved her, but her shadowy form in the woods had vanished. Maybe she knew a lost cause when she saw one. Kata caught Elín's eye. She and Týr were moving through the crowd, probably planning to carry out some plan even more slipshod than the one that had gotten them into this mess. Kata shook her head once, and they stopped. There was no point in throwing away their lives, too.

King Karvel held up his hands and waited for the crowd to calm. There was a glint in his eye, and Kata knew he would give the execution orders next. She was only a few words from death. She attempted to spin out of the king's grasp, but his fingers dug into her arm like talons. Her eyes roved the crowd and the sky, wishing for impossible things—that Nattmara would return, that Týr and Elín would find the perfect spell, that Magni would sweep down from the sky and take her away. Her father met her wild gaze, and she knew he was sorry. So sorry. She was, too.

Then Prince Stefán stepped forward. This hushed the crowd quickly. They were used to seeing him as a silent, pale boy at the king's side. He had never addressed the people directly. His steps were rigid, wooden, and she wasn't sure if it was from hiding his limp or from the weight of what he was about to say.

Kata felt one last ray of hope. Her oldest friend might still find a way to free her. Maybe, somehow, he was still on her side.

"Your Highness, I recommend imprisonment in the dungeons, for both the girl and the water-spirit." Prince Stefán spoke the words clearly and with confidence.

Maybe not, then.

The king stiffened and replied through gritted teeth, "Why?"

"It's a better punishment for them both," Prince Stefán said, his gray eyes cold. A muscle twitched in his jaw. He still wouldn't look at Kata. "The girl roams the forest with her father, and the water-spirit is used to his freedom. The dungeons will punish them for their crimes, and they may spend the rest of their lives serving as a warning to others, rather than just a few brief moments today."

The crowd seemed to like that idea. Kata did not.

The king didn't seem swayed. Stefán took another step closer to him and said, in a low voice only Kata and the king could hear, "It will also keep the people from acting on their outrage."

So *that* was why he'd spoken. Kata felt as if he'd slapped her. It didn't really matter if she were alive, imprisoned, or free, so long as the people were not on the edge of an uprising and his father remained in power.

"Very well," the king said, after he'd scanned the faces of his people and seen the truth of his son's words. "Now, step back."

Prince Stefán obeyed, and King Karvel raised his hands to the crowd again. "I sentence them both to imprisonment in the dungeons, where they will live out the rest of their days. Let this be a warning to any who would delve into the dark world of magic."

As Kata was dragged away by guards, she narrowed her eyes at Prince Stefán. But he still wouldn't look at her, and as the crowds dispersed, she saw the king grab his arm and roughly drag him into the castle, too.

PABBI

Elín

The helplessness Elín felt was immense and dark—she feared it might swallow her. There was no way into the castle, no way to save Kata. Grim, a being far more practiced in magic than she, had failed to enter the fortress unnoticed, and that was before the castle guard knew magical creatures were amidst them.

Elín stared up at the foreboding, stone-hewn castle. Yesterday, she'd stared at it in awe—it was the largest structure she had ever seen—but today, she felt only malice. Towers stood at each of its four corners, bearing arrow slits along their sides. The walls stretched high above them. She wondered how many troops patrolled those ramparts. Two of the towers had turrets growing out of them, with colorful flags waving from their peaks. It was impenetrable.

"What do we do?" she asked Týr.

"Blend in with the rest of the crowd," he answered quietly. "They're leaving, so we need to go, too. If we try to rescue Kata now, it will look suspicious."

Elín nodded and followed him as the crowd disbanded. The castle had been built along a wide bend of the river, forming a natural moat around two of its sides. The east side was perched on a cliff overlooking the sea, and the north faced the King's Forest, where they'd hidden in the hunting lodge. There was a bottleneck at the bridge over the river that led back to town, and she and Týr had to wait to cross.

Kata's name was on everyone's lips. Elín did her best to tune them out, but it was difficult when emotions were running so high. Many seemed enraged that she would be thrown in the dungeons. Others said it was due punishment for those who conspired with monsters.

"Týr," she said, grasping the sleeve of his tunic as the crowd jostled around them. He turned back. "I want to see my father."

His eyebrows shot up. "It's a great risk."

She bit her lip. "He spoke in Grim's defense. Maybe he's not as bad as Kata said. Even if he is . . . this could be my only chance to meet what remains of my family."

Týr considered this, then nodded. "If I had a chance to speak to my parents, even once . . ." He took her hand and pulled her to the edge of the crowd. Then he asked a stranger for directions to the Royal Huntsman's home.

As they crossed the bridge, he gave a friendly wave to a family of peasants who sat at the riverbank, fishing.

It was a long path through tall, ancient trees. There were no homes, though, only wild forest. A mix of evergreen scents tickled her nose, and she caught occasional whiffs of the sea when its breeze managed to wend its way through the maze of tree trunks. She was a little tired from casting the fog spell, but they trudged their way along the forest path. Just as Elín was sure they'd become hopelessly lost, they came upon Njáll's cabin.

As Týr approached to knock on the door, Njáll came along from a path behind the house. He wore a thunderous expression that made Týr take a step back and put his hand on the hilt of his sword. "Pardon, sir," he said.

When Njáll looked up and saw Týr, he took a step back, too. Up close, Elín could see he was a broad-chested man of medium height, with a short beard. His hair had once been blond, like Kata's, but large streaks of it had turned gray.

"I'm sorry, stranger," he said. "Horrid day. Can I help you?"

Týr turned aside, and Elín stepped forward. Njáll inhaled sharply, his eyes wide in disbelief. "Signý?"

Elín shook her head, tears starting to fall. "Not Signý. Her daughter—*your* daughter, Elín."

He stood in stunned silence. She hesitated, remembering what Kata had told her of his skill as a bounty hunter. But the way he was looking at her now, he surely couldn't wish for her death. She took another step forward, and he wrapped her in a hug so tight it lifted her off the ground. "Elín," he whispered into her hair, his voice strained with emotion.

"Pabbi," she said, trying the word out for the first time in her life. It was a safe, homey word. Comforting.

She breathed in the scents of beeswax and spruce trees, and embraced him tighter. The fur edging his cloak was soft against her hands. She caught Týr's expression over her father's shoulder; a small smile played over his features. There was something a little bittersweet in it, too, and she remembered with an ache that he didn't know his own parents.

When Njáll finally put her back on her feet, she was shaking. Týr seemed to notice and wrapped his arm around her. "I'm Týr. Pleased to meet you. Let's go inside," he suggested, failing to mask the ragged edge in his own voice. "You two have a lot of catching up to do."

Inside, Njáll sat them in chairs near the hearth and pressed flagons of celebratory mead into their hands. The cabin was simple but cozy, smelling of hearth-fire, roasted meat, and the woods around them. Njáll was warm and welcoming, and Elín dreaded having to bring up anything to do with snowsong, but knew it had to be faced as soon as possible.

"Thank you for this," Elín said, taking a sip and setting the mug aside on the table. "But I'm afraid there's something I should tell you now about me. I've met Kata . . ."

He flinched and put his face in his hands. "My little dove," he said. "In the dungeons now."

"Yes," Týr said. "We were there and saw it happen. We also saw you speak in defense of Grim."

Njáll's eyes flicked to the side, but he merely nodded.

"We want to get Kata out and are not sure how," Elín said. "But first, I must tell you something about myself. Kata has told me you are the king's huntsman, and that in the past, you have hunted . . . things other than game for the king's table."

"That is my reputation, yes," Njáll said steadily. "The truth is more complicated."

Elín wanted to sigh with relief. Surely, a complicated truth must be better than him being a heartless killer of those like herself. "I . . . think I am glad to hear that," she said. "Because what I need to tell you could get me thrown in the dungeons—or worse—and I dearly hope my father would not turn me over to the king for it."

He nodded. "You're a Stormsinger. I know. That's why you were sent away."

Elín's jaw fell, and she shared a shocked look with Týr.

"Yes," she said. "And with my grandmother gone, I am the last. Týr is the last Tomekeeper, but I'm afraid there isn't much of the Kirja left."

"The king told me he had killed the last Stormsinger a few years past. I thought he meant you," Njáll said, his eyes shiny with unshed tears. "But I gave offerings in the sacred forest and prayed every day to the Ladies that he never found out about you. That you would be spared."

Njáll embraced Elín again, then told her everything. How he had realized the way the king's attitude was changing toward magic years before the bounties and banishments were decreed. How he'd realized the danger to Elín and her grandmother and sent them away to the village where his friend Arn had moved.

"I wanted us all to go," he said, gazing into the fire. "To stay together as a family. But your mother thought I could do more good here—could find ways to protect magical creatures, to change King Karvel's mind." He shook his head, smiling ruefully. "If only I'd known then how little I'd accomplish."

"Why didn't we take Kata, too? Or why didn't my mother stay with you and only Amma take me?"

"Both of those choices were your mother's. It broke her heart to leave Kata, but she knew your journey would be dangerous—that you and your grandmother would be killed if found. She wouldn't put Kata in danger unnecessarily."

"But she put herself at risk," Elín said.

He nodded. "Your grandmother was old already, and she didn't want something to happen—for you to be left alone in the world."

Elín said nothing. Her heart felt both full and aching. She remembered her long-held belief that her mother had died of a broken heart. Perhaps she had;

it had broken, over time, with longing for a husband and daughter she would never see again.

He sighed. "I used my abilities to help as many creatures and magic-wielders to leave Snjoreya as I could, under the guise hunting unicorns. That let me stay above anyone's suspicion. Especially the king's."

"You pretended to hunt them?" Týr asked, speaking for the first time since entering the cabin. "But how could you . . . ?"

Njáll ran a hand over his short beard. "Many unicorns died on the crossing to Skyli. Froze to death. Even this far south it is too cold for them." His eyes dimmed at the memory, and his mouth turned down. "They allowed me to harvest the horns so I could spin tales of my hunts for the king and receive money from him that went toward funding many more escapes."

Elín shuddered at the image of this man—who she still couldn't quite believe was her father, though they shared the same deep blue eyes—removing the horns of those who had perished, packing them up, and selling them to the king.

Her thoughts and emotions were tangled. Should she feel betrayed that she hadn't met this man until her sixteenth winter, or did she owe her life to the circumstances that had kept them apart? Was it wrong for her mother and grandmother to keep all of this from her, or had they been trying to save her pain?

Most of all, though, she felt grateful. Grateful that she had a chance to meet the man she'd always wondered about, even if only for this one moment. She could be captured or killed at any time, now that the king knew of her coming to Snjoreya, but she'd received answers to so many of her questions.

She reached out and placed her hand over his. "It must have been very hard," she said softly. "But you chose well. I wondered about you, of course. But I had a happy childhood, and I never feared for my life or learned of this persecution of magic. Your friend Arn helped us whenever we needed it."

Withheld tears made his eyes glassy, shining in the light of the fire and the candles on the table. "I wondered about you often. I thought of you and Signý and Revna every day. Once every few years, Arn would find a way to send me word of how you were, so at least I knew you were alive. I couldn't communicate with you directly, lest your location be traced, but Arn had a way of telling me you were well. I both longed for and feared those letters."

He stood and crossed to the mantle, taking down a carved wooden box. When he opened the lid and offered it to her, she saw a half dozen rolls of parchment tied with string. "I want to give you these. To show you I was thinking of you all along."

"Arn's letters," she said. "Thank you." Gently, she took the box from him and ran her hands over the smooth parchment, the rough twine.

He hugged her again, kissing the top of her head. Then he sat back in his chair.

"I would love to spend more time talking, but as you saw, Kata was just imprisoned by the king." His tone turned deep and dark.

"We know," Týr said, and they briefly explained how they had come to know Kata, and Eldri's now-foiled plan.

"You're fighting for Eldri?"

"I suppose you could say that," Elín said. "He had a plan for Kata and me to carry out—a way to overthrow the king. She can speak to magical creatures in her mind."

"It's true, then." Njáll rubbed his eyes. "My little dove inherited my gift. I was never sure if she would, and I did my best to keep her away from ever finding out. But when I saw her trying to help the water-spirit, I suspected as much. And she's helping Eldri, too?"

"Well, she was going to," Elín said. "But it's all ruined now."

"Is it, though?" Týr asked. "The most important part of the plan is for Kata to get down to the dragon's lair beneath the castle. She's in the dungeon now. If we could get into the castle and help her get close to the dragon, we could see it through."

"Ah, Dreka," Njáll said. "I tried, once, to speak to her. It didn't go well. I came away gravely injured, and she has sworn to burn me alive if I dare come near her again. It's too dangerous for Kata to try."

"Kata spoke to the kraken and saved their ship from it," Elín said, a touch of pride in her voice. "I think she can manage the dragon."

"Is she willing, though?" Njáll asked. He shook his head and grimaced. "I wanted so much to tell her about our family, but it seemed safer if she knew nothing of the Stormsinger line or my abilities. She became so interested in the other bounty hunters. I know that's what she most wanted . . . Finding out she could speak to those with magic must have been a great shock to her."

Elín shifted in her seat and shot Týr a look that she hoped conveyed he shouldn't dare mention Kata's attempt on her life yesterday. "I'm sure it was, at first," she said to Njáll. "But I know she wants to help the creatures at Skyli as much as I do, now."

"And I'm sure if she had no personal grudge against the king before, she has one now," Týr added.

Njáll leaned back in his chair. "The king might allow me to see her in the dungeons, if I ask. I don't know how I'd get her out, but if I could, and she got down to the dragon's lair . . ."

Týr shook his head. "We would need to lure the king outside somehow. To the top of the castle, maybe, to minimize other damage or lives lost. We can't predict what Dreka will do. If we unleash her and she decides to avenge herself on the king, we can't expect her to save her wrath for him if there are others nearby. We must get him out of the way of anyone innocent."

Njáll grimaced. "You're right. Perhaps before I could have gotten the king to the castle ramparts on some excuse, but after I knelt and asked for mercy today . . ." He trailed off, then stood. "Let me go into the city and see if I have friends who can help us. There must be a way. At the very least, I can gather some of the good people of Linnafell. If they can catch a glimpse of the dragon kept by the king, or better yet his hoard of gold—well, we will have more allies in what comes next."

Elín stood, too. "Very well. We'll return to our hiding place and try to return this evening."

"Where have you been hiding?" Njáll asked.

"A hunting lodge in the King's Forest. Kata brought us there."

He shook his head. "You must stay here with me. If the king knows you're in Snjoreya he'll send hunters after you. They'll find you at the lodge."

"We can't stay here. We'd be putting you in danger needlessly," Elín protested.

"Don't worry about that. I'd far rather know you were safe in my own home. No one knows I'm connected to the Stormsingers—they won't look for you here. Now I'll go, hoping to return with good news, or something we can use to free Kata."

He smiled down at her for a few heartbeats, as if to save an image of her in his memory, then left the cabin.

Elín let out a long breath, placing her elbows on the wooden table and her forehead in her hands.

"How are you feeling?" Týr asked.

She leaned back in her chair and considered. "Happy. Afraid. Angry. I think if I had the Tome and a spell to tear the castle apart, stone by stone, I would use it now."

"A pity then, that we have no such spell," Týr said with a sad half-smile.

Elín ran one of her fingers along the wood grain of the table. "I just wish there was something we could *do* right now."

"For now, we wait. I hope Njáll will turn up something. Or maybe Nattmara has not truly abandoned us and will return." Then, more tenderly, he said, "Would you like me to read you the letters?"

Suddenly choked by emotion, Elín nodded and pushed the box toward him.

Týr opened it, unfurled the first scroll, and began to read.

THE BANISHED AND BOUNTIED

Kata

Kata didn't know how much time had passed. No sunlight entered the dungeons, so when a flicker of light illuminated the hall, only her hunger and thirst—dull, not overwhelming—told her she'd been there a few hours and not a few days.

The yellow light cast striped patterns through the bars of her cell as it moved closer. She'd been frustrated by being left in the dark, but now that she caught glimpses of her surroundings—the slimy walls, the rusted chains, the scampering rats—she wished she hadn't seen them.

Footsteps echoed down the passage. The dull glow grew larger. *Please be Pabbi, please be Pabbi.* The worst case would be the king. He'd been so angry, had called for her blood with no remorse. She wouldn't be surprised if he had come to finish her, away from the eyes of the crowd.

But the figure was not the king, nor her father. He was shorter than either and not as broad across the chest—though she would almost say he had grown since she last saw him.

"Stefán," Kata said incredulously, stepping up to the bars of her cell to see him better. She'd forgotten to be angry in her initial surprise, but now she screwed her face into a scowl and backed away.

He set his candle on the ground, then stood close to the bars to see her in the flickering light. His expression was stern as his eyes appraised her.

"Did they hurt you?" he asked. His hands were clenched tight at his sides.

"Why would you care?" she spat. "You're the one who got me imprisoned down here. I'll probably be killed." She crossed her arms. "I thought I could trust you. I thought we were—" The word strangled in her throat, and she looked away.

Prince Stefán's calm expression didn't waver. "Are you quite finished?"

Kata glared daggers at him. She wished for Skadi's bow, foolishly left back at the hunting lodge, so she could train an arrow on him and force him to release her. Was there anything else, hidden in the darkness of her cell, that she could use as a weapon?

But deep down, she knew she couldn't threaten Prince Stefán with any sort of weapon. He was still too dear to her for that.

"You look like you're figuring out how to kill me," he said, one side of his mouth quirking. "Really, there's no need. I'm going to help you get out of here."

Relief flooded her, and her stance softened, but questions came pouring in, too. "Then why did you tell the king to throw me in the dungeons in the first place? The crowd wanted banishment. At least I'd be away from him. And where's Grim?"

"He's in a different cell, and he's safe. For now. Kata, I overheard my father's conversation with you. I know you have powers. I know he asked you to kill the last Stormsinger."

"So?"

"Is she here? If she is, I take it you didn't kill her."

Kata took another step back, into the safety of the darkness. "Why would I tell you anything?"

"I know there's something afoot. I want to know what it is. If it will help Snjoreya, even if—as I suspect—it endangers my father, I will do what I can to help."

Kata gasped. "What?"

He nodded. "I thought I could bide my time, waiting until he grew old, and do my best to repair the damage he's done when I became king. But now I see I was wrong. Our kingdom is suffering. He hoards wealth even during harsh winters, and the banishments are cruel. Still, I wasn't ready to fight against him until—" He breathed out slowly and ran a hand over his eyes. "Until my father would have killed you. I had to do something."

"And you thought imprisoning me here would be the best 'something?'"

"It was what I had at the time," Stefán said, frustrated. "I needed to speak to you, and neither death nor banishment would allow that, would it?"

Kata pressed her lips together. "I'll give you that, but why don't you let me out *now*? If you're not here to torture me for the king, are you going to help me escape?"

His face went pale. "You thought I was here to . . ."

Kata waved her hand, stepping closer to the bars again. "I don't know what to think anymore. But no, I didn't. Not really. But it seems you're not here to get me *out*, either, or you would have done so by now."

He sighed. "I want to, believe me, I do. But I can't just yet. There must be a way out of this . . . I can join whatever plot the Stormsinger has come here to execute."

Her heart swelled—hadn't she told the council at Skyli that the prince would help? But she also had to stop herself from blurting out that she was more key to their plan than the Stormsinger. If he was still at all loyal to the king, if this was a trap, that would be her death sentence.

"I see you don't want to tell me," Stefán said, sounding hurt. "I understand why, I do. But please, trust me." He took her hand through the bars and squeezed it once.

Closer to him, she saw a dark bruise forming over his eye and cheek. There was a faint brown line above his lip where his nose had bled, and he'd wiped it away. Had he taken another beating from the king for standing up for her?

"I think I need to tell you from the beginning."

He nodded. "Your disappearance. Start there. Did it have to do with the alicorn you told me about that day when you and your father brought the elk?"

She swallowed. "In a way."

"You hunted it?" he asked, eyes narrowing as he wrapped one hand around the bar between them.

Kata hesitated. What she said next could either free her or brand her a traitor and see her executed—no narrow escape this time. It depended on what Prince Stefán really thought of magic, and maybe a little on what he believed of her. But though he was the Crown Prince, son of a wicked king, he was also her oldest friend.

He knows you best, she thought, remembering the necklace.

She suddenly realized she didn't want to live in a world where she had to trust the likes of Nattmara and Grim but keep secrets from Stefán.

"At first, I wanted to," she admitted. "But no, I didn't hunt him. I *rode* him."

His eyes widened, and he drew closer. "Really?" he breathed. "What was it like?" Then he shook his head. "I'm sorry, I shouldn't be asking you for details when my father has you locked in a cell. I'll get you out as soon as I can, but—"

"It's alright," she said. "It was amazing. Flying over the kingdom . . . I felt so close to the stars. Like I could reach out and hold one in my hand."

"It didn't try to harm you, did it?" Prince Stefán asked, but it sounded as if he already knew the answer.

"No," Kata said. "None of them did. Well, except—" She went pale.

"'Them?'" Stefán's face went serious again.

Kata tugged at her tunic and nodded slowly. This was the true test. "The alicorn took me to their hideout. For magical creatures like him." She paused, waiting for the prince to demand to know where it was, or how many creatures were there. All things she would have wanted to know only a few weeks ago, so she could calculate the bounties.

When he said nothing, only waiting for her to continue, she went on. "I met so many of them, and they're not at all what we thought. They're just like us."

Prince Stefán nodded, unsurprised.

"Actually, I—I found out I'm one of them."

He raised an eyebrow. "I overheard Helga's account of the kraken."

"Yes. I can speak to them with my mind. Or, at least, I was learning to." When he still didn't look shocked or disgusted, she added, "I think I'm good at it, too. It wasn't easy to save our ship from the kraken."

"What was it like?" Stefán asked, a hint of awe in his voice.

Kata considered the question. "Terrifying. But even he wasn't what I always thought. He's so much greater than us that, at times, maybe he cannot help but do harm. But he isn't *evil*."

"I've long thought my father was wrong about that. He fears them, but he's also madly jealous of those who can wield magic when he cannot."

Her heart lifted then. Maybe she could tell Stefán everything. "They don't deserve to be banished or hunted. And . . . I'm going to help them. There's a way."

"How? What can I do?" Prince Stefán leaned forward, his gray eyes shining.

"You were right. There is a plot. I have an important part in it, and I need to get out to see it through. But I'm afraid if I tell you . . ."

"Tell me what?"

"I might never see the light of day again." His gaze felt too warm on her, and she looked away. She dropped her voice and said, "The plot will risk your father's life."

"I suspected as much." He tried to hide it, but Kata caught the waver in his voice.

She peeked up at him then, watching his confusion. His gray eyes darted back and forth. Then, his face settled into a look of resolve. "My father has done much ill to the kingdom," he said. "He taxes the people heavily and ignores the clan elders. The banishment, the bounties . . . my mother."

His eyes flashed then, and Kata found herself unable to look away. "I'm sorry," she finally managed.

He shook his head. "Whatever the plan is, I'm sure justice will be served. Now, tell me all."

"You really want to be a part of this?" Kata said. "You must be *sure*. Because I told them they could trust you, but they'll want you to change the laws. To allow the banished and bountied back into Snjoreya, after—" She stopped, swallowed, then met his eyes again. "After your father is gone, and you are king."

He grimaced. "Yes, I must see this through. If there was a way to do this that guaranteed my father to live, I would take it. But I can't value his safety over all those in Snjoreya and Skyli. Not after what he's done. I can only hope it won't come to that." In a lower voice, he asked, "Do you think I'll be a good king? Better than him?"

"Of course," she said without hesitation. It wasn't just that his father was cruel and greedy, and anyone would be an improvement. The prince was kind and brave, thoughtful and wise beyond his years.

She was treated to one of his rare smiles then. Certainly, it was the first she'd seen since he'd come down to visit her in the dungeon.

"Tell me all, then," he said, and she did.

As quickly as she could, she summarized her time in Skyli, though she did not reveal its location, just in case. There was so much to tell: finding out about her powers, learning that she had a *sister*, attempting to rescue Grim.

"Sorry about that. I was so surprised—and happy—to see you that I didn't think it might show on my face. I didn't realize that only I could see you, and I still don't understand how . . ."

Kata shrugged, ignoring the warmth in her cheeks. He didn't need to know why the necklace hadn't worked on him. "At least my head's still on my shoulders."

Prince Stefán didn't laugh. He rubbed his eyes and wiped his hand down his face. "By Lady Destiny—you have a sister, too. You've had a lot to take in over the past week."

She shrugged. "The important thing is that Týr and Elín aren't found, that we can still carry out the plan."

A familiar, thoughtful look passed over Prince Stefán's face, but Kata knew better than to ask him about it. He never shared his ideas until they were completely worked out in his head, and this one was clearly still forming.

"Yes," he said. "I can see that, and I think I have a plan. But Kata, really, are you sure you're alright? I can imagine this has been . . . a lot."

Her mouth went dry. He was right; she hadn't spent much time processing all that she'd learned. Her powers had been upsetting enough, and then Skyli and the plight of its people, her family history, and now, being held prisoner . . . she felt on the edge of crying, but held back. Prince Stefán needed to see she was ready to carry out the plan. There was plenty of time to dissolve into tears later, after King Karvel had been defeated. *If* she survived.

She cleared her throat. "It is a lot, but I'm fine. Right now, I'm worried about my—my sister," she said, trying out those two words together. She liked the sound of it. "And, of course, about everyone at Skyli."

Prince Stefán studied her for so long that she grew uncomfortable and began to fidget, playing with the hem of her tunic. Finally, he asked, "If I can find Elín and Týr, get you out of here tomorrow morning, and get my father out of the way, to the North Tower . . . will you be ready to face the dragon?"

A chill ran through her, but she stood straighter, shoulders back. "Yes. If I can calm the kraken, I can survive a dragon." Kata spoke the words with more confidence than she felt.

"Good," Prince Stefán said. "I need to get back before I'm missed. I hope you know"—he drew closer to the bars then—"that I would stay with you if I could."

Kata's stomach did a little flip. "I know."

"Where are Elín and Týr?"

"I had taken them to the hunting lodge in the King's Forest. I think they might go back there." She remembered Elín's face when she'd seen her father. "Or . . . perhaps they might find their way to my house. I hope you can find them."

"It won't be a problem."

"Thank you." Then, thinking about what she'd just done—revealed a plot against Snjoreya's King to the Crown Prince—she looked at him and said, "I trust you."

He held her gaze, the scant flame flickering in his steely gray eyes. "I don't take that lightly." He picked up the candlestick. "Be well, Kata, and stay strong. I will come for you as soon as I can tomorrow morning."

"Goodbye," she said, realizing there was much more she wanted to say to him if she ever got the chance. But he was already gone, his silhouette and the glowing orb of the candle's flame vanishing. She sank against the wall, no longer caring that it was filthy, and let out a slow breath.

She hoped her father might convince the king to let him see her. Why had she not gone straight to him after Helga had dragged her before the king?

After Helga's betrayal, she hadn't thought she could stand to see his disgust at learning the truth about her too. But now, with her life balancing precariously, she wanted only to speak with him once more.

But the morning of the next day was marked by porridge slid between her bars, and he hadn't come.

GREAT RISK

Elín

Týr was reading one of the last letters from the box when someone knocked on the door. Elín assumed it would be Njáll returning, but opened it to find the Crown Prince of Snjoreya.

"Oh," she said, swiftly curtsying and trying to hide her surprise. "Your Highness."

Týr stood so quickly that his chair clattered against the wall and ruined his attempt at a smooth bow. "Your Highness."

"May I come in?" the prince asked.

A trill of terror ran down her spine when she recalled his father's words on magic the day before, but she couldn't very well turn him away. And the prince had spoken for Kata, had helped to keep her alive.

"Of course, Your Highness," Elín said, moving aside so he could enter. At least he'd come alone, though she eyed the sword at his waist and wondered how Týr's skills would compare. Despite all the danger they'd been through, he had not yet needed to use his sword from Brokk.

Up close, she noticed a few things about the prince that she hadn't seen from the crowd. His hair was nearly black and his eyes a light gray. One foot dragged a little as he walked. He was missing a few fingers on one hand, his leather glove sewn straight where they would have been.

The prince didn't sit when she offered. After Elín closed the door again, he asked, "Are you Týr and Elín?"

This seemed a dangerous question to answer, and Elín had to stop herself from looking at Týr in panic. *He can't know I'm a Stormsinger, can he?*

Prince Stefán must have caught on anyway. "I haven't come to turn you over to my father, if that's what you fear. I've just visited Kata in the dungeons, and she told me all about Eldri's plot on my father and of her dealings with you both. I've come to help."

Elín was so shocked she had to sit down.

"You have?" Týr asked, mouth agape.

He nodded. "My father has done a great deal of harm to the kingdom during his years on the throne. I mean to correct all that I can during my own reign."

"You just came from Kata," Elín said, still in disbelief. "How is she?"

He grimaced. "I didn't like seeing her in a cell. I think she is as well as can be expected, though, and she is ready to face the dragon if we can cover the rest of the details. I believe I see a way to do that."

Hesitating then, he looked around for a chair and sat. "It requires great risk on your part, though."

"If it frees Kata and helps right the king's wrongs, I'll do it," Elín said fiercely.

"What must we do?" Týr asked warily, sitting down next to Elín.

The prince grimaced again, and Elín wondered whether he ever smiled. Perhaps not. It can't have been easy to grow up under the wing of a tyrant.

Prince Stefán outlined his plan. The issue of getting into the castle was straightforward. Kata was already there, and the prince could lead her down to the dragon. They needed to get the king to the North Tower, though, and he was angry with the prince after he'd spoken for Kata and Grim that morning. It was unlikely he would go anywhere Stefán wanted. But there was one thing King Karvel couldn't resist . . .

"Magic," Prince Stefán said. "If there's a way he can use it for himself while keeping others in the dark about it, he'll do it. The dragon is one example, but I've seen other things hidden in the castle that he would never admit to."

"You should know," Elín said, "the Tome—the book that would allow me to use snowsong—was mostly destroyed by your father's hunters, so I don't know very many spells."

"You'll only need enough to show you're capable of some magic, and hopefully to keep him distracted long enough for the dragon to arrive."

Týr frowned, lightly drumming his fingers on the table. Elín could tell he didn't approve of the plan but hesitated to say so in front of royalty.

"It will work best if I take you both to the tower in the morning. I have a way to disguise you—don't worry about that. Then Týr finds the king and tells him he has the last Stormsinger, and that she wants to make a deal with him, but he must come alone. I know him. He'll have to go."

Týr stopped his drumming, and both of his hands tightened into fists. "I don't like it," he said. "There's far too much risk to Elín. If Kata doesn't manage to unleash the dragon, Elín is trapped on the tower with the king, and he'll know she has magic. What if he isn't interested in our proposal? What if he kills her?"

"I know," Stefán said. "It's risky. If you're not willing to try, I understand. But I can see no other way to guarantee the king will be on the tower when he needs to be. I need to get him far away from any of my people who might be harmed. I'm sorry to say it in this way, but I know you're the bait that will tempt him."

Elín placed her palm over Týr's fist. "I understand the risks," she said gently. A great many there were—death, imprisonment, perhaps being forced to use snowsong for a wretched king. "And I'll do it."

"This could end the Stormsinger line," Týr said. The fire flickered in his eyes. "Forever."

"Snowsong was given to us to protect Snjoreya," Elín said, swallowing nervously. "I don't plan to die. But if I do, at least it will be while trying to fulfill the magic's purpose." And protecting those she'd come to love as family, after losing her home and the first people life had given her to love.

Prince Stefán coughed once, and Elín removed her hand from Týr's and sat back in her chair. She'd nearly forgotten the prince was there.

"I'm glad to hear that," he said, standing and straightening his belt and tunic. "I must be going now. There's much to arrange, including with Njáll. Do you know where he has gone?"

"Into the city," Elín said. "I'm sorry, Your Highness, that's all we know."

"It's enough. I'll find him. Meet me tomorrow just after dawn, behind the castle in the corner where it abuts the sea."

"We'll be there." Elín stood and opened the door for Prince Stefán, curtsying again.

"Thank you for your help," he said, then left them.

When Elín turned around, Týr's face was in his hands. He peeked out through his fingers and asked, "I suppose there's no way you'll be talked out of this?"

She sat again and leaned back in her chair. "It seems rather fruitless to try."

"I don't like this," Týr said.

Annoyed now, Elín said, "That's nothing new. You've been trying to hold me back at nearly every step of this journey."

"I think you mean 'protect you,'" he said, eyes flashing.

"I'm a Stormsinger," Elín said. "I've embraced that now, and I'm going to do all I can to defeat this wretched king." She was more determined than ever now that she'd seen the viciousness in his eyes, his willingness to kill Kata after trying to hire her as an assassin only the day before. "That's what the Stormsingers before me would have wanted."

Týr dragged his hands down his face and slumped in his chair. "My two duties were to you and to the Kirja. I've already failed in one."

More irritation flickered within Elín. He wasn't concerned for her safety as her friend. It was all about his duty and his loyalty to Björn. "We've made it this far," she said, setting her jaw.

"Let's hope Lady Luck blesses us a little longer," Týr said spitefully.

Elín sighed. "I don't want to fight with you, Týr. Not when tomorrow is so important." *Not when you're leaving so soon.*

"I'm sorry," he said, rubbing his eyes. "I just wish we could keep you out of danger for a while. Our 'quest' has been rather harrowing."

"It has," Elín said, one side of her mouth quirking up. "But we're safe for tonight. And after this is over, and we defeat the king, I promise to stay nice and safe for a good long time."

"Really?" Týr said, the familiar teasing note creeping back into his voice. "You think you can manage it?"

"I've got a father and sister now," Elín said. She put her hands behind her head and leaned back against the wall. "I'll need time to get to know them. It'll be the settled family life again for me."

He turned his gaze on her, and it was too intense, warmed by the fire reflected in his brown eyes. She wanted to flinch away, but kept her eyes locked with his. "Is that what you want?" he asked, voice a little husky.

Elín had to think about it. When Björn and Týr had first come to her village, she'd wanted no part in this. She'd believed then that she would be happiest to stay home, on her farm, forever. But now . . . *was* that what she wanted?

No. The answer came, sure and clear. Now that she'd seen more, she wanted more, and perhaps it would never stop. Skyli, Viltland, Snjoreya—there was far more to the world than she'd ever dreamed, and there was still so much more to discover.

"No," she said, just above a whisper. "Not forever. But for now."

A Political Alliance
Kata

Kata debated whether she should eat the cold, lumpy porridge that had been shoved into her cell. She'd snatched it up before the rats could partake of it, but now she wondered if she should leave it for them. On the one hand, her stomach was hollow and growling fiercely. On the other, she thought there was a good chance it would make her sick. What she wouldn't give to have a steaming bowl of Bergdis's stew now.

Then that painful feeling came again—as if someone were grabbing her heart in her chest, squeezing it. If she made it out of this ordeal alive, would Bergdis ever allow her in the tavern again? Could she ever laugh and swap stories with her old hunter friends, knowing how much blood of Eldri's people was on their hands? And if she could forgive that, would *they* ever speak to *her* again? Or would there be too much suspicion and mistrust of her to ever truly feel a part of this kingdom again?

She set the bowl on the ground and kicked it into the corner, hearing some splash out before the rats ran for it. She shuddered. Another sound pricked her ears amid the chattering and scampering, and she perked up. Footsteps.

Please be Prince Stefán, she prayed. *Or Pabbi.* Not *the king.* She suppressed another shudder at the last thought.

"Stefán," she said when she heard his unusual gait. "*Prince* Stefán. Thank the Ladies. You've come back." He carried a torch this time, and she was grateful for it; she wasn't sure how much longer she could have held herself together in the darkness.

"I'm here," he said, rattling keys as he pushed one into the lock on her cell door. The rusty hinges squealed open. "I spoke to Elín and Týr yesterday, and they're ready to do their part, too."

She was so happy to be free that she almost threw her arms around him, but withheld as usual. He grasped her hand, though, and she squeezed back.

"How are you?" he asked, then scoffed. "A horrible question—you've just spent the night in these dungeons."

"I'm fine. Really," she said. "I'm happy to see you and to get out of here."

"Even if there's a dragon at the end of our journey this morning?"

"Even then," she said, setting her jaw. "Let's go."

As they left her cell, the prince handed her a parcel of food he'd brought. Kata found bread and a small block of cheese inside. "Thank you," she told him, now glad she hadn't been ravenous enough to try the porridge. He only nodded as she scarfed them down.

They moved quietly through the dark corridors, their sphere of torchlight passing from shadow to shadow. Kata was relieved he knew the way. She might've been lost forever in the labyrinthine dungeons without him. As they went, he explained the plan to get the king to the North Tower, using Elín as bait. It was a foolish plan, Kata could see that, but it was also their last hope.

"What about you?" she whispered as they started down a ramp-like hall. The dungeons were becoming damper and danker as they approached the dragon's lair. "Overthrowing the king, *becoming* the next king . . . it must be a lot for you, too."

One of his pensive looks passed over his face as they reached the end of the ramp. Around another corner, they darted across a hall and then were onto another down-sloped ramp, this one steeper and a little slippery.

"I'll admit that I haven't slept a wink since I saw you on the execution platform." He shuddered. "But I've known since birth that I'd be the next king, and I've known since my mother died that I must be a better one than my father."

Stefán looked down, his mouth a hard line as he continued his careful steps on the wet stones. "I wish there were another way. I don't want a hand in his death, but the kingdom won't survive if they make war on him." He shook his head. "I've studied the histories of great rulers before me, learned all I can to become a worthy king. I will try to right the mistakes of my father. Starting today, Kata."

Kata studied him, really looked at him, for the first time since she'd left Snjoreya. He looked much older than his fifteen winters—he wasn't a boy anymore, she realized, just as these last weeks had made her something more than a silly girl with dreams of bloodshed and glory. She felt a surge of gratitude for his kindness and patience with her over the years, his love of learning and his desire to lead well. "You're going to be a great king," Kata said softly.

"I hope to be," he said. "But you have a role to play, too."

"I know," she said. "The dragon. I can do it." As she said it, she wiped her sweaty palms on her trousers. He didn't need to know how nervous she was or how her heart pounded in her chest. She wished she'd had more time to learn to use her powers.

"No," he said, smiling and shaking his head. "Don't misunderstand me; that part is vital. But there's something else."

She waved a hand. "Well, whatever it is, you can tell me later. If I survive the dragon."

"I want to tell you now," he said. "I have full confidence in your abilities. But in case something else goes wrong—on my end, for example . . ."

"Fine," Kata said, her nerves translating into annoyance at the interruption. They'd reached the end of the ramp. She stopped in the narrow stone corridor and faced him. "What is it?"

He stopped, too, and smiled at her in a way that made her heart speed up.

"I'll need a queen who will do what's best for the people, whether it's best for her or not."

Kata's brow furrowed. What did she have to do with Snjoreya's next queen?

"I've always known you could become such a woman, but now you've proven it. By putting your own life at risk to save Eldri's people, by saving the hunters from the kraken." He paused, his gray eyes boring into hers with such fire that she had to look away. She fiddled with the frayed hem of her tunic, hoping he couldn't see her reddened face in the dark corridor. She couldn't quite make herself believe what he seemed to be implying.

"If we succeed today, there will be many rough winters ahead. The hunters and people of Snjoreya won't unlearn their fear of magic overnight, and Eldri's people who return may harbor animosity toward them. I think a magic-wielding queen—who grew up and hunted among the people of Snjoreya—could be key to uniting both sides."

Kata finally let her tunic hem be. "You want a political alliance," she said, not meaning her voice to fall as flat as it did.

"As Crown Prince, I've always known my marriage would be a political alliance," he said, voice steady.

She found herself unable to say anything through the stabbing disappointment. There was also yearning—to be the bridge between the two worlds he'd described, to be their queen. To be *his* queen.

Prince Stefán cleared his throat. It was his turn to look away from her. "I just never thought I would be able to choose for myself."

He took her hand then, and it was somehow so different from the many times he had taken her hand and pulled her through the hedge maze or along the ramparts as they were growing up. She remembered the way he'd taken her hand and kissed it when he'd warned her about the alicorn. Her stomach had fluttered the same way it did now.

"Will you be my queen?" he asked, and all the air left Kata's lungs.

But he didn't want *her*, not really. If he needed a queen the people would love—one who could look and act like a queen, who had powers that could serve the kingdom well—she wasn't the best choice.

"If—" She steadied her voice, tried again. "If you want to choose someone with magic, you should choose Elín. She's a Stormsinger—the last one—and people will respect and trust her more than someone who they think can control dragons and kraken and such." Her throat constricted, and she forced herself to continue. "And your—your grandchild someday could carry on the line. A powerful Stormsinger for king or queen."

Her hand fell from his. The moment stretched between them. She couldn't bear to look at him, afraid of what he'd see in her eyes. But she imagined he was weighing what she'd said, seeing the merit of her advice. She remembered how Elín had brushed her hair, had made her feel welcome in Skyli, though it was still a strange, fearful place to Elín too. She'd been willing to let Kata take her life in the woods rather than do her any harm.

She would make the perfect queen, a mother to all the people of Snjoreya.

"You do not want me," Prince Stefán said finally, and Kata stole a glance up at him. His shoulders were slumped, his tone hollow.

"What?" Kata asked tentatively.

"I thought—for years I hoped that—" He cut himself off, shaking his head, then turned to continue along the torchlit corridor.

"Wait." She grabbed his wrist but jerked her hand back when she realized what she'd done. Of course she had feelings she shouldn't for the prince; she was always crossing boundaries, doing things she shouldn't dare with someone of royal blood.

He let out a thick, exasperated sigh. "Why do you always do that now? Are my disfigurements—am *I* so distasteful to you that you can't even bear to touch me anymore?"

"*What?*" Kata repeated, more confused than ever.

"You're always drawing away from me like that. I thought at least that we were friends." He rubbed his eyes wearily.

"We *are*," Kata said, and the next words tumbled out in a rush. "I do that because you're the prince, and I'm not supposed to be so familiar with you! Half the time I forget to even call you 'Prince' or 'Your Highness,' and that's something I could be imprisoned for."

His face looked stricken as he drew his hand away from his eyes. "You think I would imprison you? You think I'd imprison *anyone* over such a small offense?"

"No, of course not," Kata said. "But the king might . . ." She was playing with her tunic's hem again, shredding it. "We *are* friends. You're my oldest and best friend, truly." She looked at him, face earnest, then weighed how much else she should reveal.

There was a good chance she would be burned to death or—she was unsure if it would be better or worse—*eaten* by a dragon in the next few hours, so she continued. "When I was gone—when Magni took me, and I was among all the magical beasts that I feared so much at first, I thought of you often. More often than anyone except for my father. I was afraid I would never see you again, and I regretted our last meeting. The last thing I said to you was so cold. I was afraid if—if I died that—"

Tears started to form, and one slipped down her cheek before she could stop it. Prince Stefán wiped it away with his thumb.

"If I mean so much to you," he said, his voice hoarse, "then why? Why won't you be my queen?"

She laughed mirthlessly. "There are so many reasons I don't know where to start. I'm a huntress; I have no idea how to be a queen. I can barely follow the royalty protocols with *you*, as I just explained. And don't get me started on the dresses and how a queen should *look*. Half your people will hate me; the hunters already think me a traitor." She caught her breath. The tears had passed now, but she still couldn't look at him. "And I've never thought about marriage much, but if I *were* to marry someone, I don't think it would work for me for any other reason than because we're in love—"

"Kata," he said, almost annoyed. "I've been in love with you for years. Since before I even knew what 'in love' meant."

Her jaw dropped in surprise, then her brows knit together. "You never said . . ."

"Because it would only have hurt," he said. "When I had to marry someone else. It wasn't until yesterday when I spoke to you in the dungeons that I realized I had the chance a prince rarely has: to marry strategically *and* for love."

Kata found herself unable to form words.

"It will be several winters yet before anyone expects either of us to marry. But I thought with a betrothal . . . with time to learn what it takes and make plans for the kind of kingdom we want Snjoreya to become . . ." He huffed out a breath and rubbed the back of his neck. "I thought you might grow to love me, too. Now I see this was an incredibly foolish thing to bring up right before you're about to face down a terrifying monster. I've upset you. Please, accept my apologies and forget I ever mentioned it."

"I don't want to," Kata blurted before she could think better of it. He looked up at her, half hopeful, half wary. "Forget it, I mean. I don't want to forget it."

"You don't?" His face brightened in a way that made her heart skip a beat.

"Ask me again after all this is over," she said. "It's too much right now."

"Of course," the prince said, looking around as if just then realizing a dark, dank dungeon was not a romantic setting for a proposal. He grimaced.

"I'll say yes," Kata said.

A slow smile crossed his face as he took a step closer to her. "You will?"

"If you don't come to your senses and choose someone else between now and then."

"As if there could be anyone else," he said, laughing softly. "You underestimate your abilities. You've been giving me sound advice since we were children."

"Like when?"

"Do you remember when I was upset because I can't wield a two-handed sword like my father, and because my footwork is not fast enough even with this one?" He placed a hand on the hilt.

"No," Kata said honestly.

"I came to you, complaining of my shortcomings, and do you know what you said? You looked me in the eye, sighed, and said, 'It doesn't matter, Stefán. You'll be king, so you need to know how to *rule*. There are others who will fight, but if you're a good enough king, you won't need them.'"

"I don't remember that at all," Kata said. "But it *is* rather sensible advice."

"Those words had such an impact, Kata, though we were so young. I was determined to read every book in the library, to learn from all the clan leaders, and to become a king who knew how to rule better than my father."

Kata smiled, though she didn't feel happy. "Well, I'm glad for that. But do listen to my sensible advice now, too: think on what is best for the kingdom. It may not be me. It *most likely* is not me. And when you've realized this, you can choose differently."

He reached up, hesitated, then put his hand to her cheek, fingers brushing her hair. "Never."

Though Kata genuinely believed what she was telling him, another part of her hummed in the background. A part that remembered growing up with Stefán—the way he was gentle when she was rough, thoughtful when she was careless. She trusted him with everything. *Choose me*, said some innermost part of her, which didn't care about the future of Snjoreya as much as it cared that their friendship would never diminish.

She wasn't sure who leaned in first, but her eyes slipped shut, and his lips pressed against hers, warm and soft. There was a taste of red wine; she wondered if he had sipped some to steel himself for this conversation. Her blood sizzled as sparks traveled through her body. She had a sudden urge to put her hand up, pull him closer, but found herself frozen.

When he pulled away, she inhaled sharply and said, "Dragon."

There was a new light in his eyes as he smiled down at her. She hoped to see smiles like that—ones that felt as if they belonged to *her*—more often now. "Yes," he said. "Let's get you to the dragon." He blinked a few times, and the relaxed look left his face. "Only a few turns more."

The corridors leading into the dragon's keep were a twisting labyrinth, the path so narrow they had to navigate it one at a time. Stefán pointed out the stones carved with dragons along the walls that were there to help the trusted servants who fed the beast find their way.

At the end of the maze was a pool of water. "I can swim," Kata said as the prince dragged a wooden board from its hiding place around the corner.

He shook his head. "Look closer."

Kata did, and beneath the dark surface she saw the white translucent domes of moon-glitter floating in the water, trailing tentacles. *Oh.* Brush against one, and she'd lose feeling and control in her limbs, then drown.

The plank it was, then. She helped Stefán position it over the moat. Peering across it, through the arch far on the other side, she caught the shine of gold but was unable to see the dragon. She thought she could hear slow, steady breaths, though, as if the dragon slept. Kata reached out and found she could sense exactly where the dragon was. This beast didn't seem as large as the kraken but then, Kata hadn't gotten so near to the greatest monster of the seas.

"Elín and Týr should be luring my father to the North Tower now, and they've promised to stall him until the dragon comes." Kata's gut twisted. If she couldn't get the dragon to fly off in a rage, what would become of Týr and Elín? "The sooner you can unleash it, the better," Stefán added. His voice was dull now, emotionless.

Kata imagined how difficult it would be to turn on one's father, even if he were as cruel as King Karvel. She squeezed his arm. "Lady Luck be with you."

"With you, too." He pulled her into a hug. She squeezed her eyes shut and prayed this would not be the last time she saw him, the last time she breathed in his scent of old books and warmth. That she would see Pabbi again, get to know Elín and Týr. Maybe even become queen.

It had been some time since she had prayed to Lady Legend. She had always thought of her most on her hunts, but she saw now that what they were doing now could go into legend, too. Who wouldn't write songs about a Stormsinger, a Tomekeeper, a prince, and a huntress overthrowing a ruthless king, allowing hundreds of exiled magical creatures to return to their homeland?

Stefán squeezed her tight again, then knelt to hold the board steady while she hurried across, careful to keep her balance. She turned back once safely on the other side. The prince gave her one last, long look before he reentered the maze, leaving her alone in the dragon's lair.

DEAL IN DISHONESTY

Elín

Njáll had led Týr and Elín to the ancestral clearing, bidding them farewell and the blessings of the goddesses, just before dawn. He had his own role to play in the day's madness, convincing as many townspeople as he could to come to the castle and see the dragon and the king's hoarded wealth, and to rally around him those who might welcome back magic creatures.

Njáll had assured them that more Snjoreyans would support a new king than they expected. The king's fear of magic had ripped apart many families, and his greed had placed heavy burdens on his people. Paying to have hundreds of creatures killed and, later, tracked even into other kingdoms, had cost Snjoreya greatly.

Elín took a deep breath and made her way around the clearing, the predawn light enough to allow her to thread her way through the trees. It was so much larger and older than her family's back in Ornfoss. She ran her palms over the rough bark, the smooth spirit-marks, cut and recut deeply into the trees by the offspring of the deceased each year, for longer than they'd walked the Earth themselves. She wondered how many had been Stormsingers like herself.

I'm your daughter, she tried to tell them as she passed by each grave. *Through many years of your children's children. And I need your help today, for your other daughter, Kata, and this kingdom.*

She finished her spiral by kneeling at the offering-stone in the center of the clearing. Týr stood off in the trees, his expression unreadable, and she wondered whether he was thinking of his own family. Whether he felt adrift and alone, unable to ask them for help. She had felt that way when she first learned of this ritual, when her mother was still alive, and there had been no one in the spirit realms she could seek for help.

Slowly, she untied the pouch at her belt and placed Amma's three locks of hair in her palm. The first rays of sun broke through the trees, making the hair shine like copper and burnished bronze. She placed them in the worn center of the stone, one at a time.

Then she withdrew Brokk's gift from her boot and slipped the dagger from its sheath. But before she could make a small cut on her arm and offer blood to her ancestors, too, Týr was beside her, his hand on her forearm. "No," he said quietly.

"I want to offer them more," she said. "I want them to know how much this means."

"The magic of snowsong is in your blood, Elín." His grip on her arm loosened, but he didn't let go. "You're going to need all the strength you have today."

His brown eyes captivated her with their warmth, especially in contrast with the snow and the dull gray trees. Slowly, she lowered the dagger. "Kata—all of us—have so much to lose today. I want to offer them more for their protection."

"Then let me," he said, reaching for the dagger.

Elín shook her head and pulled it away from his outstretched hand "It has to come from me. You're a stranger to them." And then she realized what she should give.

She smiled ruefully as she ran her hand down her braid one last time. Týr held her gaze. His dark eyes, made like molten gold by the sun, held both regret and understanding. Then she gripped the dagger and severed her last earthly connection to her mother.

"I can't do this," Týr said, wiping a hand down his face as he paced along the tower wall.

Prince Stefán had just left them, and it was nearly time for Týr to petition the king. The prince had given them servant uniforms to wear so he could guide them through the castle without raising suspicion. It was strange to see Týr in the colorful garb of a castle servant rather than his usual deep green tunic and dark cloak.

"The king will believe you. I'm sure he will," Elín said, playing with the unevenly cropped hair at the base of her skull. It was only hair. It would grow back, if she survived today, so it was foolish of her to feel like crying every time she felt the breeze on her neck and remembered its absence. Especially with how precarious the chances of living through today had become.

Týr continued to pace as if he hadn't heard her. He'd been quiet since the ancestral clearing, and Elín wondered if she should have gone without him. The practice was foreign to him, and being near the dead seemed to have brought up memories of his past that made him anxious.

"From what we know of the king, he'll jump at the opportunity. You only have to tell him I'm here." Though she wasn't sure if he would be more interested in using her powers or killing off the Stormsinger line. Either way, he'd have to come to the tower to see her.

"It's not that. It's the *lying*."

"Think of it as acting, then," Elín replied. "I'm sure even if you're a poor actor you can get by long enough to lure him up here, especially with so much at stake."

He shook his head. "That's not my concern. I can act, I can lie—I'm excellent at it, in fact."

Elín forced herself not to turn her eyes skyward, looking out at the sea far below them instead. She was nervous about her role, too, and her gaze kept darting to the stairwell on which they'd come up the tower. But she didn't see why *Týr* was so worried. He didn't have to perform any magic. "What's the problem, then?"

Týr stopped pacing and stared out over the sea and the King's Forest. "When I was a child, I often had to lie or act or con my way into people's hearts to survive. After Björn found me, I swore I'd never deal in dishonesty again."

Elín softened, stepping to his side at the tower wall. "And you haven't since?"

Swallowing, he shook his head.

After hesitating for a moment, she took his hand. "I believe that," she said. "And you don't know how much I've appreciated having someone I can trust to help me navigate all we've been through. My powers, Skyli, Snjoreya . . . all our foiled plans and reluctant alliances."

He turned toward her, taking her other hand in his. A few of his fingers were still ink-stained from piecing together spells on the knarr. "Truly?"

"Yes," she said softly. "And I know you can do this. One last part to play."

He squeezed her hands in response.

If they failed, they'd be killed. If they succeeded, Týr would leave. Elín realized this was her last chance for something she'd wanted to do longer than she would ever admit to him.

She took a step closer to him, and he rested his forehead against hers, his eyes searching and his lips slightly parted. He smelled of hearth-fire and parchment and leather. The familiarity was comforting, but it also reminded her that he would soon leave her in search of the library.

Right now, that didn't matter. They were so close that she could see the constellation of freckles on his nose. His warm brown eyes devoured her. She freed one of her hands, slid it to the side of his neck, and pulled him to her.

As she pressed her lips against his, her eyes slipped closed, and her stomach lit up with fireflies. She wanted this, wanted Týr, and there had to be a way it could happen. Tomekeeper traditions be damned.

He inhaled sharply, and one of his hands went to the nape of her neck. But then he froze, and she realized her mistake. It hadn't been the traditions and rules stopping him. He didn't want this, didn't want her—

Týr placed his other hand at the small of her back and pulled her close. His lips responded to hers, and she grabbed a handful of his servant's tunic in her fist. Elín felt dizzy with sudden happiness as he pushed her hair behind her ear and cradled her head in his hand. Their lips and breath and hands were warm, defying the cold wind up on the tower.

Elín felt in her bones that this was where she belonged. This thing between them was real—had been real for some time.

He pulled away first, and far too soon, but she let him go.

"I should be going down to the king now," Týr said, smoothing the front of his tunic.

"Yes," Elín said, her voice hoarse. "The prince said he would be in the dining hall."

"Yes," Týr said.

She bit her lip, feeling shy now, and a flame lit in her when she saw his eyes flick down to her mouth. He shook his head and made for the spiral staircase that wound around the inside of the tower.

"Týr?" Elín said quietly.

One foot was already on the first step down, but he turned back toward her. "Yes?"

"Please stay," she said, eyes fixed on a crooked stone in the tower wall. She felt exposed, vulnerable, but she went on. "If we survive this, I mean. Stay here in Snjoreya. With me."

He pressed his lips together and raked a hand through his hair. "I can't," he said. "After I know you're safe, I need to—"

"I know," Elín said, not wanting to hear him say again how much he valued all the rest over her. She found it strange that she could still speak when it felt as though her heart was tearing. "The Lost Library, the Tome. Traditions. Your duty."

He nodded. She thought he wished to say more, but as a strange tension stretched between them, he said nothing, and she couldn't bear it. This could be their last chance to say whatever they liked to each other, but Elín found there was too much to say. After all they'd been through, the weight of everything said and unsaid—or said but not meant—between them was crushing. There was no time for such long-winded confessions now.

Or perhaps that wasn't the problem. A few words might be enough, if they were the right ones. But she couldn't bring herself to say them.

"Lady Luck be with you," Elín said instead. She straightened her skirts and locked away her feelings. He still hadn't moved, so she made a shooing motion. "Go on, then. We have a king to overthrow."

OF FIRE AND BLOOD

Kata

Now that the time to face the dragon had come, an odd calm fell over Kata. Her palms ceased to sweat, her eyes stayed focused straight ahead. It wasn't like the manufactured calm Magni could give or the fiery feeling of the end of the hunt. Rather, this was a grim certainty that this day would end one of two ways: she would succeed, or she would die.

All the while, the dragon compelled her. Kata could hear her thunderous breaths now as she passed through the archway. A golden shine winked at her from the end of the dark passage.

The dragon slumbered, and Kata couldn't connect her mind with Dreka's, though she sensed her monstrous presence. She crept forward, relying on the steady, silent pace she used on her hunts. It felt strange to be stalking prey like this with no quiver slung over her back, no bow in her hands. Not that her arrows would be any use against a dragon as large and thick-scaled as Dreka must be.

When she reached the end of the passage, she stopped, frozen beneath another stone arch. Mesmerized. The lair was scantly lit by a few torches along the walls, but there was plenty to see.

The dragon was larger than she'd ever imagined. She remembered, suddenly, Gunnar's story of the castle tower-sized dragon in the mountain when he was a boy, and felt this must be the same one. Besides in Gunnar's boastful stories, she'd never heard of one so large.

Most dragons now were roughly horse-sized. Fierce, but possible to kill with a handful of hunters. Even the skeleton in King Karvel's trophy room stood only a few hands taller than the largest horses Kata had seen. Dragons now couldn't grow to this monstrous size before a hunter found and killed them.

As Dreka breathed, licks of flame leaped from her nostrils, and Kata felt the heat from each one on her face a few moments after she saw them spring up. Great, leathery wings, black and shaped like a bat's, stretched out at her sides.

Her hard black scales reflected the dashes of light from her flaming breaths. They protected every inch of her body, and some were so wide that Kata's hand couldn't have covered them. Hardened ridges sprung up from her back, and her tail, which ended in a spiked club, was coiled around her broad body.

And everywhere there was gold. Coins and bars were lumped together in heaps, the wet sheen of silver peeking out from beneath. Cautiously, Kata stepped toward an unmarked wooden chest and lifted it open. Curiosity fueled her, but she was not careless, ensuring the wood didn't creak and the hinges didn't scrape.

She stifled a gasp when she saw its contents. A heavy gold crown, almost as fine as the king's, inlaid with colorful, rough-cut jewels. Strands of pearls a woman would have to coil around her neck half a dozen times to make them fit. A handful of glittering pink gems the size of her smallest fingernail. An emerald the size of her fist.

You're not here for treasure, Kata reminded herself, pulling her eyes back to the beast and its shining scales. She considered slamming the trunk shut to wake the dragon. *No,* she decided, closing the lid gently. *Better not to startle her.*

Picking her way through the maze of coins and jewels, Kata was careful to make no sound as she crept along. When she was a stone's throw from the dragon, close enough to smell the singe of her flaming breaths, she sat and crossed her legs.

She let herself imagine what went on in the mind behind the thick, scale-protected skull with its angular ridges. Dreka's head was over half as long as Kata was tall. She remembered Gunnar telling her that dragons never ceased growing. This one would have to be hundreds of years old to reach this size. If Eldri's tales were to be believed, she was older, even, than the kingdom of Snjoreya itself.

Before Kata could follow that thought, to think of how much this dragon must have seen in her lifetime and how little chance there was she would listen to a girl who had been on this Earth for less time than she'd been in her egg, she steeled herself. Now was the time.

She screwed her eyes shut and reminded herself why she was there. For Magni. For Eldri and his people. For Pabbi, for Elín. For Prince Stefán. And—though they may not yet see it—for all Snjoreya's people. Helga and Gunnar and Bergdis.

Taking one last deep breath, Kata reached out her mind and, as strong as she could, forced out *Hello, Dreka.*

One yellow eye peeled open, revealing a snake-like black slit, and the other followed. Dreka saw her instantly and opened her mouth. The relief Kata felt at being able to wake the dragon this way vanished as she found herself staring at the flames building in Dreka's throat. The scales on her chest glowed red.

No, stop! She sent, and the flames dimmed.

What have we here? Dreka asked, and it was not the thunderous boom of the kraken or Magni's calm, ethereal voice. This was piercing. The words crashed into Kata's mind, seeming to echo through it, giving her a skull-splitting headache. She instinctively covered her ears with her hands, though, of course, that was not where the sound came from.

She gritted her teeth against the pain. *Eldri sent me.*

Dreka swung her head side to side, peering at Kata with one eye forward, then the other. *Why would Eldri send me a huntress?*

Her voice was less shattering this time, or maybe Kata just knew what to expect. When she'd untangled the words, she lost the plea for the people of Skyli she'd been preparing and blurted out in surprise: *How do you know I'm a huntress?*

Only one who stalks could enter without waking me. She raised her head higher. *I am a creature of fire and blood, more ancient almost than this land. Do you not believe I can see the lives taken by another in their eyes?*

It took Kata several breaths to calm her mind and parse Dreka's words from the pain they caused. When she did, she said, *Alright, I believe you. I am a huntress, though not of dragons, as you can see.*

She wondered how her voice sounded to this ancient creature. If Dreka's was an earthquake inside her skull, hers must be but a whisper on the wind to the dragon.

Dreka gazed at her steadily for several heartbeats, and Kata met her gaze, sitting up straighter. Finally, the dragon said, *I admire anyone with the courage to approach me, even a huntress so bold and foolish as to approach me unarmed. What is it you want?*

You must know what has been happening here. Eldri's people—anyone with magic, even dragons like you—have been banished by the king or hunted for bounties.

What have I to do with that? Her tail flicked.

Kata's jaw fell. *Don't you care for your own kind?*

Dreka adjusted her wings, sending a rush of air through the chamber. *The dragons of old—real dragons—are gone now, but for me. These young dragons are mere pups. They do not live long enough for me to spare any attention for them.*

There was so much pain that Kata thought she might lose her grasp of what was real and what was not. Maybe speaking to a dragon did that to a person. She steeled herself and attacked again. *So you've been sleeping down here for years, well-fed and hoarding your gold, while you let the man who feeds you slay the young of your own kind?* Kata was angry now, the words coming quickly. *Can you not see that you are unjust?*

Careful, girl. I am not so well-fed as you think, and you would fill my belly handsomely.

Kata stood then, scattering gold coins as she did so, and put her hands on her hips. *I came here knowing you might burn or eat me. If you do not help now, then it will be war upon this kingdom, and I shall as likely die as live anyway. I came because you can be a part of freeing magic upon this land. Lady Legend would bless you for it.*

I care not for Lady Legend. No one reigns over me.

King Karvel does!

Dreka went still. Her tail stopped flicking; her wings froze in place. *Do you dare say there is someone more powerful than I?*

Kata scoffed. *I had forgotten how vain dragons are said to be. Of course there are those more powerful than you. Only a few days ago, I spoke with the kraken.*

He may rule the depths, but I rule the land and sky wherever I choose. She raised her wings and thumped her tail onto a pile of gold, making pieces scatter and a ringing sound echo around them.

Not for the last ten years. Not for most of my *life.*

Dreka's chest glowed red again, like the embers of a fire. *I will show you what happens to those who dare insult me.*

Kata crossed her arms to hide her sweating palms. She thought the pain might split her skull into pieces, and she was more afraid than she had ever been, but she did not flinch or back away. *A dragon who can burn a girl to death? That proves nothing. The "pups" you spoke of could burn me just as easily.*

Dreka stopped then, and Kata saw a few sparks dance in the back of her throat before the glowing red scales of her chest turned black again. *What did Eldri want? Tell me before I kill you.*

She shrugged. *It doesn't matter. You won't help, and I'm not sure I believe you could, now that I see what a weak and pampered creature you have become.*

Her nostrils flared. *Of all things, I am not weak.*

Of course you're not. You let King Karvel, the cruelest man to ever rule Snjoreya, feed you and give you shelter beneath his castle, let him steal your gold—

No! Dreka screeched, and Kata put her hands to her temples and closed her eyes against the sound rattling her head. *He takes from that pile there.* The dragon pointed her tail to a small mound of gold and silver coins. *He feeds me in return for guarding his treasury. The rest is mine.*

I think you know more than that goes missing while you sleep. Those times when your food is tampered with by the king's men, and you fall into a deep slumber. When you wake up and there are pieces missing. Kata stared her down. *I didn't know you lacked intelligence as well as strength.*

The dragon's chest flamed red again, and it took everything in Kata to keep her knees from buckling, to keep from turning and running, diving into the moat to take her chances with the moon-glitter over the dragon's fire.

Your real enemy stands at the top of the North Tower now, she said with all her remaining resolve. *Avenge your gold and avenge your dragons on King Karvel, not me.*

WIND OF THE NORTH

Elín

Elín looked out over the kingdom, the one she hoped to call home soon, and lightly touched her fingers to her lips. She could feel where she'd kissed Týr and wished she didn't know it had been the last and only time.

She could not quite make herself wish she hadn't done it.

Perhaps it was for the best that he was leaving. Her life would be full enough already. Practicing incantations, being part of a family again, and—if the prince gave her the chance—helping integrate the creatures of Skyli back into Snjoreya. It would be a lie to say she wouldn't miss Týr, but she likely wouldn't have much idle time to dwell on it.

As she waited for Týr and the king to arrive, she said the ancient words of the spell they'd chosen under her breath, like a mantra, though she'd memorized it before nightfall the day before. She had repeated them in her head on the walk from Njáll's house to the clearing, from the clearing to the castle.

There was a certain comfort in the words. In knowing that generations of Stormsingers before her had sung them, too. Or at least, sung something similar. She hadn't been able to remember every word of Revna's song, hard as she wracked her memory.

Elín heard the king before she saw him.

"If this isn't worth my time, boy, to the dungeons it is with you."

She swallowed, pressed her eyes shut, and composed herself. She'd decided to act haughty. As the last Stormsinger, she had that right, and she hoped it would help the king believe the story they were spinning him. The last thing they needed was for King Karvel to realize how relatively powerless she was without the Tome and all its spells.

As Týr stepped out, he made a flourish with his hand. "I present to you, the Songstress of Storm and Snow."

Elín did not curtsy, holding her chin high while she examined the king more closely than she had been able to from the crowd at the execution stage. He was a tall, pale man who looked even paler because of his gray-streaked black hair and beard. His eyes were a cold, piercing gray. He was dressed in rich fabrics and carried himself as one who had great power and knew how to wield it. An older, steelier, and shrewder version of Prince Stefán.

"Ah," the king said, spreading his hands. "The final Stormsinger. The one that got away."

He circled her, sizing her up with a predatory gleam in his eye. Elín hadn't thought she could hate him any more than she had when first learning the history of Skyli, or when he'd been about to execute Kata, but it turned out her hate only grew the more she learned of him.

Once he stood in front of her again, he tilted her chin up and turned her head to each side, examining the angles of her face. Then he rubbed his hands together. "If her beauty is any indication of her power, then I think I'll be quite willing to allow her into my service. In utter secrecy, of course."

"You will address me directly, Your Highness," Elín said fiercely. Her temper had flared as the king directed his comments to Týr. "And you will call me by my title: Songstress."

"You're a fiery one," the king mused. "But I can't say I mind. However, I will call you Songstress only after you've demonstrated your powers and I've found them worthy of such an honor."

"Very well," Elín said with as much dignity as possible. She turned toward the ramparts. Reaching to toss her braid over her shoulder, she found it missing. It threw her off for a moment, and she placed her hands on the cold stone wall to steady herself.

Týr came to her side so he could remind her of the spell.

They'd decided on the storm incantation. Týr had done his best to fill in the missing words, but they weren't sure if it would work. Elín would not be strong enough to call multiple storms and end them in one day, so they hadn't tested it. They hoped the snow would hide the citizens of Snjoreya from the dragon as Eldri had planned. Elín also realized it could well be the last incantation she ever performed. For that reason, and to best distract the king, it seemed worth trying the most powerful spell they had.

To remind her of what she should visualize, Týr recited the song's meaning in the common tongue for her in a low voice, his tone reverent. Like her, he recognized the weight of what they were about to do.

Wind of the north, bend to my will
Blow fiercely and whip through the trees
Uproot them if they do not bend
Snow, rush down and whiten the sky
Cover the land and freeze the rivers
Blot out the sun with your fury
I command you thus
By the snowsong in my blood

The vision formed in her head as he spoke the words. She closed her eyes to help it form, picturing the trees below them groaning in the wind as snow streaked down, blotting out her view of the sea and turning the forest white.

She hesitated, remembering how happy the crowds had seemed yesterday, drenched in sunlight as they'd left the castle. The family fishing by the river, enjoying the day's unusual warmth. How many farmers wanted to plant, how many families were ready to spend days outdoors again after the long winter? She regretted stealing that from the people of Snjoreya.

I promise, she thought. *This is the last storm this spring if I can help it.*

Then, after one deep breath more, she began to sing.

She had practiced the ancient words in her head so many times that they came out clear and true now. More powerful than any other spell she had attempted, this one finally made her aware of the snowsong within her. Magic rang through her bones and set the network of veins through her body aflame.

Elín sang through the spell again, repeating a few of the lines, slightly changing the syllables of the ancient tongue until they felt right on her lips and made the snowsong within her glow brighter. Her body tingled from head to foot, and she felt strength well up within her and then drain away.

The temperature dropped, and bumps rose on her arms. Strands of her cropped hair whipped against her face. The haunting notes raised hairs on the back of her neck. She reached her hands out at her sides, and snow pelted them. When she finally opened her eyes, the blue-and-green of the spring morning had been replaced with the whites and grays of her snowstorm.

Týr's eyes were wide with wonder, and he grinned with something like pride.

Through the blowing snow, they saw the servants who had been working in the gardens behind the castle rush for shelter.

Guilt weighing heavily on her, Elín sent a prayer that no one would be killed by this storm. She would end it as soon as Dreka was out of sight—she didn't know how long it might rage on without her intervention.

She especially hoped her father would be safe. His part in the plan was to gather people from the city and bring them to the castle after the storm, so all would learn as soon as possible what had happened. Prince Stefán could show that he had survived and do his best to explain the circumstances. They didn't want chaos.

Her thoughts were interrupted by a slow clap behind her. She turned, not wanting to watch the damage she'd caused in action. The wind whipped her hair and skirts around her. This spell had taken more from her than any others she'd performed, but she braced herself against the tower wall and did not let her knees tremble.

"I'm impressed," the king said, continuing his slow claps. "You're worth keeping alive after all, *Songstress*."

He stepped toward her. Týr reached for the hilt of his sword but grabbed only air—the prince had warned them that to pass as servants, they should go unarmed.

Elín willed Kata to hurry with the dragon. She didn't know how else to stall the king now that she'd called the storm.

Týr must have had some ideas, though. He recovered from the sword-grab smoothly and approached the king. With a winning smile, he said, "This is but a small demonstration of all the Songstress can do. She will have terms, of course. Use of a power as great as hers should command a great price."

King Karvel grinned wickedly. "Oh, I'd say her life should be sufficient. A few days ago, I was willing to pay a great sum to have someone end it. But now that she comes to me as a willing servant . . ."

Týr's nostrils flared, and Elín struggled to maintain her composure. Then, over the howling wind, she caught an unearthly screech. Elín both hoped and feared it was the dragon.

The king must have heard it, too, because he whipped around and looked over the ramparts, seaward.

Please, Elín pleaded. *Find your enemy, Dreka.*

"What was that?" Elín asked innocently. Perhaps *too* innocently, because King Karvel whirled on her. Clearly, she didn't have Týr's skill with lies.

"What is this?" he hissed. Elín feared he might shove her from the tower, so enraged did he seem. But a screech broke the air again, louder this time, and all three of them turned to see the dragon appearing from the blizzard.

The creature was black and soared toward them on wide, bat-like wings. It was over the sea now but approaching rapidly.

Týr shoved Elín along, and they ran for the staircase, but another screech, this one ear-splittingly close, and a whooshing flap of wings made them duck for cover. Elín covered her head with her hands and Týr placed one of his over her head protectively as he crouched beside her.

The king had not moved so quickly. Elín looked up in time to see Dreka grab him with her talons. They sank into his flesh, spraying Týr and Elín with blood. The king cried out, but the sound was drowned out by another dragon shriek. Then both king and dragon launched into the air, leaving the tower far behind.

Elín caught her breath and wiped the blood from her face with the sleeve of her dress. She was horrified by what she'd witnessed but had no time to dwell on it now. Because she'd seen something else, too.

"Was that . . . ? Before she grabbed the king, do you think there was already blood on the dragon's talons?" Elín asked Týr, desperately hoping she had imagined it. She tasted cold, metallic fear, and her heart pounded against her ribs. *Please, don't let it be Kata's blood.*

"I think so," Týr said, but Elín was already running down the spiral stairs.

DARKNESS
Kata

Dreka shrieked, wings flapping and creating a whirlwind that blew Kata's hair back. She closed her eyes and waited for the flames. Instead, she was knocked into a pile of gold with such force that she rolled through it, a burst of pain blooming across her stomach.

Gritting her teeth against the searing pain, she rolled to see Dreka breathe fire and melt a gaping hole in the castle walls. Kata had become disoriented after her time in the dungeons, but she now saw that the side the dragon had burned was along the cliff's edge, facing the sea. Dreka's sword-like claws gripped the edge of the opening she'd made, and then she was flying, fading, gone.

Kata attempted to sit up and examine her wound, but the pain was too great, and the movement sent stars over her vision. She put her hand against her abdomen, and it came away crimson with blood.

Whether she had meant to or not, Kata wasn't sure, but Dreka had torn her open with one of those sabers attached to her feet. The pain was all-consuming; she couldn't even feel the chill of the wind that entered the lair. Her mouth tasted like metal, and her mind reeled.

Her only clear thought was, *Go back.* Back to where Stefán had left her. Where Elín would find her.

She groaned as she crawled through the dragon's lair. The strength to swim across the moat was beyond her—much less the coordination to swim through stinging moon-glitter unharmed. But she hoped if she could return to the edge, to the archway she'd passed through, Týr and Elín would be waiting as planned. They'd find a way to drag her across the wooden board and over the moat to safety. And someone—the royal physician or Eldri, if he could make it in time—could heal her.

Her mind was rattled both from the conversation with Dreka and from the loss of blood. Her skull felt bruised and hollowed-out.

Humans were not meant to speak to dragons, she thought as her head throbbed and the floor seemed to tilt beneath her. Maybe some essential part of her had shifted or broken when she'd heard Dreka's fiery voice in her mind. Reality seemed to be ebbing away, and she reached her hand out as if she could snatch it back.

This was not good.

She tried to hold on to pieces of reality as she pulled herself along, trailing blood. Things she knew to be true. To be *her*.

I am a huntress.

I am Njáll's daughter and Elín's sister.

I have spoken to alicorn and huldufólk, kraken and dragon, and they have listened.

Her vision swam. Blood still seeped through her fingers, but she realized she no longer felt the pain of the gash in her side. Her feet and hand sank deeper into the mounds of coins and jewels as she struggled to push forward. Her hand slipped and she sprawled across the pile.

Collapsing onto her stomach when she attempted to rise again, she pushed her hand harder against the wound she no longer felt. As she slipped into darkness, she remembered one last thing.

I am Kata, and I might have been queen.

DRIFTING SNOW

Elín

They met Stefán on their way down the tower stairs. He begged them to check on Kata, as she had not yet returned, but he couldn't go himself as he needed to reassure his people. He gave them rushed directions on how to find the dragon's lair. They ran, tripping down spiral stairs and getting turned around several times as they wound their way through the corridors and chambers beneath the castle. Each time they backtracked and took another route, Elín wrung her hands with worry for Kata.

The dragon's talons had been monstrous—the length of daggers and just as sharp. Could a person survive being slashed by one?

Finally, they reached the long, sloping tunnel Stefán had described. Every few stones along its walls were carved with crude dragon images. "There," she whispered, and they hurried on, twisting their way through the narrow maze. Týr stayed at her side, helping when she stumbled, still weak from wielding snowsong. A torch he'd nabbed from a sconce during one of their wrong turns lit their way.

They reached a dark pool of water with a wooden plank across it. Deep beneath the surface, Elín could see ghostly white outlines as deadly sea creatures drifted in the black water. This was the moon-glitter moat Stefán had warned them of. Not wanting to waste time balancing on the narrow plank or holding it for each other, Elín sang the freezing spell so they could run across. They hurtled on through the long hall on the other side to the archway, Týr half-supporting Elín.

Týr stopped in his tracks as the entire room seemed to reflect the torchlight back to them. It glanced off hills of gold and silver, chests and chalices and other treasures Elín had no words for.

"Where is she?" Elín scrambled over heaps of wealth, sending priceless treasures rolling and clanging against each other. "Kata!" she called. There was no answer.

Týr eyed a shaft of light, snowflakes drifting in through it. He climbed up a mound of treasure with some difficulty. The pieces slid beneath his feet, and he sank a hand into the coins to steady himself.

Elín followed, and they both stared at the gaping hole in the castle wall, the red-hot rock that had melted and pooled like lava. Through the blizzard they could see the ocean waves out to the horizon.

"You don't think she . . ."

It was too horrible to consider, so she shook her head. "She's here," Elín said with conviction she didn't feel. She waded through more treasure, calling Kata's name. Týr slid down the mound of coins and joined her.

Elín caught a glint of gold. Not the deep, rich gold of the dragon's hoard but the sunny gold of Kata's hair. As she rushed to her side, Týr a step behind, the torchlight illuminated another color: Kata's blood had stained the gold beneath her deep red.

She lay prone, her face twisted to the side, her eyes closed. One arm lay beneath her, blood-soaked, and the other reached toward the moat.

"No. No," Elín pleaded, kneeling beside her and pushing Kata's hair from her face. As she did so, she felt a faint warmth on her hand. "She's still breathing."

Relief washed over Týr's face. Then, helping Elín to roll Kata on her side and seeing the wound across Kata's body, he said, "Not for long if she doesn't get help."

"Are there any spells I can use?" Elín asked, her hand grasping his forearm desperately, her eyes wide. Then she let go and removed her cloak, using it to staunch the bleeding from the wound.

"No. Snowsong is for the wind and waves, not for healing." Týr said, standing. "I'll find someone. Stay with her." Then he ran back to the moat. She heard the ice creak under his feet, but he made it across.

When she'd finished wrapping Kata and tied the cloak around her bleeding torso as tight as she could, she sat and cradled Kata's head in her lap.

She felt suddenly very alone, down in the castle's depths. There was no sound but the waves of the sea, the howl of the wind, and their breaths: hers rough and fast, Kata's weak and staccato.

Remembering her promise, she thought of the spell she'd heard Revna use to end storms. Her previous spells had taken much from her, but she told herself this would be the last for some time and sang on anyway. It was a calming, tender song with a lilting melody, like a lullaby, and she hoped it would be some comfort to Kata. If she could hear it.

The howling wind, faint as it was down below the castle dungeons, faded away. Elín said, softly, "You did well. Stay here with me, Kata. I want to know my little sister."

Then she let her pent-up tears fall as she stroked Kata's hair and watched the drifting snow float in through the hole the dragon had made, slowly covering the gold.

Kata slept deeply through the night after they moved her to an elegant room in the castle that had once been the Queen's. She was never alone. All manner of castle servants and attendants bustled about her, ensuring the fire roared and a mound of fresh fruit was ready in case she awoke hungry. Njáll, Elín, and Prince Stefán scarcely left her side.

But for Kata's injury, all had gone according to plan. The king and the dragon he'd tricked for years had last been seen flying west, over the sea, and the king had still been alive then. By morning, he likely no longer was.

Few tears were shed yesterday for King Karvel. Although the future king's intentions to repeal the banishment and end the bounties were not well-received in all quarters, his plan to redistribute much of the hoarded wealth among his people *was*. Many were happy, also, that he had given the clan leaders more power, as they had held with the first kings of Snjoreya.

The royal physician left Kata early that morning. After she had finished cleaning, stitching, and binding Kata's wound, she declared, "I've done all I can. It's up to her now."

Kata still hadn't opened her eyes.

"My little dove," Njáll moaned when the physician left, putting his face in his hands and openly weeping. "My brave Katrín."

Elín put a hand on his shoulder to comfort him, though she still disbelieved at times that this man, who was a stranger still, could truly be her father. Being no longer alone in the world took some getting used to.

She gazed at Kata and hoped with such a ferocity that she felt it burn in her chest. The girl seemed so pale against the richly embroidered blankets, and she was dwarfed by the giant bed. Indeed, she looked so ill that Elín dared not give voice to her hopes.

"She will not die," the prince said. His voice was commanding, fitting for the future king. Elín almost believed he could force the things he spoke to be true, the way she could with her spells. As the Crown Prince he probably often could. She prayed to all three goddesses and all their ancestors that it would work this time.

He turned back to Kata and added tenderly, "She is to be my queen."

Njáll withdrew his hands from his face. "What?"

"I asked her yesterday morning," Prince Stefán said. "She didn't believe me serious, and told me to ask again after she faced the dragon." He looked up at Njáll, then at Elín. "So you see, she must survive."

"She's so young," Njáll said.

"As am I," he said. However, Elín had noticed the loss of the boyishness she had seen in him at their first meeting. Perhaps it could be attributed to the betrayal and loss of his father, or Kata's illness, or the weight of the kingdom and his people.

The prince continued, "Kata knows what this kingdom needs and can be a link between Snjoreya and Eldri's people. I also intend to appoint you, Njáll, as a member of my council. If you are ready to leave your Royal Huntsman days behind you, that is."

Njáll was stunned. When he got control of his faculties again, he said, "I am honored, Your Highness."

"I mean to appoint you to the king's council as well, Elín," Prince Stefán said, fixing her with his steady, gray-eyed gaze. "Týr, too. His knowledge of the ancient tongue and the kingdoms beyond mine would serve me well."

"Of course, Your Highness, if that is what you wish," Elín said, inclining her head. Despite her powers, she felt much less qualified than Týr to be on the council. She had so little knowledge outside of Ornfoss, even after her recent adventures.

The thought of Týr made her wince. He'd said he would leave so many times. She reminded her traitorous heart that those moments on the tower had changed nothing. He had been holed up in the royal library all morning, looking for resources to help him repair the Tome or find the hidden library in Stórborg. It was clear what was important to him now.

As if her thought had summoned him, Týr burst into the room. "Your Highness," he said. "Skyli's chosen leader, Eldri, has arrived. With a . . . friend of Kata's. Can I let them in?"

"Of course," Prince Stefán said, standing. "See them in."

Only when she had seen the huldufólk leader in the middle of the castle did Elín realize how natural he'd looked among the mountains and forest of Skyli, especially the first time she saw him, astride a mighty ice bear. Inside these walls, he seemed less real somehow, his crystal eyes and translucent skin almost frail. He looked as if a strong gust of wind might blow him away.

Behind him walked Magni. His broad wings were pulled in, but even so, he almost didn't fit through the doorway. Njáll gasped when he saw him. "Magni," he said. "It has been years, my friend."

The alicorn inclined his head to Njáll, but his focus was not long kept from where Kata lay in the bed. He approached her and put his nose to her hand, but she did not stir.

Elín knelt in front of Eldri. "Please," she said. "You have healing powers; heal my sister. After she did so much for your people, she cannot—"

"Oh, Songstress. My child," he said, wrinkles forming at the corners of his wise eyes. "Why do you think we've come?"

Prince Stefán left his chair beside Kata's bed so Eldri could kneel upon it. Elín began to weep and to pray, and Njáll wrapped a warm, strong arm around her. Eldri placed a hand against Kata's forehead and his other on the blanket covering her midsection.

The room fizzled, but Elín was not sure if it was with the anticipation and hopes of everyone in it or some effect of Eldri's magic. The huldufólk leader closed his eyes, and the moments stretched long.

When he pulled his hands away, Elín stepped forward to see Kata's face. It was perhaps not as pale as it had been before. The room waited with bated breath.

Then, after being both wounded and healed by magic, surrounded by finery and the people she loved, Kata opened her eyes.

GRANDER, BETTER

Kata

"There," Elín said as she pinned the last braid to Kata's head. "You look lovely."

"Thanks to you, I'm sure." Kata felt the crown of interwoven braids on her head. She swallowed back emotion. Elín had done all she could to make her look—and feel—like a future queen.

"I'm headed down to the throne room," Elín said, smoothing the skirts of her own lovely dress. Her now-short chestnut hair was loose and wavy, shot through with braids in the style favored by female vikings. "But I shall see you at the banquet."

Kata smiled, hoping she was hiding her nerves well enough. Despite her sister's work, she wasn't sure she'd ever feel worthy to be Snjoreya's queen.

After fidgeting with her dress, Kata left her chambers and found her father waiting for her in the hall.

Njáll already had tears in his eyes, probably from seeing Elín. When Kata came out, he said, "My little dove," and held his arms out to her. His embrace crushed her, and her nose filled with the scents of chimney smoke, spruce trees, and the beeswax they used on their bowstrings.

"Let me have a better look at you," he said, pulling away. "I thank Lady Destiny every day for giving me two perfect daughters. And my youngest is so grown up now." He smiled warmly.

"Not *too* grown yet," Kata said. They'd argued so many times before about whether she was old enough for various things. Now she feared time was moving too fast, that she was taking on more than she was ready for.

"Too grown for my taste," Njáll said, laughing. "What I wouldn't give for another day with you trailing behind me on the hunt, your head and shoulders hardly above the snow."

"Hunting *is* much easier at my current height," Kata pointed out. "Now come, you must go down to the throne room. I'm sure Elín has saved you a good seat."

He embraced her once more and left her. Then, she took another corridor that led to the Great Hall. Now the true test: whether she could descend the grand staircase of the palace in this trailing gown.

Kata placed a hand on the railing and descended the steps carefully, sweeping the long train of her gown to the side the way the women of court had taught her. It was tricky; Eldri's magic had saved her the week before, but it couldn't repair all the damage done by Dreka. It would be some time still before she was freely roaming the woods again.

The dress she wore bared her shoulders, making her feel a little exposed. Her hair was bound into braids and piled on top of her head, thanks to her sister, and in combination with the dress, it made her stand straighter.

Prince Stefán awaited her at the bottom of the staircase, arm extended to escort her to the coronation. Or, since it was his coronation, maybe she was escorting him.

His eyes had seemed warmer lately, she'd noticed. Not the pale ice-gray they had often been before. Now, as he watched her, they seemed to glow.

"Well," he said as she hopped off the last step and took his arm. "Your fears of not looking how a queen should were certainly baseless."

She swatted his arm—something she hadn't allowed herself to do since they were children—and laughed. "The second this is over, I'm putting my hunting clothes back on."

He sneaked a kiss onto her cheek and said, "I wouldn't have you any other way."

She did her best to hide her blush. "Are you ready?"

"As ready as I'll ever be."

As they reached the massive wooden doors, two servants opened them, bowing. The future King and Queen of Snjoreya entered the throne room together.

The banquet proceeding Prince—*King* Stefán's coronation was a sight to behold. The castle cooks had outdone themselves, and the hall was filled with as many Linnafell citizens as it could hold, all intent on eating their fill and making merry. The air was thick with the scent of roasted meat spiced with thyme and marjoram.

The king's council sat at the broad front table. Its new members included Njáll, Elín, Eldri, and Skadi, who had just arrived with the first ship of Skyli residents to return to Snjoreya. Each clan leader had made it for the coronation, too, and were seated at the tables nearest the council's.

Kata sat next to King Stefán, who kept looking over at her and smiling contentedly. She had to look away, embarrassed. Turning to Elín at her other side, she asked, "Have you ever seen such a feast?"

"No," Elín said, attempting a smile. "I certainly haven't."

Her plate was untouched other than her bread, which she'd torn to shreds. Kata frowned and asked, "What's wrong?"

"Nothing. I'm happy—especially for you." She squeezed Kata's forearm.

"This is about Týr, isn't it? Where is he? Still holed up in the library?"

Elín looked up, eyes widened in surprise. "He's gone. He left a few days ago." She breathed out slowly. "And he didn't say goodbye."

"What?" Kata asked, her anger flaring at this injustice. "After everything . . . do you want me to track him down?"

Laughing, Elín shook her head. "Of course not. And anyway you're still healing. No hunts for lost Keepers for you."

"I meant I could send someone to find him. Now that I'm the future queen and all. I *think* I have the power to do that."

"I appreciate it," Elín said. "But he's in search of the Lost Library of Safni, which is supposed to be hidden somewhere in Stórborg. The Tome of Incantations, repairing it . . . it's important to him. He's where he wants to be."

"Surely he'll come back, once he is done there?" Kata had seen the way Týr looked at Elín, even back in Skyli. The way he'd pushed her out of the path of Kata's arrow. His sudden departure didn't make sense. She was determined to do something about it.

Elín shrugged. "Perhaps. But please, don't let me dampen your enjoyment of this day." Glancing across the table at Njáll, who was laughing heartily at something Eldri had told him, Elín added, "Pabbi certainly seems to be enjoying himself."

"He is." Kata smiled. Njáll was adjusting well to castle life. He was no longer so tired as he had been after all-day hunts in the winter woods, and he got along well with Stefán, Eldri, Skadi, and the other advisors.

He'd insisted, however, on doing his duty as Royal Huntsman one last time before this feast. "Let me fulfill my role, just once, to a king I respect and love," he'd said, and Stefán had permitted him. Kata had gone with him, though she'd had to move slowly and stop often to catch her breath, a hand pressed to her aching side. At least, thanks to Elín, the snow had gone, and spring had since bloomed in full force.

The three great boars they'd taken were the centerpiece for the feast, and it made Kata's heart feel warm and glowing to see her people fill their bellies. She glanced at the rightmost table, where Bergdis and Gunnar and some of the other hunters sat. Several were glancing anxiously at Skadi and her ethereal beauty, but all seemed to be enjoying the feast nonetheless. Gunnar had been happy to take on the mantle of Royal Huntsman when Njáll had asked him. Now, when he caught Kata's gaze, he approached the front table.

He bowed to his king, then smiled at Kata. "Your Future Highness," he said, winking. He was one of the few people in the kingdom who already knew of the betrothal.

"Royal Huntsman," Kata said, grinning back. "Where's Helga?"

His face fell, and he sighed. "I'm sorry, Kata. She and some of the other hunters have left Linnafell for the western mountains . . ." He shook his head. "It will take time."

"I know," Kata said, even as her heart ached for the huntress who had been her friend, if not quite a mother. She wondered if Helga would ever give her another gift from the woods, a bear claw or flowers or sweet mushrooms, or if that time was gone. Kata wasn't the hunters' little pet anymore. She was no longer a girl, either; in a few winters, she would be queen.

Gunnar bowed and turned to go, but Kata added, "Make sure they know about King Stefán opening the King's Forest to them. They may hunt game to sell in the markets. The warden knows all the details."

"Very good," Gunnar said, bowing once more to her and to King Stefán. "Your Highness." Then he returned to his table.

Stefán squeezed Kata's hand then, under the table where others couldn't see, and smiled sadly at her. He understood about Helga. She'd never realized before how well they could communicate without speaking. How they knew each other better than perhaps anyone else in the kingdom. A useful skill now that her days would be spent with him seeing supplicants and attending council meetings, rarely alone together.

Still, they had their moments. When she took him into the King's Forest, and Magni had taken them both for a flight. When he showed her the chair by the hearth in the castle library where his mother used to read to him, and she finally appreciated what that room meant to him. When they stood on their old balcony, overlooking the hedge maze, and reminisced on their childhood misadventures.

After it seemed everyone had filled and cleaned their plates at least once, King Stefán stood and raised wine cup to the room. Everyone else stood, too, wooden cups and drinking horns and wineskins in their hands.

"To Snjoreya," he said. "And to my future queen. Queen Katrín."

Then he turned to Kata and raised his cup to her. She tried to glare at him—they had agreed to wait until things were more settled to announce the betrothal—but found she couldn't when the whole room was cheering for their union.

The new king drank, and his subjects followed. Elín squeezed Kata's hand briefly, and their father and Eldri beamed at her. Bergdis, Gunnar, and their other friends were hollering and clapping, having downed their wine.

She caught sight of Grim among the crowd. When he'd first seated himself at one of the long tables, he had been given a wide berth and many suspicious glances. Now, he seemed to have charmed those around him and was surrounded by people whose cheeks were rosy with wine and laughter. He looked no worse for wear after his time in the dungeon.

As the applause died away, Kata thought of the way her dreams had changed. Once, she had wanted nothing more than to become a bounty huntress, to gain riches for her father and herself and admiration from the other hunters. But Lady Legend had different plans for her, and now Kata was filled with other dreams. Grander, better ones. To be a good queen for this kingdom, to help shape it into a good home for all its subjects, was first among them.

In that moment, Kata felt very *real* and alive and more excited for the future than she had ever been. She sat down again, between the best friend who would become her husband and the once-stranger who had become her sister, and smiled out at her kingdom.

EPILOGUE: ANOTHER QUEST

Elín

The salt breeze of the ocean had done Elín good. It made her feel hearty and whole again, as if she would never lack the strength to face what she set out to do. She tried to imagine how only last winter she'd seen the vast waves and tasted sea salt on her tongue for the first time. It was autumn now; that journey had not *really* been years ago, though at times it felt so.

A merchant vessel was certainly more respectable, but she found she missed the feel of the viking ship. The gruff captain, the loyal, hardworking men and women. The sense of adventure that the merchant vessel severely lacked.

And perhaps she also missed the company of the boy who had first shown her the sea.

Kata, Elín, and their father had made the journey to Ornfoss so she could bring Ský back to Snjoreya with them. What little there was in the cottage she would take back, too, but she had already decided to leave the farm to Haakon and his future wife. Who would *not* be her.

Elín had a home now in Snjoreya, with her father and her sister and a role on the king's council. Though her heart ached when she remembered her warm childhood days in Ornfoss with her mother and grandmother, she knew she couldn't return to that life. Revna and Signý would not be staying across the sea from those they had loved either. Their bones would travel back with their family, and be laid to rest among their ancestors in the sacred forest.

So, Elín knew this would be the last time. She would move on.

Of course, there was the tiny snag in her new life, the one she did her best to ignore. The feeling that "home" was not so much a place now as a person, one she hadn't seen in over half a year. She'd dreamed of him last night, probably because she had returned to the place where she'd first seen him. After greeting her mother and grandmother, while giving her father and Kata time to pay their respects, she had stared off into the trees, wishing a boy with brown eyes and dark robes would step through them once more.

Njáll and Arn were catching up back at Arn's house, the ale and laughter flowing easily between them despite all the years apart. Kata sat with them, listening and content. Later Elín would show her sister her childhood home, but first, she wanted to revisit it and regain her bearings by herself.

When she arrived, she ran a hand over the place where the arrow had stuck in the door. Someone—Arn or Haakon, most likely—had removed the arrow and carved a piece of wood to fill the hole. A pang of homesickness and loss gripped her heart. She couldn't shake the memory of Björn dying just outside the door, in the snow.

She turned back toward her fields and the trees that broke the wind around their cottage. It was a grim, cloudy day, and Elín didn't need any more reason to be melancholy. She sang a spell she'd been practicing—one to clear the clouds—and smiled to herself as the sun broke through. The clouds slowly dissipated, revealing blue sky. She turned back toward the cottage.

You're ready to say goodbye, Elín told herself as she opened the door.

How small it was! And so dark without a fire in the hearth. She had seen many things now—the wonders of Skyli's market, the bustle of a ship at sea, the richness of the rooms in Snjoreya's castle—that it was hard not to see her home with new eyes. The rickety chairs, the packed earth floor, the sparseness of the shelves.

She sat on Amma's side of the bed and opened the drawer of her bedside table. It was empty, of course. Only the birch bark drawing remained, where Elín had pinned it on the wall. She ran her thumb over it, smiling fondly, before putting it in her bag. In many ways, she no longer felt like the girl who had grown up here, the girl who had etched the horse out of charcoal.

From the foot of the bed, she removed the blanket her mother had carefully crafted and folded it. Now she understood why it had taken so long, why she had been so careful to dye the wool the perfect shades of green. Signý had been recreating the colors of the King's Forest, and perhaps with it, a piece of the man she loved.

There was nothing else to take. The other things would be of more use to Haakon and his future family than to her.

She turned, still sitting on the bed, and let her eyes drift to the open door. The trees outside had turned brown and red and gold as they felt the coming winter, and she let herself remember other times here. Especially the cherished times, softened by memory, when Revna and her mother were both alive.

"I shall carry you with me, always," she said softly to the empty house.

Then she stood and took one last look around, noticing something on the mantle. Her mouth fell open as she realized it was her mother's hairbrush, in its usual place. Somehow, it had returned to her. *What magic is this?*

Stepping forward slowly, she picked up the brush and ran her fingers over the carvings, the boar bristles that were made soft by time and use. It was the same one she'd used every night for most of her life.

Then someone darkened the doorway.

He cleared his throat. "Elín."

"Týr?" she asked, taking a step back. She wanted to throw her arms around him, but she didn't quite believe he was there. She'd resigned herself to never seeing him again. Indeed, she'd been doing her best to convince herself that she did not *want* to see him again.

Elín held the hairbrush out. "Did you do this?"

He stepped into the cottage then, the afternoon sun she'd revealed lighting the angles of his face. "Yes," he said. "I found its buyer with information from Captain Axel. But someone else had bought it from them, and then they'd sold it to someone in Virki . . . It ended up being a much longer detour than I'd intended."

"You did that—you tracked this silly old hairbrush halfway across the world—for me?" Clutching it to her chest, she tried to stop the flow of tears before it could start. Tried to remember the pain of the way he'd left, with no goodbye and no hope of seeing him again.

"Of course," he said, as if it should have been obvious. She noticed then that his hands held a bound book. He held it out to show her. "It's the Kirja," he said. "Or as much of it as I could put together."

She set the brush down and took the book gently in her hands. It was bound in embossed leather, but not quite as beautiful as the old one must have been before the fire. "So you found the library, then. The Lost Library of Safni."

He shook his head. "No. I made it halfway to Stórborg before realizing I was going the wrong way entirely. This was put together from our notes on your grandmother's songs and some texts in the ancient tongue I found in King Stefán's library."

"You didn't even try to find it," she said softly. Schooling her expression into one she hoped conveyed indifference, she asked, "Why are you here?"

He attempted one of his familiar, crooked smiles. "Didn't you miss me?"

Elín did her best to keep her expression frosty. It should be no matter to be as frigid as her powers. But he was *here*. And he was looking at her almost as if—she didn't dare think it.

Once, she'd asked how Kata managed her icy looks. After all, Kata never had these issues, and Elín suspected her glare would be an important tool in Snjoreya's future diplomatic relations. But Kata had only given her a strange look and said, "No, Elín, I don't expect you can manage it. You're always warm."

So, when she finally responded to Týr, her, "You left," didn't come out icicle-sharp as she intended, but heavy with emotion. She continued despite the tremble in her voice, "You didn't say goodbye. You didn't send word."

"I know. I'm sorry. I was confused."

She stepped forward, her gaze meeting his. He hadn't yet answered her question, and she wasn't sure she could repeat it without bursting into tears.

"I'm here because . . . well, it was rather difficult."

"What was?"

Though their time together had been short, Elín had seen many sides of Týr. She hadn't seen this one, though. He was hesitant and fidgety and couldn't meet her eyes for any length of time. His mouth, usually on the cusp of a grin, was now downturned.

Remembering the way their kiss on the tower had felt, Elín found it was better not to look at his mouth.

He blew out a long breath. "It was difficult to be away from you."

Elín's chest over her heart suddenly felt rather tight. "Because you were worried about me, being the last Stormsinger. I might still be a target."

"No," he said abruptly. Then, considering, he said, "Well, yes."

She turned away. "You mustn't worry. I'm quite safe in Linnafell, and I won't be visiting Ornfoss again after this."

Týr grabbed her sleeve, gently, turning her back toward him. "I, uh . . ." He let go of her and rubbed the back of his neck. "Kata told me you'd be here. I had to find you because . . . because I had another quest in mind."

She crossed her arms and arched an eyebrow. "Another quest?"

"Of a sort."

Her heart leaped, but she didn't allow herself to hope. "You need my powers." A statement, not a question.

"No, no," Týr said, stepping closer. "It's not that kind of quest. It's not your powers I need." His smile grew larger, more crooked. "It's you."

"And why, exactly, would I want to go on another life-endangering quest with you?" she asked, eyes widened by the sudden, concerning realization that she would go anywhere with Týr. "What could we be looking for this time?"

"When I was hunting that down," he said, indicating the hairbrush, "I was happy. Much happier than I was when I put together this new, partial Kirja. It mattered so little to me in the end."

He took a step closer to her. "The hairbrush mattered because I knew it was a reason to find you again. I wanted, more than anything, to see you again. And I realized how foolish I had been, to think being apart would change that. If anything, it made it worse. Much worse."

Elín didn't know what to say. But the tightness in her chest was gone. She felt light all over, as if she might float away. She cleared her throat. "The quest?"

"The quest is us, Elín." He met her eyes, finally. "Us, together. I know you're upset with me, and you might not think this makes sense. When I went away—"

"Without saying goodbye," she interjected, voice steady.

He inclined his head. "Yes, without saying goodbye. That was horrid and born of a misplaced belief that it would make things easier. And, I suppose, I also thought if I had to *tell* you goodbye, I couldn't go through with it Now, I only hope you can forgive me. That we could try spending our days together again, like we did on our last 'quest.' Perhaps, in time, and with a great deal of help from Lady Luck, I might trick you into marrying me."

She didn't quite believe her ears. "What about tradition? You said the Storm-singers and the Keepers . . ."

He waved a hand. "It was hopeless for me from the start. I was just as enchanted as Arn's cows, that first day we met, and it only got worse from there. There's no curing it now. But, in any case, I've had time to do a great deal of thinking about the tradition. Perhaps it mattered when there were so many Stormsingers and only one Keeper and an apprentice or two. They couldn't make the one they loved more powerful than the rest. But now . . . why should it matter? As long as you don't mind."

It was only then she started to believe him, allowed herself to hope. And the hope made her throat constrict, tears threaten.

When she didn't answer right away, he said, "Besides, I'm not truly a Keeper. I never finished my training, remember?" This time when he said it, there was no bitterness or disappointment in his voice. In fact, he was grinning.

"You had to journey for half a year, halfway across the world, to figure all that out?" Elín asked, laughing breathlessly. She had thought she would never see him again, and now she could see him every day—maybe even for the rest of her life. Her eyes were glassy, a few tears fell loose, and a smile threatened to break through her defenses. "I think you may be the most frustrating person I have ever met."

"Please, I will take that as a compliment if you say 'yes.'" He pulled her closer and kissed her wet cheeks. "I will do my best not to frustrate you *too much* from now on."

"Will we live in Snjoreya?" Elín asked, searching his eyes. She couldn't imagine living far from her new family, and she had embraced her role as one of King Stefán's trusted advisors. "You can serve on the king's council with me."

"Of course," he said, brushing her hair behind her ear. "We'll live anywhere you want." Then he slid his hand back, cradled her head, and kissed her.

Elín's breath caught in her throat as his thumb stroked her ear. She wrapped her arms around him, pulling him closer as she responded to his kiss. Her eyes fluttered closed, and she breathed in the scents of forest and leather and sea salt. She and Týr were together again, and everything felt perfectly as it should be. Except for one thing.

Withdrawing, she said, "The king might still require us to go on quests sometimes. And there is that lost library which *just might* exist, and *just might* help us create a complete copy of the Kirja." Elín studied him, the pull of adventure on her heart stronger, even, than his.

He smiled against her lips. "Perhaps. We are rather good at them."

"Are we?" she asked, pulling away to look into his eyes. They seemed lit from within, aflame. "We've only had one, and we almost died. More than once."

"Well," he said, "we'll find out. Practice makes perfect, after all. But wait—you haven't actually answered me. Do you accept the quest I've proposed? One that, as you pointed out, is just the first of many to come?"

Laughing, pulling him to her again, Elín whispered, "I accept."

AUTHOR'S NOTE

First, thank you so much for taking a chance on and reading this book! I really hope you enjoyed spending time with Elín and Kata in their world. If you did, please consider leaving a review on Amazon, Goodreads, Barnes & Noble, or your favorite book review platform.

Second, I wanted to share a few notes about the inspiration behind this story. My aim was to capture the feel of a time when, never having seen any of them with their own eyes, a unicorn seemed just as likely to exist as a giraffe or a camel to the average person. I therefore combined traditional Nordic and Icelandic creatures (nykur, huldra, griffins, huldufólk, frost giants, the kraken) with traditional mythological creatures of Western Europe (unicorns, phoenix, gnomes, dragons). This is also how ice bears—the same animal as the polar bears we know today—became caught up in King Karvel's banishments. As one of the fiercest land creatures, who's to say they aren't imbued with some magical abilities of their own?

All creatures in the story come from mythology, whether Icelandic or Western European. Fossegrim is a fiddle-playing troll or water-spirit from Scandinavian folklore. Nattmara represents the Mara, who appear as creepy young women and bring nightmares to people. They have some loose associations with werewolves that I used when developing Nattmara's character. Eldri is the main character representing the huldufólk or "hidden folk" of Iceland. Sometimes translated as "elves", these supernatural beings live in a parallel world to ours, and are the subject of many Icelandic legends.

The landvaettir or "Four Protectors of the Land" story is an Icelandic legend, but snowsong, the Stormsingers and Tomekeepers, and the Ladies Luck, Legend, and Destiny are all my own invention. Elín's family tradition of ancestor veneration was inspired by Finnish paganism. Very little knowledge of this tradition survives, but I've incorporated a few things that have, like the *karsikko* burial markings on trees and offering-stones in sacred forests.

The various locations described in *Songs of Snow* are inspired by the landscapes of Iceland, Sweden, and Norway, as well as the forests of Northern Minnesota and Wisconsin, where I spent many happy days as a child. The setting is inspired by the Viking Age, and I tried to keep most details accurate to that historical time period, though of course this is a second-world fantasy and not a historical one.

I've chosen not to capitalize the word "viking" or "vikings" to better reflect the more recent understanding that it was not a separate culture or ethnic group, but a vocation similar to "raiders" or "pirates" in which people of many backgrounds participated.

Elín's song to call the cows home is based on a real Scandinavian herding call tradition called *kulning*. These haunting melodies recently inspired some of the vocals for Disney's *Frozen* movies.

For further reading about Icelandic mythology, check out:

The Guardians of Iceland and other Icelandic Folk Tales by Heidi Herman

Icelandic Folk Tales by Hjörleifur Helgi Stefánsson

Nordic Tales: Folktales from Norway, Sweden, Finland, Iceland, and Denmark from Chronicle Books, beautifully illustrated by Ulla Thynell

ACKNOWLEDGEMENTS

This story was many years in the making, so there are a multitude of people who helped improve and influence it over time.

First, I want to thank my friends and family for their love and support. Thank you to my husband Ryan for being steadfastly supportive of my writing and publishing journeys.

I'd like to thank my writers' networks, including the Rochester MN Writers Group, the Mothman Stans critique group, and my Plague Year Query Wenches for all their assistance and encouragement! Beta readers were also vital to improving and polishing this story, and I would like to thank Hester Steel, Erin Leo, Michelle Tang, Shawna Barnett, Anthony W. Eichenlaub, Ben Green, Angela Vartanian, Dorothy Robinett, Cate Pearce, Ruby Martinez, and Olivia Woods for all their advice and suggestions. Some of you were so good as to read multiple versions of this story or have *Songs of Snow* brainstorming sessions with me, and I can't thank you enough.

I'm also so grateful to my street team for helping me promote *Songs of Snow*. Thank you Ruby Martinez, Johanna Randle, A.R. Frederiksen, Elizabeth Bane, G.W. Prouse, Olivia Woods, and Scarlet for sharing this book so enthusiastically!

I'd also like to thank Vicky Brewster for their editing savvy, Elaine Ho for her gorgeous cover illustration of Elín and Kata, and Mallory Rock for pulling it all together into the wonderful cover design.

Thank you to Villimey Mist for helping me find the perfect Icelandic names for my two main characters. Thank you to Of Monsters and Men and Sigur Rós, two Icelandic bands whose music formed much of the soundtrack as I wrote and revised *Songs of Snow*.

Finally, thank you to all my readers, especially those who have ever reviewed my books or recommended them to others. Without you, I wouldn't be here, publishing my third novel!

About the Author

L.J. Thomas is a writer of speculative fiction and the author of *We Survivors*, *The Bloody Key*, and *Songs of Snow*. She lives in Minnesota with her husband and adopted dog, where she works as an engineer by day and writes by night. In her free time, she enjoys the great outdoors, traveling, reading, and daydreaming about other worlds.

Let's Connect!
ljthomasbooks.com
Twitter/X: @ljthomasbooks
Instagram & Threads: @ljthomasbooks
Email: author@ljthomasbooks.com